THE
EXECUTIONER

About the author

Born in Brazil of Italian origin, Chris Carter studied psychology and criminal behaviour at the University of Michigan. As a member of the Michigan State District Attorney's Criminal Psychology team, he interviewed and studied many criminals, including serial and multiple homicide offenders with life imprisonment convictions.

Having departed for Los Angeles in the early 1990s, Chris spent ten years as a guitarist for numerous rock bands before leaving the music business to write full-time. He now lives in London and is a *Sunday Times* bestselling author.

Visit www.chriscarterbooks.com

Also by Chris Carter

The Crucifix Killer
The Night Stalker
The Death Sculptor

CHRIS CARTER

THE EXECUTIONER

SIMON &
SCHUSTER

London · New York · Sydney · Toronto · New Delhi

A CBS COMPANY

First published in Great Britain by Simon & Schuster UK Ltd, 2010
A CBS COMPANY

First published in paperback, 2011
This new edition first published, 2013

3 5 7 9 10 8 6 4 2

Simon & Schuster UK Ltd
1st Floor
222 Gray's Inn Road
London WC1X 8HB

www.simonandschuster.co.uk

Simon & Schuster Australia, Sydney
Simon & Schuster India, New Delhi

A CIP catalogue record for this book is
available from the British Library

Paperback ISBN 978-1-47114-307-6
Ebook ISBN 978-0-85720-013-6

Typeset by M Rules
Printed and bound by CPI Group (UK) Ltd, Croydon CR0 4YY

For Samantha Johnson . . . always.

Acknowledgements

Though authored by a single individual, I have found that a novel is never the achievement of one alone.

Many people have contributed in different and generous ways to this work and, though a simple acknowledgement page cannot fully express my gratitude, I'd like them to know that this novel would never have been possible without them.

I owe a special debt to Samantha Johnson for her love, undying patience, understanding and for being there every step of the way. To the most extraordinary agents any author could hope for, Darley Anderson and Camilla Bolton. They are indeed my literary Guardian Angels. Staying on the subject of angels, my most sincere thanks also goes to all at the Darley Anderson Literary Agency – the extremely hard-working Darley's Angels. Thanks, too, to the superb team of creative and talented professionals at Simon & Schuster UK for all their relentless work. To my fantastic editor, Kate Lyall Grant, and my incredible publishers, Ian Chapman and Suzanne Baboneau, my eternal gratitude.

I would also like to say thank you to all the readers and everyone who has so fantastically supported me since the release of my first novel.

One

'Ironic how the only certainty in life is death, don't you think?' The man's voice was calm. His posture relaxed.

'Please . . . you don't have to do this.' In contrast, the man on the floor was petrified and exhausted. His voice strangled by tears and blood. He was naked and shivering. His arms were stretched above his head, chained by his wrists to the raw brick wall.

The dark basement room had been transformed into a medieval-looking dungeon, all four walls fitted with heavy metal shackles. A sickening smell of urine lingered in the air and an incessant buzzing sound came from a large wooden box in the corner, placed there by the attacker. The room was sound- and escape-proof. Once locked inside, there was no way of getting out unless someone let you out.

'It doesn't matter how you've lived your life,' the other man continued, disregarding the bleeding man. 'It doesn't matter how rich you are, what you've accomplished, who you know or what hopes you have. In the end the same thing will happen to all of us – we'll all die.'

'Please, God, no.'

'What matters is how we die.'

The man on the floor coughed, spitting out a thin red mist of blood.

'Some people die naturally, painlessly, as they reach the end of a natural cycle.' The man laughed a bizarre, gurgling laugh. 'Some people suffer for years with incurable diseases, fighting every minute to add just a few more seconds to their lives.'

'I . . . I'm not rich. I don't have much, but whatever I have you can take.'

'Shhhh.' The man brought a finger to his lips before whispering, 'I don't need your money.'

Another cough. Another mist of blood.

An evil smile parted the assailant's lips. 'Some people die very slowly,' he continued. His voice was cold. 'The pain of death can drag on for hours . . . days . . . weeks . . . If you know what you're doing, there's no limit, did you know that?' He paused.

Until then, the chained man hadn't noticed the nail gun in his attacker's hand.

'And I really do know what I'm doing. Allow me to demonstrate.' He stepped on the bone protruding from the victim's fractured ankle, bent over and quickly fired three nails into the man's right knee. Intense pain shot up the victim's leg and sucked the air out of his lungs, blurring his vision for several seconds. The nails were only three inches long. Not long enough to puncture through to the other side, but sharp enough to shatter bone, cartilage and ligaments.

The chained man took quick, shallow breaths. He tried to speak through the pain. 'Plea . . . please. I have a daughter. She's ill. She suffers from a rare condition and I'm everything she's got.'

The strange gurgling laugh filled the room again. 'You think I care? Let me show you how much I care.' He grabbed the head of one of the nails lodged into the man's knee and, as if using a screwdriver to pop open a can of paint, slowly forced it to one side as far as it would go. The crunching noise was like stepping on broken glass.

The victim roared as he felt the grinding of metal against bone. His attacker applied just enough force to overcome the resistance and splinter the kneecap. Shards of bone perforated nerve and muscle. Nausea flooded through the chained man's body. His assailant slapped his face several times to keep him from passing out.

'Stay with me,' he whispered. 'I want you to enjoy every moment of this. There's more to come.'

'Why . . . Why are you doing this?'

'Why?' The man licked his cracked lips and smiled. 'I'll show you why.' From his pocket he produced a photograph and held it inches away from the chained man's face.

The man's eyes rested in confusion on the picture for several seconds. 'I don't understand. What . . .?' He froze as he finally realized what he was looking at. 'Oh my God!'

His tormentor moved closer, his lips almost touching the bleeding man's right ear.

'Guess what,' he whispered as he glanced at the wooden box in the corner, 'I know what scares you to death.'

Two

Christmas was a week or so away and Los Angeles was embracing the festive spirit. Streets and shop windows everywhere were decorated with colorful lights, Santa Clauses and fake snow. At 5:30 a.m. the drive through south Los Angeles felt eerily calm.

The white front of the small church glowed against the tall, naked California walnut trees on either side of the arched wooden doorway. Picture-postcard scenery. Except for the police officers swarming around the building and the yellow crime-scene tape that kept curious onlookers at a safe distance.

Dark clouds had started to gather as Robert Hunter stepped out of the car, stretched his body and blew onto his hands before zipping up his leather jacket. Bracing himself against the strengthening cold Pacific wind and studying the sky, Hunter knew that rain was no more than a few minutes away.

The Homicide Special Section (HSS) of the LAPD Robbery-Homicide Division is a specialized branch. It deals with serial killers and high-profile homicide cases requiring extensive time and expertise. Hunter was its most accomplished detective. His young partner, Carlos Garcia, had worked hard to make detective, and he'd done it faster than most. First assigned to the LAPD Central Bureau, he'd spent a few years busting gang members, armed robbers and drug pushers in northeast LA before he was offered a position with the HSS.

As Hunter clipped his badge onto his belt, he spotted Garcia talking to a young officer. Despite the early hour, Garcia looked bright and alert. His longish, dark brown hair was still damp from his morning shower.

'Weren't we supposed to have today off?' Garcia said under his breath as Hunter approached them. 'I made plans.'

Hunter nodded a silent 'good morning' at the officer, who returned the gesture. 'We're Homicide Special, Carlos.' He tucked his hands into his jacket pockets. 'Words like "day off, pay rise, holiday and vacation" don't apply to us. You should know that by now.'

'I'm learning fast.'

'You been inside yet?' Hunter asked as his pale blue eyes focused on the church.

'I just got here.'

Hunter faced the young officer. 'You?'

Six foot two and well built, he ran a hand through his short-cropped black hair nervously under Hunter's attentive eye. 'I haven't been inside either, sir, but apparently it isn't a pretty sight. See those two over there?' He pointed to two pale-faced police officers standing to the left of the church. 'They were first response. I heard it took 'em less than twenty seconds to come running out puking their guts all over the place.' He mechanically checked his watch. 'I got here five minutes after they did.'

Hunter massaged the back of his neck, feeling the rough, lumpy scar on his nape. His eyes scanned the crowd already gathered behind the yellow tape. 'Do you have a camera with you?' he asked the officer, who shook his head, frowning.

'How about a phone cam?'

'Yeah, my personal cell phone's got a cam. Why?'

'I want you to take a few pictures of the crowd for me.'

'The crowd?' the officer asked, confused.

'Yeah, but do it discreetly. Pretend you're taking crime-scene pictures of the outside of the church or something. Try to get the whole crowd. And from different angles. You think you can do that?'

'Yeah, but . . .'

'Trust me,' Hunter said calmly. 'I'll explain later.'

The officer nodded eagerly before reaching inside the police vehicle for his cell phone.

Three

'The vultures are already here,' Garcia observed as they approached the yellow tape. Behind them, reporters were pushing their way to the front of the crowd, their camera flashes exploding every few seconds. 'I think they get the call before we do.'

'They do,' Hunter confirmed, 'and they pay very well for the information too.'

The policeman standing behind the tape nodded as Hunter and Garcia stooped under.

'Detective Hunter,' a short, round and bald reporter called out. 'Do you think this is a religious kill?'

Hunter turned to face the squad of reporters. He understood their apprehension. Inside that small church someone had been robbed of his or her life, and they all knew that if Robert Hunter had been assigned to the case, the murderer had used overwhelming violence to do it.

'We just got here, Tom,' Hunter answered evenly. 'We haven't even been inside yet. At this point you probably know more than we do.'

'Could this be the work of a serial killer?' A tall, attractive brunette asked. She was wearing a thick winter coat and holding a small tape recorder. Hunter had never seen her before.

'Did I stutter?' he murmured, looking at Garcia. 'I'm gonna

say it slower this time for those of you who have trouble keeping up.' He stared straight at the brunette. 'We-just-got-here. We-haven't-been-inside-yet. And you guys know the drill. If you want any information, you'll have to wait for the official police press conference. If there *is* one.'

The brunette met Hunter's stare before disappearing towards the back of the crowd.

A crime-lab agent waited on the worn stone steps of the church's entrance, ready to hand Hunter and Garcia white Tyvek coveralls.

As they stepped inside, they were hit by the smell. A combination of perspiration, old wood and the sharp, metallic odor of blood.

Two long rows of red oak pews were separated by a narrow aisle that ran from the entrance to the steps at the altar. On a busy day, the Seven Saints Catholic Church could receive close to two hundred worshippers.

Its small interior was brightly lit by two large forensic powerlights mounted on separate metal pedestals. In their unnatural brilliance everything was harsh and clinical. At the end of the aisle three crime-lab agents were photographing and dusting every inch of the altar and the confessional on the right-hand side.

The door closed behind them. Hunter felt the anxiety that came with the first steps into every new murder scene.

Hearing their approach, the crime-lab agents paused and looked up uneasily. The two detectives walked towards them, stopping at the altar steps.

Blood was everywhere.

'Jesus Christ!' Garcia murmured, covering his mouth and nose with both hands. 'What the hell is that?'

Four

Winter in the City of Angels is mild compared with most of the USA. Temperatures rarely go below fifty degrees Fahrenheit, but for Los Angeles residents that's certainly cold enough. By 5:45 a.m. a cold drizzle had started. Police officer Ian Hopkins wiped his cell phone on the sleeve of his uniform jacket before snapping another picture of the observers outside the church.

'What the hell are you doing?' asked Justin Norton, one of the two officers first at the scene.

'Taking pictures,' Hopkins replied facetiously.

'Why? Do you have a morbid fetish for crime scenes or something?'

'Homicide Special asked me to do it.'

Officer Norton looked at Hopkins sarcastically. 'Well, I'm not sure if you've noticed, but the crime scene is that way.' He used his thumb over his shoulder to point to the church behind him.

'The detective doesn't want pictures of the church. He wants pictures of the crowd.'

A worried frown this time. 'Did he tell you why?'

Hopkins shook his head.

'And why are you holding the camera around chest height instead of bringing it to your eye?'

'He doesn't want the crowd to know I'm taking pictures of them. I'm just trying to be discreet.'

'These Homicide Special detectives . . .' Norton tapped his left index finger against the side of his head. 'They're really fucked up in the head, d'you know what I mean?'

Hopkins shrugged the comment away. 'I think I've got enough now anyway. Plus this rain will screw up my phone if I'm not careful. Hey . . .' he called as Norton started to walk away. 'What happened in there?'

Norton turned around slowly and locked eyes with Hopkins. 'You're new to the force, right?'

'It'll be three months this week.'

Norton gave him a cheesy smile. 'Well, I've been a cop for over seven years,' he said calmly, pulling his cap lower over his eyes. 'Believe me, this city has thrown some messed-up shit my way, but nothing like what's in there. There are some evil people in this city. For your sake, just take your pictures and move onto the next job. You don't want the image of what's in there burned into your memory right at the beginning of your career. Trust me.'

Five

Hunter stood perfectly still. His eyes absorbing the scene as the adrenalin flooded his senses. On the stone floor just outside the confessional, surrounded by a pool of blood, the decapitated body of a slim and average-height man dressed in a priest's cassock lay on its back. It'd been purposely positioned. Its legs were stretched out. Its arms crossed over its chest. But Hunter's main focus was on the head.

A dog's head.

It'd been attached to a wooden spike and then rammed down the neck's stump, making the body on the floor look like a grotesque, human/dog mutation.

The dog's lips were dark purple. Its thin, long tongue had stained black with blood and was hanging to the left of its deformed mouth. The eyes were wide open and a dull milky white. Its short fur was caked a dark red. Hunter took a step forward and crouched down next to the body. He wasn't an expert in dog breeding, but he could tell that the head used was that of a street mutt.

'A shocking sight, isn't it?' Mike Brindle, the lead forensic agent at the scene asked as he approached both detectives.

Hunter stood up to face him. Garcia kept his eyes on the body.

'Hi, Mike,' Hunter replied.

Brindle was in his late forties, stick thin and doorframe tall. Certainly one of the best forensic agents Los Angeles had to offer.

'How's the insomnia going?' Brindle asked.

'Same as always,' Hunter answered with a shrug.

Hunter's chronic insomnia was no secret. It'd started mildly after his mother's death when he was seven. As the years went by it intensified. Hunter knew it was nothing more than his brain's defense mechanism so he didn't have to deal with the ghastly nightmares. Instead of fighting it, he simply learned to live with it. He could survive on three, if needed two, hours of sleep a night.

'What do we have?' Hunter asked in a calm voice.

'We just started. We got here fifteen minutes ago, so at the moment I know just about as much as you do, with one exception.' Brindle pointed to the body. 'It looks like that used to be Father Fabian.'

'Looks like?' Hunter instinctively allowed his eyes to search the area. 'You haven't found the head yet?'

'Not yet,' Brindle answered, casting a questioning look towards the two other crime-lab agents, who shook their heads.

'Who found the body?'

'The altar boy, Hermano something. When he came into the church this morning he was greeted with what you see here.'

'Where's he?'

'In the back,' Brindle answered with a head tilt. 'There's an officer with him, but not surprisingly he's in a bit of a shock.'

'Approximate time of death?'

'Rigor mortis is well on its way. I'd say somewhere around eight to twelve hours ago. Definitely sometime last night. Not this morning.'

Hunter kneeled down and studied the body for a while longer. 'No defensive wounds?'

'Nope.' Brindle shook his head. 'It looks like the victim has no other wounds of any nature. He was killed quickly.'

Hunter switched his attention to the trail of blood that started at the body and moved up the steps leading to the altar.

'It doesn't get any better once you get up there,' Brindle commented as he followed Hunter's stare. 'In fact, I'd say it gets more complicated for you guys.'

Six

Garcia tore his eyes away from the body and faced the forensic agent. 'What do you mean?'

Brindle scratched his nose and faced him. 'Well, you're the ones who'll have to figure out what all this means. The pattern of blood splatters up there—' he shook his head, considering '—it doesn't seem random.'

'Human blood?' Hunter asked.

'As opposed to dog's blood?' Brindle countered, pointing to the dog's head.

'Uh-huh.'

'Can't say for certain yet. Very hard to tell just by looking at it. Their properties are very similar.'

Hunter climbed up the altar steps in one smooth movement. Garcia and Brindle followed. The place was covered in blood, but Brindle was right – there was definitely a pattern. Some sort of symmetry. On the floor, a thin continuous crimson trail created a circle all around the altar. On the wall directly behind it, there was a long, uneven diagonal splash, as if someone had dipped a paintbrush in the blood and flicked it against the wall. Hundreds of smaller splatters littered the once-crisp white altar cloth.

'Usually when the distribution of blood covers such a large area, it's due to one of two types of struggle,' Brindle explained.

'A fight, where both parties involved run around punching each other and bleeding all over the place, or an injured victim struggling to get away from his attacker.'

'The splatters aren't consistent with a fight scenario or a runaway struggle,' Hunter said, analyzing the pattern. 'The distance between them – the shapes – it's all too symmetric, almost calculated. This blood trail was intentionally created by the killer, not the victim,' he added calmly.

'I agree,' Brindle said, folding his arms over his chest. 'This wasn't a fight, and Father Fabian didn't get a chance to run away from anything.'

'What gets me is, if the priest was killed down there—' Garcia pointed to the body '—how did all this blood get up here?'

Brindle shrugged.

Hunter approached the altar and carefully walked around it, studying the thin blood trail on the floor. He stopped when he'd completed a full circle.

'How tall are you, Mike?'

'Six-four, why?'

'How about you, Carlos?'

'Six-two.'

'Come here.' Hunter motioned Garcia closer. 'Walk with me slowly,' he said as his partner joined him. 'Stay about a foot away from the trail. Take one step at a time and walk naturally. Start from right here.' He indicated a point on the floor directly behind the center of the altar.

The two other crime-lab agents stopped what they were doing and joined Mike Brindle by one of the powerlights.

Garcia had taken only four steps when Hunter asked him to stop. Bending over, he quickly checked Garcia's foot position in relation to the trail before allowing him to continue. Four steps later, Hunter stopped Garcia once again. Four steps after that, the circle was completed.

'Twelve steps in total,' Garcia said with an intrigued look.

Hunter called Brindle over and asked him to do exactly the same as Garcia had just done.

'Eleven steps from me,' Brindle said when he reached his starting point after a full circle.

'I'd say the killer's Garcia's height,' Hunter concluded. 'Six-two, give or take half an inch.'

Seven

Brindle's inquisitive stare stayed on the blood trail for a moment before moving to Hunter. 'And how did you come to that?' he asked.

'Because of these breakaway splatters over here.' Hunter pointed to two separate points on the floor around the altar where several drops of blood created a foot-long, outbound, breakaway line from the circular trail.

Brindle was joined by the two other crime-lab agents.

'I don't follow,' one of them said.

'If you had to draw a circle of blood around this altar, but you had no paintbrush, what'd you do?' Hunter asked.

'With this much blood,' the crime-lab agent offered, looking at the pool that surrounded the body, 'you could fill a cup with it and pour it onto the floor.'

'Too messy,' Hunter disagreed. 'You wouldn't be able to control the pouring, unless you had a container with a beak.'

'It's a drip trail, anyway,' Brindle said confidently. 'Blood wasn't poured onto the floor. It dripped onto it.'

'That's also my understanding.' Hunter nodded.

'OK. Still, how does that give you the UNSUB's height?' The crime-lab agent pressed.

'Imagine someone walking around the altar holding a small

object saturated with blood,' Hunter explained, moving to the front of the altar. 'The excess dripping onto the floor.'

'A small object like a candle?' the shorter of the two agents asked, lifting a half-melted altar candle by its wick. Its bottom half was stained red as if it'd been dipped in a shallow glass of blood. 'I found it to the left of the altar.' He brought it closer, allowing both detectives and Brindle to have a look at it.

'This is it,' Hunter agreed.

'Bag it,' Brindle commanded.

'So the killer dips the end of the candle into some blood and uses it to create the circular trail,' the agent said, dropping the candle into a cellophane bag. 'What about the breakaway splatters?'

'A candle isn't absorbent enough,' Hunter explained. 'It can hold only a very limited amount of blood before it stops dripping.'

'So the killer had to re-dip it,' Garcia confirmed.

'Exactly.'

Brindle thought about it for a few seconds. 'So you figured the killer managed only four steps before having to re-dip the candle in blood.'

Hunter nodded. 'I'd say he was holding the blood container close to his body. The breakaway lines are the drips from the blood container back to the trail.'

'And they come at exactly four of Garcia's steps apart,' Brindle concluded.

Another nod from Hunter. 'Your steps overshot it and mine fell short of the mark. I'm six foot tall.'

'But why create the circle around the altar?' Garcia asked. 'Some sort of ritual?'

There was no answer. Everyone went quiet for a while.

'As I've said—' Brindle broke the silence '—you're the ones

who'll have to figure out what all this means. The blood splatters, the dog's head shoved down the priest's neck . . . It looks like the killer is trying to get a message out.'

'Yeah, and the message is *I'm a fucking psycho*,' Garcia murmured, looking back down at the body.

'Have you ever seen anything like this before, Mike?' Hunter asked, tilting his head towards the body. 'I mean, a dog's head shoved down someone's neck?'

Brindle shook his head. 'I've seen a lot of bad and weird stuff, but this is a first for me.'

'It's gotta mean something,' Garcia said. 'No way the killer did it just for the heck of it.'

'I'm guessing if you haven't found the head, you haven't found a weapon either,' Hunter said, now studying the blood splatters on the wall.

'Not so far.'

'Any guess what it could be?'

'Hopefully, the autopsy will be able to answer that question, but I can tell you the cut looks smooth. No edges. No signs of hacking. Definitely a very sharp instrument. One that could've performed the cut in one clean sweep.'

'An axe?' Garcia enquired.

'If the killer is skillful and strong enough, sure.'

Hunter frowned as he studied the altar again. Other than the bloodstained cloth, there was only one object left on it. A gold-plated chalice adorned by silver crucifixes. It was lying on its side, as if someone had knocked it over. Its shiny surface was sprinkled with blood. Hunter bent down and twisted his body so he could have a look inside its bowl without touching it.

'There's blood inside this chalice,' he said as his eyes carried on analyzing the holy cup.

'Does that surprise you?' Brindle asked with a chuckle.

'Look around. There's blood everywhere, Robert. It's like a blood bomb exploded in here.'

'I'd say that's what the killer used as a blood container to dip the candle in,' Garcia emphasized.

'I agree, but . . .' Hunter made a come here gesture with his left hand. Garcia and Brindle joined him, both bending down to draw eye level with the chalice. Hunter pointed to a faint print on its border edge.

'I'll be damned. It looks like a mouth print,' Brindle said, surprised.

'Wait a sec,' Garcia shot back wide-eyed. 'You think the killer drank the priest's blood?'

Eight

The room was small, badly lit and devoid of any luxury. The walls were papered in a dull blue and white pattern with several framed religious drawings hanging from them. Against the east wall stood a tall mahogany bookcase lined with old-fashioned hardcovers. To the right of the entrance door, the room extended out into a small kitchen. A terrified-looking boy was sitting on an iron-framed single bed that occupied the space between the kitchen and the back wall. He was small and skinny; around five foot six, with a narrow chin, tiny brown eyes set closely together and a pinched nose.

'We'll take it from here. Thank you,' Hunter said to the officer standing next to the bookcase as he and Garcia entered the room. The boy didn't seem to notice them. His stare was cemented on the untouched cup of coffee in his hands. His eyes were bloodshot and puffy from crying.

Hunter noticed a kettle sitting on a two-burner hotplate.

'Can I get you another cup of coffee? That one looks to have gone cold,' he asked, once the officer had left.

The boy finally looked up with terrified eyes. 'No, sir, thank you.' His voice a whisper.

'Do you mind if I sit down?' Hunter asked, moving a step closer.

A shy shake of the head.

He took a seat on the bed next to the boy. Garcia chose to stand.

'My name's Robert Hunter. I'm a detective with the Homicide Division. That tall and ugly guy over there is my partner, Detective Carlos Garcia.'

A hint of a smile graced the boy's lips as his eyes stole a peek at Garcia. He introduced himself as Hermano Cordobes.

'Would you rather we spoke in Spanish, *muchacho*?' Hunter asked, leaning forward to mimic Hermano's position. Both elbows resting on the knees.

'No, sir. English is fine.'

Hunter breathed, relieved. 'I'm glad, 'cos *muchacho* is pretty much the only word I know in Spanish.'

This time the ice-breaker worked and they got a full smile from the boy.

For the first few minutes they talked about how Hermano came to be the altar boy at the Seven Saints church. Father Fabian had found him begging on the streets when he was eleven. He'd just turned fourteen two weeks ago. He explained he'd run away from home and from a violent father when he was ten.

Daylight had started to crawl into the room through the old curtains covering the window just behind Hermano's bed when Hunter decided the boy was relaxed enough. It was time to get serious.

Nine

'Can you run me through what happened this morning?' Hunter asked in a calm voice.

Hermano looked at him and his bottom lip quivered. 'I got up at a quarter past four, showered, said my prayers and made my way to the church at a quarter to five. I always get here early. I have to make sure everything's set up properly for the first Mass at six-thirty.'

Hunter smiled kindly, allowing him to continue in his own time.

'As soon as I entered the church I knew something wasn't right.'

'How come?'

Hermano brought his right hand to his mouth and chewed on what was left of a nail. 'A few of the candles were still burning. Father Fabian always made sure they were all put out after closing the church.'

'Did Father Fabian always close the church by himself?'

'Yes.' He started chewing on another nail. 'It was the only time of day he had the church all to himself. He liked that.' Hermano's voice trailed off as tears started to roll down his cheeks.

Hunter fetched a paper tissue from his jacket pocket.

'Thank you, sir. I'm sorry . . .'

'There's no need to be sorry,' Hunter said understandingly. 'Take your time. I know how difficult this is.'

Hermano wiped the tears from his face and drew another deep breath. 'I could tell that the altar was a mess. The candle-holders were on the floor. The chalice was tipped over on its side, and the altar cloth looked dirty. Smeared with something.'

'Did you notice if there was anyone else in the church?'

'No, sir. I don't believe there was. The place was as quiet as it's always been at that time. The front door was locked.'

'OK, what did you do after that?' Hunter asked, his eyes taking in every reaction from Hermano.

'I walked up to the altar to check what was going on. I thought that maybe someone had broken into the church and sprayed paint everywhere. Like graffiti, you know? This isn't the best of neighborhoods. Some of the gangs around here don't have no respect for nothing. Not even Our Lord Jesus Christ.'

'Have you had problems with gangs in here before?' Hunter asked while Garcia checked the kitchen.

'That's the funny thing, sir. We never had any trouble. Everyone loved Father Fabian.'

'How about break-ins? Either into the church or into these sleeping quarters?'

'No, sir. Never. We don't really have anything of value.'

Hunter nodded. 'So what happened next?'

'I didn't know what to do. I knew there was no way I'd be able to get the church cleaned and ready for the six-thirty Mass. When I got to the other side of the altar I saw it, on the floor next to the confessional. I panicked. I thought it was the devil.'

'The devil?' Hunter arched his eyebrows.

Hermano was crying again. 'The man with a dog's head all covered in blood. It looked like the devil. But it was Father Fabian.'

'How could you tell?' Garcia asked.

'The ring.'

'What ring?'

'Big gold ring with the image of Saint George slaying a dragon on the left hand,' Hunter said, lifting his hand and dangling his ring finger.

Garcia bit his bottom lip, half annoyed he'd failed to notice the ring back in the church.

'That's right, sir,' Hermano said, impressed. 'Father Fabian never took it off. A present from his grandmother, he told me. When I saw the ring I knew it was him. It was Father Fabian.' Hermano broke down, burying his head in his hands. His sobs were violent enough to jerk his body every few seconds.

Ten

Grief and silence are perfect partners. Hunter understood this very well. He'd been around people suffering from the shock of discovering a dead body too many times. Words, no matter how comforting, rarely made a difference. He offered the young altar boy a new paper tissue and waited as he dried his tears. When he turned to face Hunter, his eyes were cherry red.

'I don't understand, sir. Who'd do something like that to Father Fabian? He never hurt a soul. He was always willing to help. No matter who. No matter what time. If anyone needed him, he'd be there.'

Hunter kept his voice calm and steady. 'Hermano, you look like an intelligent boy and I'm not gonna lie to you. We don't have the answers right now, but I promise we'll do our best to find them. If it's OK with you, we still need to ask you a few more questions.'

Hermano blew his nose into the paper tissue and nodded nervously.

Hunter retrieved a pen and a small black notebook from his jacket pocket. 'When did you last see Father Fabian?'

'Last night, sir, just before confessions started.'

'And what time did it start?'

'At a quarter to nine.'

'That late?' Garcia cut in.

'Usually confessions go from four to five in the afternoons,' Hermano explained. 'But on the weeks leading up to Christmas it gets a lot busier. The afternoon sessions aren't enough to deal with the number of people who come in. Father Fabian runs a second session around an hour before closing time.'

Hunter scribbled something down in his notebook.

'After I left the church I came back to my room, said my prayers and went to bed. I'd got up at four-thirty yesterday.'

'Did you hear anything at all after you went to bed?' Hunter's eyes roamed the room.

'No, sir, I didn't.'

Hunter wasn't surprised Hermano hadn't heard anything. His room was in a separate small building at the back of the church. Through closed doors and thick walls, unless the killer had broadcast his attack over loudspeakers, nothing would've been heard.

'I take it Father Fabian's room is just down the hall. The next door along?' Hunter asked with a slight tilt of his head.

'Yes, sir.' Hermano massaged his closed eyelids while nodding slowly. A new tear rolled down to the tip of his red and sore nose.

Hunter gave him a few more seconds before carrying on. 'Did you notice if Father Fabian seemed different in the past few days? Anything at all, maybe agitated or nervous?'

Hermano sucked a deep breath through his nose. 'He wasn't sleeping well. Sometimes I heard him in his room in the early hours, praying.'

Hunter leaned back on the bed and used his pen to lift the bottom edge of the heavy curtain. 'You said you clean the church, right? Do you also clean this building, including Father Fabian's room?'

'Not his room, sir.' He shook his head. 'Father Fabian was a very private man. He always kept his door locked. He cleaned it himself.'

Hunter found that peculiar. 'Do you know how we could get access to his room?'

A timid head shake. 'Father Fabian was the only one who had the key.'

Hunter closed his notebook and placed it back in his pocket. As he stood up, his eyes quickly scanned the religious drawings on the walls. 'Do you know what his real name was?' he asked as Hermano got to the door.

Garcia shot Hunter a questioning look.

Hermano turned to face both detectives. 'His real name was Brett.'

Garcia frowned. 'And where did the name Fabian come from?'

'Saint Fabian,' Hunter replied, nodding towards one of the religious drawings – a man dressed all in white with a white dove on his right shoulder.

'That's right,' Hermano commented. 'Did you know that before becoming a saint he was elected Pope and . . .' He froze, suddenly realizing something. His eyes widened. 'Oh my God!'

'What?' Garcia asked, surprised. His stare moved back and forth between the boy and Hunter.

'Saint Fabian,' Hermano said in a weak voice.

'What about him?'

'That's how he died. He was beheaded.'

Eleven

Hunter went back to the church after he left Hermano. Brindle had found Father Fabian's room key in the left pocket of his cassock. That wasn't what the killer was after.

The priest's room was larger than the altar boy's but just as simple. Another bookcase lined with hardcovers, an old desk and a small bed. In the far corner, a private shrine was over-loaded with religious figures. On the opposite side of the room sat a small wardrobe. The place was spotlessly clean, but an old, musty smell lingered in the air. The bed was perfectly made. No one had slept in it last night.

Father Fabian's closet revealed work clothes, a few long-sleeved shirts, jeans, a dark blue pinstriped suit and worn-out shoes.

'This room smells like my grandparents' house back in Brazil,' Garcia commented, checking the desk while Hunter slowly browsed through the titles on the bookcase.

'Hermano was right,' Garcia said, lifting his latex-gloved right hand to produce a passport. 'Our priest's real name was Brett Stewart Nichols. Born 25 April 1965 right here in Los Angeles. I'm not surprised he went for a different name. Father Brett doesn't have a good ring to it, does it?'

'Any stamps on the passport?' Hunter asked with interest.

Garcia flipped through the first few pages. 'Only one. Italy, three years ago.'

Hunter nodded. 'Anything else from the drawers?'

Garcia rummaged through them a little more. 'A few notes, Saint George cards, pens, pencils, an eraser and . . . a newspaper clipping.'

'What about?'

'Father Fabian.'

Hunter joined Garcia to have a look at it. The article was eleven months old and it'd come from the *LA Daily News*. A photograph of a kind-looking priest surrounded by smiling children topped the article. The headline read COMPTON PRIEST – THE REAL SANTA CLAUS. The rest of the article went on to explain how Father Fabian had saved out of his own allowance to put a smile on the faces of homeless children in six different orphanages by handing out presents.

'It sounds like he was a good man,' Hunter commented, walking back to the bookcase.

Garcia agreed with a nod and returned the news clipping to the drawer. 'I guess tonight won't be such a party for us after all,' he said, now looking through the figurines on the small shrine.

Captain Bolter's leaving do was scheduled to start at five in the afternoon at the Redwood Bar & Grill.

'I guess not.' Crouching down, Hunter pulled a leather-bound volume from the bottom shelf and flipped through a few pages before putting it back and repeating the process with the next one.

And the next.

And the next.

They were all handwritten.

'What've you got?' Garcia asked, noticing Hunter's interest as he read through a few pages.

'A whole bunch of journals, or something like it,' Hunter

answered, standing up again. He flicked back to the first page and then all the way to the last one. 'There are exactly two hundred pages here.' A few more flicks. 'And they're all filled from top to bottom.'

Garcia joined Hunter by the bookcase, twisting his body to get a better look at the bottom shelf. 'There are over thirty-five volumes. If every page means a day's entry, he's been documenting his life for what?'

'Over twenty years,' Hunter said, flipping open the volume in his hand. 'His days, his thoughts, his doubts. They're all here on paper. Listen to this,' he said, turning towards Garcia.

'*With a heavy heart I prayed today. I prayed for a woman – Rosa Perez. For the past five years she'd been coming to this church. She'd been praying for one thing and one thing only. To be able to bear a child. Her womb was severely damaged after she'd been sexually assaulted by four men almost eight years ago. It happened only a block away from here. She was sixteen then. Rosa got married three years after the assault. She and her husband, Antonio, have been trying for a child ever since, and last year her prayers were finally answered. She became pregnant. I've never seen anyone so happy in all my life. Two months ago she gave birth to a baby boy, Miguel Perez, but there were complications. The baby wasn't born healthy. He fought bravely for ten days, but his lungs and heart were too weak. He died eleven days after his birth.*

'*Rosa came back to this church only once after she left the hospital. She brought with her a single question – WHY?*

'*I saw it in her eyes. There was no belief anymore. Her faith had died with her son.*

'*Today – alone – she took her own life inside a small apartment in East Hatchway Street. I now fear for Antonio's sanity. And though my faith is indisputable, I long to know the answer to Rosa's question. WHY, Lord? Why do you give only to take away?'*

Hunter looked at Garcia.

'When was that?'

'There are no dates,' Hunter confirmed.

Garcia shook his head as he pinched the bridge of his nose. 'That's a sad story. It seems that even priests question their faith from time to time.'

Hunter closed the diary and placed it back in the bookcase. 'If Father Fabian feared for his life, or if anything bothered him lately, it will be in one of these books.'

Garcia slowly blew out a deep breath. 'We'll need some extra manpower to read through all of them.'

'Maybe,' Hunter said, retrieving the first diary from the right. 'I'm hoping Father Fabian was an organized man. If that's the case, the journals should be in order. If anything bothered him "lately", it'll be in the most recent one.'

Twelve

The party was already in full swing by the time Hunter arrived. Everyone was there. From the chief of police to the Robbery-Homicide Division's mail boy. Even the mayor was expected to turn up. That wasn't surprising given that William Bolter had been the Robbery-Homicide Division's captain for the past eighteen years. Most of the division's detectives had never been under a different captain. Everyone owed Captain Bolter a favor or two – everyone including Robert Hunter.

The Redwood Bar & Grill was bustling with law-enforcement officers. The ones on duty had their beepers securely clipped onto their belts. The ones off duty had beer bottles and whiskey glasses in their hands.

Hunter and Garcia had spent the entire day at the Seven Saints Catholic Church and its neighborhood. But the house-to-house turned up nothing but scared and distressed people. Hunter's mind was overflowing with questions, and he knew the answers would take time.

'Believe it or not, they have a ten-year-old bottle of Macallan behind the bar,' Garcia said, coming up to Hunter with two half-full whiskey tumblers.

Single-malt Scotch whiskey was Hunter's biggest passion. But unlike most people, he knew how to appreciate it instead of simply getting drunk on it.

'To Captain Bolter.' He raised his glass. Garcia did the same. 'Where's Anna?' Hunter asked, looking around.

Anna Preston had been Garcia's high school sweetheart and they'd married straight after graduation.

'She's at the bar chatting to some of the other wives.' Garcia made a silly face. 'We ain't staying long.'

'Me neither,' Hunter agreed.

'Are you gonna go back to the church?'

'Roberrrrt,' Detective Kyle Byrne interrupted, grabbing Hunter by the arm and raising the bottle of Bud in his hand. 'A toassst to Captain Bolterrr.'

Hunter smiled and touched his glass against Kyle's bottle.

'Where're you going?' Kyle asked as Hunter started towards the bar. "ave a drink wizz us,' he slurred, pointing towards a table where a handful of detectives sat drinking. They all looked wasted.

Hunter nodded to everyone at the table. 'I'll come back in a minute, Kyle. I just gotta say hello to a few people, but Carlos here can hang around with you boys for a while.' He patted Garcia on the back, who gave him a 'you didn't just do that to me?' look.

'Carlosss. Come and 'ave a drink.' Kyle dragged Garcia towards the table.

A firm hand grabbed Hunter by the shoulder before he reached the bar. He turned around ready to raise a new toast.

'So you finally decided to show up.'

Captain Bolter was an impressive-looking man. Tall and built like a rhinoceros. Despite being in his late sixties, he still had a full head of silvery hair. His thick mustache had been his trademark for the past twenty years. His menacing figure demanded respect.

'Captain,' Hunter replied with a pleased smile. 'Did you actually think I wouldn't turn up?'

Captain Bolter placed his right arm around Hunter's shoulders. 'Let's step outside, shall we? I can't bear to raise another toast to myself.'

Thirteen

Clear skies made the night feel even colder. Hunter zipped up his leather jacket while Captain Bolter pulled a Felipe Power cigar from his jacket pocket. 'Want one?' he offered.

'No, thanks.'

'C'mon, it's my leaving do. You should try one.'

'I'll stick with Scotch.' Hunter raised his glass. 'Those things make me dizzy.'

'You sound like a big girl.'

Hunter laughed. 'A girl who kicked your ass in the shooting range.'

Captain Bolter's turn to laugh. 'You know that I let you win on Friday, don't you?'

'Of course you did.'

'I'll take one of those.'

Hunter and the captain turned to face the man standing behind them. In his early sixties, Doctor Jonathan Winston, the Los Angeles Chief Medical Examiner, was dressed in an expensive-looking dark Italian suit with a white shirt and a conservative blue tie.

'Jonathan!' Captain Bolter said, already retrieving another cigar and handing it to the doctor.

'You look like you just came from church, doc,' Hunter said with a smile.

Doctor Winston lit up his cigar, took a long drag and blew the smoke out slowly. 'From what I've heard, so have you.'

Hunter's smile faded fast.

'I've heard about this morning,' the captain said in a more ominous tone. 'By the look on your face, I can tell you don't think this was a random killing, do you?'

Robert shook his head.

'Religious hate?'

'We don't know yet, captain. There are some clues that point to a religious motive, or a religious psycho, but it's too early to say.'

'What do you have?'

'At this point the only thing we know for sure is that the killer was extremely brutal, probably ritualistic.'

Hunter's split-second hesitation was quickly picked up by Captain Bolter. 'C'mon, Robert, I know you. There's something else bothering you.'

Hunter sipped his Scotch and breathed in sharply. 'They talked.'

'Who talked? The priest and the killer?'

Hunter nodded.

'How do you know that?' the doctor asked.

'The body was found a few feet from the confessional. Both doors were open and so was the small window on the partition that separates the two small cubicles.' He paused for a second. 'In the Catholic Church when a confessor is done confessing his sins and is given his penance, the priest always closes the partition window. Something about symbolizing that the door has been shut on those sins and the person's been forgiven.'

'Are you Catholic?' Doctor Winston asked.

'No, I just read a lot.'

Captain Bolter moved his cigar to the right edge of his

mouth. 'So you think the killer confessed before . . .' He shook his head, giving Hunter a chance to fill in the blank.

'Dragging the priest out of his cubicle and decapitating him.'

The captain closed his eyes, threw his head back and let out a slow and heartfelt sigh. 'Forgive me, father, for I'll rip your head off.'

'Something like that.'

'We all know what that means,' the doctor said, taking another puff on his cigar.

'That this is just the beginning,' Captain Bolter said. 'And if we don't catch up with this killer soon, he'll claim another victim.'

Fourteen

The wind had strengthened, and Doctor Winston pulled the collar of his suit blazer tighter around his neck before cocking a questioning eyebrow at the captain. 'We?'

'He's right, captain.' Hunter smiled. 'From midnight tonight, you're a retired man. You don't have to worry anymore.'

'Your work here is done, my son,' Doctor Winston said in a low, Darth Vader-like voice.

'It's gotta feel good, hasn't it?'

The captain gave Hunter an unconvincing smile. 'Force of habit, I guess. I've given fifty years of my life to law-enforcement agencies in this city. It's not something I can drop overnight, but I'll get there.'

Hunter saw straight through the captain's brave face. He was sad to be leaving.

'So what're you gonna do with your life now that you don't have to worry about catching criminals anymore?' Doctor Winston asked.

'Beth wants to move.'

'Really? Where to?'

'Somewhere far away from here. She's had enough of this city and I don't blame her. LA has gotten too violent.'

'I can vouch for that,' Doctor Winston agreed. 'As the years go by, what we see down at the morgue just gets more gruesome and sadistic. It's like there's no respect for life anymore. And the numbers are rising. We can barely keep up with our daily workload.'

Hunter quickly saw the need for a change of subject. 'Maybe you won't miss LA.' He turned towards Captain Bolter. 'But I know you're gonna miss us.'

'Like a hole in the head,' he replied, puffing on his cigar.

They all laughed.

'At least the new captain is a lot better looking than I am.'

'That wouldn't be hard,' Hunter joked. 'So, are you finally gonna end this goddamn mystery about who the new captain is?'

'They don't know it yet?' Doctor Winston asked, biting his bottom lip.

'Do you?' Hunter asked, surprised.

'Uh-huh.'

Hunter pinned Captain Bolter with a hawk-sharp gaze.

'Don't gimme that pissed-off housewife look,' Captain Bolter said derisively. 'I get enough of that at home, plus I wanted it to be a surprise.' His grin made Hunter squint with a new worry.

'Oh, she'll surprise them alright,' Doctor Winston laughed.

'She?' Hunter looked from one man to the other.

Captain Bolter held the suspense before conceding. 'Her name's Barbara Blake.'

'You *are* kidding me, right?' Hunter leaned back against the beechwood table.

'Why? Because she's a woman?' the captain asked with a frown.

'No, because her name's Barbara. Are you telling me that the RHD will have Captain Barbie from now on?'

'Ooh, don't ever call her Barbie.' Doctor Winston shook his head.

'Definitely not,' Captain Bolter added. 'Unless you've grown tired of your balls. Don't let the fact that she's a woman fool you, Robert. She's a great captain and a vicious bitch when she needs to be. She's proven it many times. We were partners for two years before she asked to be transferred to Sacramento.'

Hunter detected sadness in the captain's voice. 'Just work partners?' he asked as he finished the last of his single malt.

'Don't even think about psychoanalyzing me, Robert. Not anymore.' Captain Bolter shook his head and pointed his cigar at Hunter.

'Wouldn't dream of it.'

'There you are, captain.' Lieutenant Sheldon appeared at the door. 'They're calling for you. It's speech time. And we all wanna know who's taking over. No more suspense.'

'I guess not.'

Hunter didn't follow them in.

Fifteen

The main facility of the Los Angeles County Department of Coroner is located on North Mission Road, number 1104. The building is an outstanding piece of architecture with hints of Renaissance. Old-fashioned lampposts flank the extravagant entrance stairway. Terracotta bricks and light gray lintels fronted the large hospital-turned-morgue. The whole building looked like it should be part of a prestigious Oxford college.

Criminalistics students Nelson Fenton and Jamaal Jackson still had another hour to go before the end of their night shift. Despite their job being part time and relatively simple, it required a very strong stomach. As forensic technicians for the LACDC, they were expected to transport, undress, photograph, clean and prepare bodies for autopsies.

'How many more bodies do we have on the list?' Jamaal asked, pulling his surgical mask down from his mouth and letting it hang loosely around his neck. They'd just finished preparing the body of a sixty-five-year-old man who'd been stabbed fifty-two times by his own son.

'Two.' Nelson pointed to the two black polyethylene body bags on the steel tables at the far end of the room.

'Let's just get on with it, then.'

First they needed to undress the bodies before thoroughly hosing them down in preparation for the post-mortem. While

Jamaal was adjusting the strap on his surgical mask, Nelson approached the larger of the two body bags and unzipped it.

'Oh shit!' Nelson said, lifting both hands to his mouth and taking a step back.

'What's the matter?'

'Have a look.'

Jamaal checked the unzipped body bag. 'Oh crap.' He made a face as if he'd just tasted something bitter. 'Headless.'

Nelson nodded. 'But have a look at what he's wearing.'

Only then Jamaal noticed the priest's cassock. 'Oh man, that's bad. Who the hell would do this to a priest?'

'Someone with a lot of anger,' Nelson said, stepping forward again.

'I'm not Catholic or nothing, but this is just . . .' Jamaal shook his head without finishing the sentence. 'This city's messed up, man. Violence everywhere.'

'The whole world's messed up, dude. Let's just finish this and get the hell out of here. I've had enough for today.'

'You can say that again.'

They unbuttoned the cassock, pulled it open and froze.

'Holy shit,' Nelson whispered.

'I think we better get Doctor Winston on the phone. Right now.'

Sixteen

Insomnia is a very unpredictable condition and it affects people in different ways. It can kick in before you go to bed or it can torture you, allowing you to fall asleep for an hour or so before creeping in and keeping you awake for the rest of the night. In the United States, one in five people suffer from it.

After spending most of the night researching on the internet, Hunter managed only a couple of hours' sleep before his brain was wide awake again. The images of the church and Father Fabian's murder played at the back of his mind like a film stuck on an agonizing loop. To disconnect, Hunter hit the gym at 4:00 a.m.

At 6:00 a.m., after a heavy workout and a hot shower, Hunter was staring out of the window of his small one-bedroom apartment in south Los Angeles. He was trying to organize his thoughts when his cell phone rang.

'Detective Hunter speaking.'

'Robert, it's Jonathan Winston here.'

Hunter checked his watch. 'What's the matter, doc? Can't sleep?'

'At my age I rarely sleep past five in the morning anyway, but I ain't calling to discuss my sleeping habits.'

The ominous tone in Doctor Winston's voice cleared the grin from Hunter's face. 'What's wrong?'

'Well, you'd better get your partner and get here. I need you to see something before I start the autopsy on the decapitated priest.'

'*Before* you start the examination?' Hunter enquired skeptically.

'That's right.'

'Are you at the County Coroner's?'

'Yep.'

'I'll call Carlos. We'll be there in half an hour, doc.'

Seventeen

'So what's this all about?' Garcia asked as he met Hunter in the parking lot to the County Department of Coroner at 6:35 a.m. 'This place ain't even open yet.'

Hunter shrugged. 'The doctor didn't say, but I guess we'll find out soon enough.'

Doctor Winston greeted both detectives with a firm handshake by the entrance door.

'So what happened, doc?' Hunter asked as they entered the building.

'Well, last night when I got to the Redwood Bar & Grill for William's leaving do, I turned my cell phone off. After all, I'm a pathologist not a surgeon. I don't get called for emergencies in the middle of the night.'

'OK.' Hunter said the word slowly.

'When I turned my cell phone back on this morning I had a rather peculiar message from one of my forensic technicians.'

They walked through an empty front lobby, past the reception desk and into a long and well-lit corridor.

'As you might expect, we're one of the busiest coroners' departments in the entire United States. Most of the gritty, autopsy-preparatory jobs are delegated to forensic technicians, who are usually university students.'

They reached the stairwell at the end of the corridor and went up to the first floor.

'The corpses arrive here in a regular polyethylene body bag. In the specific case of your priest's body, the coroner's investigator at the scene was kind enough to remove the dog's head from the body before sealing the bag.'

'I can imagine a student's surprise as he unzips a bag to find a human body with a dog's head stuck to it,' Hunter said.

'Exactly,' the doctor confirmed. 'I haven't seen the head yet.'

'Where's it now?' Garcia enquired.

'In the lab. It will be undergoing forensic tests this morning. If we're lucky, we might get something.'

They stopped in front of the changing-room door.

'Suit up,' the doctor said. 'I'll meet you at autopsy 2B. Second to last door on the left.' He pointed down the corridor.

After Hunter and Garcia rejoined him, Doctor Winston continued, 'OK, so last night the forensic technicians were preparing bodies for this morning's examinations.' He opened the door to room 2B and switched on the lights. Immediately, the smell of ammonia hit them and burned their lungs. A stainless-steel table occupied the middle of the spotlessly clean tiled floor. On one wall there was a large double sink and a metal counter with several tools neatly lined up on it, including a Stryker saw. On the opposite wall, shelves held numerous microscopes, vials and test tubes. Two state-of-the-art computers sat on two separate small desks.

'The body needs to be washed before the examination is carried out,' Doctor Winston said, stepping closer to the stainless-steel table. A body lay on it covered by a long white cloth. 'Needless to say that before being washed, the body needs to be undressed.'

Hunter could already predict what would come next.

'When the forensic technicians undid the priest's cassock, this is what they found.' Doctor Winston uncovered the body. All three men stared at it in silence for a few seconds.

'Fuck,' Garcia whispered, breaking the tense silence. On the priest's chest, painted in red and about six inches long, was the number three.

Eighteen

It was past 9:30 a.m. by the time Hunter and Garcia arrived at the RHD headquarters in North Los Angeles Street. Usually the main squad room would be at least two-thirds empty at this time, with the majority of detectives out in the field. This morning it was surprisingly full.

'Wow! Busy in here today,' Garcia commented, looking around the open-plan office.

'And there's a reason for it,' Hunter countered.

'Homicides are finally on a slope in LA?' Garcia joked.

'Not even God could make that happen.' Hunter pointed to the door at the far end of the squad room. 'That's the reason.' The placard on its door read CAPTAIN BARBARA BLAKE.

'Damn! I forgot all about the introductory meeting with the new captain this morning at eight.'

'We had more important things to do,' Hunter said, taking off his jacket and placing it on the back of his chair as he reached his desk.

Before he had a chance to sit down, the door to the captain's office was pulled opened and Captain Bolter poked his head through. 'Robert, Carlos, get in here.'

Without knocking, both detectives entered the spacious office. A stylish rosewood desk was positioned by the large back window. Casebooks lined the various shelves on the wall to the right of the desk. Most of the framed photographs that once decorated the room were now gone. Hunter guessed they were packed inside the boxes neatly arranged against the west wall. Captain Bolter was by the coffee machine in the corner. Standing beside the desk was a striking-looking woman.

'Robert Hunter, Carlos Garcia, meet your new captain, Barbara Blake,' William Bolter said as he stirred the cup of coffee in his hand.

Captain Blake's long dark hair was elegantly styled into a twisted bun. Her skin, under light makeup, looked smooth and well cared for. She wore a pale shade of lipstick, a pearl necklace and matching earrings. Her designer white silk shirt was neatly tucked into a black tube skirt. Hunter knew she was in her early fifties, but she looked no older than forty.

'Please have a seat.' She pointed to the two leather chairs in front of her desk. 'This will be the last time any of you two walk into my office without knocking,' she said as both detectives sat down.

William Bolter chuckled. 'I told you she can be a right bitch.'

Hunter kept silent. His eyes studied the new captain. She was playing her cards right. Straight away she was making a stand. Showing she wouldn't take crap from any of her detectives. The right thing to do on her first day in such a powerful and male-dominated job.

'I'm gonna skip the bullshit speech I gave the other detectives earlier. I'm sure you've heard it all before and I'm not here to patronize you,' she said, taking a seat behind her new desk. 'Nothing's gonna change. You'll carry on doing your job and you'll report to me as your captain just as you did with William.' She nodded towards Captain Bolter.

Hunter liked her style. First show you mean business then play your friendly hand. Barbara Blake was no first-timer.

She tossed a neatly folded newspaper towards both detectives. 'Your new case is already causing a stir.'

Hunter picked it up and checked the headline.

DECAPITATED PRIEST MADE TO LOOK LIKE THE DEVIL. There were no pictures.

Hunter handed the paper to Garcia without reading the rest of the article. 'That was expected, captain. Reporters were already there by the time we got to the church. We're just lucky none of them managed to sneak in and snapshot the body.'

Captain Blake leaned back on her chair. 'I just came off the phone with Mayor Edwards. As you probably know, he's a Roman Catholic. He's also very good friends with Bishop Patrick Clark, who's the Episcopal Vicar of the San Pedro region. The Seven Saints Catholic Church belongs to that region.' She paused and locked eyes with Hunter. 'Mayor Edwards called to pressure me. He wants this investigation to be the very definition of swift justice. I reassured him that, as always, we'd be doing our best. He asked who I had on the case, and when I gave him your name he freaked out.'

Carlos frowned.

'He demanded I handed the investigation to someone else.'

'What?' Garcia looked at Hunter.

'He's got some issues with you.' She continued staring. 'I'd say he hates your guts. What did you do, bed his wife?'

A slight head tilt from Hunter. William Bolter kept his eyes on his coffee cup.

'Oh hell no,' she said as her eyes widened. 'Please tell me you didn't bed the mayor's wife.'

Garcia cocked both eyebrows.

'With all due respect, captain, I don't see what my personal life has to do with the case.'

The captain's lips twitched. She stood up and walked around

to the front of her desk. 'I'd have to agree with that statement. William tells me you're the best he's ever commanded. I trust his judgment. And I'll be damned if on my first day as the RHD captain I'll allow some snob-ass politician to try and intimidate me, much less tell me which of my detectives I should or shouldn't assign to an investigation.'

William Bolter smiled.

'I told the mayor the case was being handled by extremely competent and experienced detectives. And never to try and tell me how to run my division again.'

'You defied the mayor of Los Angeles on your first day?' Hunter asked calmly. 'Most people would prefer to have him on their side.'

Captain Blake leaned against her desk directly in front of Hunter. 'Do you think I made a mistake, Detective Hunter?'

Hunter held her gaze. 'Do *you* think you made a mistake, captain?'

Captain Blake's smile was full of confidence. 'Let's get one thing straight from the word go, shall we? I'll always stand by my detectives. So don't even think about starting with that *Miami-Vice, I don't give a crap* bullshit attitude. It doesn't bother me pissing politicians off. What bothers me is not having the trust of the people I work with.' Her voice was steady and firm. Her stare moving between both detectives. 'If the mayor's only beef with you is because you tapped his wife, that's something he's gonna have to live with. I don't have time for that crap. So in answer to your question, Detective Hunter – no, I don't think I made a mistake.'

Hunter couldn't fault her. She really knew how to play her cards right.

Nineteen

Barbara Blake didn't allow the silence to settle.

'So what have we got on this new case?'

Hunter proceeded to tell her the little they had so far on Father Fabian's murder.

'Goddamnit,' she spat the word. 'So this killer's probably killed twice before?'

'It's possible, but it isn't a certainty,' Hunter replied, pinching his chin.

Captain Blake lifted her eyebrows, inviting him to carry on.

'The number three could mean Father Fabian's the third victim or it could mean something else.'

'Like what?'

'I'm not sure. Something important to the killer, or Father Fabian, or both. The truth is that we don't know yet and it's irresponsible to make assumptions this early.'

'OK, I can go with that,' Captain Blake agreed. 'Do you think the altar boy could be involved? It's not unheard of.'

'I don't think so,' Hunter replied.

'Why not?'

'It takes a certain kind of person to be able to kill someone the way Father Fabian was killed. Hermano isn't physically or mentally strong enough. He's only fourteen.'

'We'd also be missing motive,' Garcia cut in. 'And we

already deducted the killer is about six-two. Hermano is five-six, five-seven tops.'

'How did you figure out the killer's height?'

Garcia started explaining, but after thirty seconds the captain raised her right hand, stopping him. 'Forget I asked.' She returned to her seat and faced Hunter. 'What're your initial feelings on this?'

'We have only one victim so far, and that gives us nothing to establish a consistent pattern. Initial analysis of the crime scene indicates the UNSUB is very strong, skilled, intelligent, methodical and brutal. Despite the savagery of what we found in the church, Father Fabian's murder was well planned.'

'Methodical and planned?' She frowned. 'From what I've heard, there was blood everywhere. An extremely messy crime scene. Doesn't that indicate rage and loss of control?'

'In most cases, yes.'

She waited for Hunter to go on. He didn't. 'Care to develop, detective?' she pushed.

'The Seven Saints crime scene might appear messy to an outsider, but not to the killer. The bloodstains and splatters were exactly where he wanted them to be. It was a controlled and planned mess.'

'Ritual?'

Hunter leaned forward on his seat and ran his hand over his nose and mouth. 'What we have so far indicates so.'

'Baptism of fire for you, Barbara,' William Bolter said, approaching the window behind her desk.

'I'll assign an extra officer to you,' she announced, looking at Hunter. 'It should help with the legwork. If you need any more, let me know. I've also already moved you two to the special operations room upstairs. You'll need the extra space. I've set up an anonymous tip line. I know they usually cause more headaches than anything else, but who knows? We might get lucky.' Captain Blake paused and flipped through a few pieces of paper on her desk. 'With the press already all over this case and a pissed-off mayor, there'll be a lot of pressure on us to come up with answers . . . and fast.'

Twenty

The special operations room was spacious and well lit. Two metal desks already equipped with computer terminals and telephones occupied the center of the room. A fax machine sat on a small wooden table in the corner. A large, nonmagnetic marker board and a half-empty bookcase covered most of the west wall. In the opposite corner was an old-fashioned cork-board. It was mounted onto wheeled pedestals and stood next to two battered gray metal filing cabinets.

Crime-scene photos and witnesses' statements had already been placed on Hunter's desk ready to be organized. He fired up his computer as a knock came at the door.

'It's open,' Hunter called.

Officer Ian Hopkins stepped into the room carrying a brown paper envelope.

'Detective Hunter. These are the photographs you asked me to take of the crowd in front of the church yesterday.' He handed the envelope to Hunter.

Garcia had forgotten all about that.

There were twenty-five pictures in total. Hunter spread them on his desk, bending over to look at each one attentively for a few seconds.

'Do you think the killer could've been watching from the crowd?' Hopkins asked with a hint of excitement.

'It's possible,' Hunter agreed, his eyes moving to another photograph.

'If you don't mind me asking, detective, why would he do that?' Hopkins's curiosity increased.

'It's basic human nature. We all want recognition for things we've done. Many killers enjoy watching the drama of the aftermath of their actions unfold. They're very proud of their work.'

'Proud?' Hopkins smiled nervously. 'That's pretty sick.'

'Serial killers usually are,' Garcia commented from his desk.

'Serial killer?' Hopkins asked a little too enthusiastically. 'Was that the work of a serial killer yesterday?'

Garcia laughed.

Hunter kept his eyes on the photos.

'Do you think the killer is in one of those photos, Detective Hunter?' Hopkins insisted.

'It was already raining by the time you took these.' Hunter shook his head. 'Everyone had either a hood on or an open umbrella. If he is, we wouldn't know.'

'I messed up,' Hopkins said, running his hand through his hair. 'I should've gotten closer, shouldn't I?'

Hunter turned and faced him. 'It's not your fault the rain came down, Officer . . .?'

'Hopkins, sir. Ian Hopkins.' He extended his hand and Hunter shook it firmly.

'You did what I asked you to do, Officer Hopkins.'

Hopkins gave Hunter an unconvincing smile. He felt he should've done better.

'How long have you been a cop, Ian?' Hunter asked, studying Hopkins.

'Three months this week, sir,' he answered proudly.

'Do you like it?'

'Yes, very much.'

'Yesterday, was that your first crime scene?'

'No, sir. A couple of gang shootouts and an armed robbery. All of them with fatal victims.'

'At the church yesterday,' Hunter continued, 'I know you were very curious to have a look at the crime scene. Why didn't you?'

'Because my orders were to stay outside and deal with the onlookers. And then to take some pictures of them.' He gestured to the photos on Hunter's desk.

Hunter glanced at Garcia and they exchanged an unspoken agreement. 'OK, how'd you like to carry on helping with this investigation?'

Hopkins's eyes lit up.

'That'd be fantastic . . . sir.' He couldn't believe his luck. To police officers a serial-murder case is the champagne of homicides, and he'd just been given a VIP invitation to join the party.

'OK. Captain Blake said she'd assign an officer to us. I'll request you.'

'Thank you, sir.'

'I'm not sure *thank you* are the words you'll be using in a week's time.' Hunter leaned back and interlaced his fingers behind his head. 'This won't be easy.'

'I don't like *easy*, sir.'

Hunter smiled. 'Good, so let's start with you dropping the "sir" crap. I'm Robert and this is Carlos.' Hunter gestured towards Garcia. 'Are you any good with computers? I mean, internet searching, research, that sort of stuff?'

'Yeah, I'm very good at it.'

'Great. I'll introduce you to Jack Kerley, the main guy in our IT unit. He'll get you set up.'

'OK, that sounds great to me.'

'One more thing,' Hunter said, stopping Hopkins before he left the room. 'This case and everything related to it is to be discussed with no one other than Carlos and myself, do you understand?'

'Yes, sir.' He nodded eagerly before reaching for the door.

The phone on Hunter's desk rang.

'Detective Hunter.'

It was Doctor Winston. 'Robert, I've got the results of the autopsy together with a few of the lab tests. I can email them to you, but . . .'

Hunter sensed the uneasiness in the doctor's voice. 'It's OK. We'll be right over, doc.'

Twenty-One

In the Los Angeles lunchtime traffic, it took them over twenty-five minutes to cover the two miles between the RHD headquarters and the LACDC. Doctor Winston was waiting for them in room 2B, the same autopsy room they were in earlier.

'So what have you got for us, doc?' Hunter asked, covering his nose with his right hand.

'Would you like a mask, Robert? We've got plenty,' Doctor Winston said, reading Hunter's discomfort.

'No, I'm fine, but if we could speed this up, it'd be great.'

'OK, follow me.' The doctor walked up to the stainless-steel table. Hunter and Garcia followed. The headless priest's body had been washed clean. The familiar Y incision that ran from the front of each shoulder to the pubic bone had already been sewn shut. Large black stitches stuck out of the ghostly-white flesh like poisonous thorns.

'Fingerprints have confirmed that the victim is indeed Brett Stewart Nichols, aka Father Fabian. Time of death is estimated to be somewhere between 10:00 p.m. and midnight on Wednesday.'

Hunter nodded. 'Closing time at the church.'

'Except for where the head's been severed, the body is clean of traumas,' the doctor said, putting on a new pair of latex gloves. 'Decapitation didn't occur after death. In layman's terms, it was the cause of death. Now here's the interesting fact: there's nothing to indicate that the victim's been restrained. No abrasions or marks on the wrists or ankles.'

'Was he sedated?' Hunter asked, bending down to look at the neck stump.

A slight head shake. 'Toxicology came back negative for any type of anesthetic.'

'Why do you think he could've been sedated?' Garcia turned to Hunter.

'Most people would put up a fight if they were about to be beheaded.'

Doctor Winston agreed with a nod. 'With no defensive wounds, we know the priest didn't fight back. It's not easy to decapitate a moving target.'

'Could the priest have been knocked unconscious?' Garcia asked.

'That's a possibility I've considered,' Doctor Winston replied, circling the table to the other side. 'Without the head, I won't be able to confirm it.'

Garcia nodded.

'There's only one glitch with that possibility,' the doctor continued, pointing to the neck stump. 'The head was severed with a single, powerful strike. Undoubtedly a very sharp and precise weapon. No hacking, no sawing. According to the forensics team, there were no marks, no dents, nothing on the floor surrounding the body. If the victim was lying unconscious on the floor, a blow from a sharp, decapitating weapon would've surely left some sort of impression. The cut line on the neck suggests the priest was in an upright position, probably kneeling or sitting down. The blow came from above and from the victim's left, suggesting the killer's right-handed.'

Hunter considered the doctor's words for several silent seconds. 'I don't believe the priest was knocked unconscious.' He stepped away from the body and leaned against the microscope counter.

'Why not?' Garcia asked. 'It would've made things a lot simpler for the killer.'

'This killer isn't after easy or simple. You saw the brutality of the crime scene. Sadistic killers rarely show compassion. Killing an unconscious victim would've given him no satisfaction. This killer wanted the victim's fear. I bet he was looking straight into Father Fabian's eyes when he delivered the fatal blow.'

Garcia felt a shudder run through his body. 'So if he was conscious, why didn't Father Fabian fight back? Or at least lift his hands to protect his face? It's only natural.'

'Too scared to move,' Hunter offered.

'Very possible,' Doctor Winston admitted.

'Are you suggesting that he just sat there like a statue while the killer took a swing at him?'

'It happens.' Doctor Winston nodded. 'Depending on how terrified a victim is, it's not uncommon for the brain to simply shut down. No motor stimuli get sent anywhere. And even though the victim might want to, he won't be able to move.'

'Hence the terms *scared stiff* and *petrified*.' Hunter confirmed.

Garcia's stare rested on the priest's body once again. 'Poor man. How about the weapon used, doc? An axe?'

'An axe is an easy weapon to obtain, but very hard to handle and control,' the doctor clarified. 'It's bulky, heavy and, contrary to what you might've seen in movies, the length of its blade isn't ideal for decapitation. The killer would have to be a master lumberjack to achieve this sort of precision with a single swing.'

'Any suggestions of what we should be looking for, doc?' Both detectives faced Doctor Winston.

'Because we haven't found the head yet, I can only analyze the neck side of the cut. Judging by how smooth and precise it is, I'd say it's very consistent with the type of cut achieved by a samurai sword.'

'Samurai?' Garcia's eyes widened. 'Like ninja style?'

Doctor Winston laughed. 'They're not the same thing, but you've got the idea.' The doctor studied both detectives for a moment.

'I wanna show you something that might just help.'

Twenty-Two

From the counter behind him, Doctor Winston retrieved a remarkable-looking sword. Its long, slightly curved blade had a distinctive mirror-polish finish.

'Goddamnit, doc,' Hunter said, taking a step back. 'You gotta lay off those cheesy late-night kung-fu movies.'

Doctor Winston paid no attention to the comment. 'This is a typical samurai sword, also known as katana. It can be easily purchased over the internet – no identity checks necessary. The blade is made out of carbon steel. Its length can vary, but it's usually somewhere between twenty-two and twenty-nine inches.' He stepped closer to the priest's body. 'This is a precise and laser-sharp weapon. Ideal for a decapitation job. If the sword handler is skilled enough, the strike can be lightning fast. Almost impossible to evade.' He held the sword with both hands and slowly moved it down towards the body's neck stump. 'But the great thing about this weapon is that it's so light the killer could've used a single hand for the fatal blow. And it would've been just as precise.'

'Great,' Garcia commented.

'Some of the lab results are in.' Doctor Winston changed the subject as he returned the sword to the counter. 'As we expected, there were hundreds of fingerprints all around the church and the confessional.' He pulled a few sheets of paper out of a manila envelope. 'At the moment they're being run against the national fingerprint database, but I wouldn't expect any great breakthroughs.'

Hunter nodded. He knew they'd probably get positive matches for petty crimes, robbery, maybe even firearms offences. Compton is an underprivileged neighborhood, still heavy with gang activity. Most of its residents are no strangers to violence. 'Did we get anything from the altar?' he asked, his eyes scanning the sheets Doctor Winston had handed him.

'Two sets of prints. They belong either to the victim or to the altar boy. Nothing from an unidentified source.'

'How about the chalice?' Garcia asked. 'Didn't the killer allegedly drink the priest's blood from the chalice?'

'Yes.'

'So we can get the killer's DNA,' Garcia said with excitement.

'No, we can't.' Hunter rubbed his tired eyes.

'Why not? Can't DNA be extracted from saliva?' Garcia faced Doctor Winston.

'Yes, it can.'

'But the blood inside the chalice belonged to Father Fabian, right?' Hunter asked.

Doctor Winston nodded.

'That means that our killer's DNA, taken from the saliva, would've mixed with the priest's DNA in the blood. Once DNA gets mixed together . . .' Hunter shook his head. 'It can't be split apart anymore.'

Garcia looked at Doctor Winston for confirmation.

'Robert's right.' He nodded. 'The lab will be able to tell you that there're two different sources of DNA. But they won't be able to split them.'

'Fantastic.' Garcia cupped his hand over his nose. The

nauseating smell was getting to him. 'This gets better by the second. Do we have anything conclusive?'

Doctor Winston took a deep breath. 'The blood the killer used to draw the number three on the priest's chest. It's human, and it's not Father Fabian's.'

Hunter raised his eyebrows in anticipation.

'It belongs to a woman.'

'A woman?' Garcia looked baffled. 'I didn't know you could tell gender from a simple blood test?'

'You can from DNA tests, or if you specifically test for levels of estrogen.'

Hunter instinctively checked his watch. 'There's no way you would've gotten DNA results this fast, doc. And you had no reason to test for estrogen levels.'

'So how do you know the blood came from a woman?' Garcia pressed.

'Unless . . .' Hunter's questioning eyes moved back to Doctor Winston.

'Unless what?' Garcia asked eagerly.

'Unless she was pregnant.'

Doctor Winston closed his eyes and nodded slowly.

Twenty-Three

Amanda Reilly re-entered the numbers into her spreadsheet and pressed the RETURN button.

Nothing changed.

The final calculation was still way short of what was needed to cover her estate agency's bills for the month. She placed her reading glasses on the desk in front of her and pinched the bridge of her nose. This was the fourth consecutive month she'd have to default on several payments. The week was drawing to a close, and the two viewings they'd had this week hadn't produced an offer. According to her calculations, if she didn't get a sale soon she'd only be able to afford to keep the agency open for a few more weeks – maybe a month.

Amanda had dropped out of high school at the age of seventeen after flunking tenth grade for the second time. She was an intelligent girl, but when it came to exams and answering questions her heart would take off like a fighter jet, her mind would go blank and she couldn't get a single answer out.

Amanda knew she was very good with people. And she had charisma – bundles of it. Her first job was as a trainee broker in a small real estate agency in central LA. It didn't take her long to get the gist of things, and within a year her sales figures were topping everyone else's in the agency.

She didn't stay in central Los Angeles for long, accepting a job with Palm Properties, one of the largest real estate agencies in Palm Springs.

In California, businesses don't come much more cutthroat than real estate, but Amanda knew how to use her assets to her advantage. Other than being smart, charismatic and charming, she was also very attractive, with shoulder-length blond hair, sky-blue eyes and porcelain-smooth skin. Some would say she slept her way into her partnership just three years after joining Palm Properties.

Amanda stayed with the agency for eleven years before giving up the partnership and opening her own agency – Reilly's – in West Hollywood. She was a hard-working woman, and during the following ten years three other Reilly's opened across Los Angeles. But just over a year ago, the booming American property market came crashing to a halt. Repossessions were at an all-time high. Bank loans were nonexistent. No one was buying. Not even the super-rich.

Amanda tried every trick she'd learned over the years to keep her head above the waterline, but nothing seemed to work. She had to close all but her flagship agency in West Hollywood. The past four months had been particularly hard for Amanda and her company. She had to let everyone go except for her best friend and first ever Reilly's employee, Tania Riggs.

Despite the gloomy week, Amanda was feeling lucky. Late yesterday she'd received a call from a potential buyer who sounded very interested in one of her most expensive properties. A seven-bedroom, nine-bathroom, four-million-dollar mansion on Pacific Coast Highway in Malibu. The caller had seen the property advertised on their website and loved the features – the swimming pool, the large eccentric fireplace in the living room, the tennis court, the beautiful grounds – the house was perfect. He had requested a viewing for late this afternoon.

'Here you go,' Tania Riggs said, handing Amanda a dark green plastic folder.

Amanda had asked Tania to prepare a 'killer' package on the property.

'I've included everything.' Tania said. 'Photos, detailed information on the house and grounds – even a list of celebrities who live within two miles of the place. There's also a CD with that PowerPoint presentation I showed you earlier.'

Amanda smiled. 'That was a fantastic presentation, Tania, thanks. I have a good feeling about this.' She wiggled the folder in her hand.

'Me too. It's such a beautiful house, and if you have the money . . . a bargain.'

Amanda admired Tania's optimism. For someone who hadn't received her wages in five weeks, she sure knew how to stay positive.

The phone rang and Tania ran back to her desk to pick it up.

'Amanda,' Tania said, after placing the caller on hold. 'It's Mr. Turner for you.'

Amanda nodded and reached for the phone on her desk. The conversation took less than a minute.

'Please tell me he didn't cancel,' Tania said nervously, after Amanda hung up.

'No, no.'

'Thank God for that.'

'But he'll be about an hour late.'

'Oh, that's OK, then.' Tania smiled. 'Do you want me to wait with you?'

'There's no need. I'm all set here.' She pointed to the dark green folder Tania had given her. 'Go home, girl. And try to have a good rest over the weekend.'

'I sure will. Good luck.'

Tania buttoned up her coat all the way to her neck before closing the door behind her.

Amanda placed her right elbow on her desk, rested her chin on her closed fist and stared at the spreadsheet on her screen once again. Things were about to change, she could feel it.

Twenty-Four

Hunter and Garcia were studying the forensic photographs taken at the church when Captain Blake entered the room without knocking and closed the door behind her. Her eyes rested on the piles of leather-bound notebooks on both detectives' desks.

'Are these the priest's journals?' she asked, approaching Garcia's desk, picking a volume up and flipping through the first few pages.

Hunter nodded.

'Anything interesting?'

'Depends what you consider interesting.'

Captain Blake gave Hunter a look that told him she didn't have time for bullshit.

'We're going through them as fast as we can,' Hunter explained. 'But there's a lot of stuff in those books. They're not proper journals or diaries. They're just books the priest used to write his thoughts, the way he felt, things he'd done . . . There's no sequence. Most of the entries read like dissertations, and they go back a long way.' He walked back to his desk. 'The problem is we're not really sure what were looking for. It could be anything, a word, a phrase . . . or it could be hidden between the lines. If Father Fabian feared for his life, we were hoping to find something in the most recent diary, but they aren't dated.

The idiots who brought them over after forensics were done dusting them didn't think to number the books in the same order they were found on the shelves inside Father Fabian's room.'

'They've been shuffled like a deck of cards,' Garcia commented.

'So if by interesting you mean stories of a tormented priest, then yes, they're very interesting,' Hunter continued. 'But if you mean "have we found something that might give us a clue why he was murdered?", then the answer is – not yet.'

Captain Blake closed the diary and placed it back on the pile. Only then she noticed how neat and tidy Garcia's desk was. Nothing was out of place. No clutter. All the objects on it were arranged symmetrically. 'What do you mean by a tormented priest?'

'It seems like he'd questioned his faith more than once,' Garcia offered.

'We all do that every now and again,' she replied with a shrug.

'That's true.' Hunter looked for something inside his top drawer. 'But it looks like what Father Fabian saw and heard over the years made him doubt priesthood was really his call.'

'Why?'

'You need to believe in God if you're gonna be a priest. At times he questioned God's existence.'

'Plus, there're a few passages that make it clear that he was struggling with the whole celibacy concept,' Garcia noted.

'How many of these have you been through so far?'

'Three each, and we've been reading through the night.' Hunter answered.

The captain folded her arms and exhaled a deep breath. 'Bishop Clark is worried about these journals.'

'Worried how?' Hunter cracked his knuckles and Captain Blake cringed.

'He fears Father Fabian might've written things he shouldn't have.'

'Can you be a little more specific, captain?' Hunter asked. 'We don't have a lot of time for guessing games.'

'The celibacy dilemma for one.'

Garcia coughed. 'So Bishop Clark is more worried that Father Fabian could've jumped the fence than with the fact that he was brutally decapitated inside his own church? That's messed up.'

'He's also very worried that Father Fabian might've written down things he heard in confessions. To the Catholic Church, that's like a felony.'

'Only if Father Fabian had verbally discussed any of his confessions with someone else.' Hunter disagreed. 'Writing them down in a private diary constitutes no sin or Catholic crime.'

'Are you Catholic?' she asked with a frown.

A shake of the head.

'So how do you know that?'

'I read a lot.'

Garcia smiled.

'I suggest you read faster then.'

'Why?'

'Bishop Clark is pressuring to get the journals back.'

'Let him pressure.' Hunter wasn't worried. 'The contents of these journals may turn out to be evidence in an ongoing investigation. The last I heard the police still had the authority to seize any evidence from a crime scene.'

'He ain't going through a court of law.' Captain Blake faced Hunter.

'Let me guess. My old friend, Mayor Edwards?'

'Who no doubt will talk to his old friend, the chief of police. After that it gets complicated.'

'Complicated is what we do, captain. We need to go through those journals.'

'Just get through them as fast and as thoroughly as you can, will you?'

Twenty-Five

Captain Blake approached the corkboard and studied the photographs that were pinned on it. 'I can see what you meant about this being ritualistic. The decapitation, the dog's head, the circle around the altar, the blood-drinking theory, the numbering of the victim . . . It's all there, isn't it?'

Neither detective replied.

'You see, that bothers me,' the captain carried on. 'Rituals are never rushed, and it doesn't seem like this one was either. That tells me the killer would've needed at least twenty to thirty undisturbed minutes to achieve his goal.'

Hunter agreed with a slow nod.

'Risky, isn't it? Especially when you take into account the murder was committed in a public place. Anyone could've walked in on the killer.'

'He had it under control,' Hunter confirmed.

'How so?'

'It looks like the killer was inside the church dressed as a priest just before closing time.'

'What?'

'The estimated time of death coincides with the church's closing time – around ten o'clock.' Hunter searched through a few pieces of paper on his desk. 'Confessions were due to end at ten to ten. At twenty to ten the church was almost empty, except for two people – a Mrs. Morales and a Mrs. Willis. According to their statement, they were asked to leave at that time by a priest they didn't recognize.'

Captain Blake squinted.

'The priest told them he was there to help Father Fabian, and that they were closing early because they needed to prepare the church for a special Mass the next morning. Hermano, the altar boy, knows nothing about a priest helping out. And he said there was nothing special about any Mass.'

'Have you talked to these two women? Do we have a sketch of this mysterious priest?'

'I've talked to them, yes, but no sketch.'

'Why not?'

Hunter picked up two sheets of paper from his desk and handed them to Captain Blake. 'These are the witnesses' statements concerning the priest who asked them to leave.'

The captain read them attentively. Her brow creased as her eyes jumped back and forth from one page to the other. 'Is this serious?'

'Afraid so,' Hunter said.

'So Mrs. Morales says the priest was a Caucasian young man, tall with short blond hair and a long nose.' Captain Blake waggled the sheet in her left hand. 'While Mrs. Willis thinks the priest was "not so tall" and looked Hispanic with short cropped brown hair, a rounded nose and a thin mustache. Are they both blind?'

'No,' Hunter replied casually. 'They're old. Mrs. Morales is seventy-two and Mrs. Willis is seventy-seven. Their memories aren't what they used to be. And you know that our visual memory is our weakest one. No two witnesses ever see the same thing.'

'Great.' Captain Blake handed the statements back to

Hunter. 'But the killer still took a big risk by talking to two different people and asking them to leave the church. He had no way of knowing what their description of him would be like.'

'It was a calculated risk,' Hunter replied, massaging his neck. 'If he took the trouble to disguise himself as a priest, it stands to reason that he'd change his appearance as well. Contact lenses, wig, false nose and mustache . . . whatever. I don't believe he left anything to chance.'

'Very methodical.'

'Ritualistic killers usually are.'

'What if the killer wasn't disguising himself as a priest?' the captain asked, leaning against Garcia's desk. 'What if he *was* a priest? Priests are usually very methodical people.'

'We're also looking into that.' Hunter poured himself a glass of water.

'You don't sound very sure.'

'At the moment I'm not sure of anything, captain. There're too many loose ends.'

'Like what?'

'The importance of the ritual, for one.'

'You lost me already.'

Hunter left his glass on his desk and approached the picture board. 'In a ritual, the ceremony itself is the most important thing; the victim comes second.'

'And you don't believe that's the case here, do you?' the captain asked, joining Hunter by the board.

He subtly shook his head. 'The victim was the most important thing in this murder. The killer specifically wanted Father Fabian dead. And he gave us a clue to that.'

'What clue?' She looked at Hunter.

'The number three drawn on the priest's chest.'

The captain pouted her lips as she thought about it for a few moments. 'The fact that the killer went through the trouble of undoing Father Fabian's cassock, writing the number on his chest and then buttoning him back up.'

Hunter nodded. 'That means that the attack was very personal.'

Captain Blake pulled a strand of loose hair from over her right eye. 'Do you think all that could've been a diversion? The killer made the murder look like a ritual, when in fact it was just a plain sadistic homicide?'

'To divert us from what?' Garcia asked.

'It wasn't a diversion,' Hunter said confidently as he returned to his desk and had a sip of his water. 'If the killer wanted to stage a ritual, the decapitation and the circular blood trail around the altar would've done the job. He didn't have to go as far as drinking the priest's blood or shoving a dog's head down the body's neck. There's a deeper meaning to all this.'

Captain Blake closed her eyes and let out a long sigh. 'So what's your next move?'

'We need to find out as much as we can about Father Fabian, including his personal life.'

'Any family?'

'Father Fabian was an only child,' Garcia replied, reading from a sheet on his desk. 'His father's unknown and his mother died of liver cirrhosis six years ago.'

'Our best bet is Father Malcolm,' Hunter cut in.

'Who's Father Malcolm?'

'He's the head priest at the Our Lady of the Rosary Catholic Church in Paramount. He was also Father Fabian's closest friend.' Hunter instinctively checked his watch. 'I'm taking a drive there later on.'

'I'll stay and get on with the journals.' Garcia pointed to the pile of books.

'How about this?' the captain asked, pointing to the dog's head photograph. 'Any leads?'

'Not yet,' Garcia replied. 'We've found references to Greek mythology and the Eastern Orthodox Church, but nothing relevant so far.'

They were interrupted by the phone on Hunter's desk. It rang twice before he picked it up. 'Detective Hunter.' He turned towards Captain Blake. 'It's for you.'

'Yes . . .' she said, bringing the receiver to her right ear. 'Put him on hold and transfer the call to my office. I'll take it in there.' She handed the phone back to Hunter. 'Just a few days on the job and the mayor is already becoming a pain in my ass.' She headed for the door.

Twenty-Six

Ryan Turner arrived at Reilly's Estate Agency in West Hollywood an hour and fifteen minutes late. Amanda had only talked to the prospective buyer over the phone and she wasn't really sure of what to expect. She was pleasantly surprised.

Ryan was around six-two, in his early forties and well built. His dark brown hair was short, conservative and clean, in harmony with the rest of him. He was executively dressed in an expensive-looking dark suit with perfectly polished shoes. He spoke with a hint of a southern accent.

'I'm sorry for being late,' he said as he firmly shook Amanda's hand. 'Business people always babble on more than they should.'

'It's no problem at all, Mr. Turner,' she replied, giving him her warmest smile. 'I'm glad you could make it.'

'I'm really looking forward to seeing this house. From what I saw on your website, it looks perfect.'

Amanda's smile widened.

'And please,' he continued, 'call me Ryan.'

'Only if you call me Amanda.'

'Deal.'

Ryan convinced Amanda to ride with him. With traffic, the drive took them just over an hour. Amanda spent the first twenty-five minutes telling Ryan how wonderful the property was. Her rehearsed speech rolled off her tongue like poetry. For the rest of the drive they talked about everything, from business to Christmas presents.

The first thing Ryan noticed as they drove through the grand electronic iron gates of the property in Malibu was the tennis court to the left of it.

'Impressive,' he said.

Things were going just as Amanda hoped they would.

The rest of the house didn't disappoint Ryan. Over six thousand square feet of living space with high wood-beamed ceilings in places and magnificent marble floors. Its interior had been luxuriously decorated with modern and stylish furniture. Ingenious light fixtures made every room relaxed and warm. Outside, the spacious entertaining and seating area and large pool with spa provided the final touches to the house.

As he explored each room, Ryan tried to conceal his excitement by keeping his leather-gloved hands tucked into the pockets of his long black overcoat. But the smile on his face gave him away. In this case, the house was literally selling itself.

'Do you mind if we take another look in the living room before we go?' he asked as he stared out of the window of the master bedroom on the second floor, overlooking the beach.

'Of course not,' Amanda replied, trying hard to curb her enthusiasm.

As they entered the living room, Amanda stood by the large, hand-carved wooden double doors. She seemed a little apprehensive.

Ryan was standing behind a lavish white leather sofa positioned just off the center of the immense room, his eyes glued to the ostentatious river rock fireplace that occupied part of the south wall.

'I take it that the fireplace works?' he asked, turning to face Amanda.

'Yes. Everything in this house works perfectly.'

'And I'm guessing it's a gas fire instead of log. Or else I'll need a small forest to fire up this thing.'

Amanda noticed he said 'I'll need' and bit her lip to conceal her smile. 'You're right. It's a gas fire.'

'Could we light it up so I could have a look?'

The question caught Amanda by surprise, and she stared at Ryan wide-eyed.

'Are you OK?'

'Umm . . . yes, I'm fine.' It took her a few seconds to regain her composure. 'I guess it'll be OK if you wanna light it up, but if you don't mind I'll wait in the kitchen.'

Ryan narrowed his eyes and took a couple of steps towards Amanda. 'Is there something the matter?'

'Not at all. Everything is just fine.' Though she put on a brave face, she failed to convince him.

'Everything isn't just fine. The color is gone from your face, Amanda. Did I miss something?' Ryan's eyes searched the room.

'No, no . . .' Her reaction had startled him and she knew it. 'There's nothing wrong with the house or the fireplace. I guarantee it.'

'So what's wrong? I'm very good at reading people, and something is definitely bothering you.'

Amanda took a deep breath. 'I . . . I don't like fires very much.' Her eyes found the floor like a timid little girl.

Ryan let out a nervous chuckle. He stepped within two feet of her and tried to catch her eyes once again. 'Really?'

Amanda lifted her head and stared into Ryan's caring eyes.

'A bad experience?' he asked in a soft voice.

Her lips made a thin line as she nodded.

Ryan placed a comforting hand on Amanda's left shoulder. 'Do you wanna know something?' he said after a short silence. 'I'm petrified of spiders.'

Her lips widened into a tentative smile.

'When I was a young kid, I had an attic room in this old timber house,' he said calmly. 'One night, I fell asleep reading. It must've been around three or four in the morning when I felt something tickling the back of my neck.'

'Oh God!' Amanda exclaimed with a quick shiver.

'Still half asleep, I tried to scratch the annoying tickle. I ended up pissing the spider off and pushing it into the collar of my shirt.'

'Urgh!'

'It was a common brown recluse spider, the type that bites more than once. I guess the one in my shirt was really hungry because it bit me several times.'

Amanda made an 'irk' face and rubbed her hand urgently against her nape.

'Unfortunately, my body reacted really badly to the bites. I had fever, chills, nausea and these large white blisters popped up where I'd been bitten. Since then, every time I see a spider I act like the biggest wimp you'll ever see. Even my voice changes to a high-pitched one and I sound like a Barbie doll.'

'Really?' Amanda chuckled.

'Trust me.' He nodded and smiled. 'It's very embarrassing.'

She didn't like talking about what happened, but she felt comfortable with him. She also needed to convince Ryan that there was nothing wrong with the house.

'I was young when it happened,' she said, brushing her fringe from her face. 'My friend and I were playing. Pretending we were cooking. I don't really know how it happened, but my clothes caught fire.'

Ryan's interest grew.

'In a way, I was lucky,' she continued. 'Only the back of my dress lit up. Have you ever been burned?' she asked.

Ryan shook his head. 'Not in that way.'

'The pain is hard to describe.' She paused, searching for words to illustrate it. 'It's not like scalding or touching a hot iron. It's not a stinging kind of pain. It's something so intense your brain ceases to work and you pray for death. I felt my skin melting. I could smell my hair burning.' Amanda softly touched her hair with her right hand. Her gaze distant. 'We were alone in the house that day. By the time my friend managed to find some water and throw it over me, most of my back and neck had burned.'

They looked at each other in silence for a while.

'I'm truly sorry,' he said.

'It's OK. It's not your fault. I should learn to control it, really, but I just can't. Any type of fire simply freaks me out.'

Ryan walked back to the center of the living room. Amanda followed him.

'I did see a psychologist about my fear of spiders,' he announced. 'You know, they have these special therapies that are supposed to help you get rid of any phobias.'

'What happened?' she asked curiously.

'The psychologist talked a lot and after a few sessions he decided I was ready to face my fear. He brought in this huge hairy spider and placed it in my hand to try and prove they were harmless.'

'Did it work?'

'Did it hell. I peed myself before running out of the room screaming like a lunatic.'

Amanda laughed.

'Maybe some fears are not meant to be conquered.' He

stepped closer to the leather sofa. Amanda was standing about two feet in front of him, staring at the fireplace.

His hand wrapped around something inside his pocket.

'You know when you told me about the incident when you were young and how scared you are of fires?' he asked.

'Yes,' she replied without turning around.

His voice suddenly changed: 'I already knew.'

Before she was able to turn and face him, he grabbed her from behind, covering her nose and mouth with a wet cloth.

Twenty-Seven

Father Malcolm had agreed to a meeting at 7:30 p.m. At twenty past seven Hunter parked his Buick Lesabre in front of the Our Lady of the Rosary Catholic Church in South Paramount Boulevard. The street lights, together with the Christmas decorations, created a warm carnival of colors.

The church was a large white building flanked by two small green yards. Above its hand-carved rosewood double doors sat a life-size, light gray statue of Our Lady of the Rosary.

A cheery-looking priest in his late sixties was standing by the entrance door talking to a short and stout woman. His hairline had totally receded on top, and all that was left were two small islands of gray hair. One over each ear.

He said goodbye to the woman as Hunter made his way up the four short steps in front of the church.

'Father Malcolm?' Hunter asked.

'You must be the detective I talked to earlier on the phone,' the priest said with a warm smile.

'I'm Detective Hunter.' He had his credentials in hand. 'Thank you for agreeing to see me.'

The priest quickly checked Hunter's ID before ushering him inside. The interior of the church was large, and the altar shone with hundreds of candles. The main hall was able to hold around five hundred worshipers, and a handful of people were scattered among the many red oak pews. Some were praying, some were reading the Bible and some looked to be asleep.

'Shall we talk in my office?' the priest asked with a hand gesture. 'It's just out back.'

'Sure.' Hunter nodded.

Father Malcolm's office was small but comfortable. The walls were painted in white, very lightly tinged with gray. The furnishings were classic, with a distinct European influence. A heavy wooden desk sat at the back of the room facing the door. In front of it were two replica Victorian armchairs. There were saints' prints on the walls, and religious books lined the large bookcase to the left of the desk.

Father Malcolm showed Hunter to a seat before taking his place behind the desk. Neither spoke for a few seconds. 'I can't believe what's happened. Fabian was a good man, a good priest.' Father Malcolm's voice was frail and sad.

'I'm very sorry,' Hunter replied. 'I understand you were good friends.'

The priest nodded. 'I used to teach seminary. Fabian was one of my students. I've known him for over twenty years.'

'What was he like?'

'Kind, devoted, compassionate. As I've said, he was a good priest.'

'When did you last see him?'

'About two weeks ago. We had a seventh- and eighth-grade bake-sale here. He came over to help.' A shy smile appeared on the priest's lips. 'Actually, he came over to eat. He loved banana cake.'

'Did he seem different at all? Maybe worried or nervous about something?'

'Not at all. He was as calm as he'd always been. Very

talkative, joking with the students all the time. He looked a bit tired, but that had always been the case with Fabian.'

'How so?' Hunter gently rubbed the scar on the back of his neck.

'As far as I know he never really slept very well.'

'Any particular reason why?'

A slight shake of the head. 'We deal with many hardships, detective, and they sometimes creep up into our minds in the middle of the night and keep us awake. Fabian told me once he had bad dreams quite regularly.'

Hunter remembered reading several passages in Father Fabian's journals about bad dreams, but he never described them. 'Did he ever talk to you about these dreams?'

'Never. He was a very reserved man.'

Hunter scribbled something down in his black notebook. 'Did he ever talk about any worries he had?'

'As priests we have many worries, Detective Hunter. We deal with people in need, and in today's world troubles are plenty. But I guess you mean the type of worry that could've cost him his life?'

Hunter didn't reply, but his silence was understood.

'No.' Father Malcolm sounded confident. 'He was a simple man. He lived for the church and to help others. Whatever worries he had, I assure you they weren't life threatening.'

Hunter thought about his next words. He knew he was about to venture into dangerous territory.

Twenty-Eight

'Did Father Fabian ever talk to you about doubting his decision to become a Catholic priest or his intention to leave it all behind?' Hunter asked and saw Father Malcolm's demeanor change. He looked offended. He narrowed his eyes and surveyed Hunter.

'What we do is based solemnly on faith and on the desire to serve Our Lord, Detective Hunter.' The priest's voice was steady but firm, as if reprimanding a disobedient child. 'We don't do it for money or thrills. It's a call. I must admit that sometimes it gets tough. We're humans and as such we have our moments of weakness, our uncertainties. It's not uncommon for those of us who choose a life of servitude to God to question that decision every now and then. But our faith always proves stronger than any doubt. Do you understand what faith means, detective?'

'I think so,' Hunter replied with a nod. 'Blind belief without questioning or proof.'

Father Malcolm smiled, showing yellow-stained teeth. 'That belief keeps us on the right path. It drowns our doubts. So in answer to your question, detective – yes, Father Fabian and I talked about his uncertainties and his dilemmas. Just because we decide to serve God it doesn't make us immune to temptation and unclear thoughts. And just because cloudy thoughts enter our minds, it doesn't mean we're gonna go through with them. He was a man of unquestionable faith.'

'Please don't get me wrong, father,' Hunter said, leaning forward and resting his elbows on his knees. 'I'm not questioning his or your faith. I was just wondering if there was a reason for these "unclear" thoughts. If there was, it could give us a lead. Did Father Fabian ever tell you he was thinking about giving up the priesthood?'

Father Malcolm scratched a small scar above his right eyebrow. Hunter could see he was debating if he should answer the question or not. 'It really is important,' Hunter pressed.

'Yes,' Father Malcolm said after several unsettling seconds. 'After Fabian's mother passed away, his faith was unbalanced.'

'Were they close?'

'He tried.'

'Tried?'

'Fabian never knew his father. His mother brought him up on her own, but she was a bitter woman. She expected her only son to become a lawyer or a doctor or something that would make him rich so he could pay her back.'

Hunter shifted on his seat.

The priest looked down at his clasped hands. 'She had problems. She battled with alcoholism for many years. Even though she resented him for becoming a priest, he loved her. He prayed for her every day, for as long as I can remember. When she got ill, it all happened very fast. She was taken into hospital and within a week she passed away. He took it very badly.'

'How badly?'

'He was angry.' Father Malcolm bit his lip and rethought his words. 'No, I think the correct word would be *discontent*. He was discontent with God. He hoped that after so many years praying for the same thing, God would've listened. He kept on saying he never asked for a miracle. He only wanted God to give his mother a fighting chance. But instead, God took her away.'

Hunter sat motionless battling with his own memories. His eyes were fixed on the priest but unfocused. '*I know exactly how he felt.*'

Father Malcolm noticed pain in Hunter's expression and leaned forward. 'Can I ask you something, detective?'

'Of course.'

'Is it true what the papers said? About Fabian being decapitated? About the dog's head?'

'Yes.'

The priest let out a deep sigh. 'You probably already know that Saint Fabian, who Father Fabian got his pseudonym from, was beheaded.'

Hunter nodded.

'Do you think there's a relation?'

'It's a possibility.' Hunter leaned back again. 'What do you think, father? Do you think the killer wanted Father Fabian to die the same way Saint Fabian did?'

The priest stood up and approached the bookcase next to his desk. 'In years gone by, a great number of people who were misunderstood were arrested and tortured before being sentenced to death,' he said, reaching for a book on the top shelf. 'For centuries, most death sentences in the Western world meant decapitation.'

Hunter considered this. 'So if Father Fabian had chosen any other saint's name, death by decapitation would've probably matched the saint's death anyway,' he concluded.

A slow nod.

'How about a dog's head? Does it mean anything to you, or to the Catholic faith?'

The priest took a deep breath. 'The devil,' he replied. As he spoke a cold draft entered the room. Hunter instinctively pulled the collar of his jacket tighter around his neck.

Father Malcolm returned to his seat. 'Without being insolent, detective, I think that maybe you're going down the wrong path.'

'How's that, father?' Hunter asked, meeting the priest's eyes.

'I believe that this has been an aggression against the Catholic Church. Someone who wants to hurt the Church as a whole, not an individual priest. Fabian was a tragic casualty. It could've been any of us. The killer could've chosen any of our churches for his act of anger.' He paused as his next words worried him. 'And something tells me he will kill again. Maybe he already has.' The priest's tone caused the tiny hairs on Hunter's arms to rise.

Twenty-Nine

Amanda Reilly felt incredibly cold and thirsty. Her head thumped with such ferocity that she thought her temples would explode. As she tried to move she realized she was tied down. Her wrists had been bound to the arms and her ankles to the legs of an uncomfortable metal armchair – so tight the wires were cutting into her skin.

Her eyelids felt heavy and sticky. As far as she could tell she wasn't blindfolded, but something was keeping her from opening her eyes. She tried to scream but her lips wouldn't come apart. There was a bitter and sickening taste in her mouth. Instinctively, she pushed her tongue against her lips and felt a rigid, thin layer of something unidentified between them. She tried forcing her mouth open and felt the tender skin on her lips start to tear.

Oh my God!

Shivering, she finally understood what'd happened.

Her mouth had been super-glued shut.

Panic took over and she jerked her body violently from side to side, kicking out, trying to free herself. Blood started dripping from where the wires had cut into her wrists and ankles.

The chair didn't budge. It was either too heavy or it had been nailed to the floor. Her screams, muffled by her tightly shut lips, sounded like animal grunts.

An uncontrollable shudder came over her body, and she fought to keep her teeth from chattering.

Tears sprang in the corners of her closed eyes, forced their way through and started rolling down her face, washing away some of the sticky substance that had been smothered over her eyelids. She felt them coming unstuck. Very slowly, she managed to get them open. They stung as if burned by fire, forcing her into a blinking frenzy.

It took several minutes for the pain to subside and for her eyes to regain some focus. They were puffy and their whites had turned crimson. At first everything was blurred, but the candlelit room looked familiar. She recognized some of the furniture, but where from?

The thumping in her head had intensified, and her muddied thoughts weren't making any sense. She took deep, steady breaths and forced herself to concentrate on her heartbeat. Her memory slowly started putting together images of what had happened.

She convulsed with fear as she finally remembered. The blurred image in front of her was that of the immense river rock fireplace in one of the properties on her roster.

She'd brought a prospective buyer here for a viewing.

What was his name?

'How's the head, Mandy?' The voice that came from behind startled her rigid. Mature and firm like an army sergeant. 'The thumping will go away soon enough.'

She started shivering again.

The focus in her eyes was almost back to normal. Amanda looked down and finally realized why she felt so cold. She was naked.

A tall figure stepped out from behind her and into her line of vision. It was the same man she'd brought to the house for a viewing, but she still couldn't remember his name. He was dressed differently, though. Instead of the long overcoat and the professional tailored suit, he was wearing tight-fitting black sports clothes. His hands were still gloved, and his hair was now hidden under a knitted hat.

Once again she fought her restraints, franticly twisting her body and trying to kick her legs.

He calmly watched her in silence for a few minutes until she realized that her efforts were pointless.

'Unfortunately, I don't think you'll be able to free yourself,' he explained as he started pacing in front of her.

'*Oh please. Why are you doing this to me?*' She said the words in her mouth, but all that came out was an oscillating humming sound.

With his lips compressed tightly together and shaking his head from side to side, he mimicked the sound back to her before laughing.

'If you wanna speak to me, you're gonna have to try harder. C'mon, you can do it. Open your mouth.'

She stared at him, paralyzed. Her fear so intense she thought she would faint.

He bent down, his face just a few inches from hers.

'OPEN YOUR MOUTH.'

The shout was so loud the air from his breath blew her hair away from her forehead.

Amanda lost control. She'd gone way beyond terrified. Every hair on her body was standing on end when she wet herself.

'Oh, that's disgusting,' he said, standing up again and taking a step back from the puddle quickly forming on the floor under her chair.

'Maybe I can help you open your mouth.' He picked something up from the fireplace mantelpiece. 'What do you say? Do you wanna give it a try?'

He showed her a glistening silver letter opener.

Amanda's eyes widened in terror, and she jerked her head back as far as it would go. A new, high-pitched shriek came from her sealed lips.

'It might rip your lips from your mouth, but, hey, who cares, right? Just nod and I'll start tearing.'

Amanda shook her head fiercely.

'Or maybe I should use this down there.' He pointed to her groin. 'It might stop you from being a dirty bitch and wetting the floor again. What do you say?' He slowly ran his tongue along the length of the shining blade. 'Shall I stick this inside you? I promise I'll make you enjoy it first.'

Amanda's body wrenched forward violently, and she felt the few contents of her stomach come rushing through her throat and into her mouth. Her eyes rolled back into her head as she started to choke.

'Did you just vomit into your mouth?' he shouted, rushing towards her. 'You filthy little whore.' He pressed his hands against both of her cheeks, pushing her head back. 'Swallow it back down. Swallow it back down, now,' he ordered, applying more pressure to her cheeks.

Amanda tried shaking her head, but her attacker had it firmly between his hands in a tight vice-grip.

'SWALLOW IT BACK DOWN,' he shouted again.

She coughed, but the air pressure had nowhere to go except up through her nose. Bloody mucus spurted out of it, spraying the man's gloves and sleeves.

'You bitch,' he said, massaging her throat. 'You're not gonna die on me like this.'

Amanda hadn't had any food for several hours. Whatever her stomach had regurgitated into her mouth was little more than a soup spoon full. With her attacker applying pressure to her cheeks and massaging her throat, she finally swallowed her own sick back down.

'Good girl,' he said, retrieving a paper tissue from his pocket and attending to her nosebleed. He waited in silence for about five minutes while Amanda sat shivering.

'I can see you're cold,' he finally said, his voice changing. He sounded serene. He stepped closer. 'I have something to show you.'

From his pocket he pulled an old black and white photograph and held it in front of Amanda's face.

'Look at it. Do you remember?'

She was weak, dehydrated and feeling too dizzy to concentrate.

'C'mon, Mandy.' He snapped his fingers a couple of times. 'Pay attention to the photo. Do you remember?'

Still feeling confused, she stared at it with unsteady eyes. Nothing was making sense.

And then she saw it.

'*It can't be.*'

'Welcome to your fear, Mandy,' he whispered. 'I know what scares you to death.'

Thirty

Some say Los Angeles Union Station is America's last great railway station. Built in 1939 to consolidate passenger terminals from three different railways, the station still serves as a transit hub. Though its exterior is a successful merging of Spanish Mission, Moorish and Streamline Modern architectural styles, Los Angeles Union Station is best enjoyed from inside. It's been carefully renovated, with original light fixtures, inlaid stone floors and tiled walls.

Beauty aside, the station is a constant hustle of passengers and tourists, but today it seemed busier than normal.

The girl ran as fast as she could, constantly swerving her body to avoid colliding with other commuters. People were coming from all directions, and everyone seemed to be in a hurry. After successfully negotiating her way around a large woman pushing a baby in a pram, she almost ran over a little girl in uniform, who seemed to have detached herself from her parents. By the time she reached the escalator going down to the station's underground, she was puffing and sweating.

'Excuse me, please,' she called in a hurried voice as she squeezed her way through, skipping down the steps.

She saw the doors of the Red Line subway train closing as she stepped onto the platform.

'Oh no, no!'

The train started to move away.

She dashed towards it, but she knew it was no good.

'Late again . . . great,' she whispered. 'Just what I need.'

Her eyes searched for the noticeboard. At least fifteen minutes before the next Red Line service. Despite the departing train, the platform was still rammed.

Where the hell are all these people going today? she thought, looking around. Her eyes rested on an empty glass poster box and she caught a glimpse of her reflection. Her long dark brown hair was still neatly tied back in a ponytail, but beads of sweat had formed on her forehead, and her nose looked pink from a combination of the cold outside and her running effort. She desperately needed a makeup retouch.

The main floor was heaving with people. Tourists were noisily walking around, marveling at the many twinkling lights and shining baubles. She hadn't even noticed the colorful Christmas decorations until now. They reminded her of her hometown and of her parents' house. Places and people she'd do anything to forget. She checked her watch before making her way towards the ladies' room at the far end of the hall. No hurry this time. A tall, skinny man carrying a red leather briefcase gave her a malicious smile and her whole body shuddered.

'*Ladies and gentlemen,*' a voice announced through the loudspeakers, '*due to a signal failure in Pershing Square, there'll be a five-minute delay to our next Red Line service. We apologize for the inconvenience.*'

'Fantastic,' she murmured. 'This just isn't my day.'

Suddenly, she felt her chest tighten around her heart. A burning heat took over her body with incredible speed as her throat knotted, making it hard for her to breathe. The station started to spin. Her vision was invaded by tiny circles of light, but they quickly got bigger and brighter until all she could see was a blinding white light. And then it happened.

The bright light was replaced by grainy black and white images, like a short segment from an old movie. But what she saw was no classic.

'Oh God, no.' Her voice was drowning on tears. 'Please, not again.'

The images played for only a few seconds, but it was enough to fill her with terrifying fear.

Her nose started bleeding. Something pirouetted inside her stomach, and she gagged on the bile as it surged into her mouth. She desperately needed to get to the ladies' room.

'*Someone please help me.*' Her lips moved but no sound came out. Her legs buckled beneath her, and she fell to her knees as something erupted from her stomach. Right there, in the middle of the main floor of Los Angeles Union Station, she lost control and vomited.

Thirty-One

Hunter lived alone. He'd never been married, and the relationships he had never really worked out. They'd always start well. The women he dated, at first, seemed very understanding of the pressures of his job and the commitment it demanded. But soon they wanted more. A lot more than he was prepared to give. And although he felt lonely sometimes, long-term relationships simply didn't fit into his lifestyle. Hunter's sexual life consisted exclusively of one-night encounters or short-term, no-strings-attached affairs.

He enjoyed spending time by himself. He felt comfortable in his sparsely decorated one-bedroom apartment. A good book and a double dose of one of the many single-malt Scotch whiskeys from a very well-accomplished collection always made him relax. But not tonight. This was only the second night since they'd found Father Fabian's body, but the pressure was building up fast. He felt the need to go out and see other people talking, laughing and living life. The world of the dead had a habit of getting under his skin.

Los Angeles has one of the liveliest and most exciting nightlifes in the world. From luxurious and trendy clubs where A-list celebrities hang out, to dingy and sleazy underground venues. There are themed bars and lounges scattered all over the city. You can have a drink in a hospital ward where cocktail waitresses run around in skin-tight black nurses' uniforms, or in the most traditional of Irish pubs, where the barman leaves the Guinness to settle before topping up the glass and drawing a shamrock in the froth.

Hunter wasn't looking for anything crazy or loud, so live music venues and bars with dance DJs were out. He also decided to stay in Downtown Los Angeles instead of taking a drive to any of the many beach bars. He settled on the Golden Gopher on West Eighth Street. Its low-key and relaxed atmosphere was just what Hunter had in mind.

He got there at about 9:00 p.m. The place was busy but not crowded. He took a seat at the end of the old-West saloon-looking bar and ordered a single dose of single malt. The barman, a tall, short-haired Puerto Rican with a goatee trimmed to perfection, dropped two cubes of ice into the glass and Hunter stared at them as they cracked. His mind methodically going over the case. Two days and they had nothing so far.

He finished his Scotch and his stare fell on a small group huddled around an old Space Invaders game machine.

Without him noticing it, the barman poured another dose and slid the glass towards Hunter.

'Wow, you're quick,' he said with a nod.

'This one's paid for, sir.'

Hunter frowned.

'The lady at the far table to your right,' the barman said with a slight head tilt.

Hunter turned to face the table the barman had indicated. A tall, attractive brunette was sitting by herself. Streaked hair fell in ringlets over her shoulders. She had olive-tanned skin and seductive brown eyes. The top two buttons of her cream blouse were strategically undone, revealing a jaw-dropping cleavage.

Hunter lifted his glass and accepted the drink with the most subtle of smiles.

She held his gaze, blinked and then smiled back, gesturing for him to join her.

'You're in luck,' the barman said.

'Does she do this often?'

'I've never seen her in here before,' he replied, running a hand over his goatee.

'She looks like a maneater to me,' Hunter said without breaking eye contact with the brunette.

The barman grabbed a glass and started polishing it. 'She could eat me any time.'

Hunter gave the barman a friendly wink. 'OK, here goes nothing.' He made his way towards the brunette's table.

Thirty-Two

'Thanks for the drink. It's very kind of you,' Hunter said, taking the seat directly in front of her.

She gave him a dentist's magazine smile. 'It's no problem. It's good to find a man who appreciates a real drink.'

Hunter noticed she was drinking the same as he was.

'You're a Scotch drinker?'

'I like my drink strong.'

She had a sip of her single malt under Hunter's watchful eye.

'I'm Robert,' he said, extending his hand.

'I'm Claire, Claire Anderson.'

They shook hands, and Hunter noticed how smooth her skin felt.

'Do you come here often?' she asked.

'Not really. I needed a drink tonight, and I didn't feel like going to a hip or noisy place. They serve good single malt in here, and the atmosphere is . . . sedated. How about you?'

'I come in here every once in a while. My apartment's just a block from here.'

'Great location, but this isn't really a reporter's drinking joint, is it?' he said casually.

Her smile didn't disappear. It simply morphed into a more believable one. 'I guess you've recognized me, then?'

'Your hair is different. Curlier. But I remember you from the

Seven Saints church. You asked me if I was attributing the murder to a serial killer even before I had a look at the crime scene.'

Claire arched her eyebrows, accepting it. 'So, now that you've seen the crime scene, do you think it could be the work of a serial killer?'

'You started so well,' Hunter said, shaking his head disappointedly. 'Buying me a drink and all. Wasn't there supposed to be a little bit of sweet-talking, maybe even flirting, before the questions start?'

'We can do that if you like.'

'I think that would be better.'

'So what would you like to sweet-talk about, Detective Hunter?'

'You can call me Robert. It's OK.'

'So what would you like to sweet-talk about, Robert?'

'Let's start with this.' He leaned forward, reached for her glass and poured its contents into his own. 'What do you really drink?'

She regarded him for a second. 'How do you know Scotch isn't my drink?' A tone of defiance in her voice.

Hunter cocked his eyebrows.

She held his gaze for a second before her lips broke into a new smile. 'OK, you got me. Gin and tonic.'

A moment later Hunter came back to the table with a tall, icy glass of G&T.

'Thanks,' she said before sipping her drink. 'Let's try this again, shall we?' She offered her hand. 'I'm Claire.'

'Oh, so you did give me your real name?'

She nodded.

Hunter made no effort to shake her hand this time. 'So which paper are you with?'

Claire put her hand down without looking offended. 'The *LA Times*.' She thought about it for a second. 'Actually, I'm on a trial period.'

'Oh, I see. And you're thinking that maybe a serial killer story would provide the key you need to cruise through your trial period with flying colors.'

'It wouldn't hinder my chances, let's put it that way.'

Hunter had another sip of his drink. 'Unfortunately, I don't think I can help you.'

'C'mon, Robert. I just need a little lead. Something that the other reporters don't have. And that won't be difficult since no one has anything.'

'That's because there's nothing to have.'

'Are you joking? Someone decapitated a priest and shoved a dog's head down his neck. The killer practically painted the church with blood. That's the behavior of a deranged psychopath, not a one-off killer, and you know it. The whole thing was well planned. I think he's gonna do it again or he's done it before. What do you think?'

Hunter smiled. 'That's clever. Trying to induce me into a comment by disguising the question as your own opinion. Did you learn that in journalism class?'

Claire ran her left hand through her hair. 'Two semesters of psychology at Idaho State University.'

'You're from the potato state?'

'There's more to Idaho than just potatoes,' she replied, un-amused.

'I'm sure there is.'

'I've also read your book.'

Hunter looked up, allowing the silence to stretch. 'I've never written a book,' he shot back, shaking his head.

'OK, your PhD thesis on criminal behavior and conduct. It

was made into a book and it's still mandatory reading at the FBI's NCAVC.' Claire noticed Hunter's questioning look. 'I dated an FBI trainee,' she explained indifferently. 'Your thesis makes for very intense reading, but it's extremely good. No wonder every FBI profiler has to study it. I'm surprised they don't have you as a lecturer.'

She's switching tactics, Hunter thought. *She's gone for the flattering approach now*.

'I did a quick check-up on you as well,' she continued. 'A prodigy, a whiz kid. You attended Mirman School for the Gifted, sped through university and got your PhD when you were twenty-three – impressive. How does someone like you end up as a detective instead of a millionaire?'

Guns and Roses started playing on the jukebox.

'My life story won't make a bestseller.'

'I'm not looking to write one,' she replied casually. 'But about your book, I'm intrigued. I was particularly fascinated by the part about ritualistic murderers. I really do believe your theories are right on the money, but there's something that bothers me.'

'And what would that be?'

'Unless you've drastically changed your mind, or you're willing to contradict your own thesis, I know you don't believe the church murder was a one-off. Am I right?'

'See, there you go again,' Hunter replied. 'Pushing your thoughts onto me and expecting me to agree or disagree with them.'

'C'mon, Robert. Let me work this story with you. I'll do a great job. I can make you famous.'

Hunter chuckled, crossed his legs and let his arms slump down onto his knees. 'Famous?'

'You're a great detective. I know it because I researched you.

Your track record when it comes to catching criminals, especially tough ones, is outstanding, but no one except a handful of people knows that. You deserve recognition. Los Angeles is in desperate need of a hero.'

Hunter had a slow sip of his Scotch. Claire Anderson was certainly very good at the flattering game; he had to give her that. 'I'm happy the way I am,' he replied. 'I don't wanna be a hero. And I don't need to be famous.'

'You're happy? I don't buy that.'

Hunter crossed his arms. 'I like my life the way it is. I like being—'

'A loner?'

Hunter kept silent.

'OK.' Claire leaned forward and placed both elbows on the table. 'Off the record, answer me this, not as a cop but as a criminal psychologist just to quench my curiosity.'

Hunter arched his left eyebrow with interest. 'Off the record?'

'Yes. I promise.'

'Shoot.'

'Let's suppose you weren't investigating this case, but simply studying it. If you had to create a profile of the killer judged solely on what you saw inside the Seven Saints church. Wouldn't that profile indicate an UNSUB that'll probably offend again, or has already offended in the past, or both?'

Hunter let out a constricted laugh. 'You don't give up, do you?'

'I wouldn't be a good reporter if I did.' The answer came with a wink.

Hunter finished his drink and placed the empty glass on the table with an emphatic smack. Claire did the same.

'One more round?' she asked.

Hunter glanced at his watch with a doubtful look.

'C'mon, you don't have a wife to go back home to, do you?'

'Somehow I think you already know the answer to that question.'

She giggled. 'As I said, I did check you out a little bit.' She realized how crazy that sounded and was quick to reiterate. 'Not in a psycho, stalker way. Research is part of being a journalist.'

Silence.

'C'mon, it's my round. Look, I promise I won't ask any more questions about the case.'

Hunter pulled a face. 'I sincerely doubt that.'

'I'll tell you what,' Claire said, standing up. 'I've gotta tab going at the bar. Order whatever you like and get me another gin and tonic while I go to the ladies. We'll have one more drink here, and then maybe we can go someplace else. My flatmate is out of town for the weekend.' Her lips stretched into a seductive smile.

Wow, she's prepared to go all the way. Claire would be amazing in bed, Hunter decided, but her performance would be in direct proportion to the information her lover could provide. It was the information she was making love to, not the man.

'Look, Claire. You're a very attractive woman. I'm sure you know you could take your pick out of all the guys in this joint to take home.'

'I pick you.'

Hunter laughed. 'And I'm flattered. But this would be for the wrong reasons and you know it.'

'Sometimes the wrong reasons are the best ones.'

'And most nights I'd agree with that. But tonight I'll have to take a rain check.'

'You're blowing me off?' She sounded genuinely offended.

'Not really.' Hunter paused for a second. 'Let's do this. When this investigation is over, I'll take you out for dinner. Let's see if you still wanna take me back to your place for drinks then.'

Thirty-Three

Hunter managed to get only three and a half hours of sleep. Though he'd been up since 4:30 a.m., it was just past eight by the time he walked into his office. Garcia was at his desk reading one of Father Fabian's journals. His eyes were bloodshot framed by dark circles.

'What time did you get here?' Hunter asked, closing the door behind him.

Garcia placed the journal on his desk, leaned back on his chair and massaged his stiff neck. 'Seven-thirty, but I was up half the night, reading.'

Hunter nodded. 'Yeah, me too.'

Garcia noticed he had two journals under his arm. 'How far did you get?' He nodded towards the books.

'I read through both of them.' Hunter placed them on his desk.

'You read four hundred pages in one night?'

'I read a lot, I read fast and I don't sleep much.'

'Did you find anything?'

'Nothing that could really help the investigation. But Father Fabian was a troubled man.' Hunter leaned against his desk and shoved his hands deep into his pockets. 'He thought about suicide – twice.'

Garcia rubbed his eyes with the tips of his fingers. 'Well,

I'm getting cross-eyed. And I still haven't found anything either. Any joy from the tip lines?'

Every night, before going home, Hunter personally went through the day's tips collected by the tips team.

'Nothing. Over two hundred calls so far and all of them bullshit.'

A knock came at the door.

'Come in,' Hunter called.

Officer Hopkins stepped into the office carrying a blue plastic file. He also looked tired.

'I have some preliminary results to the searches you asked me for,' he told Hunter, who raised a hand, stopping him before he was able to continue.

'I think we could all use a break from the office and from computer screens. It's not a bad day out there. What do you say we go grab a coffee in Little Tokyo? A change of scenery would do us good.'

'I'm in.' Garcia raised his hand.

'Sure. I love that place.' Hopkins nodded.

Little Tokyo is a small district in Downtown Los Angeles, just across the road from Parker Center and the RHD. It's one of only three official Japantowns in the United States, and if you like Japanese food there's no better place to be in LA.

Hopkins suggested Poppy Coffee Shop, on the south side of Little Tokyo. He'd eaten there many times and their coffee was the best.

Despite the early hour, the café was packed. They all ordered black coffees, and Hopkins had a chocolate-sprinkled donut to go with it.

'You guys should try one of these donuts,' Hopkins said as they took the last available table by the door. 'They're so rich they're practically a food group.'

'I'm good,' Garcia said, lifting his right hand.

'Knock yourself out.' Hunter smiled and frowned at the four cubes of sugar Hopkins dropped into his coffee. 'So what have you got?' he asked.

'Not much.' Hopkins sounded disappointed. 'I researched what you've asked. Any acts of violence against any churches in the past five years.' He retrieved a few sheets from his file and started flipping through them. 'I've got vandalism, graffiti, a few broken windows, stolen objects, a few attempted arsons, but no significant physical violence against any priests. There have, however, been a few cases of rape against nuns.'

'That doesn't fall into the category we're looking for.' Hunter sipped his coffee too quickly and burned the roof of his mouth.

'I know, but still, that's just fucked up.' Hopkins took a bite of his donut and wiped the sprinkles from his lips onto a green paper napkin. 'The second search you asked for; homicides with ritual and torture characteristics. The list is long.'

Somehow Hunter was expecting it to be.

'I filtered the results using the criteria you gave me. One, criminals that haven't been apprehended yet, and two, the use of any animals.'

'What did you get?'

'Murders with excessive spillage of blood – there've been many. Most of them attributed to gangs, turf and drug wars. But other than lots of blood, they carry no other ritualistic characteristics at all.'

'Anything with animals?' Garcia asked, blowing into his coffee.

'Yes, but no dog's head. Actually, the only case I could find where an animal head was left at the scene of a crime in the last five years involved a horse's head.'

'Italian Mafia,' Hunter said.

'That's the theory,' Hopkins agreed. 'The case has never been solved.'

'So what other animals, if any, have been used in crimes?' Garcia asked just as Hopkins had another bite of his donut. They had to wait while he chewed and swallowed it down.

'A few. Rats, pigs, pigeons, cats – but apparently the preferred animal is chicken. Especially its blood. Used a lot in black magic – voodoo. And these were mostly attributed to Jamaicans and—'

'Brazilians.' Garcia nodded.

'Brazilians?' Hunter turned towards his partner.

'Yes. In Brazil it's called macumba. Something Brazil inherited from the many slaves who came from Africa.' Garcia shook his head, indicating he wasn't about to go into much historical detail. 'They have lots of rituals, and many of them involve sacrificing chickens and using their blood.'

'I've searched the net for hours,' Hopkins said, shaking his head, 'trying to find anything that justified replacing someone's head for a dog's – I got nothing. As you've asked—' he tilted his head towards Hunter '—I've checked with every animal welfare agency in Los Angeles. No street mutt's body missing a head has been found. I'll keep checking, but at the moment that's turning out to be another dead end.'

Hunter rubbed his face with both hands. He hadn't shaved this morning, and his day-long stubble prickled his palms.

'I've also checked with detectives in every bureau, as you asked me to do,' Hopkins continued. 'Nothing on a decapitation, a dog's head or a numbered body. If this killer has claimed two previous victims, no one's found them yet.'

Thirty-Four

As soon as they entered their office, Garcia reached for another of Father Fabian's journals.

'Have you come across any passages in these journals about a bad dream that pestered Father Fabian for years?' Hunter asked, flipping open one of the leather-bound volumes on his desk.

'I have, actually.' Garcia searched for a specific journal. 'And I meant to ask you the same question. Some reoccurring dream that scared him senseless.'

'That's right.'

'I made a note of it. Here it is.' He found the journal and opened it to a marked page. 'Listen to this.

'*3:00 a.m. I just woke up again. For minutes I could barely breathe. My hands are still shaking and my clothes are soaked in cold sweat. I am too scared to go back to sleep. Too scared to close my eyes. It's the dream again. All these years and it has never left me. Why, Lord? Why am I tormented by these visions? Is it a warning of what's to come?*'

'I've been through several passages that sounded just like that,' Hunter observed.

'It seems this dream came back to haunt him frequently.' Garcia placed the open diary on his desk. 'Maybe it's nothing.' He shrugged. 'We all have bad dreams every now and again.'

Hunter leaned back on his chair. 'Do you know many people who wake up from dreams short of breath, shaking, sweating and too scared to go back to sleep on a constant basis?'

Garcia thought about it for a moment before conceding with a slight head tilt.

'Dreams that have that kind of effect on a person are usually based on reality. Farfetched, maybe, but a reality nonetheless.'

'I'm not sure I know what you mean.'

'If you have a dream based on fantasy,' Hunter explained, 'a fire-breathing dragon, for example. No matter how shocking or violent the dream is, your subconscious knows it's an impossible fantasy. It might scare you, but it shouldn't trigger a severe panic reaction.'

'But if you have a dream based on reality, like being stabbed—' Garcia caught up with Hunter's line of thought '—your subconscious knows that the chances of it actually happening are very real.'

Hunter nodded. 'Most nightmares are spin-offs of lived traumatic experiences. We have no control over them.' He gestured towards the open diary. 'I know about such dreams. I have them.'

Garcia looked at the scars on his hands for a long moment. 'Since the Crucifix Killer's case, so do I.'

They read the journals in silence for a while before Garcia cursed under his breath. 'Shit!'

Hunter's head snapped up. 'What have you got?'

'Father Fabian's disturbing nightmare. And you won't believe this . . .'

Thirty-Five

Hunter waited for Garcia to continue, but his partner's catatonic eyes were glued to the open journal in his hands.

'Carlos. What have you got?'

Garcia leaned back on his chair and drew a deep breath. 'Listen to this.' He flipped back a page.

'*It's very late and I can't sleep. I woke up from the dream maybe an hour ago, and this time it felt more real than ever. I threw up all over myself.*

'*I'm scared.*

'*Once I read somewhere that one way to extradite fear is to write it down. It's supposed to symbolize the act of pushing it out of your mind.*'

Garcia looked at Hunter.

'It's a well-known technique,' he confirmed.

Garcia flipped to the next page and continued reading.

'*This is the first time I'm writing about this.*

'*I didn't always have my faith. When I was young, I thought I was invincible. Me and my gang of friends.*

'*We terrorized everyone, from school students to teachers and families in our neighborhood. We thought we were cool – real badasses.*' Garcia's lips stretched into a thin, nervous smile. He found it hard to think of Father Fabian as a 'badass'.

'*One evening, we were hanging out by the park as we always*

*did. We were bored. We'd been drinking since the afternoon
and some of us were high. Someone saw a stray dog rummag-
ing through a trashcan. It was a skinny old mutt with thinning
gray fur. Its body was covered in dried blood scabs as if it'd
been fighting. Suddenly, one of the guys in the gang jumped to
his feet and started chasing the dog. That got us all going. It
was like we were possessed. We were waving our clenched fists
in the air and yelling "get him . . . get him". There was something wrong with one of its legs. It couldn't run properly, so it
hopped away, trying to escape.'*

Hunter placed both elbows on his desk, leaning forward.

'It didn't take us long to catch up with the frightened dog.'
Garcia carried on reading. *'We cornered it against a wall of
hedges. The poor thing was shivering all over. Too weak and
scared to put up a fight, it just lowered its head and its sad eyes,
as if begging us to leave it be.*

*'I tried telling everyone to leave the poor thing alone. It was
only looking for some food, but no one listened.'* He paused for
a deep breath before continuing.

*'One of the guys in the group bent down and offered the dog
his hand. The trembling mutt lifted its head and gingerly took
a few steps forward. When it got close enough, my friend
grabbed it by the fur on its head and violently lifted it off the
ground. Its tiny body kicked and writhed in the air. Everyone
could see the dog was in pain. It was so weak that it couldn't
even bark. It tried, but the sound that came out was more like
a petrified shriek.'* Garcia stretched his neck awkwardly, as if
trying to fight off an incoming migraine.

*'I told my friend again to put the dog down and let it go. The
rest of the gang was cheering him on – "Fuck him up, gut the
old bag of fleas."*

'I didn't even see where the knife came from. All I know

was that all of a sudden my friend had a meat cleaver in his hand.'

Garcia's eyes left the page and wandered over to Hunter for a second.

'Under shouts of "do it . . . do it," he raised the crying dog high in the air. Its eyes were filled with dread. It knew what was about to happen. My friend swung the meat cleaver hard at its neck. Blood gushed everywhere. I was sprayed across the face and chest, and my stomach knotted. The dog's small body slumped to the ground. For another thirty seconds or so it twitched and kicked, draining the last breaths of life out of it. They all cheered and laughed until their eyes rested on me. Without realizing, I'd started crying.' Garcia leaned forward and placed the book on his desk before running the tip of his finger slowly over his eyes.

'Soon after that, I started distancing myself from the group. I haven't seen any of them since then. I couldn't say for sure how long after the park incident the nightmares started. Maybe a couple of months, but they've never left me.'

'Get ready for this,' Garcia said, making a face as if what he was about to read was hard to believe.

'In my dream, instead of the dog, it's me who's held by the hair. I'm as petrified as the poor animal was. I try, but I can't escape. I can't see my attacker's face, but I know it's not my friend, the one who beheaded the dog. He has a sword in his hand. As the blade comes towards me, I freeze, unable to move. I open my mouth and try to scream, but no sound comes out. I'm terrified. In slow motion the cold blade strikes me at the base of my neck.' A new pause. A new awkward neck movement. *'I feel it gradually slicing through my flesh, tearing my head from my torso. The pain is unbearable. I feel my blood soaking my clothes. My body starts to get cold. The strike is*

clean, but for some reason I'm still not dead. My head tumbles to the ground, rolling several times, just like the dog's that night in the park. But my body isn't headless.' Garcia placed both elbows on his desk and rested his forehead on his closed fists.

'Above my shoulders there's a mutt's head – its eyes wide, its tongue black and sticking out of its crooked mouth. The person with the blade spills my blood all around me, like a ritual. My head is taken away to be burned. That's when I wake up.'

Garcia rubbed his exhausted eyes. 'No fucking way this was a coincidence,' he said, shaking his head. 'The decapitation, the mutt's head, the splattering of blood . . . Father Fabian's been dreaming his own grotesque murder for years. How can that be?'

Hunter thought about it for a moment before looking up slowly. 'You're looking at it from the wrong angle, Carlos. Father Fabian hadn't been dreaming his own death. The killer knew about the nightmare and decided to make it come true.'

'Well, listen to the next line.' Garcia leaned forward over the book. *'I've never told anyone about that day in the park or about the dreams that torment me.'*

Thirty-Six

Hunter went silent for a few seconds while his mind kept going over the facts, digesting what Garcia had just told him. A secret nightmare that had tormented and scared Father Fabian for over twenty years. A nightmare that someone had gone to great lengths to make a reality.

Garcia spoke first.

'The killer could've read the journal just like we did, but the altar boy told us that there'd never been a break-in and no one had access to the priest's room, except the priest himself.' He stood up, approached one of the windows and pushed it wide open. Their office wasn't particularly stuffy, but he suddenly felt the need for some fresh air.

Hunter let out a constricted breath. 'I don't believe the killer found out about the nightmare through the diaries.'

'Why not? We did.'

'Exactly. There are two of us.' Hunter leaned back on his chair. 'We read solidly for almost three days. How many journals did we get through before you came across the pages that told us about the dream?'

'Several,' Garcia admitted, slowly running his right hand over his face.

'The killer would've needed either a lot of luck, or a lot of undisturbed time with the journals to have found out about the dream the same way we did. And if that's the case, why didn't he just take the book with him? Why leave it behind? The journals aren't numbered or dated. We would've never known one was missing.'

'So how?' Garcia stopped in front of Hunter's desk, his hands resting on his hips.

'The journal entries aren't dated.' Hunter gestured towards the books on his desk. 'The priest could've written that specific entry you read last week or five years ago.'

It took Garcia only a few seconds to catch up with Hunter's line of thought. 'So you're thinking the priest could've told someone after he wrote the entry.'

Hunter nodded. 'The dream had obviously gotten too much for the priest. He tried the *writing down* therapy. That didn't work.'

'So the next logical stage would've been to step it up a notch and tell someone,' Garcia concluded, and Hunter agreed.

The phone on Hunter's desk rang and he picked it up before the second ring. He looked concerned as he listened.

'We'll be right down.'

'What's up?' Garcia asked.

'There's someone downstairs, a member of the public, who wants to talk to us.'

'About what?'

'Father Fabian's killer.'

Thirty-Seven

The girl was in her late teens. She sat alone in one of the interrogation rooms on the second floor. Hunter and Garcia were watching her from the other side of the two-way mirror in the adjacent observation room.

She could've been attractive, but it was clear her appearance wasn't the most important thing in her life. Her disheveled brown hair fell over her shoulders in an overly casual way. Her beautiful, big brown eyes were bloodshot. She wore no makeup and her face was pale. The long winter coat she had on had certainly seen better days.

'She's just a kid,' Hunter said, frowning. 'Who's she again?' he asked the police officer who had initially talked to the girl and brought her up to the room.

'She said her name is Monica, but you don't need to be an expert to figure out that's made up.'

'And she said she had information on the Seven Saints Catholic Church murder?'

The officer nodded. 'She said she'd only speak to the detectives in charge. I tried taking a statement downstairs, but she refused.' He looked unsure for a moment.

'Anything else?' Hunter asked, sensing the officer's uneasiness.

'Something about her—' he looked from one detective to the other '—gave me the creeps.'

Garcia stepped closer to the mirror, his eyes scrutinizing the girl. She looked frightened.

Monica lifted her eyes as both detectives entered the room. Her stare bypassed Garcia and settled on Hunter.

'Hello,' Hunter said with a warm smile, extending his hand. 'I'm Detective Hunter and this is Detective Garcia.'

She stood up, smiled back and shook their hands, holding Hunter's just a little longer than she did Garcia's. 'I'm Monica.' Her voice was soft but padded with grief.

'Just Monica?' Garcia asked, his eyebrows arching slightly.

She bit her bottom lip, and her worried eyes reverted back to Hunter.

'It's OK,' he said in a comforting tone. 'I'm Robert and that's Carlos.' He tilted his head towards his partner. 'I also prefer when people call me by my first name. It's much less formal, isn't it?'

She smiled thinly.

'Could we get you a drink of something? Water, coffee, soda . . .?'

'Some water would be great, thank you,' she said as she sat back down.

'I'll get it,' Garcia offered, already reaching for the door.

Hunter pulled a chair and sat across the table from the girl. Her hands were clenched, and she was rubbing her thumbs against each other.

'These rooms are very intimidating, aren't they?' Hunter said in a relaxed tone. 'The bland walls, the metal table and chairs, the big mirrored window . . . Some say we could do with an internal decorator, a few flowers, maybe some incense. I tend to agree. What do you say?'

Her mouth didn't move.

'I'd offer to talk in my office, but I'm afraid it looks even worse than this. If you can imagine such a place.'

Her mouth twitched with a possible smile.

'If you don't mind me asking, how old are you?'

She hesitated for a second. 'I'm nineteen.'

Hunter nodded. She knew he hadn't bought her lie. Despite her young age, Hunter saw something in her eyes that told him that she was forced to mature faster than most.

The door opened and Garcia walked in with an aluminum jug of icy water on a metal tray. He placed it on the table before pouring her a glass.

'Have a seat, Carlos,' Hunter said, pointing to the chair next to him.

'It's OK, I'll stand. I don't mind.'

'I do,' Hunter hit back.

If Monica was a suspect in an ongoing investigation, Hunter would've stood up himself. Interrogations demand a certain degree of intimidation. Standing up, being able to move around freely and looking down on a subject who's restricted to his or her chair puts the detective in a psychologically authoritative position. One thing Hunter definitely didn't want was for Monica to feel any more intimidated than she already was.

Garcia pulled a chair and sat down.

'We were told you might have information that could be of some value to us,' Hunter said.

Monica had a sip of her water before locking eyes with him. 'I saw something.'

'You saw something?' Garcia's voice raised half an octave as he leaned forward. 'You were inside the church on Wednesday night?'

Monica gave Garcia a subtle head shake.

'Did you see anyone leaving the church late that night? Were you walking by or something?'

'No. It wasn't like that.' She held Garcia's gaze for a couple of silent seconds. 'I saw it in a vision.'

Garcia's posture stiffened defensively and he shook his head as if he hadn't heard her correctly. Hunter didn't react.

'I'm sorry?' Garcia frowned.

Monica took a deep breath to steady her voice. 'I know how this might sound, but please just listen to me for five minutes. I'm not crazy. I'm not a clairvoyant. I can't see the future. I don't read minds or talk to spirits either. But unfortunately I can sense certain things deeper than most people.'

Garcia glanced at Hunter, who was sitting back in his chair. His legs were crossed casually with his hands resting on his lap. He was concentrating on the girl.

'What sort of things?' Garcia asked.

Monica nervously pulled a loose strand of hair from her face and hooked it behind her ear. Even though Garcia had asked the question, she stared at Hunter before answering.

'Pain.'

'You can sense pain?' Garcia asked with a dubious expression.

'I can sense other people's pain,' she explained.

Garcia shifted his weight in his chair. Almost without fail, every time a high-profile case hits the news, the police get tens of people dropping in or calling and saying they can help with the investigation because they had a dream or a vision. He knew it was only a matter of time before it happened in this case, but he wasn't expecting it to happen so soon.

Since Garcia took point on questioning, Hunter had limited himself to listen and observe. He was taking in the girl's reactions, analyzing her eyes and physical movements together with voice intonation and quivers. Experience told him that when people walked in from the streets claiming they had a vision that could help the police catch a criminal, they usually fell into one of five categories – a lonely person looking for attention – a drug user who had hallucinations – someone with mental problems, most probably schizophrenia – a charlatan looking for money and/or publicity – or they had been involved in the crime themselves. Monica, so far, gave no indication of any.

Garcia once again glanced at Hunter, half hoping for some sort of reaction. When he didn't get one, he checked his watch before leaning forward and placing both elbows on the table.

'I'll tell you what we'll do, Monica,' he said calmly. 'I hope you understand that at the moment we're stretched thin and really pressed for time. But I'll ask an officer to take down what you think you saw, and if you leave us your details we'll get in touch if we have any questions . . .'

'I'm not trying to waste your time, detective,' she said firmly, reading Garcia's reluctance to believe her.

'And we appreciate that,' he replied in the same tone, but she didn't break stride.

'Whether you believe it or not, detective, it happens. Unfortunately, it happens to me. I see other people's suffering. I see their pain and tears and what makes them sad. It's not a gift; it's a curse that makes me scared of closing my eyes every night. I don't wanna be here either. I've never done this before, but I really think I can help.'

Monica went back to staring at Hunter. Something shifted in her eyes.

'Helen . . .' she whispered, '. . . it wasn't your fault.'

Hunter raised an eyebrow. 'I'm sorry?'

'You just wanted the crying to stop. She just wanted the pain to go away. You did what you thought was right. What she asked you to do. You freed her from the pain.' She shook her head. 'It wasn't your fault.'

Hunter stiffened. His eyes fixed on the brunette in front of him. He felt his mouth go dry and his stomach churn as images of a long time ago flooded his memory.

Garcia sensed the change in Hunter, but before he could say anything the door to the interrogation room was pushed open by Captain Blake.

'You guys better wrap it up in here,' she said, ignoring Monica. 'It looks like he claimed another one.'

Hunter looked up. 'Our man?'

Captain Blake nodded. 'In Malibu.'

Garcia jetted out of his chair. 'Thanks for coming,' he said before hurrying out of the room.

Hunter turned and faced Monica. 'I'll get an officer to write down your details.' He quickly placed one of his cards on the table in front of her.

'Detective,' she called as Hunter got to the door.

'He knew about the fire. He knew what scared her.'

Thirty-Eight

Hunter sat in silence staring out of the window as Garcia sped down Hollywood Freeway. Night had already fallen over Los Angeles, and with it came rain. Not your typical, heavy Californian downpour, but a steady, annoying English-type drizzle. The sky was covered by gray clouds. The wet weather would go on for hours.

Hunter was softly massaging between his eyebrows with his index finger, focusing his attention on the raindrops on the passenger's window. His thoughts were tangled in a tight cluster, and he was trying hard to unwind them. In the space of half an hour, the whole complexion of the case had changed. Now that they knew about the priest's dream, the idea of the killer being ritualistic took a knock. Hunter was certain that what happened a few days ago inside the Seven Saints church was not a ritual. The killer had simply acted out Father Fabian's nightmare, but why?

Garcia's attention was on the road, but he'd noticed his partner's change in mood inside the interrogation room. Something that girl said had really got to Hunter.

'Can I ask you something?' Garcia asked tentatively.

'Shoot,' Hunter said without breaking his stare.

'Who's Helen?'

'Sorry?'

'Monica, the—' Garcia searched for the correct word '—psychic girl we just talked to. She said something about Helen and it not being your fault. Who's Helen?'

Hunter closed his eyes.

Garcia knew better than to push for an answer. He allowed the silence to stretch.

'My mother,' Hunter finally replied, returning his attention to the window. 'Helen was my mother.'

He'd only been seven when it happened, but the memories crowding his mind now were still fresh.

Thirty-Nine

He sat alone in his room watching the heavy rain hammering against the window. He liked rain, especially heavy rain. Its thundering noise was almost enough to cover the crying, the moans of pain that came from the room next door – almost. He'd asked his father why the doctors didn't do something. Why they didn't take her into hospital and make her better.

'There's nothing more that can be done,' his father had said with tearful eyes as he placed two tablets next to a glass of water before hiding the medicine bottle deep inside the highest cupboard in their small kitchen.

'Can't we give her some more tablets, Dad? They help with her pain. She doesn't cry so much when she takes them.'

'No, Robert,' his father replied in a nervous voice. 'Too many aren't good for her.'

He had to take care of her when his father wasn't home, and back then his father worked nights.

Nights were always worse. Her screams sounded louder, her groans deeper and heavier with pain. They always made him shiver. Not like when he felt cold, but an intense shiver that came from deep within. Her illness had brought her so much pain, and he wished there was something he could do to help.

He cautiously opened the door to her room. He felt like crying, but his father had told him he mustn't. She was curled up on the bed. Her knees pushed up against her chest. Her arms wrapped tightly around her legs. She was crying.

'Please help me,' she whispered. 'It hurts so much.'

He was shivering, trying to keep his tears locked in his throat. 'What can I do, Mom?' His voice was as weak as hers.

She curled up into a tighter ball.

'Do you want me to call Dad?'

She shook her head. Tears were streaming down her face.

'Dad can call the doctor. He'll come and help you.'

'Dad can't help, honey. Neither can the doctor.'

His mother looked like a different person now. She was so thin he could see her bones poking at her sagging skin. Her eyes had the darkest bags under them. Her once-beautiful long blond hair was now fine and frizzled and sticking to her sweaty face. Her lips were cracked and crusted.

'I can heat some milk up for you, Mom. You like hot milk.'

She managed a delicate shake of the head. Her breath was coming in short gasps.

'Would you like me to get you some biscuits? You haven't eaten much today.'

She winced as a new surge of pain took over her body. 'Please, baby. Help me.'

He couldn't hold his tears anymore and they started rolling down his cheeks.

'You can help the pain go away,' she said in a trembling voice. 'You can get me my pills. You know where they are, don't you?'

He ran the back of his right hand against his running nose. She could see he was scared and shaking. 'They're very high up,' he said, hiding his eyes from her.

'Can't you reach them for me, baby? Please, the pain has been going on for so long. You don't know how much it hurts.'

His eyes were so full of tears everything appeared distorted. His heart felt empty, and he felt as if all his strength had left him. Without saying a word, he slowly turned around and opened the door.

His mother tried calling after him, but her voice was so weak that only a whisper left her lips.

He came back a few minutes later carrying a tray with a glass of water, two cream biscuits and the bottle of medicine. She stared at it, hardly believing her eyes. Very slowly and through unbearable pain, she pushed herself up into a sitting position. He stepped closer, placed the tray on the bedside table and handed her the glass of water.

She gave him the most honest smile he'd ever seen.

'I'm not strong enough to open the bottle, darling. Can you do it for me?'

He took the bottle, pressed down on the cap and twisted it anticlockwise. Pouring two pills onto his hand, he offered them to her. She took them, put them in her mouth and swallowed them down without even sipping the water. Her eyes pleaded for more.

'I read the label, Mom. It says you shouldn't have more than eight a day. The two you just had make it ten today.'

'You're so intelligent, my darling.' She smiled again. 'You're very special. I love you so much and I'm so sorry I won't see you grow up.'

His eyes filled with tears once again as she wrapped her bony fingers around the medicine bottle. He held on to it tightly.

'It's OK,' she whispered. 'It'll all be OK now.'

Hesitantly, he let go. 'Dad will be angry at me.'

'No, he won't be, baby. I promise you.' She placed two more pills in her mouth.

'I brought you these biscuits.' He pointed to the tray. 'They're your favorite, Mom. Please have one.'

'I will, honey, in a while.' She had a few more pills. 'When Daddy comes home,' she whispered. 'Tell him I love him. Can you do that for me?'

He nodded. His eyes locked on the now almost empty medicine bottle.

'Why don't you go read one of your books, darling? I know you love reading.'

'I can read in here. I can sit in the corner if you like. I won't make a noise, I promise.'

She extended her hand and touched his hair. 'I'll be OK now. The pain's starting to go away.' Her eyelids looked heavy.

'I can guard the room. I'll sit by the door.'

She smiled a pain-stricken smile. 'Why do you wanna guard the door, honey?'

'You told me that sometimes God comes and takes ill people to heaven. I don't want him to take you, Mom. I'll sit by the door and if he comes I'll tell him to go away. I'll tell him that you're getting better and not to take you.'

'You'll tell God to go away?'

He nodded vigorously.

She smiled again. 'I'm gonna miss you so much, Robert.'

Forty

As they drove down Pacific Coast Highway, the scenery had changed from the hustle and bustle of Downtown Los Angeles to the tranquility and breathtaking ocean views of Malibu. Hunter continued to stare out of the window.

Malibu is famous for its warm sandy beaches and for being the home of countless movie stars and celebrities. A place reserved for the rich and mega-rich.

'No need to check for the address,' Garcia said, slowing down. 'I guess that's it.'

About a hundred yards ahead on the left, several police vehicles were parked at the gates to a large mansion. News vans from various channels were already at the scene. Satellite antennas raised high in the cold and wet night sky.

Garcia slowly zigzagged his way around the cars and came to a stop in front of the intimidating electronic iron gates. An officer wearing a standard-issue LAPD vinyl raincoat came up to the driver's side.

'Detectives Garcia and Hunter,' Garcia said after lowering his window. 'Homicide Special.'

The officer nodded and used the remote control in his hand to open the gates. 'Forensics and the two other detectives have been in there for a while now,' he said.

'Two other detectives?' Hunter asked, leaning across Garcia.

'That's right,' the officer replied, stepping back from the car and gesturing for them to drive through.

As Garcia drove forward, Hunter caught a glimpse of Claire Anderson standing under a large white umbrella with the other reporters.

The perfectly cement-paved driveway must've been at least a hundred yards long, flanked by numerous palm trees. Just past the gates, on the left, there was a tennis court. The large green area between the court and the impressive two-story mansion had been impeccably mown, and the hedges around it were neatly cropped.

Garcia entered a circular parking bay and pulled in next to a forensics unit van, just in front of a four-car garage.

'Wow, would you have a look at this place,' Garcia said, stepping out of his car. 'Someone knew how to live in style.'

The house was white and modern with a terracotta-tile roof and large glass windows. On the second floor, the room at the corner of the house had a wrap-around balcony offering panoramic views of the beach. A few police officers were standing on the stone steps that led up to the front door, sheltering themselves from the rain.

With his badge in hand, Hunter took the steps two at a time. All the officers at the house's entrance were unnaturally quiet. The look on their faces was a mixture of sorrow and skepticism.

Double doors led them into a reception area that was bigger than Hunter's entire one-bedroom apartment. It was a rich, sterile room, full of money and devoid of character – the kind of elegant space in which it was hard to believe people actually lived.

A strange, unidentifiable smell lingered in the air. The sort of smell that could make you sick if you were exposed to it for long enough.

A short and bulky man in a white Tyvek coverall noticed the two detectives as they stepped into the house.

'Detective Hunter?' he asked, approaching them.

'Yes.' Hunter turned around.

'I'm Detective Martin, Thomas Martin, from the LASD Malibu/Lost Hills station.'

They shook hands firmly.

Malibu is actually an incorporated city in Western Los Angeles County. Any homicides committed in that city initially fall under the Los Angeles Sheriff Department jurisdiction.

'What do we have?' Hunter asked, looking around.

'A fucking mess, that's what we have. It started as a missing person's call to the West Hollowood station.'

'West Hollowood?' Garcia enquired, surprised.

Martin nodded. 'I suggest you guys suit up while I fill you in.' He pointed to two coveralls on a table together with surgical masks and latex gloves.

Forty-One

'A realtor called Reilly, Amanda Reilly,' Detective Martin continued after Hunter and Garcia stood ready. 'She owned her own estate agency called, funny enough, Reilly's, in West Hollywood. This morning she didn't turn up for work. Her work colleague . . .' Martin snapped his fingers a couple of times as he tried to remember her name. 'Aw damn. It's on the report, I'll check it later. Anyway, her colleague got worried. She said she's never known Miss Reilly to come in late in over ten years they'd worked together, never mind not turning up.'

A tall and skinny black man, also wearing a Tyvek coverall, entered the reception area from the door at the far end of it.

'Hey, CJ,' Martin called, gesturing for him to join them.

'What's up, Tom?' CJ said, freeing his nose and mouth from the surgical mask he had on. 'Are these the Homicide Special guys?'

Martin nodded before turning towards Hunter and Garcia. 'This is my partner, Detective CJ Simmons.'

'Call me CJ, everyone does.'

They all shook hands.

'CJ, what's the name of the lady who reported Miss Reilly as missing. I can't remember it for the life of me.'

'Mrs. Riggs, Tania Riggs. The report's in the car. I'll go and get it before we hand the case over to you guys.'

Hunter noticed a look of relief on CJ's face.

'Miss Reilly's car is parked back in West Hollywood,' Martin continued. 'It's been in the same spot for two days.'

CJ took over. 'The last Mrs. Riggs knew about Miss Reilly was that she was supposed to show this house to a prospective buyer on Saturday – early evening.'

'So this house is for sale? No one lives here at the moment?' Hunter asked, zipping up his overall.

'That's right.' CJ nodded. 'You know the protocol. So in the middle of the afternoon, a request was sent to our station asking us to dispatch a black and white unit down here to check it out. And then . . .' CJ shook his head slowly without finishing the sentence.

'And then all fucking hell broke loose,' Martin picked up. 'What's in there's just fucking insane. Someone had a lot of hate for this Miss Reilly.'

'How do *we* come into all this?' Hunter asked curiously.

'That's what I was wondering,' Garcia added.

'Forensics,' CJ replied. 'When they got here and had a good look at the body, the lead agent said that we needed to contact Homicide Special and ask for the two of you. Apparently, this case's linked to one that you're already investigating.'

'Mike Brindle the lead forensic agent?' Hunter asked.

'That's him,' Martin agreed with a nod.

'And the victim's this Amanda Reilly?' Hunter pressed on.

Martin and CJ exchanged a nervous look.

'We can't tell.'

'OK, let's go have a look.' Hunter knew he wouldn't get any more answers out in the reception area.

CJ smiled as he noticed that Hunter and Garcia were all suited up, but neither of them had a surgical mask. 'I strongly recommend you wear the mask.' He pointed to the one hanging from his neck. 'And I hope you really enjoyed what you had for dinner today. 'Cos you'll probably have it all back in your mouth as soon as you get in there.'

'He's right.' Martin nodded sarcastically. 'Have you noticed a terribly unpleasant bouquet in the air that sort of tickles your stomach?' He didn't wait for a reply. 'Well, in there it's fully matured.'

'And if the smell doesn't do it,' CJ cut in. 'Wait until you have a look at the victim.'

Frowning, Hunter and Garcia took the LASD detectives' advice and grabbed a surgical mask each.

'Through that door.' Martin pointed to the door CJ had come through earlier. 'There's a round foyer. Take the door to the right of the stairwell and follow the corridor to the end. You can't miss it; there are forensic agents everywhere.'

CJ and Martin were right. With every step, the smell got stronger and more sickening. They reached the last door and stepped into a nightmare.

The room was massive, furnished with delicate sofas and modern units. Mike Brindle and three other forensic agents were busy at work.

Hunter felt a sting in his eyes. He wasn't sure if it'd been caused by the nauseating and repulsive smell, or by what lay before him.

Garcia's body convulsed as he tried to keep himself from being sick, but the combination of the stench together with the ferocity of the scene became too much for him. He quickly stumbled back out of the room and Hunter heard him empty his stomach by the door.

'My God!' Hunter closed his eyes.

Forty-Two

At first Monica didn't know why she'd said those words to Hunter. They simply came out, as if she had no control over what she was saying. But just a minute after Hunter and Garcia had rushed out of the interrogation room, she had her answer.

The same sickening feeling she'd experienced just a few days ago inside Los Angeles Union Station came back, and it came back stronger.

A hurricane seemed to have started in her stomach as her vision blurred. The large mirrored window in front of her was substituted by grainy, flickering images. She blinked several times, trying desperately to get rid of them. She didn't want to see them. She didn't want to be part of any of it. But she had no choice. Again, they lasted only a few seconds, but a few seconds was all that was needed.

As the images faded, she sat shivering and crying. Her breathing came in short, fast bursts and catatonically she repeated the words 'please, no' over and over again.

It took her two minutes to get her breathing back to normal and another two to stop shivering. On unsteady legs she stood up and stared at her reflection in the mirror. She looked dreadful. Her hair was a mess. Her skin looked dry and badly cared for and her lack of recent sleep showed in her tired-looking eyes. She was wearing no lipstick, which made the scar on her lips more noticeable. Her coat looked dirty and old with tiny tears on the sleeves. No wonder both detectives looked at her as if she was a drug addict on a bad trip looking for some attention.

'What am I doing here?' she whispered to herself as if waking up from a strange dream in an unknown place. 'I must be insane thinking someone would've believed me.'

She checked her watch and wondered what to do next. The detective had said that he'd send an officer to take her details, but no one had showed up yet. Maybe that was a sign. Maybe telling others about the appalling things she saw wouldn't help them. It wouldn't help her.

Deep down she had hopes that if she could help any of the people she saw suffering, then, maybe, the images would go away and she could go back to having a normal life. But standing there, alone, in a police interrogation room, all she had were doubts.

'I need to get out of here, this is crazy,' she said as her eyes rested on Hunter's card on the table.

Forty-Three

Mike Brindle was in a crouch position next to a large white leather sofa when he noticed Hunter standing by the door. Getting to his feet, he approached the detective in silence.

Brindle had been with the Los Angeles Scientific Investigation Division for over fifteen years, but the look in his eyes told Hunter that even he hadn't seen anything like what had happened in that room.

They stood face to face without saying a word for a while before Brindle checked his watch.

'I guess you take the prize,' he finally murmured through his surgical mask.

Hunter narrowed his eyes and faintly shook his head.

'Other than "yours truly", nobody who's come through that door has managed over forty seconds in here before losing their dinner,' Brindle explained.

'I didn't have dinner.'

'I guess he did.' Brindle nodded towards Garcia, who had just re-entered the room. His surgical mask was back over his mouth and nose. His face was drained of all color.

'What in the world's happened here, Mike?' Hunter asked once Garcia had rejoined them.

'A lot of pain,' Brindle said, turning to face the enormous river rock fireplace on the south wall. Just over a foot in front of it and tied to a metal high-back armchair sat the naked body of a woman. Most of the skin on the front of her torso, arms and legs had blistered, crinkled and burst open, revealing her bloody, now burned flesh. Parts of her body had completely carbonized, displaying a crusty texture and charcoal color, but all eyes were on her face.

Garcia felt his stomach play up again as they stepped closer to the body.

The skin on her face had been burned so badly that it seemed to have melted into crumpled and clustered lumps, like hot wax. Her exposed flesh and muscle tissue had severely wrinkled and hardened, as if her face had been deep-fried. Her eyeballs had exploded inside their sockets from the intense heat.

'From what I've gathered so far,' Brindle said, carefully side-stepping the small pool of blood, urine and feces that surrounded the armchair. 'She was brought here on Saturday evening, tied to this chair and left in front of a blazing fire. She died long ago, but the fire was never turned off.' He pointed to the fireplace. Heat still emanated from it.

Hunter's stare quickly moved from the dead woman to Brindle. 'The killer . . . cooked her?'

Brindle's lips thinned as his head bobbed down. 'Given her proximity to the fire, more like roasted her alive.'

'This is fucking sick,' Garcia commented, turning his head away.

'This is a gas fire,' Brindle continued. 'Which means its intensity is controlled. Worst of all, it's constant. It won't die down unless somebody turns it off.'

'Was it on when the body was found?' Hunter asked, kneeling in front of the fireplace.

'Yes.' Brindle nodded. 'But on a very low setting. Just enough to—' he bit his lip '—simmer her. But look at the size of this fireplace, Robert. On its higher setting, it would feel like a proper bonfire.'

Hunter cleared his eyes, took a deep breath and forced himself to study the body for a moment. Garcia stayed a few steps behind. His right hand cupped over his nose. His face screwed up as if he'd tasted something sour.

The smell of burned human flesh is quite different from that of other animals because of our diet. Humans are the only animals who eat such diverse foods as meat, vegetables, sweets and chemically altered products. The combination of their smells gets embedded in the human flesh and then released, together with several toxins when the flesh burns.

Garcia felt something start to rise in his throat again.

'We cut her loose,' Brindle said, noticing Hunter's look as he studied her severed restraints. 'And that's the reason why the two of you are here.'

Hunter's brow creased in anticipation.

'We've been here for a while. Her body and the scene have already been photographed. The two local detectives we thought would be taking the case had seen enough. The body was ready to be taken to the morgue.'

Brindle gestured for one of the crime-lab agents to come and give him a hand. Very carefully, they moved the dead woman's back away from the armchair's backrest.

'And then we saw this.'

Hunter and Garcia repositioned themselves so they could have a better look.

'Oh fuck,' Garcia murmured through gritted teeth, pinching the bridge of his nose.

Forty-Four

Hunter massaged his temples with the tips of his fingers, trying to rub away the headache he knew was on its way.

'Shit,' he said softly.

His eyes were focused on the victim's back and neck. They had been badly scorched. But these were old burn marks. The skin had already healed, showing lumpy, leathery and irregular patches. But the surprise in both detectives' faces wasn't caused by the disfigurement. Halfway down her back, painted in red and about six inches long, was the number four.

'There's more.' Brindle lowered her body back to the original sitting position before asking one of his agents to bring him the large evidence bag they'd collected earlier. He lifted the clear plastic bag in the air so Hunter and Garcia could have a look at its contents. Inside lay a badly burned skull.

'This was found in the fire, after it was turned off.'

Garcia looked confused for a moment.

Hunter let out a deep sigh. 'Father Fabian's head?' he asked, already knowing the answer.

'You've gotta be kidding.' Garcia's eyes widened. Then he remembered what he'd read in the priest's journal – *My head is taken away to be burned.*

'We'll have to wait for the test results, but I'd put money on it,' Brindle replied.

Garcia turned his attention back to the burned woman. 'What I don't get about this is – how come it looks like she's got different degrees of burns all around her body?' He cautiously moved a step closer. 'The skin on her torso, arms and thighs has blistered and ruptured open. You can tell that the exposed flesh has simply cooked, as you've put it.' He nodded at Hunter. 'But her lower legs, feet and hands have burned to a fucking crisp. Most of it has carbonized for chrissakes. And what in God's name has happened to her face? It's like different parts of her body have been exposed to different intensities of heat.'

'And they have,' Brindle admitted. 'As I've said before, this thing at full tilt would feel like a forest fire.' He pointed to the fireplace. 'She was just about a foot away from it. I'm sure the killer was controlling the heat, torturing her, but because of her armchair sitting position, her lower legs and hands are about a foot closer to the fireplace than the rest of her body. That extra proximity could mean a rise of two, maybe three degrees Celsius. Given the probable amount of time she was exposed to such intense heat, the body parts closer to the fire would've sustained considerably more damage, as you can clearly see. Now, when it comes to her face—' he shook his head with uncertainty '—I've seen enough burn victims, but I've never seen anything quite like this before. The skin on her face has crumpled into melted-looking lumps, like a dinner candle.'

'Could the killer have used an accelerant?' Hunter asked.

'In my view, that's the only explanation,' Brindle admitted.

'Something like cooking oil?'

'Cooking oil?' Garcia repeated in a disbelieving tone. 'You think the killer smothered her face with cooking oil, placed her in front of a fire and watched it sizzle?'

Brindle tilted his head and shrugged in a 'who knows?' gesture. 'You'll have to wait for the autopsy and the lab results to be certain, but something had to have helped the skin on her face burn the way it did, causing it to look like it's melted away. Fire and heat alone wouldn't have done it.'

'Why not?' Garcia asked.

'Skin can't melt,' Hunter said, bending down and having a closer look at her face.

'That's right,' Brindle confirmed. 'I'm not gonna get scientific on you, but it's a biological and physical impossibility. It'll burn and carbonize, but it won't melt.' He paused for a second and rubbed his left eye with the heel of his hand. 'We checked the whole house, Robert. That's all the blood we found.' He pointed to the small pool under the armchair. 'If this is the same killer who got to the priest a few days ago, there was no ritual this time. If there was, it certainly didn't involve blood. It's like this is an entirely different killer. His MO has changed completely.'

Hunter nodded, but saw no point in revealing to Brindle what they'd found out earlier in Father Fabian's journal.

'Anything from dusting?'

'No prints yet, just a few fibers, but they could've come from anywhere in this house.' Brindle shrugged. 'There're rugs, carpets, curtains and fabrics just about everywhere in this place.'

Hunter walked around the room, checking the furniture for anything out of the ordinary. He found nothing. 'Who else has seen the number on her back?'

'Only the people in this room,' Brindle replied confidently. 'The two Malibu detectives decided to wait outside while we cut her loose. They didn't look too well.'

'And you haven't told them that's the reason why we're here.'

'Nope. I told them the skull found in the fire was the reason I wanted you two to have a look at this case.'

'Let's keep it this way,' Hunter said, approaching the door. 'Have you found her clothes and bag?'

'Not yet, but I wouldn't be surprised if the killer took them with him.'

Forty-Five

Hunter closed the door to his apartment behind him, leaned back and shut his eyes. The headache that had started at the house in Malibu had intensified on the way home. It now felt as if a rat had woken up inside his skull, panicked and tried to scratch its way out through his eyes.

The obnoxious smell of burned flesh had managed to bypass his coverall and it'd impregnated his clothes. A bitter tang so strong that it unsettled his stomach, stung at his eyes and constantly made him gag. He needed a shower – urgently.

Hunter undressed quickly. He grabbed a black trash can liner from the kitchen and dumped his clothes into it, knowing that washing them, no matter how much detergent he used, would never fully get rid of the smell.

In the bathroom, he ran the shower as hot as he could tolerate and leaned against the white tiles, letting the water sluice over his head, shoulders and back. Now, away from everyone's eyes, his chest heaved and he finally threw up. By the time he turned off the water, his skin had gone a dark shade of pink and his fingertips were soft and wrinkled. He'd been through almost an entire bar of soap, but still the smell lingered. It wasn't on his skin, he knew that. The unsettling odor had clung to the hairs inside his nose and no amount of blowing was getting rid of it. For the time being, the only solution he could come up with was to numb his brain.

The first two shots went down neat and in one single gulp. The third, a double, was poured over a single cube of ice and sipped slowly.

It was late, but Hunter knew sleep would be bordering on impossible. It was already hard enough on a regular, non-eventful day.

He paced the room for a while before stopping by his living room window. He stood there for a moment, staring at the empty street. His mind full of thoughts. Nothing made sense.

The single malt seemed to be doing the trick where the smell of burned flesh was concerned, but his head still felt like a ticking bomb. Headache tablets had never really worked for him, so he discarded the thought as it entered his mind. But pills reminded him of something else, and it made his pulse race – Monica, the girl who'd dropped by the station earlier.

Over the years, he'd seen his fair share of crazy people and charlatans, all of them positive they could lead the police to an unfound body or to an elusive killer, but something told Hunter that wasn't the case this time.

There was something different about Monica. Hunter saw a conviction in her eyes he'd never seen before in any of the so-called psychics. She wasn't after a free publicity ride or attention. In fact, she looked scared, as if talking to the police would expose her to something or someone she'd been running away from.

Hunter took a deep breath and ran his hand through his wet hair. Her words still echoed in his ears. *Helen . . . it wasn't your fault.* 'How could she know?' he said out loud. 'No one does.'

He felt the same old destructive guilt creep up on him, and he finished the rest of his Scotch in one large swig. It burned the back of his throat, and that's when he remembered the last thing she'd said to him.

'*He knew about the fire. He knew what scared her.*'

Forty-Six

Hunter was leaning against his car in the empty LACDC parking lot. His hands deep inside his jacket pockets. It was a clear day, but cold according to LA standards. A cup of flavorless machine coffee purchased from a gas station rested on the hood of his old Buick. It was 7:10 a.m. Doctor Winston had called him about half an hour ago saying he'd already concluded the autopsy on the new body.

Hunter had been waiting less than five minutes when Garcia pulled up and parked next to him. As he stepped out of his Honda Civic, Hunter noticed his reddish eyes and pale complexion.

'I guess I wasn't the only one who got no sleep last night,' Hunter said, reaching for his coffee.

Garcia shook his head slowly. 'I freaked Anna out last night.'

'What do you mean?' A slight head shake.

'I called Anna to let her know I'd be home late yesterday, but she decided to wait for me so we could have dinner together.'

'That's nice.' Hunter sipped his coffee and pulled a bitter face.

'When I got home, Anna was in the kitchen.' Garcia buttoned up his coat. 'As soon as she heard me walk in, she threw two steaks onto the grilling pan. The sizzling noise, together with the smell of cooking meat, hit me like a ton of bricks. I puked right there on the kitchen floor.'

'Oh shit! That can't be good.' They started walking towards the LACDC building.

'Obviously, I didn't tell her about the investigation and the real reason why, all of a sudden, a sizzling steak was making me throw up.' He paused and pulled his longish hair away from his eyes. 'I was born in Brazil, Robert. I was practically brought up on steak. It's my favorite food.'

'What did you tell her?'

Garcia laughed tensely. 'I came up with some bullshit about a stomach bug going around at the station.'

'Did she buy that?' Hunter's eyebrows arched.

'Hell no. Anna's too smart for that kind of crap. But she pretended she did.'

Hunter gave Garcia an understanding smile.

'That's not all. I needed to have a shower. That godforsaken smell was all over me like zits on a teenager, and I was sure Anna could smell it too. I passed on dinner and locked myself in the bathroom for about an hour. My skin was red-raw from all the scrubbing, but the smell just won't go away.' He brought his right wrist to his nose.

'It's not on you, Carlos,' Hunter said without going into details.

'And then came the tossing and turning in bed,' Garcia continued. 'It was like her melted face and burned body were hiding behind my eyelids. I couldn't close them. Not only did I get no sleep, but I kept Anna up all night. I know I'm starting to scare her again, Robert. She ain't exactly over what happened during the Crucifix Killer's case, you know.'

They reached the main building and were allowed in by the security guard, who told them Doctor Winston was waiting for them in autopsy room 2A. They suited up and Garcia popped two anti-acid tablets in his mouth before making his way to the room on the far end of the corridor. The doctor was sitting at the microscope counter, flipping through some result sheets. His shoulders were hunched forward, his hair in a mess.

'Did you pull an "all-nighter", doc?' Hunter asked, closing the door behind them.

Doctor Winston looked up slowly. 'Almost.' He gave them a faint smile before approaching the stainless-steel table where the woman's body lay. Hunter and Garcia pulled their surgical masks over their noses and mouths and followed.

'What we have here is—' Doctor Winston paused and shook his head, as if words weren't enough to explain '—a master-piece of evil. Whoever this killer is, he must've hated this woman with every fiber in his body.'

Forty-Seven

With the woman's body stretched over the autopsy table, Hunter could see the extent of her injuries more clearly. The blisters on her torso had all burst open, and the edges of the scabs were black and curled up. The exposed flesh had dehydrated from the intense heat, but some of it still kept a deep pink, sunburned-type color. Her lower legs and hands were crusty and charcoaled. Some bone parts were now visible. But still, the injuries to her face mesmerized Hunter. Mike Brindle was right. It looked like the skin had melted into clumps, just like a candle.

'My guess is that she was probably unconscious when she was tied to the armchair,' Doctor Winston explained. 'But there are no bumps on her head.'

'Drugged?'

'That's the logical conclusion. I'm still waiting for the results from the lab, but I'm certain the killer didn't use a hard intravenous drug.'

'Why not?' Garcia questioned.

'It'd be overkill. The killer needed only to knock her out for a few minutes so he could undress her and tie her down. Any longer than that and he'd be losing precious time.'

'The killer wanted her to be conscious so she could suffer,' Hunter concluded, walking around to her left side.

'It all points that way,' the doctor agreed. 'The killer knew that by Monday he had to be out of that house. He knew exactly how long he had to torture her, and I bet he used every second of it.'

'Drugged cloth over the nose and mouth?' Hunter asked.

'Most probably.' The answer came with a sequence of quick nods. 'A common volatile agent, almost certainly ether based.'

'Any names?'

'Huh,' Doctor Winston chuckled. 'Anything like Enflurane, Desflurane, Sevoflurane, Insoflurane. I can get you a list if you like.'

'That easy to come by?' Garcia this time.

'Easy enough. And those are the most common, non-irritant when inhaled ones. I don't think the killer was really concerned if the skin around her mouth got little acid burns from the wet cloth. He could've used almost anything.'

'Great!'

'Due to the state her body's in, we won't be able to tell if she was sexually assaulted, but I don't believe she was.'

'Neither do I,' Hunter agreed. 'Whatever satisfaction this killer is after, it isn't sexual.'

'The main torture here is unseen, Robert,' the doctor said, lifting his eyebrows.

'What do you mean?' Garcia looked intrigued.

'She suffered a lot from the skin and subsequent flesh burns, but what the killer was really doing was roasting her alive.' Doctor Winston paused, allowing the full extent of what he was saying to be absorbed. 'If you put someone in front of an intense fire for long enough without allowing them to move, without giving them water, consequently their internal organs will start to cook.'

'Oh Jesus Christ.' Garcia ran both hands through his hair and interlaced his fingers at the back of his head.

'That's right. Liver, kidneys, pancreas, stomach, lungs, heart, every organ in her body would've responded to dehydration and the constant increase in temperature.' The doctor bit his lip and shook his head in disgust. 'Her blood literally boiled.'

Hunter closed his eyes for an instant.

'Her liver and kidneys were still hot when I pulled them out of her body during the autopsy. And every organ I looked at had some severe damage caused by heat and dehydration. It was like a race to see which organ would give in and burst first.'

Silence settled, and Hunter allowed his eyes to drift back to the woman's face.

'Now that was ingenious,' Doctor Winston said, following Hunter's stare. 'Evil, but ingenious nonetheless.'

'You mean, causing her face to melt?' Garcia asked and felt his stomach go rigid again.

'Achieving that effect, really. Skin won't melt.'

'Yeah, I was told.' Garcia nodded. 'So how the hell did the killer get her face to look like that?'

'He used an accelerant.' Doctor Winston paused and raised his right index finger to emphasize a point. 'Actually, it looks like he used a combination. And that's where the ingenious part comes from.'

Hunter made a face, as if he couldn't wait to hear it.

'Again, I need confirmation from the lab, but a quick first test showed the killer could've used something as common as lard.'

'You're kidding?'

'Nope. Your everyday supermarket lard.'

'That would've . . .'

'Fried her face.' The doctor completed Hunter's sentence.

'OK, but that wouldn't have caused the melting effect.' Hunter bent over to get a closer look at her disfigured face.

'No, it wouldn't.'

'So?' He stood back up as the stinging smell made his eyes water.

'So we definitely need the lab to confirm it, but it looks like the killer could've used a combination of something like lard together with a rubber compound.'

'Rubber?' Garcia repeated, frowning.

A confident nod from the doctor. 'Maybe even foam latex prosthetics. Just like they use in films. It's actually quite clever. The rubber compound attaches itself to the skin like glue.' The doctor ran the tips of his fingers down his face as if applying a moisturizing cream. 'With the heat, it melts, running down the victim's face, creating the desired candle wax clump effect. The skin just behind the rubber compound is covered in the accelerant, which would've drastically sped up the burning process, completely destroying the skin on her face, causing unimaginable pain. The final effect . . .' He pointed to the body, '. . . the melted face.' Doctor Winston took a step back and faced both detectives. 'And that's not all.'

Forty-Eight

Hunter braced himself. *What else could this killer have done?*

'I have indications that the injuries to her face were caused while she was still alive,' Doctor Winston continued. 'He tortured her by *melting* her face first.'

Hunter frowned. 'How?'

'A guess – heat lamps. The victim was tied to an armchair, right? Now imagine the killer had one or even two heat lamps mounted onto a pedestal or a tripod or something, very close to and pointing directly at her face – old interrogation style.'

It suddenly seemed as if there wasn't enough oxygen in the room.

'The UVB rays together with the accelerant and the rubber compound used would've caused her face to fry and *melt*, but the injuries wouldn't be enough to kill her. Unbelievably painful, but not life threatening. Not for hours.'

Garcia coughed twice, trying to clear something from his throat. 'So you're saying the killer allowed her to suffer grotesque pain for many hours before finally turning on the fireplace and cooking her alive.'

The doctor used his thumb and index finger to rub his eyes and he nodded slowly. 'That's my theory anyway.'

Hunter circled the autopsy table.

'What about her back, doc?'

'Yes. She's no stranger to fire.' The doctor stepped away from the body, approached a metal cabinet by the west wall and retrieved a paper envelope from the top drawer. 'Her body's in a very fragile state and I don't wanna keep on moving it. So let me show you on these pictures.' He pulled four photographs out of the envelope and arranged them neatly over his desk. 'She's been severely burned before. As you can see, most of her back and neck are scarred.' The doctor pointed to the first two photographs.

'Any idea of how long ago?'

'Very hard to be precise, but she was probably a young girl or a teenager.'

'That long?'

Doctor Winston nodded. 'The skin has stretched quite a bit since it's healed. Meaning she's grown. I'm certain those burn marks aren't from her adult life.'

'The number drawn on her back.' Hunter pointed to the third picture. 'Did the killer use blood again?'

'Definitely. It's already been sent to the lab, and I'll have a result sometime today.'

Both detectives looked at all four photographs.

'How long would you say she was exposed to the heat, doc?' Hunter asked.

'Probably from Saturday night all the way until when she was found. I heard the fire was still on when the police came into the house yesterday.'

Hunter bit his lip and nodded.

'The killer didn't stop cooking her after she died, Robert. This was more than torturing a victim. This was a demonstration of his resolve. He knew we'd find her. And he wanted us to find her looking like this. He's showing off how evil and brutal he can be. I'm just not sure why.'

'Maybe he isn't showing off, doc,' Hunter shook his head. 'Maybe he only stops when the monster inside him is satisfied. That's not uncommon. Sometimes death alone isn't enough to soothe a killer's rage or evil or whatever the hell it is that made him wanna kill. There're cases upon cases of killers who carry on shooting, clubbing, stabbing, cutting their victims or whatever, way after they're dead. Some even keep them for days, weeks, months . . .'

'Maybe you're right,' Doctor Winston agreed. 'Maybe just killing them isn't enough for him.' He took a deep breath and let it out slowly. 'There's something else I need to show you.'

The doctor's tone made Hunter stare in his direction.

Pulling a round magnifying lamp mounted onto a pedestal towards the autopsy table, the doctor summoned Hunter and Garcia closer. He positioned the lamp sideways, its beam illuminating the right side of the victim's abdomen. 'Have a look.' He moved out of the way.

Hunter stared through the magnifying lamp unsure of what he was looking for. A few seconds later his eyes narrowed as they locked their focus on something just under her right breast.

'No way!' he exclaimed, feeling a chill electrify his body.

Doctor Winston nodded calmly.

'You've gotta be shitting me, doc.'

Forty-Nine

Two distinct groups of crime-scene photographs, separated by a white marker line, were now pinned onto the corkboard in Hunter and Garcia's office. On the left, the Seven Saints Catholic Church and the brutality of a priest's decapitation; on the right, the mansion in Malibu and the sadism of a body left to roast in front of an enormous fireplace.

With the discovery of a new body, Captain Blake had demanded a team meeting from now on, every day, at nine in the morning. Hunter and Garcia made it to the office with ten minutes to spare.

The forensics report from Amanda Reilly's crime scene revealed that they'd found a partial print in one of the rooms upstairs. They'd also found a utilities room and a vacuum cleaner that'd apparently been used recently. The lab report would take a few days to come through.

The information they had so far on Amanda Reilly was basic. Born and raised in Los Angeles. Left high school before graduating and had been in the property business ever since. Her mother passed away seven years ago. Her father was never a strong presence in her life – alcohol and gambling problems. His location is unknown. Amanda was divorced. Ex-husband ran his own restaurant in San Diego. He'd been living there for six years. He was working all through the weekend. Alibi verified. She was also experiencing heavy financial difficulties. Her agency wasn't doing well. The house in Malibu is owned by a stock market investor millionaire named Dan Tyler.

At 9:00 a.m. Captain Blake entered the room without knocking, carrying a copy of the *LA Times*.

'Have you seen this?' she asked Hunter.

'I tend not to read newspapers. They depress me.'

'Well, then this will make your day.' She calmly placed the paper on his desk with the front-page headline facing up.

Hunter let his eyes glide towards the paper without reaching for it. Garcia stood up and approached Hunter's desk, curious to read it himself.

THE EXECUTIONER STRIKES AGAIN. NEW VICTIM SCORCHED TO DEATH BY SADISTIC SERIAL KILLER. LOS ANGELES POLICE BAFFLED.

Hunter read the headline in silence before quickly checking the reporter's name – Claire Anderson. *I could've guessed that.*

As Hunter made no attempt to read the rest of the article, Garcia was quick to snatch the paper from his desk.

'My question is,' the captain said, annoyed, 'how the hell have they linked these two murders together?'

'She's got contacts in the police and probably at the morgue,' Hunter replied casually.

'She?' the captain asked with a worried frown.

'Claire Anderson, the reporter who wrote the article.'

Captain Blake stared at Hunter with inquisitive eyes. 'By the look on your face, I gather you know her.'

'We've met.'

The captain held Hunter's gaze for a few seconds, but he was giving nothing away. 'No one else at the RHD, apart from the three of us, knows that these two cases are connected.' She started pacing the room. 'If neither of you talked to her, the tip couldn't have come from here. Doctor Winston has guaranteed me that only he and three very reliable forensic agents know about the connection. He's sure the leak isn't on his side.'

'It says here,' Garcia interrupted, reading from the paper. '*Special Homicide Detective Robert Hunter is leading the investigation. Though he's declined to comment, there's no question that both murders have simply baffled the police. The Executioner . . .*' he paused and raised his eyes at Hunter. 'Cute name. Who the hell comes up with these?'

Hunter shrugged indifferently.

Garcia continued reading. '*. . . The Executioner is now roaming the streets of our city, and once again the police seem to have no real direction, no suspects and, as we understand, no clues. For all our sakes, this reporter sincerely hopes that Detective Hunter gets to the Executioner faster than he did to the infamous Crucifix Killer.*'

'Bitch,' Hunter said under his breath.

'All this doesn't really bother me . . . yet,' the captain said, locking eyes with Hunter. 'I don't care if this reporter somehow managed to link both cases together. What we must, at any cost, keep from the press is the numbering on the victims. If the press gets hold of that, we're screwed. We'll have a citywide panic on our hands. Not to mention the nuclear pressure to find the first two victims.'

'They obviously don't know anything about that,' Garcia said, waving the paper in his hand. 'Or else it would've made the headlines.'

'And we'll do our best to keep it that way,' the captain countered. 'I want this case completely sealed off. No one else is to have access to this room or the investigation files without you clearing it with me first. Is that understood?'

Fifty

Captain Blake approached the corkboard and studied the new photographs. Hunter noticed she visibly flinched before falling back into her usual controlled demeanor. 'Did the killer use blood again to draw the number?' She pointed to one of the pictures.

'Yes,' Hunter replied, pushing his chair back with a scraping sound and standing up.

There was a knock at the door.

'Come in,' the captain called ahead of Hunter and Garcia.

Ian Hopkins entered and was instantly surprised to see Captain Blake in the room.

'Oh I'm sorry. I didn't know you were having a meeting.'

'It's OK,' Hunter said, motioning him to stay.

Captain Blake turned to face Garcia with a questioning expression.

'He's OK.' Garcia gently shook his head. 'He's the officer you assigned to us to help with the legwork, remember?'

'I just came in to tell Detective Hunter that no one took down the Monica girl details,' Hopkins said. 'When the officer got to the interrogation room, she was gone.'

'Monica?' the captain asked, turning around. 'Is this the girl who came in yesterday saying she had some information on the Seven Saints church murder?'

'That's her,' Garcia replied, leaning against his desk.

'So what came of that?'

'We had just started talking to her when we were told about the new victim.' Hunter joined the captain by the photo board. 'She never got a chance to tell us what she came here to tell us.'

'Was she at the church? Did she see anything?' The captain's interest grew.

'No to the first and in a way to the second,' Garcia replied, scratching his chin.

'And what the fuck does that mean?'

'She wasn't at the church,' Hunter said calmly. 'All she told us is that she had a vision.'

The captain's posture tensed. 'Hold on,' she said firmly, lifting her right hand. 'She came in claiming she was psychic?'

'Not as far as we know,' Hunter replied.

The captain stared around the room and came to rest on Garcia. 'Somebody better tell me something.'

'According to the officer who first talked to her, she didn't say anything about being a psychic or having any visions. She claimed she had some information, but she'd only talk to the detectives in charge.'

The captain took a packet of mints out of her dark blazer's breast pocket and popped one in her mouth. 'I'm sorry.' She turned to Hunter. 'But if she is a crackpot claiming she's psychic, why are we after her?'

'She's not a psychic, captain,' Hunter said cautiously. 'She seems to feel things deeper than most people.'

'She what?' The captain almost choked on her mint.

'Extrasensory perception.' Hunter didn't hesitate.

'Please tell me you're joking,' she shot back. Her hands on her hips. Her voice half an octave higher.

'I'm as skeptical about this as you are, captain,' Hunter

replied, 'but the fact is, whether we believe it or not, people with ESP do exist.'

'It doesn't matter, Robert.' The captain crushed her mint with a loud crunch. 'We're not the supernatural freaking police. The press is already out in force to get us, and so is the mayor. We are under severe pressure. Now imagine what would happen if they found out we enlisted the help of a psychic. How incompetent would we look?'

'I'm not enlisting anyone's help, captain. I just wanna talk to her. Find out what she has to say. If it all turns out to be bullshit, we'll disregard it like we've done with one hundred percent of the tips that have come in so far.'

She popped a new mint in her mouth and rolled it from one cheek to the other. 'What makes you think she's the real deal?'

Hunter stood behind his chair and leaned his elbows against it. 'As I was rushing out of the interrogation room yesterday, she stopped me to tell me something.' He looked at Garcia. 'You'd already left.'

'And what was that?'

Hunter paused for a moment. 'She said, "He knew about the fire. He knew what scared her."'

Fifty-One

The room went silent and all eyes fell on Hunter.

'It couldn't have been a guess.' He shook his head and moved from behind his desk. 'But at that moment I had no idea what she was talking about.'

'Maybe she's using this hyper-sensitivity thing as a smoke-screen,' the captain said. 'Maybe she's more involved than she'd like us to believe.'

'Whatever the reason is, I think we should talk to her.'

'Unfortunately,' Hopkins interrupted, 'as I've said, no one got her details. She left no last name, address or phone number at the front desk.'

'Yes, but we have CCTV in the interrogation room.' Hunter nodded at Hopkins. 'Ask the tech guys to get a snapshot of her from the tape and run it against the MUPU database.'

'The Missing Persons database?' Hopkins asked, looking puzzled.

'I have a hunch she's a runaway. Start the search with Pennsylvania.'

'Why Pennsylvania?' the captain asked.

'She had a slight Pennsylvania Dutch accent. I think that'll be the best place to start.'

'I'll get right on it.'

The captain waited for Hopkins to leave before turning to

face both detectives. 'If you find her, you bring her here, do you understand?' she said firmly. 'This has to run by the book, Robert. If she has information about any of our investigations, psychic crap or not, she has to be interviewed under caution and I wanna be in the observation room. Am I clear?'

Hunter nodded.

'Am I clear, detective?' She pressed him for a vocal answer.

'Yes, captain.' Hunter didn't break eye contact.

'OK.' She furtively checked her watch. 'Brief me on what we have so far on this Amanda Reilly.'

Hunter quickly explained what the autopsy had revealed.

'The killer took a bite out of her body?' the captain asked, feeling a wave of nausea starting to surge.

'The doctor found indentations just under her right breast.' Hunter retrieved a photograph from a paper envelope and handed it to Captain Blake. 'A small chunk of flesh is clearly missing.' He indicated what he meant on the picture. 'Due to the state the body is in, it'll be impossible to confirm the teeth marks, but the doctor is as certain as he can be.'

'This is insane,' the captain responded, rubbing her face.

'It's one of the very few things that's consistent with the Seven Saints church murder,' Hunter replied. 'The killer drank some of the priest's blood and now it looks like he ate some of Amanda Reilly's flesh.'

'Why?' Captain Blake asked with a disgusted look. 'Why would the killer do that?'

Hunter massaged his eyes with his thumb and forefinger. 'History and textbooks will tell you that the most common reason why a killer would consume his victims' flesh or blood is because he feels that by doing so the victims become a permanent part of him. Sometimes it gives the killer a sick sense of sexual pleasure.'

A disturbing silence followed.

'But we know this killer is not after sexual pleasure.' The captain handed the picture back to Hunter. 'Why would he want to make the victims a permanent part of him?'

'Only the killer can really answer that, captain.'

'Humor me with the psychology stuff,' the captain said in a commanding voice. 'Who might we be facing here?'

Hunter pinned the photograph to the board, took a deep breath and faced Barbara Blake. 'A killer who knew the victims very well. Whose hate for them is so complete that having absolute control over their life and death wasn't enough for him. He needed more.'

The captain exhaled. 'And by more you mean drinking their blood and consuming their flesh?'

Hunter nodded, approached the window and looked out into a sunny, cold day.

'But why the change?' The captain wasn't giving up. She wanted to understand the possible reasons behind all this. 'If the killer drank the priest's blood, why not do the same with Amanda Reilly? Why go for a bite?'

'Again, only the killer can answer that, but he might be evolving. Moving up the ladder.'

'Come again?'

Hunter stretched his body and his muscles tensed. 'Many serial killers usually escalate in one way or another. It could be the violence, the time interval between kills . . . This one could be escalating from drinking blood to true cannibalism.'

'Oh, that's just great,' Captain Blake said, raising a hand to her forehead as if fighting a headache. She checked her watch. 'Shit. I have to be in a press conference in ten minutes. For now, I'll play dumb and say I can't confirm both murders are linked, but I won't be able to hold that position for long. If need be, I'll lie my ass off and say we have very reliable leads we're pursuing, but you two better come up with something – and quick. And find this Monica girl. I wanna know why she said what she said.'

'Me too,' Hunter said as the captain let the door slam behind her.

Fifty-Two

The press conference room at Parker Center was large enough to comfortably accommodate the herd of hungry reporters that had turned up.

Barbara Blake had to admit that when she took the RHD captain's job only a week ago she never expected to be facing the LA press on a serial killer case so soon. She also never expected to have to see eye to eye with the Los Angeles mayor on her first day at the job. But if this was what the job demanded, this was what she was prepared to give.

As she entered the room, the loud murmur of animated voices died to a whisper. Captain Blake was wearing stylish straight-legged black pants with a light red satin blouse and a black blazer that was the perfect backdrop for her long dark hair. Her makeup, as always, was subtle and elegant. She took her position behind the speaker's stand, looking completely at ease and self-confident. Without saying a word, she let her eyes travel around the room, waiting for everyone's attention. It took her less than ten seconds to get it.

'I'll answer questions for five minutes and five minutes only. Maybe we'll be able to do away with some of the fantasy that's been published in today's paper.' Her voice was as firm as it was seductive, combining a soft, girlish tone with a level of self-assurance that was disarming. 'Before you start, let me say this.

I will not discuss any aspect of any of our ongoing investigations, so please don't even bother asking. If your questions don't come in a civilized and orderly fashion, this conference is over.'

Hands flew in the air as reporters started shouting questions and thrusting forward microphones emblazoned with insignia from CNN, Fox, CBS, NBC, Court TV and several of the major newspapers.

The captain gritted her teeth. *They didn't hear a damn word I said*.

'Captain Blake,' an attractive, long-dark-haired female reporter called from the corner of the room.

'Claire Anderson from the *LA Times*.' She identified herself, and the captain turned her attention to the reporter with interest. Claire was tall, slender and her tone of voice carried a distinct arrogance. 'Are you saying that last week's Seven Saints church murder and yesterday's Pacific Coast Highway one aren't connected?'

'At the moment we have nothing to link these two investigations together,' the captain replied in a steady, non-hesitant voice.

'So why assign the case to Detective Hunter?' Claire insisted.

'What do you mean?'

'I mean I have a very reliable source who tells me Detective Hunter is supposed to be dealing exclusively with the Seven Saints church investigation. If the cases aren't connected, how come he's been assigned to the Malibu murder as well?'

So that was it, the captain thought. *There's been no leak or tip. Claire had simply deducted that if Hunter had been assigned to the Malibu murder, the cases must be connected. Quite clever, really*.

'That's why your paper printed what it did this morning?'

the captain demanded furiously. 'Because of your assumption? You chose to spread panic around this city because you made a silly deduction?'

Claire shrugged without shying away from the captain's angry stare. 'As I said, my source is very reliable.'

'Really? Well, if you're paying this source of yours more than a buck ninety-five, you've been had.'

Restrained chuckles echoed throughout the room.

'Let me clarify this for you,' Captain Blake said confidently. 'In an ideal world, this department would have as many detectives as it has cases, and the ratio would be one to one, but this isn't an ideal world, is it? This is a world where someone enters a church during confession time and decapitates a priest. This is a world where someone ties an innocent woman to a chair and tortures her in front of a large fire until she's dead.'

The room went completely silent.

'Unfortunately,' the captain continued, 'the number of violent crimes committed in this city surpasses that of detectives exponentially. Detective Robert Hunter and Detective Carlos Garcia were supposed to deal exclusively with the Seven Saints church investigation, you're right.' She nodded at Claire, widening her eyes. 'But all my other detectives are overloaded with cases. Maybe the *LA Times* could publish a request to all violent murderers out there, asking them to take a few years' break so we can catch up. How does that sound to you?'

Nervous laughter came from around the room. Claire kept her face steady.

'So you're admitting Detective Hunter is leading the Malibu investigation as well?'

'Detective Hunter brings us the advantage of also being a forensic psychologist. His knowledge and understanding of how the mind of a violent criminal might work proves indispensable in many of my department's investigations. Due to the extreme brutality of the crime committed in Malibu over the past weekend, I have asked Detective Hunter to take the investigation, yes,' the captain finally admitted.

'Why isn't he attending this press conference?'

'I can answer all your questions at this moment. Time is of the essence and Detective Hunter has to use it wisely. He's not needed in this press conference.'

More hands shot up and shouts filled the room once again.

'I guess Mayor Edwards won't be best pleased,' Claire said, raising her voice above all others. 'It's my understanding that he wanted your best detective to work exclusively on the Seven Saints church murder.'

'In this department,' Captain Blake hit back fiercely, 'we don't have a best or a worst detective. We all work just as hard and we all do our job to the best of our abilities. Rest assured both cases will be solved.' She hoped the slight uncertainty in her voice wasn't as noticeable to everyone as it was to her.

Fifty-Three

Studio City had gotten its name because of its proximity to the major movie corporations and broadcasting systems. Universal was only ten minutes away. Paramount, CBS and all of old Hollywood were just across the canyon, and if you took a quick fifteen-minute freeway drive you could be in Burbank and NBC. Most of the young and beautiful Hollywood elite liked to spend their free time wandering around the many boutiques, clubs, bars and coffeehouses in the Greenwich Village – a place to see and be seen.

Tania Riggs lived in a wood-sided complex surrounded by tens of lacy elms and giant sycamores. Every apartment had its own private balcony, and the complex had a communal pool, gym and recreational rooms.

Hunter and Garcia climbed the stairs to Tania's second-floor apartment in silence. Both wrestling with their own thoughts, trying to organize them in their heads.

Hunter's knock was answered by a woman in her forties; brunette, average height and quite overweight. Her shoulder-length hair was pinned back into a ponytail, and her dark brown eyes seemed heavy and tired, mostly from crying, Hunter deduced. She was wearing dark blue cotton pants and a black sweater. Hunter and Garcia introduced themselves and waited patiently while Tania Riggs studied their credentials.

'Please come in,' she said in a quiet voice, taking a step to her left.

There was a hint of scented candles in the air – Hunter guessed jasmine.

'Please have a seat.' She indicated a low-slung, mattress-style blue sofa tufted with buttons. Her living space was open and the furnishing sparse. Besides the sofa, there were two arm-chairs, a wooden coffee table, an acrylic four-seater dining table and a half-full bookcase against the far wall.

'Can I get you a drink?' she offered timidly.

'No, thank you, Mrs. Riggs, we're fine,' Hunter replied, taking a seat on the sofa. It was surprisingly comfortable.

'Please call me Tania. Mrs. Riggs makes me feel even older than I am.' She took a seat at the armchair furthest from the sofa. A clear sign that she wasn't comfortable having people around.

'We're very sorry about Miss Reilly,' Hunter said in a sub-dued tone of voice.

Tania squeezed her eyes tightly and two tears rolled down her face.

'Were you longtime friends?'

She nodded sadly. 'Almost thirty years. I started working at Palm Properties just a week before Mandy. We clicked straight away. I was probably the only one who didn't hate her.'

'Hate her?' Garcia asked with interest.

Tania hesitated for a moment as if she'd said something she shouldn't have. She offered an explanation. 'Mandy was very pretty, very ambitious and very good at what she did. She was also very charming and she certainly knew how to win clients over. Right from the start, everyone could see she'd go places, and it didn't take long for the envious looks to start flying around. Every male employee and client wanted to sleep with her.' Tania thought about it for a second. 'I'm sure some of the female ones did too. The real estate business is a very tough business, detective. Everyone's fighting to do better than the next person, and sometimes the punches come very low.' She anxiously ran a hand from her forehead up to her hair and kept it there for an instant. 'No one's ever happy for you if you're doing well, unless they own the company and you're bringing them money. And Mandy always did well, very well.'

'So when you say "hate", you mean people were envious of her?' Hunter asked.

'Yes. Of her beauty and of her success.'

'But you weren't?' Garcia this time.

Tania shook her head. 'Look at me,' she said with a coy smile. 'I'm no Miss America and this isn't something of late. I've always looked like this. I've always been a big girl. I knew I could never be like Mandy, so it didn't really bother me. I never had the sort of ambition she had either.' She paused and used the back of her right hand to clear her tears. 'Truthfully, I was happy that she became my friend. In school I had very few friends. People made fun of me all the time because I was fat and not very pretty. I pretended it didn't affect me, but deep inside it was awful. I'd never cry in school, but when I got home I broke down almost every night.'

Hunter nodded understandingly, and for a brief moment he remembered how skinny and awkward he used to be in school.

'I knew how Mandy felt in the office with everyone giving her the eye and whispering behind her back. I think that's probably why we became such good friends.'

'How was she as a boss?' Garcia asked, crossing his legs and leaning his elbows on them.

'Fantastic. The best boss I ever had. I guess because of what she went through, she had no patience for bullies. She treated everyone equally.' Tania reached for the box of tissues on the coffee table.

'Did she ever have a problem with an employee?' Garcia asked. 'She had to let a lot of people go, didn't she?'

'Everyone who worked for Mandy loved her. She did everything she could to keep every job in the company intact, but it wasn't up to her. The property market in LA has collapsed, and everyone in the business knows that. No one held her responsible.'

A brown cat appeared at the kitchen door, looked at both detectives for a long while and decided it didn't want to come any closer, disappearing back into the kitchen.

'Do you know if she was seeing someone?' Hunter asked.

'Since her divorce, Mandy didn't care much for relationships. She had flings, but nothing serious.'

'Any recent ones?' Garcia asked.

'Not that I know of.'

'Did she date clients?'

'No, never.' Tania shook her head vigorously. 'She might've flirted with some, but that's part of the job. We've gotta be charming, sometimes flirty, but that's all. As far as I know, Mandy never broke that rule.'

'I understand Mandy showed the house in Malibu to a prospective buyer on Saturday evening,' Hunter said, now using Amanda's nickname as if they were chatting about an old friend.

Tania dabbed the corners of her eyes with a paper tissue and nodded. 'He was the killer, wasn't he?'

Fifty-Four

Hunter leaned forward and held Tania's gaze for a short moment before tilting his head. 'We can't say for certain, but he's a person of interest. What can you tell us about him?'

'Not very much,' Tania replied in a strangled voice.

'Anything would help,' Garcia insisted.

'He booked the viewing over the phone. He said his name was Turner, Mr. Ryan Turner.'

Hunter wrote it down in his black notebook. 'When was that? When did he call to book the viewing?'

'On Friday.'

'Who talked to him, you or Mandy?'

'I did the first time.'

'Was there a second?' Hunter pressed.

'Yes. He called on Saturday to say he'd be a little late.'

The cat appeared at the kitchen door again. This time it moved into the living room tentatively and laid down under the acrylic table.

'Do you remember the conversation you had with him?'

She nodded. 'It wasn't a very long one, though.'

'Do you remember his voice? Was there anything particular about it? An accent, for example?'

'Yes,' she said with a series of quick nods. 'He definitely had a southern accent, like a hillbilly twang. Maybe Texas or Mississippi.'

'Was his tone of voice aggressive . . . subtle? Was the voice high pitched . . . low?'

She shook her head. 'Not aggressive at all. Very polite, actually. There wasn't anything particular about his voice.' She looked down at the floor. 'I'm sorry.'

'That's OK, Tania,' Hunter reassured her. 'You're doing great. Did it sound to you like he could be someone you and Mandy knew from before? A client . . . someone who visited the agency recently, maybe?'

A new pause. Tania stared at her unsteady hands for a moment before shaking her head. 'I don't think so. We haven't had that many clients come in lately.'

'Did he come to Reilly's before going up to the house in Malibu or did Mandy meet him there?' Garcia enquired.

Tania dabbed her eyes with the paper tissue again. 'We have a policy of not giving out our property addresses to clients we've never met. He came to the agency.'

'Did you meet him?'

'No,' Tania said in a deflated breath. 'He'd booked the viewing for late afternoon, but called saying he was running an hour late. I asked Mandy if she wanted me to wait with her.' A new wave of tears started rolling down Tania's cheeks. 'But she said that she'd be OK. She told me to come home as it was the weekend.' She took a deep breath and her voice faltered. 'I should've stayed with her.'

'There's nothing you could've done, Tania,' Hunter said, comforting her.

'Mandy was so petrified of fires,' Tania said as she stared at the floor again.

Hunter and Garcia exchanged a quick look.

'How's that?' Hunter asked.

Tania took her time. Her bottom lip quivered as she spoke. 'When she was a young girl, she was badly burned.'

'Do you know what happened?'

'Not exactly. Mandy never really talked about it. She just told me that when she was young her dress caught fire. Since then, she developed a terrible phobia of fires. In her house, she doesn't even have a gas stove or anything. It's all electric. Even candles made her nervous.' She paused for a deep breath and then started sobbing. 'Why . . .? Why would anyone do something like that to Mandy or to any human being? I don't understand. You'd have to be a monster to burn someone alive.' Her breathing now came in short bursts. 'She must've suffered so much.' Tania broke into a high-pitched hysterical crying, burying her head in her hands.

Hunter moved off the sofa and knelt down in front of her. 'We're really sorry for your loss, Tania,' he said, touching her shoulder. 'I know how difficult a time this is and we're very grateful to you for talking to us.'

The front door to the apartment opened and a man in his mid-forties in a decently fitting blue suit with a white shirt and a conservative tie stepped inside. He was Garcia's height and in good physical shape. The man paused for a second as his eyes quickly took in the scene.

'Tania, are you OK?' he asked, dropping his leather briefcase and rushing to her side.

Tania lifted her head. Her eyes were swollen and red. 'I'm alright, Doug.'

Hunter got to his feet, making way.

'This is my husband,' Tania said to Hunter and Garcia. She turned back to Doug. 'These are detectives from Homicide,' she explained.

Hunter and Garcia tried introducing themselves, but Doug wasn't listening.

'What the hell are you guys doing?' he demanded. 'Can't you see what she's going through?'

'We're very sorry, Mr. Riggs,' Hunter said.

'It's OK, Doug,' Tania intervened. 'They're simply doing their job and I wanna help if I can.'

'But you don't know anything. You said you never saw the man.'

'Any kind of information is always helpful, Mr. Riggs,' Hunter said, taking a step back. 'Tania was able to give us some background on Amanda Reilly, and that'll certainly help us with the investigation.'

Doug cradled Tania in his arms. 'I should've stayed home with you today. You're in no condition to be by yourself, and certainly in no condition to be interviewed by the police.' He shot Hunter and Garcia a furious look.

'I'm not handicapped, Doug. I'm just upset.'

'You were very helpful, Tania,' Hunter said before nodding at Garcia. 'We have to be going anyway. Once again, we're sorry for your loss, but if I could ask you just a couple more questions.'

Tania nodded, despite Doug's irritation.

'Mandy's bag is still missing. We'd like to have a look in her house. Do you know if she kept a spare key in the office?'

Tania wiped her tears with the heels of her hands and looked at Doug for an instant. 'Yes. In her bottom drawer. She was always locking herself outside her house, so she started keeping a key in the office, just in case.'

Hunter nodded. 'We'll check it. One last thing. Was Mandy Catholic?'

Tania shook her head nervously. 'She wasn't religious at all. I don't think she even believed in God. Why?'

'Just wondering.' Hunter gave her a comforting smile and placed a card on the coffee table. 'If you remember anything you think might be important, no matter how small, please give me a call at any time.'

Tania's eyes rested on the card for several seconds. 'I'm sorry I couldn't be more helpful.'

Hunter and Garcia got off the sofa and walked towards the door.

'Wait!' Tania suddenly called. 'He called her Mandy.'

'What do you mean?' Hunter asked.

'On the phone, when he called to let us know he'd be late for his viewing, after he said hello to me, he said – *can I speak to Mandy?*'

Fifty-Five

Claire Anderson had wanted to be a reporter for as long as she could remember. Born in Hailey, Idaho, she was a country girl with a big city woman mentality. Her parents still lived in Hailey, with thick accents and country ways. In school, Claire had been an exceptional student, but her size made her unpopular with boys. She started gaining weight very early, fuelled by her mother's extraordinary talent for baking the most amazing cakes. By the time she finished high school she'd become positively tubby.

Her excellent grades gave her a wide choice of universities. She picked Idaho State University in Boise simply because she liked being close to home. Hailey was home, but the big city became her playpen, the place where she first experienced drugs and decided they weren't for her. The place where she lost her virginity to someone she only saw twice. And the place where she decided she didn't want to be overweight anymore. With irrefutable determination, she changed her eating habits and jogged herself down to a hundred and eighteen pounds. Her transformation was astounding, and she went from 'unpopular' to the girl everyone wanted to sleep with.

Upon graduating top of her class, Claire was offered a job with the *Idaho Statesman*, the highest-circulation newspaper in

Boise. Through the paper she met Noah Jones, a freelance reporter from Los Angeles, who told her he could put in a good word for her with some of his friends at the *LA Times*. She had to sleep with him for that, but Claire considered it a small price to pay to join one of the biggest newspapers in the USA.

Claire sat perched on the edge of Matt Pasquier's desk. Pasquier was a legend when it came to crime reporting in Los Angeles. He was old school, condescending, a heavy drinker and thought nothing of journalism degrees, but he was very smart and he liked Claire Anderson. She had something he hadn't seen in years – raw ambition to be a good reporter. She wasn't doing it for the money.

'OK, what's the problem?' Pasquier let go of his cup of coffee and leaned back in his chair.

'I'm doing something wrong,' she said in a half-defeated voice. 'I can't get an angle on this story and now the TVs are getting involved.'

'I take it you met Robert Hunter. I mean, properly met him.'

Claire nodded. 'He blew me off.'

Pasquier let out an animated but strange laugh. 'You tried to seduce him? Oh Claire. Robert certainly saw you coming a mile away. He doesn't fall for those tricks.'

'I could've used that information a few days ago,' she replied, looking around the newsroom. Everyone looked busy staring at computer screens or talking on telephones.

'I'll tell you what, let's go talk someplace else,' Pasquier said, rolling his chair away from his desk and standing up. He scowled sadly at the large room. 'This place depresses me. It's full of university geeks who know shit about journalism.'

'Hey.' Claire tried to look offended. 'I'm a university geek.'

'Yeah, but you're *hot*.' He winked at her.

The cafeteria was in the mezzanine floor of the building. The food was by any standard crap, typical slop under heat lamps. A wall of vending machines offered just about anything, from apples to slightly bruised bananas, pie slices, yogurts, salads, candy bars and, obviously, triangular sandwiches.

'Can I buy you anything?' Pasquier offered, nodding at the machines.

'I'll have a coffee.'

Pasquier bought a pastrami and cheese sandwich from one of the machines and ordered two coffees at the counter. The food was so bad the place was almost deserted, and they easily found a vacant beige Formica table. He took a large bite of his sandwich and used a paper napkin to wipe some mayonnaise off his chin.

'What do you have?' he asked.

Claire had a sip of her coffee and met Pasquier's gaze. 'No one's talking, but I know that what we're dealing with is a serial killer, maybe a ritualistic one. Savage in a way we've never seen before. This guy is different.'

'If no one's talking, how can you know that?' He dropped four sugars in his coffee.

'I don't know.' She shook her head and looked away. 'Intuition, maybe. A gut feeling.'

'I see.' He had another bite of his sandwich and spoke with his mouth full. 'You said you think this killer is different – different how?'

'Just look at the facts, Matt. What sort of killer decapitates a priest inside his own church and shoves a mutt's head down the corpse's body? What sort of killer takes almost two days cooking his victim alive in front of a fireplace?' Claire tucked her hair behind her ears using both hands. Pasquier liked when she did that. He thought it very charming. 'They are keeping the bodies under strict lock and key. I can't get a picture, but I heard the killer melted Amanda Reilly's face.'

Pasquier queried with his eyes.

'Amanda Reilly was the second victim.' Her forehead creased. 'Do you read our paper?'

'Not lately. No good reporters to read.'

'Oh, very funny.'

'You see, the difference between you and most of the other deadbeat reporters on this paper is that you still have that *intuition* you just talked about. That *gut* feeling.' He smiled and Claire pointed out that he had a piece of lettuce stuck to one of his teeth. He used his little finger to scrape it off. 'And that's probably because you're a nice country girl. You didn't grow up in a metropolis where money talks and bullshit runs the marathon.' He did his best to forge a country accent. 'Us folks here in the big cities have forgotten all about intuition, guts and what it is to do somet'ing just 'cos we loves doing it.'

'Aw damn, mister, intuition and them guts on its own don't help me none.' In contrast, Claire's country accent was perfect.

Pasquier laughed and swallowed the rest of his food down. 'You won't get a peep out of Robert Hunter. He's a city folk with a country man's heart. The only cop I know who actually likes his job. And he certainly doesn't like reporters.'

Claire played with her hair again. 'Well, I'm open to suggestions. There's no way I'm giving up on this.'

A wicked smile spread across Pasquier's face. 'I was hoping you'd say that. OK, here's what you've got to do . . .'

Fifty-Six

Downtown LA's financial district is just south of Bunker Hill and north of South Park – this is where LA's instantly recognizable skyline resides. The area concentrates around Fifth, Sixth, South Flower and Figueroa Streets and remains the southland's most influential financial and business center. Tyler Financial Services had their office on the seventeenth floor of number 542 South Flower Street.

Dan Tyler sat in the elegant leather chair behind his mahogany desk. He was a kind-looking man in his forties. His brown hair, graying at the temples, was neatly combed back, and the strong lines that shaped his strangely attractive face indicated strength, experience, self-confidence and a degree of suffering. He wore an elegant dark suit and a pale blue shirt complemented by a gray striped tie. His dark brown eyes sat behind thin-rimmed glasses. His office bore the trappings of his profession – expensive-looking furniture, an impressive bar at the corner, several framed photographs on the walls and three interlinked computer monitors on his desk that were constantly displaying the stock market flow. His secretary announced the arrival of the two detectives, and he stood up to greet them by the door.

Dan Tyler showed them inside, indicating the two armchairs in front of his desk and offering both detectives a drink – they declined.

'I know this is an awkward situation, Mr. Tyler,' Hunter began. 'We'll try to get through it as fast as we can.'

'Call me Dan, please,' Tyler said, taking his seat behind his desk. His voice was serene and pleasant, like a storyteller's.

Hunter quickly explained that it would still be a few days before the house in Malibu was released by forensics.

Tyler nodded. He knew that putting the house back on the market now wasn't a clever idea.

'The house didn't look like an investment property,' Hunter said. 'Did you used to live there?'

'Yes. For many years.'

Hunter noticed a distinct tone in Tyler's voice and allowed a few silent seconds to go by before nodding towards a silver-framed photograph on Tyler's desk. An attractive woman with windswept hair and an infectious smile standing by a swimming pool. A beautiful black dog was asleep by her feet. 'Was that taken at the house?' he asked, recognizing the pool.

Tyler looked at the photograph. 'Yes,' he said with a mixture of pride and sadness.

Hunter intuited the woman in the picture was the source of the sadness. 'Is that your wife?'

Tyler looked back at him. 'Kate. Yes.' A pause. 'She passed away.'

'I'm sorry,' Hunter said and sensed that Tyler's emotional wound was still raw. 'Recently?'

'Twelve months ago.' He pressed his lips together. 'It feels recent to me.'

'I understand.'

Tyler took a deep breath. 'A lot of people say that, but surviving the woman you love—' he gave Hunter a quick head shake '—I guess it's something you have to live through to really understand. We were married twenty years.' Tyler's eyes were back on the picture.

'And the house in Malibu was your home?' Hunter asked.

'It was her pride and joy,' Tyler said, nodding. 'We built it from scratch. Kate was involved in every aspect of the architectural design. It was her dream house. She chose every piece of furniture, every curtain, every color, every detail. Kate's in every inch of that house.' Tyler paused and looked down at his clasped hands. 'After she was gone, I just couldn't live there anymore. I tried for a while but . . .' His eyes drifted away. 'Without realizing, I used to find myself talking to the walls, curtains, pictures . . .' He smiled. 'I don't need the house or anything else to remind me of what Kate and I had.'

'No children?' Hunter asked, already guessing the answer, judging by the lack of any other family pictures in the office.

'Unfortunately, no.' A different sorrow coated Tyler's words, and Hunter understood that having no children hadn't been his choice. He allowed the awkward moment to subside before proceeding.

'Did you know Amanda Reilly?'

'We met a couple of times when I approached her company to handle the sale of the house,' Tyler replied, glad to change the subject.

'How long ago was that?'

Tyler tilted his head to one side and scratched his temple. 'About eight months ago, when the house first went up for sale.'

'Not since?'

'There was no need. Her company was recommended to me. One of my clients had his house sold through Reilly's. I didn't wanna have anything to do with it. I wanted someone who could handle everything. She came across as a very genuine and trustworthy person, and her track record spoke for itself.' Something changed on his computer screen and Tyler glared at it for a second. 'We talked on the phone a few times. She'd call me every now and then to update me on any viewings.'

'Did she call you last week about a viewing this past Saturday?' Hunter asked, checking his black notebook.

Tyler nodded. 'She called me on Friday.' He pulled himself closer to his desk. 'She sounded really excited. More excited than she did about any of the previous viewings. She said that the prospective buyer—' Tyler reached for a stylish leather-bound diary on his desk and flipped back a few pages '—someone called Ryan Turner, was really eager to see the house.' He paused and slowly lifted his eyes from the diary. 'She said she had a good feeling about this guy.'

Fifty-Seven

An unpleasant silence took over Dan Tyler's office, and Hunter and Garcia looked at each other.

'Do you have the names of everyone that requested a viewing of the house?' Hunter asked, nodding at Tyler's diary.

'It's a habit of mine. I don't go into business with anyone I haven't checked out. Even though I can't bring myself to live there anymore, that house is still very dear to me and I wouldn't sell it to someone who wouldn't appreciate it. A property developer, for example. Someone who'd knock it down to build something else.'

'I'm guessing you'd only run background checks on buyers if they'd actually made an offer?'

Tyler nodded halfheartedly. 'There's no point spending time and money on someone who's only window-shopping.' He shook his head as if he'd made a mistake. 'I should've checked him anyway.'

'He most certainly used a false name,' Hunter said. 'You probably wouldn't have found anything on him.'

'And that would've gotten every alarm bell in my head going.' Tyler looked straight into Hunter's eyes. 'I deal with a lot of rich people, Detective Hunter. They're all "proud" of what they've achieved and who they are. It's a show-off game for most of them. Mine is bigger than yours kinda thing. A person going for a four-million-dollar house with a nonexistent past is a clear "be aware" sign to me.'

Hunter nodded his understanding. 'If you don't mind, I'd like a copy of the list of names Miss Reilly has given you over these eight months.'

'Sure.' Tyler reached inside his top drawer and handed Hunter a printed list. Seven names in total. Hunter studied Tyler through the top of the list. His eyes questioning.

Tyler smiled thinly. 'That's how I make my money, detective. I have to be logical, practical and, above all, think ahead. It was only logical to deduct that you'd want that list of names.'

Hunter read the names in silence. None stood out.

'None of them made an offer,' Tyler continued. 'I never requested a background check on any of them.' He stood up and approached the bar. 'Are you sure I can't get you anything?' he insisted.

'No, thank you. We're fine.'

Tyler poured himself a shot of bourbon. 'It's hard to believe that a place that'd brought me the happiest days of my life housed such a monstrous act.' He sipped his drink. 'Is it true what I read in the paper?' He hesitated for a second. 'Did the killer really use the fireplace to burn her?'

Hunter nodded in silence.

For a second Tyler's stare became distant, and Hunter knew his memory had gone back to the house. To the living room and the fireplace he knew so well. He swallowed and quickly took another sip of his bourbon.

'And is this really the same killer who decapitated that priest last week?'

'You shouldn't believe everything you read in the papers,' Garcia replied.

'I don't. That's why I'm asking.'

'At the moment it's all speculation,' Hunter lied.

Tyler walked up to the large glass window that offered a panoramic view of LA's financial district. 'This city has changed so much. I don't think I understand it anymore.'

'Did you ever?' Garcia asked.

Tyler smiled. 'You've gotta point there.'

'If it's OK with you, I'd like to show you some photographs that were taken at the house,' Hunter said and was quick to sense Tyler's uneasiness. 'Don't worry,' he clarified. 'They aren't photos of the victim.'

Tyler stared at his glass. There was something else worrying him. Hunter realized what it was. The pictures would bring back memories of the house and his wife. 'I know this is hard . . .'

Tyler shook his head and returned to his desk. 'It's OK, detective.'

Hunter placed several photographs on Tyler's desk. They all showed the main living room of the house in Malibu. 'We were wondering if you could have a look at these pictures. See if anything strikes you as odd or being out of place?'

Tyler allowed his eyes to study each photograph for a few seconds. 'It's hard to say. I haven't been to the house for eight months. The cleaning company might've moved things around.'

'We understand that,' Hunter agreed. 'But maybe there's something that really catches your eye.'

Tyler finished his drink, gathered all the photographs into a single pile and sat back in his chair. He flipped through them carefully, sometimes frowning, sometimes squinting as if trying to remember. Both detectives sat quietly observing his reactions. Halfway through the pictures he stopped. Something had grabbed his attention.

'Do you see something?' Hunter asked.

Tyler lifted his right index finger, asking for a minute. He then searched through the rest of the photos until he found the one he was looking for.

'What do you see?' Hunter pressed.

Garcia leaned forward, stretching his neck.

Tyler placed the photo on his desk facing the detectives. It showed the large river rock fireplace.

'Something different about the fireplace?' Hunter asked.

'On the mantelpiece,' Tyler replied.

Both detectives' eyes shot to the photos. The fireplace mantelpiece was decorated with several objects – small vases, a couple of picture frames, a few figurines . . .

'What's different about it?'

'My memory can be hazy at times, but one thing I remember well is that Kate never kept any picture frames in the living room.' He tapped the picture with his index finger. 'In the reception entrance yes, but not in the living room. She was superstitious like that. She thought it was unlucky. Those picture frames on the fireplace—' he shook his head vigorously '—they certainly weren't there when we lived in the house.'

Fifty-Eight

'Excuse me, honey,' the tallest of the four men sitting at the corner table in the old-fashioned diner said to the brunette waitress as she walked past.

'Yes?' Mollie turned to face him, trying her best not to look annoyed. The four of them had been pestering her for the past fifteen minutes.

'Are you tired?' he asked. The other three were already giggling.

'Why?' she replied, a little puzzled.

'Because, babe, I want you to know that as long as I gotta face, you gotta place to sit.' They all burst into laughter.

'Order up,' came the call from the busy kitchen. Mollie walked back to the counter to collect the order and felt their eyes burn a hole in the back of her red and white dress.

Every table in the small diner was taken. Most of them by sleazy scumbags like the four in the corner who thought every waitress in south LA was dying to go to bed with them. She didn't like her job and all the abuse that came with it, but she didn't have a choice. She desperately needed the money.

She took the order to a middle-aged man sitting by himself, and as she placed the plate on the table he grabbed hold of her hand. 'Excuse me, Miss Candy Pants, but this ain't what I fucking ordered.'

'Didn't you order a double cheeseburger and fries?'

'Yes, but I specifically said no goddamn pickles. I hate pickles. What the fuck do you call these?' He lifted the top bun and pointed to three long pickle slices.

'I'm very sorry, sir,' she said, embarrassed, reaching for the plate. 'I'll get the cook to take them off.'

'No, not take them off,' he said angrily between clenched teeth. 'I want him to cook me a new one. This one is ruined.'

'No problem, sir. I'll get you a new one right away.'

'Stupid bitch,' he murmured as she took the plate.

On her way back to the kitchen, Mollie noticed a Mexican-looking man in his early thirties wearing old, dirty and ripped clothes standing by the entrance door. He caught her eye and as she walked past he asked in a timid voice: 'Excuse me, miss. Is it OK if I come in for some food? I have some money.' He tapped his trouser pocket and she heard the rattle of coins.

'Yes, of course.' She frowned at the strange question. Turning around, she scanned the busy diner. A table had just vacated by the door where they were. 'Why don't you take this table right here and I'll get you a menu.'

He smiled a sincere smile. 'Thank you very much, miss. That's very kind of you. I won't be long. I'll eat quick.'

Mollie smiled back, not understanding why he sounded so thankful. She got to the kitchen and was about to explain to Billy, the large Texan cook, about the whole pickle incident when she heard loud yelling coming from the diner floor.

'Who the hell told you you could sit in here?' Donna Higgins, the restaurant owner was standing by the entrance table, yelling at its occupant.

'I'm sorry,' the Mexican man said shyly. 'The waitress said it was OK.'

'Which waitress would that be?'

He looked down shyly without answering. 'I won't be long. I'll eat quick, I promise.'

'I don't care how you eat, as long as it's not in my restaurant.'

'I'm not asking for charity, miss. I have money. I can pay for my food.'

'Of course you have money,' Donna shot back, gesticulating frantically. 'You probably stole it.'

'No, I didn't. I helped someone push his car out of the road and he was kind enough to give me a few bucks.' He showed her a handful of coins and one-dollar bills. 'I can eat outside or out the back, miss. I don't mind. I just want a hot meal, maybe some eggs and bacon and a glass of milk. I haven't eaten in a few days.'

'Well, you ain't getting it here. I bet you're a fucking illegal immigrant, aren't you?'

The man tensed.

'That's what I thought. Get your stinking self outta my restaurant—' she pointed to the door '—before I call immigration on you.'

His sad eyes wandered the diner. Everyone was looking at him. Without a word, he returned the little money he had back to his trouser pocket and left.

'Hey!' He heard someone call as he turned the corner. 'Hey, wait!' The female voice called again. He stopped and looked back. The brunette waitress had come out of the diner's back door carrying a brown paper bag.

'Do you like pickles?' Mollie asked.

He frowned.

'You know, pickles. Like cucumbers.'

He nodded. 'Yes, they're nice.'

'Here.' She offered him the paper bag. 'It's a double cheeseburger with fries and a bottle of milk. There're pickles in the cheeseburger.' She smiled.

He stared at her with thankful eyes before reaching into his pocket.

'No, no,' she said, shaking her head. 'You don't have to pay me. It's OK.'

'I don't want no charity, miss. I have money to pay for my food.'

'I know. I saw your money.' A new comforting smile. 'But this ain't charity. They made me too much food for my dinner break. I'm on a diet,' she lied and offered him the bag once again. 'Here, take it. I can't eat all this food. It'd only be thrown away.'

He hesitated for a moment before taking the bag and smiling. 'Thank you very much. You're a very kind person.'

Mollie watched him walk away before returning to the diner.

'You can find yourself another job, you little bitch,' Donna Higgins told her as soon as she walked through the back door into the kitchen.

'What? Why?'

'Who told you you could take a break when I have a packed floor in there?'

'It was only a three-minute break.'

'I don't give a shit. You took a break when you weren't supposed to and you stole food.'

The waitress's jaw dropped. 'I didn't steal any food.'

'Oh no? How about the cheeseburger and fries and the bottle of milk you took from the fridge?'

Her face tightened. 'I was gonna pay for that.'

'Of course you gonna pay for that. That's why you're getting no wages for today.'

'What?' She could feel panic starting to take over. 'Please,

Mrs. Higgins, I'm very sorry. I shouldn't have taken the food and I'll pay for it. I'll work extra hours if you like. I really need the money for my rent.'

'Oh poor you.' Donna Higgins made a silly face. 'You should've thought of that before stealing from me. Now get your stuff and get the hell outta my restaurant.'

He'd been sitting at the same table by the front window of the small diner for over eight hours. His deep-set eyes checking the faces of every passenger who boarded or stepped off any bus that stopped directly opposite the diner entrance.

He ordered another coffee and checked his watch. Three minutes until the next bus was due to arrive, enough time for a bathroom break. He'd been following the same routine for the past few days – arriving at around noon and leaving only when the diner closed at eleven o'clock but so far he'd had no luck.

He splashed some cold water on his face and ran the tip of his right index finger over the ugly scar on his forehead. 'It won't be long now,' he whispered to his reflection.

The bus was just driving away when he stepped out of the bathroom. It had come at least a full minute ahead of its scheduled time. He cursed himself and ran to the front of the diner, his eyes frantically searching, but most passengers had already scattered away.

The brunette in a red and white waitress uniform had to run, but she made it to the bus stop just as the bus was ready to leave. Taking a seat by one of the front windows, she buried her face in her hands and wondered what excuse she could give her landlord.

The man in the diner never saw her.

Fifty-Nine

The smell of burned flesh was still just as strong as the night before, and it made both detectives gag as they re-entered the house in Malibu. Garcia chewed on two anti-acid tablets before cupping his hands over his nose and mouth. His stomach retched as they approached the living room, and he stopped by the door. Bending over, he held onto his knees, concentrating hard not to be sick again.

'Why don't you wait here?' Hunter suggested, pulling a pair of latex gloves over his hands. 'I'll check the fireplace.'

'That sounds like a plan,' Garcia replied, exhaling a long breath.

Pulling the collar of his shirt up like a mask to cover his nose and mouth, Hunter approached the room's south wall and the fireplace. Fingerprint powder was everywhere. The armchair Amanda Reilly had been tied to had been taken away for further forensic examination. The once-beautiful living room now felt like a torture chamber, and it made the hairs on the back of Hunter's neck prickle. He took a deep breath and moved the focus of his flashlight onto the large fireplace. It was decorated with several figurines, four color-coordinated vases and two candleholders, but Hunter's attention was on the two silver-plated picture frames. One at each end of the mantelpiece. The frames themselves looked pretty common, probably standard issue in any department store. Hunter first checked the one at the far right. There was a gap between the frame and the wall of about eight inches, enough for him to check the back without having to pick it up – nothing out of the ordinary. He checked the second frame, and again found nothing. Finally, he picked them both up.

The photographs weren't of Dan Tyler or his wife. The first one he examined showed a woman with a pretty smile sitting comfortably on a black leather sofa. A glass of red wine in her right hand. She was attractive in a high-maintenance way; short blond hair, way too much makeup and enigmatic baby-blue eyes. There was something arrogant about her. The second photograph was of a man leaning casually against a white wall. Slender, with neatly trimmed fair hair and unexpressive hazel eyes, he was dressed in a light green T-shirt and faded blue jeans. At first look, there was nothing extraordinary about any of those two characters. But who were they?

'Everything OK in there?' Garcia called from the door, startling Hunter.

'Yeah, yeah. Gimme a minute.'

Turning one of the frames over, Hunter slowly lifted the four security clips that held its back in place. All of a sudden he felt cold. As if someone had opened a window in the room, allowing a chilling draft in. He looked up, his eyes and flashlight searching the room – nothing but the putrid smell of death.

'Carlos, are you still out there,' he called firmly.

'Yeah, what's up?' He coughed a couple of times before poking his head through the door.

'Nothing. Just keep an eye out.'

Something in Hunter's voice worried Garcia and his hand instinctively moved towards his gun. He pointed his flashlight down the eerie corridor and listened attentively for a long moment – nothing.

Hunter returned his attention to the picture frame. Carefully, he pulled the back cover of the first one apart. As it came unattached, his eyes rested on the underside of the photograph.

'Oh fuck!'

Hunter closed his eyes for a moment as adrenalin rushed through him.

He put the first frame down and quickly reached for the second one and repeated the process of lifting the security clips. Even though he was certain of what he'd find, Hunter held his breath as he slowly pulled the back cover apart.

'Sonofabitch.'

'Everything alright in there, Robert?' Garcia called, concerned. 'Have you found the pictures?'

Hunter slowly searched the dark room again. A luxurious room, now forever tainted with evil. The sickening smell was starting to burn at his nostrils and cause havoc in his stomach. He needed to get out of there.

'Did you find anything?' Garcia asked as Hunter stepped out of the room.

'Yeah, I'll show you outside,' Hunter replied, pulling his shirt from over his nose and mouth. 'I need to get some fresh air.'

'Amen to that.'

Outside, Hunter faced Garcia. 'I found these.' He handed his partner both photographs. 'Those are the photos that were in the picture frames Dan Tyler said shouldn't be here.'

Garcia studied them carefully for a moment. 'Who are they?' He shook his head.

Hunter took a deep breath and let it out slowly. 'Take a look at the back.'

Garcia turned them over and his pulse surged under the skin of his neck. 'You're shitting me.'

'Apparently not.'

Garcia stared at the photos again. Their faces now taking on a whole new meaning.

Sixty

It was late by the time they left Malibu. Hunter checked in with Hopkins and told him to meet them at Footsie's in North Figueroa Street.

Take all the snobbish fakery out of most Los Angeles bars and you might be left with Footsie's. Just a small, cozy drinking joint with a few pool tables, a comfortable lounge with half-circle red leather booths, a jukebox playing classic rock and a friendly and relaxed atmosphere. Footsie's was one of Hunter's favorite drinking spots.

Hopkins was already there, nursing a single shot of Jack Daniel's when Hunter and Garcia arrived. 'What can I get you guys?' he offered.

'It's OK.' Hunter gave him a subtle nod. 'I'll get these, Ian.'

'I'll have whatever you're having, as long as it's single malt,' Garcia said. 'I'll be right back.' He pointed to the men's rest-room door.

A booth emptied at the back of the bar and Hunter told Hopkins to grab it before someone else did.

He ordered two single shots of Laphroaig with a cube of ice each. The person standing next to him at the bar was reading through a copy of the *LA Daily News*, and as he flipped a page something caught Hunter's attention. The headline on the small article read SLASHER CLAIMS SECOND

VICTIM. Hunter craned his neck awkwardly and skimmed through the article before the man flipped the page again. A second prostitute had been found dead inside a squalid room in South Gate. Her hands had been tied together in front of her, her fingers interlaced in a prayer position. Just as the first victim a few days ago, she was found naked, on her knees with her throat cut open. The press had already nicknamed the killer the Slasher. '*This city's out of control*,' Hunter thought as he took his drinks and joined Garcia and Hopkins at their booth.

'Are you guys OK?' Hopkins asked with concern, noticing a heavy air about both detectives.

Hunter had a sip of his Laphroaig and swirled it around in his mouth until its strong alcohol started to burn the edges of his tongue. He placed four evidence bags on the table. The first two containing the disassembled picture frames, the other two the photographs. Hopkins's brow lifted and Hunter explained about their meeting with Dan Tyler and why they went back to check the misplaced pictures.

'So who are these two?' he asked skeptically.

Garcia reached for the evidence bags with the photographs and turned them over. Hopkins's eyes widened and he let out an excited gasp. On the back of the man's photograph, written in blood and about six inches long, was the number one. On the back of the smiling woman's, the number two.

Hopkins kept his eyes on the photographs for a while, his jaw half open. 'I don't get it.' He locked eyes with Hunter. 'Why would the killer do this? I mean, why would he leave the pictures of the first two victims on the fireplace? Obviously, he knew that sooner or later we'd find them.'

Hunter sat back and ran his fingertips over his whiskey tumbler rim. 'He wants to make sure we know these two victims are his. He doesn't want their murders attributed to someone else. He's a proud killer.'

Hopkins twisted uncomfortably in his seat. The world of the evilly sick was going way over his head.

'So where are these two victims?' he asked after a moment's silence. 'And if they'd been numbered like Father Fabian and Amanda Reilly, why don't we know about them?'

Hunter had another long, slow sip of his Scotch. 'Why do you think?'

Hopkins's eyes reverted back to the photos on the table. Hunter could almost hear him thinking. 'Maybe the numbering thing is something the killer only started doing after victim number two,' Hopkins offered tentatively.

'Go on,' Hunter urged him.

'Of course he couldn't go back and number the first two bodies. This is the best he could do, given the circumstances.'

'Why would the killer only start numbering from victim number three on?' Garcia asked.

'I'm not sure.' Hopkins gave him a slight shrug. 'Maybe he never thought of it at first. Maybe he expected the police to realize the first two victims were killed by the same person, and that never happened.'

'It's a good theory,' Hunter said, giving Hopkins an approving nod.

'Yeah, but I don't buy it,' Garcia said, shaking his head. 'We know this killer is extremely organized and methodical. He plans his kills to the very last detail, leaving nothing to chance. He's proven that with Father Fabian and Amanda Reilly.'

'That's right.' Hunter nodded.

'Such an organized killer wouldn't change his plan halfway down the line. I'd say he's been numbering them from the word go.'

'OK,' Hunter agreed. 'So going back to the question, where are these two victims? And why don't we know about them?'

'Maybe we just haven't found them yet,' Garcia ventured, leaning forward. 'The order in which they were killed isn't necessarily the order in which they'll be found. Maybe they're still missing, locked inside a car trunk somewhere or in a ditch up in the mountains.'

'That's possible,' Hunter agreed, stretching his neck. 'There's just one thing that bothers me about that theory. The killer made no effort to hide the bodies of victims three and four. They were found the day after they were killed. So why would he hide the bodies of victims one and two in a car trunk or up in the mountains somewhere? It doesn't go with his MO. He wants us to know about them.'

'That's why he left the pictures on the fireplace.' Hopkins half stated it, half questioned.

'Exactly,' Hunter confirmed. 'He wants to be credited with their murder.'

They all went silent for a few seconds.

'What do you think, Robert?' Hopkins asked eagerly. 'Why don't we have victims one and two yet?'

Hunter watched a long-legged brunette approach the jukebox on the corner, slide a few quarters into it and make a selection. An old Skid Row song started playing.

'I think you hit on a very good point in your theory,' Hunter said to Hopkins.

'Which point was that?' he asked, intrigued.

'The fact that the killer couldn't go back to the bodies. That's why he used the photos. The bodies have already been found.'

Sixty-One

Garcia and Hopkins exchanged a quick, uneasy look. Skid Row was still blasting through the speakers at Footsie's.

'If the bodies have been found, what happened to the numbers?' Garcia tapped the evidence bags with his index finger.

Hunter pointed to the picture of the first victim and the number one on its back. 'Have a look at the way the killer wrote this number. Anything peculiar?'

Garcia and Hopkins studied it for a moment.

'It's very simplistic,' Garcia admitted. 'There's no horizontal base line or anything. This is really nothing more than a single vertical line.'

'Holy shit!' Hopkins exclaimed. 'He's right. On a body this would've looked like a simple splash of blood. Anyone could've missed it.'

'OK, that might explain number one,' Garcia said, dragging the next picture to the center of the table. 'How about number two?'

Hunter shook his head as if anything was possible. 'Maybe the number washed off.'

'What?' Garcia and Hopkins asked in unison.

The brunette returned to the jukebox and this time her stare lingered on Hunter for several seconds before she followed it with a sparkling smile. Bon Jovi started playing.

'The killer doesn't carve the numbers onto the victims; he uses blood to draw them.' Hunter explained, leaning forward. 'What if victim two was left in a humid or unsheltered place, like the woods? What if something happened after he left the body that smudged the number?'

Garcia and Hopkins looked thoughtful.

'Rain would've easily washed the number off, or at least enough for it to be unrecognizable,' Hopkins admitted.

'And it's been raining a hell of a lot lately,' Garcia noted.

Hunter checked his watch. 'I'll get this to forensics and get you digital copies of the photos,' he said to Hopkins. 'I want you to run a search against the Missing Persons and the Homicide databases.'

'Damn!' Hopkins slapped his forehead with the palm of his hand. 'That reminds me. You were right on the money when you suggested starting the missing person's search for the Monica girl with Pennsylvania.' He handed Hunter a black and white photograph printout. 'This is what I got from the Pennsylvania Missing Persons archive.'

Hunter and Garcia analyzed the photo for just a few seconds.

'Wow,' Garcia said. 'With the exception of her hair and that scar on her lips, she hasn't changed much at all. Unless she's got an identical twin.'

'Not the case here,' Hopkins confirmed, handing them a new sheet of paper.

The girl on the photo was Mollie Woods, born on Christmas Day, seventeen years ago in Huntingdon County, Pennsylvania. She's been missing for almost four years. Her father, John Woods, reported her missing two days after her mother was run over by a drunk driver. She died instantly. John Woods moved from Huntingdon County to York, still in Pennsylvania, shortly after his wife's death.

'I haven't tried to contact her father yet,' Hopkins said as Hunter finished reading the report.

'Don't. At least not yet,' he agreed.

Garcia looked concerned. 'Don't you think we should? He's probably worried sick about his daughter. It's been almost four years.'

'There's a reason why she ran away from home.' Hunter gave Garcia a quick head shake. 'She's seventeen. If she wanted to get in touch with her father, she would've done it herself. In the interrogation room, I got a feeling she was really scared of something. And it wasn't just her visions.'

Sixty-Two

The LACDC's official public opening time is 8:00 a.m. Monday to Friday, but Hunter had no intention of waiting until then. Knowing that he was an early riser, Hunter rang Mike Brindle at around a quarter to seven. The forensics agent was already on his way to the coroner's, and Hunter met him by the staff entry door at 7:00 a.m. Brindle was surprised by Hunter's discovery of the two photographs, but he couldn't hide his disappointment for his team not having found them.

Brindle told Hunter they'd already had a few results from the house in Malibu. The partial print they'd found in one of the rooms upstairs had yielded no matches against the National Fingerprint Database so far. The fibers retrieved from the vacuum cleaner found in the mansion's utility room were too common to really give them any sort of lead. Dental records confirmed that the skull found in the fireplace belonged to Father Fabian, but the blood used to draw the number four on Amanda Reilly's back, unlike the blood used on the priest, didn't come from a pregnant woman.

'So what have you got?' Hunter asked.

Brindle handed him the lab report.

Hunter speed-read it and frowned. 'It's Father Fabian's blood?'

Brindle nodded.

Mechanically, Hunter checked the number on the back of the two photographs they found on the fireplace. His thought process went from A to Z in two seconds flat. 'The woman was number two,' he said to himself, but Brindle picked up on it.

'So what're you thinking?'

Hunter quickly shook his head, as if snapping out of a trance. 'The killer uses the blood of the previous victim to number his next one.'

Brindle pinched his bottom lip as he thought about it.

Hunter pointed to the woman's photograph. 'Number two; this is the pregnant woman whose blood was used to draw the number three on the priest's chest. I'd bet on it.'

Brindle agreed it made sense. 'I'll get the blood used on the back of these photos analyzed straight away,' he said. 'You'll have a result soon.'

Captain Blake was already waiting in Hunter's office for their nine o'clock meeting when he arrived. Garcia had brought her up to speed on all that'd happened last night, and before he was able to get rid of his jacket there was a knock at the door and they were joined by Hopkins.

'Do you think this is the real deal or could this killer be messing with us?' the captain asked calmly, staring at the pictures on the corkboard.

'Messing with us how?'

'Giving us two unknown people to run after. I'm sure he's well aware it will take us time to come up with their identities. Even longer to confirm they're really dead. By placing these two pictures on the fireplace, he's tied our hands together. He could be trying to slow us down, throwing us into a completely bogus investigation while he's free to find his next victim.'

Hunter shook his head. 'This killer's actions seem to have

more purpose than that. I don't think he's interested in diverting us. The reason he gave us the photos of the first two victims is because he wants to make sure we know they were killed by him.'

'Why?' Captain Blake sounded irritated. 'Is he saying we're not competent enough to find that out on our own?'

'If for some reason the numbers have washed off the victims, maybe we wouldn't be able to find out on our own, captain,' Hunter agreed, to the captain's surprise. 'Take the two last victims, for example. The only reason why we know Amanda Reilly was murdered by Father Fabian's killer is because the killer wanted us to know. Take the numbering away, and her case would've been sitting on the desk of two detectives from the Sheriff's Department in Malibu. At least until the skull found in the fire was processed and we got confirmation it belonged to Father Fabian.'

'That's true,' Garcia agreed, leaning against his desk.

'We thought Father Fabian was murdered by a ritualistic killer, remember? Everything pointed to it.' Hunter turned to face the picture board. 'Amanda Reilly's murder has a completely different MO. Father Fabian was killed quickly with almost zero pain. One clean strike to the neck and he was dead instantly. Messy, I agree, but nothing indicates he was tortured. Amanda Reilly, on the other hand, was cooked alive. She suffered for hours. Half of her internal organs exploded inside her body, captain.'

Captain Blake grimaced and popped a mint in her mouth.

'Without the numbering, not even Sherlock Holmes would've been able to attribute these two victims to the same killer.' Hunter cleared his throat before continuing in a calm voice. 'We're dealing with a very different type of serial killer.'

'How so?' the captain asked.

'Serial killers very rarely divert from an MO they're comfortable with. When they do, it's just a small deviation, mainly a steady progression into something crueler. This killer's cool and organized enough to totally change his tactics from one victim to another without panicking.'

'Aren't serial killers usually after some sort of satisfaction?' Hopkins asked.

'Yes.'

'What satisfaction is this one after?'

Hunter rubbed his face slowly, taking his time. 'Their fears.'

Sixty-Three

'Their fears?' The captain echoed Hunter's words.

'You read Garcia's report on what he found in Father Fabian's journal, right?' Hunter asked.

'The dream thing?'

'Yeah, the dream thing. It might seem crazy to all of us, but to the priest it was something that scared him out of his skin for over twenty years. In Amanda Reilly's case, she was so petrified of fires she wouldn't have a gas stove in her house.' Hunter searched his desk for his report on their interview with Tania Riggs and handed it to Captain Blake.

'Or candles,' Garcia added.

'She's been that scared since she was a teenager.' Hunter paused, allowing Captain Blake some time to reflect and scan the interview transcript.

'There's no way in hell the killer guessed that, right?'

Hunter gave her an almost imperceptible head shake.

'So how does the killer know about their fears? Does he force them to tell him before killing them?'

'I don't know how yet, captain, but he knows about them beforehand,' Hunter stated.

'How can you be so sure?' she challenged.

'The amount of research and planning he puts into his kills.' He tapped one of Father Fabian's photos on the board. 'To bring Father Fabian's nightmare to life, the killer needed a sword and a dog's head.'

'Which he had with him,' Garcia cut in.

'In Malibu,' Hunter continued, 'the killer picked the perfect empty house where he wouldn't be disturbed. A house with an intensity-controlled fireplace so big he could've cooked a hippo. This is LA, captain. Our winter sucks. Large fireplaces aren't exactly a common residential feature in this city.' He leaned shoulder first against the wall to the right of the photo board. 'The killer knew them well.'

'How well?'

'That's the money question. Tania Riggs told us that when the killer called to say he'd be late for his appointment with Amanda Reilly, he asked to speak to *Mandy*.'

The captain narrowed her eyes and searched the interview transcript in her hands. 'That's an affectionate nickname.'

'Precisely,' Hunter agreed. 'Not your regular customer/client way of addressing each other. A slip of the tongue, maybe.'

'Have we run the two new pictures against the Missing Persons and the California Homicide databases?' She addressed Hopkins.

'I started this morning. Nothing yet,' he replied shyly, 'but it's still early.'

'Dan Tyler, the owner of the Malibu house, has no idea who the two on the pictures could be. He never saw them before. I ran the pics by him.' Hunter paused as his gaze locked onto the four faces pinned side by side on the corkboard.

Garcia recognized that look. 'What have you got, Robert?'

Hunter lifted his hand in a 'wait a minute' gesture. 'If the killer knew the victims well . . .' He let his words float in the air for a moment.

'There's a chance they knew each other,' Garcia deducted.

'I think there's a good possibility,' Hunter confirmed.

'But Amanda wouldn't have known Father Fabian from the Seven Saints church,' Garcia continued.

'Why not?' Captain Blake questioned.

'Tania Riggs said Amanda wasn't religious at all. She didn't even believe in God. If she knew Father Fabian from somewhere, it wasn't from his church.'

'And that knowledge can save us some time,' Hunter said.

'How's that?'

'From what we found out so far, Father Fabian was some sort of recluse,' Hunter clarified. 'He lived for the church and its community, but that was all. His social life outside the Catholic Church was nonexistent.'

'Yeah, so?' The captain deposited the report back on Hunter's desk.

'So we know Amanda Reilly didn't go to church. It will be easy to find out if she was a charitable person, linked to any of the charities Father Fabian was involved with.' He tilted his head in Hopkins's direction, who made a mental note of finding that out. 'If not, then when would they have met?'

Nobody answered.

'They didn't live in the same part of town; they didn't shop in the same stores,' Hunter carried on. 'I'm certain Father Fabian never rented or bought a house from Reilly's real estate agency. Their paths had no reason to have crossed other than by extreme coincidence.'

'So if they knew each other, they must've met a long time ago.' The captain finally picked up on what Hunter was getting at.

He turned to Hopkins. 'Find everything you can about Amanda Reilly and Brett Stewart Nichols.'

'Who?'

'Brett Stewart Nichols was Father Fabian's real name,' Garcia explained.

'Find out where they lived, where they went to school, anything you can. Starting from when they were teenagers.'

'I'm on it.'

Hunter's cell phone rang. He returned to his desk and retrieved it from his jacket pocket – unknown caller. 'Detective Hunter.' The conversation was hurried and hushed. When he disconnected, Hunter had a surprised look on his face.

'What's wrong?' Garcia asked.

'I gotta go.' He reached for his jacket.

'Go where?'

But Hunter was already halfway down the corridor.

Sixty-Four

Hunter exited Parker Center, the eight-story building that housed the RHD offices in North Los Angeles Street, and turned left towards the large parking lot, Garcia right behind him. Before reaching the cars, though, he turned right in the direction of East First Street.

'Where're you going?' Garcia asked, his car keys at the ready. 'The car is right over there.' He pointed to his spotlessly clean metallic-blue Honda Civic parked at the north end of the lot.

Hunter disregarded the question and hurried his step, crossing to the other side of the road. Garcia had to wait for a gap in traffic before dashing across to join his partner.

'Are we going somewhere in particular or are we just playing follow the leader here?'

'Starbucks.'

'You mysteriously rushed out of the office to get a coffee?' Garcia joked, waiting for the real answer.

'We're meeting someone,' Hunter said as they turned the corner.

There were a few dark clouds hovering over them; though the unmistakable smell of wet soil filled the air, rain hadn't started yet. A crisp cold wind made sure that the many tables in the European-style square that fronted the coffee shop were empty. All but one. Garcia spotted her first.

'Is that the Monica or Mollie girl?'

Hunter nodded. 'She was the one who called me a minute ago,' he explained.

Garcia slowed his step. 'Shouldn't we have told the captain?' he asked, uncertain. 'Doesn't she want this to go by the book?'

Hunter nodded but didn't break stride.

'How's this telling the captain?' Garcia whispered before rushing after Hunter.

They approached the small table at the far end of the square. The brunette girl didn't notice them until they were right beside her.

'Hello,' Hunter said in a kind voice, offering her his warmest smile.

She looked up and both detectives did a double take. Her brown hair was neatly pulled back into a ponytail. Her delicate makeup expertly highlighted her impressive brown eyes, adding maturity and a charming sparkle to her face that wasn't there the first time they met. The scar on her fleshy lips was barely noticeable. Her shabby clothes were also gone, substituted by a white T-shirt with a cropped black jacket, faded blue jeans and black cowboy boots. She looked totally different.

'Thanks for calling. I really appreciate you getting in contact with us again.'

She returned the smile, but hers had a nervous edge to it. Hunter noticed that the cup of coffee on the table was empty. 'Let me get you another one,' he offered. 'What're you having?'

'Hot chocolate.'

'I'll have an espresso,' Hunter said, facing Garcia, who hesitated for a moment before shaking his head and making towards the shop.

Hunter took the seat across the table from the girl and zipped up his jacket. 'Aren't you a little cold sitting out here?'

She shook her head.

Hunter crossed his arms over his chest in a tight hug. 'I'm freezing.'

She pulled a face and he cringed.

'Wow, I just sounded like a big girl then, didn't I?' He chuckled. 'That's what you get when you live in a hot place all your life. As soon as the temperature drops under fifty-nine, we're covering ourselves with the thickest coats we can find.'

Garcia returned with the coffees and the hot chocolate. 'Are you sure you wanna stay out here?' He shuddered, nodding towards the coffee shop. 'It's nice and warm in there.'

'See what I mean?' Hunter smiled.

'Did I say something funny?' he asked, handing the girl her drink.

'Carlos here was born in Brazil. He moved to LA when he was just a kid. This is arctic temperature for him.' Hunter tried to break the tension.

Garcia frowned as he took his seat. 'What, you don't think it's cold?' The question was directed at Monica.

'Good God, don't ever go to Pennsylvania if you think this is cold.' As soon as those words left her lips, her face tightened and she looked away nervously.

'It's OK,' Garcia said in a comforting tone. 'If it's any consolation, Robert already knew where you were from, from your accent.'

She threw Hunter a questioning look. 'Really?'

'Pennsylvania Dutch, right?' he said matter-of-factly.

'He's full of those little tricks,' Garcia noted. 'That's why he's not invited to many parties.'

She smiled. The double icebreaker was working. Hunter saw

her shoulders relax and she let go of the breath she'd been holding since they arrived.

'You're right. I'm from Pennsylvania.' She looked from Hunter to Garcia and paused for a moment. Without being asked to, she decided to start at the beginning.

Sixty-Five

Mollie Woods was born on Christmas Day in Huntingdon County, Pennsylvania. Though she was born a healthy baby, her lengthy and complicated labor had put too much strain on her mother's womb, and Mollie was to be her first and only child.

Mollie's birth brought changes to her deeply religious family. Her father, John, found it hard to come to terms with the fact that he would never have the son he always wanted. In his eyes, God had punished him and his wife with a daughter. And that punishment had to be passed on.

As soon as she was able to speak, Mollie was taught to pray. And pray she did. Three times a day, naked in the corner, kneeling on dried corn kernels.

As time went by, John Woods's bitterness grew. He used his faith as a hiding place for his anger and little Mollie was always at the receiving end of it all. During her childhood, her skin was mostly black and blue.

When it came to looks, Mollie took after her mother, with a delicate heart-shaped face, plush pink lips, big hypnotic brown eyes and long, wavy brown hair. At thirteen, she was taller than most girls her age and her womanly body was developing fast.

John Woods saw Mollie's beauty as a new test from God.

She was already attracting the attention of older boys, and John knew it was only a matter of time before she gave in to temptation and sin. He had to teach her right from wrong.

The teachings started just after her thirteenth birthday. Twice a week her mother worked the night shift at a twenty-four-hour supermarket in the city center. Mollie dreaded those nights. In the darkness of her room, she'd curl up in bed and pray, but no God would listen. Time and time again she had to endure her father hammering his body against hers, showing her what boys wanted to do to her.

The nightmares began around the same time her father started invading her room. And with them came the nosebleeds. At first Mollie could make no sense of the violent images she saw, but they felt real. Falling asleep was so frightening she'd do anything to stay awake. But soon her troubling visions expanded. They weren't confined to her nightmares anymore. She started having them in broad daylight – kids being beaten and abused by their parents, wives by their husbands – the images just kept on coming, until the day one petrified her soul.

She had a vision of her mother being run over by a drunk driver. That night, in vain, she begged her mother not to go to work. Her father had slapped her across the face and sent her to her room. He'd had enough of her crazy dreams. He smiled the secret smile and told her that once her mother had gone to work, he would go to her room and pray with her.

The knock on the door from the police came an hour after Mollie's mother had left. She'd been involved in a hit-and-run accident and died instantly.

That was the night Mollie ran away. The night something snapped inside her father's head.

Sixty-Six

Both detectives listened to Mollie's story in silence, but she didn't tell them everything. She was careful not to mention her real name, anything about the beatings she received or any of the abuse and humiliation she was subjected to at the hands of her father. She was ashamed.

Hunter had been right. Having run away at the age of fourteen, Mollie had to mature faster than most.

She told them how the nightmares and visions had stopped once she'd left Pennsylvania, and how she thought she'd finally got rid of them. But a few days ago, inside Los Angeles Union Station, the visions came back.

'What exactly did you see?' Hunter kept his voice low and even.

She tensed and cupped her hands around her hot chocolate mug. 'Unfortunately, I can't control anything about these visions. The images are hazy and not always clear. Most of the time I see them as if I was watching a movie on a screen.'

'Like a spectator?' Hunter suggested.

'Yes.' A quick nod. 'But that day inside Union Station was different.'

'Different how?'

She breathed deeply and her gaze lowered. 'I was part of it. I was the one attacking him.' Her voice weakened.

'You saw it in the first person?' Garcia asked.

A subtle nod. 'I was the killer.'

Garcia looked uneasy for a second.

'Wait,' Hunter interrupted. 'Attacking him – who?'

Another deep breath. 'A priest.'

Hunter kept a steady face, knowing that sudden emotional reactions, even facial expressions, could make this even harder for her.

'We were inside some dark church, I don't know where. The priest was just kneeling in front of me, crying.' She had a sip of her hot drink and Hunter noticed her shaky hands. 'I showed him something . . . a piece of paper, I think.'

'A piece of paper?' Garcia queried.

She nodded.

'Could it have been a picture or maybe a drawing?' Hunter asked.

'It could have. I can't be sure.'

Traffic was heating up. A car stalled on East First Street and a barrage of horns came alive. She waited for them to die down.

'I never got to see it. I just showed it to the priest.'

Hunter noted something down in his black notebook. 'What did you see next?'

She hesitated for a second, as if what she was about to say made no sense. 'A dog's head. I showed the priest a dog's head, and it terrified him.'

'Where did the head come from?' Garcia this time.

'I don't know.' She shook her head. 'I just had it with me.' Another quick hesitation. 'Together with the sword I used to . . .' Her voice trailed off.

Hunter allowed a few silent moments to go by before asking her if she remembered which hand held the sword.

'The right one,' she said with conviction.

'Can you remember anything specific about the hand? Skin color? Were there any rings on the fingers? A watch?'

She thought about it for a second. 'Black gloves.'

The wind had picked up as more dark clouds gathered in the sky. It was getting colder, but the girl didn't seem to notice it.

'Anything else you remember from your vision?'

She nodded as she stared straight into Hunter's eyes. 'The number three. I drew it onto the priest's chest after I killed him.'

This time it wasn't the cold wind that made Garcia shiver.

Hunter held her gaze. Up to now, all the information Mollie had given them could've been obtained from the papers. The story that the killer had showed his victim a piece of paper could've been made up. They had no way of confirming it. But not the numbering. There was no way she could've known about the numbering.

'When you came to see us.' Hunter broke the uncomfortable silence. 'Just before I left the room, you said something to me, do you remember?'

He got no response.

'You said, "He knew about the fire. He knew what scared her." Do you remember saying that?'

'Yes.'

'What did you mean by that?' Hunter pushed his empty coffee cup to one side and leaned forward.

'At first I didn't know. It was like I had no control. Those words simply shot out of my lips. But just a minute after you left I saw it. And this time it was even stronger than the previous one.' Her voice wavered for a second.

'What did you see?'

'A woman tied to an armchair. She was as scared as the priest was, but she couldn't scream.'

Garcia ran his hand over his mouth and chin as if stroking a goatee. 'Was she gagged?'

'No. Her lips had been—' the girl shook her head, hardly believing her own words '—glued shut.'

'Glued?' Hunter asked surprised. 'Like with crazy glue?'

She nodded. 'Her face was also covered in something sticky, like some weird type of gel.'

She couldn't have known that either. Hunter pulled the collar of his leather jacket tighter against his neck.

'Did you see this as a first person again?' Garcia pressed.

'Yes.' She looked away as if it were her fault.

Hunter wanted to explore the picture story further. 'Did you show the woman a picture, like you did with the priest?'

'Yes, but again I didn't see what it was.'

'You said this vision was stronger than the previous one, stronger how?' Garcia asked.

Mollie took a moment and Hunter understood her hesitation. She hadn't had a vision in almost four years. Now they'd come back. And in the form of the most hideous murders Hunter had ever seen.

She squeezed her eyes tightly shut. 'The visions I have are usually silent – images only, but not this one.' She paused. 'I said something to the woman.'

Hunter kept silent, allowing her to continue in her own time.

'I said, *Welcome to your fear, Mandy . . .*'

Hunter's heart raced.

'*. . . I know what scares you to death.*'

Sixty-Seven

The statement was so surprising that it took several seconds for it to register with both detectives.

'Was it your voice?' Hunter queried, still a little stunned by how much she knew. 'When you said those words to the woman. Was it your voice or somebody else's?'

'My own,' she whispered.

Garcia rubbed his face vigorously, lost for words.

'Somehow I knew the woman in the chair was scared of fires,' the girl continued. 'That's why I said those words to you.'

Hunter leaned back in his chair and thought about it for a moment.

'These visions last only about thirty seconds, maybe a minute. I don't know why I see them. I don't know why they feel so real. I don't know why I wasn't a spectator like all the previous ones. I wish I did, but I don't have all the answers.' She paused and looked away from Hunter. 'What I'm trying to tell you is: whoever this killer is, he knows about their fears.'

Click, click, click. The person holding the camera on the other side of East First Street quickly snapped three consecutive pictures without anyone noticing.

'Is there anything else you remember about these visions, Mollie?' Garcia asked and saw the girl's eyes widen in shock.

She looked uncertain for a split second before reaching for her bag.

Hunter reached for her hand. 'Wait.'

Mollie looked at him, then jerked his hand away angrily and stood up.

'Please listen to me.' Hunter and Garcia shot to their feet at the same time.

'This has all been a mistake.'

'No, it hasn't.' Hunter's tone was firm but unthreatening. 'Just give me one minute to explain. Then, if you still wanna go, no one will stop you.'

She paused just long enough for Hunter not to allow her uncertainty to settle. 'I didn't know if you'd ever call again. You left before an officer had a chance to write down your details. You left us nothing, so I had to go with the only thing we had – your Pennsylvanian accent. We did a quick search. Your name came up as a missing person.'

She went rigid.

'We didn't tell your father.'

Earlier on, when she told them about her obsessively religious parents, she kept the story centered around her mother, rarely mentioning her father. When she did, her body tensed, her posture shifted and her movements were nervy. Hunter saw how scared she was of him.

'And we won't tell him,' Hunter said positively.

Her eyes held Hunter's gaze for a while longer before shifting towards Garcia. He nodded and gave her a confident wink as if saying 'we won't tell if you don't'.

Her body relaxed slightly.

'I promise you, Mollie, we weren't intruding.' Hunter paused. 'And we could really use your help.'

There was something calming, something trustworthy about

the man standing in front of her. The tense moment evaporated and she sat back down. 'The reason why I called you today . . .'

'You had another vision?' Garcia guessed.

'No. Not a vision, a flash.'

Click, click, click. Three more pictures.

'What do you mean a flash?'

'Sometimes I have quick flashes of one of my previous visions. Something that wasn't there before. They last only a couple of seconds.'

'They're called residual flashes,' Hunter said without going into a detailed explanation.

Mollie looked at him curiously.

'He reads a lot,' Garcia explained. 'So what was this flash about?'

'Something I said.'

'Something you said to who?' Hunter this time.

'To the priest. Just before I killed him.'

Click, click, click.

'But you said there was no sound in the priest's vision,' Garcia said.

'There wasn't. Not in the vision.'

'But there was in the flash,' Hunter acknowledged.

Mollie nodded and sighed.

'So what did you say?'

A deep breath.

'*They will all die.*'

Sixty-Eight

Fifteen days before the first murder

Staring at his reflection in the mirror, he ran his tongue over his dry and cracked lips. It's been almost four years, but he looked to have aged at least ten. His face now showed several deep lines, and his eyes seemed to have sunken further into his skull. But anyone who knew John Woods knew that the lines weren't an indication of age, but of heavy anguish.

After his wife's death, he'd relocated from Huntingdon County to York, in South Central Pennsylvania. He couldn't stay in Huntingdon anymore. Everything about the place reminded him of his daughter. Her demonic dreams had cursed his life.

He splashed a handful of cold water on his face and combed what was left of his thin black hair back over his ears. Tonight, the York Catholic High School and Church was hosting a Christmas charity event. Over three hundred students and parents were expected.

John worked as a janitor at the school, and he always helped Father Laurence with anything needed, from plumbing to gardening and party decorations. There was still an hour before the party was due to start, but various parents were already arriving, bringing with them a variety of baked goods ready to be sold at the massive bake-sale that'd take place inside the school gymnasium. John's task was to keep the bathroom floors and toilets clean during the party.

With his eyes still fixed on his reflection, he crossed himself and said a quick prayer before leaving the small apartment he rented just a block away from York Catholic High School.

Father Laurence had asked John to concern himself only with the bathroom inside the gymnasium. That's where everyone would be. The main classroom building had been deemed out of limits, but John knew students liked to break rules.

It was past eight o'clock when John walked into the dark hallway of the main building. After checking the two bathrooms on the ground floor, he moved upstairs to have a look at the one right at the end of the hall. He'd walked those corridors so many times he didn't need a flashlight.

As he approached the door to the bathroom, John could hear giggling coming from inside. He slowed his step and listened for a moment. There seemed to be at least three voices – one of them female. The lights were off, allowing John to sneak in quietly without being noticed. Slowly, he tiptoed his way towards the last cubicle, where the sounds were coming from.

The door was wide open, and in the faint light that came from a cell phone he could see someone standing behind a girl who was bent over the toilet. They were both naked and the boy standing behind her slapped her bare butt with his right hand while thrusting himself into her. They were both moaning with pleasure.

John was wearing dark trousers and shirt, which helped hide him in the shadows. With his back tight against the wall opposite the cubicles, he took a step closer. Sitting on the toilet, in front of the girl, another naked boy held a cell phone with his left hand, while pushing her head down onto him with his right. She took him into her mouth eagerly. The boy was filming everything.

John felt himself getting hard.

'Nick, I want you inside me now,' the girl said, lifting her mouth from the boy in front of her. 'And Shawn—' she faced the boy behind her '—I want all that in my mouth.' She pointed to his erect penis.

John moved two steps back as quietly as he could. He didn't want to disturb them.

The two boys swapped positions and everything started again. Nick, the boy now standing behind the demanding girl, still had his cell phone firmly in his left hand. Her moans quickly got more urgent, and John knew she was about to climax. And so was he.

John eased himself into one of the cubicles. Two from where the boys were. He didn't need to see them; her moans were enough to drive him crazy. He closed his eyes and allowed his imagination and his hand to do all the work, but his mind didn't bring back the images he'd seen just a few seconds ago. All he could think of was Mollie and the nights he'd walked into her room and delivered her from the temptations of this world.

With his thoughts of those nights, it took John only a few seconds to climax.

He sat there for a few minutes trying to control his body. It wrenched every couple of seconds from his ecstasy. When he was steady enough to stand, he cleaned himself up and left the bathroom as quietly as he'd come in. The students were still going at it.

'John.' He heard someone call as he walked back into the gymnasium.

Keeping his head low and his eyes on the floor, he carried on walking, pretending he didn't hear it.

'John Woods.' A hand touched him on his right shoulder. 'Didn't you hear me call?'

John turned around nervously and his eyes widened in surprise. The old man standing in front of him had thin white eyebrows that matched the little hair he'd combed over from left to right. His round nose and rosy cheeks, together with his kind-looking eyes, gave him the friendliest of looks.

'Father Lewis?' John said, looking shocked before kissing the old priest's right hand.

'God bless you, my son.'

'I didn't know you were coming.'

'It was a last-minute decision, John.'

Father Lewis had been the priest at the Most Holy Trinity Catholic Church in Huntingdon for as long as anyone could remember. John Woods had worshiped there his whole life.

'How's the church, father?'

'Fine, John. We had a new coat of paint about a year ago. You should come back to visit us sometime.'

John's eyes saddened.

'I know, I know,' Father Lewis said before John was able to form a reply. 'The memories are still too vivid, right?'

A shy nod.

'I've known you since you were a little kid, John. You've always been a very devout Catholic, and I have you in my heart as family. It pains me to know that you needed to leave us to be able to cope with your loss.'

John couldn't bring himself to lock eyes with the priest.

Father Lewis smiled a comforting smile. 'But the reason I'm here is to bring you good news.'

John finally looked up.

'Can we step outside for a moment? It's a bit too noisy in here.'

They found a quiet corner outside the school gym.

'Do you remember Sarah Matthews?' Father Lewis asked.

John squinted.

'Short lady, curly blond hair, nice eyes, laughs real loud every time I tell one of my not very funny jokes,' the priest reminded him.

He shook his head.

'She always brought apple pies to all our bake-sales. Has a very pretty daughter named Emily.'

John smiled. He remembered Emily Matthews very well. A slender and tall girl, who at fourteen had all the boys drooling over her already voluptuous figure. John remembered the way she used to look at him during Sunday Mass. Like she knew she was a bad girl and she wanted him to deliver her from carnal temptation, just the way he did with Mollie.

'Oh, I remember her now,' John said, hiding his excitement. 'The woman with the apple pies and the very loud laugh.'

'That's her.' The priest nodded. 'Well, Emily, her daughter, moved to Los Angeles about two years ago. She wants to go to drama school and become an actress.' Father Lewis shook his head disapprovingly. 'Kids these days, they all want fame and stardom, no matter what we try to teach them.'

John didn't comment.

'She came back this past weekend. She'll be spending Christmas with her family in Huntingdon. I was talking to her after Sunday's Mass, and she told me something that I just needed to come and tell you. It might bring some comfort back into your heavy heart.'

John frowned, not really knowing where the priest was going.

'To pay her rent,' Father Lewis continued, 'Emily has taken a job as a waitress in a diner in a busy area of Los Angeles.' He paused, as if what he was about to say filled him with joy. 'And she swears she saw Mollie just a week ago.'

John's heart skipped a beat. He stared blankly at Father Lewis.

'I know.' The priest nodded enthusiastically. 'It's hard to believe, but Emily said she was very sure. There's a bus stop just in front of the diner where she used to work, and that's where she saw Mollie. Apparently, Mollie hasn't changed much, apart from her hair and a small scar on her lip.'

John remembered the night Mollie ran away. He'd given her that scar.

'Emily didn't manage to speak to her. She was serving customers, and by the time she was done with their order Mollie had already boarded a bus. They used to be friends in school, remember?'

John felt his body starting to shiver as words evaded him.

'Isn't that just great news, John?' The priest smiled. 'Mollie is alive and well. I was so overjoyed when Emily told me that I had to come over and see you. I know how worried you've been.'

John wasn't listening anymore. The voices in his head now doing all the talking.

Sixty-Nine

It was early evening when Hunter received an email with an attachment containing the latest lab results sent from the LACDC. The combination used on Amanda Reilly's face to produce the melted wax effect was similar to what Doctor Winston had suggested, but not quite. The killer had created a mixture of rubber and petrolatum that was of a soft jelly consistency. The jelly, when mixed with a small amount of lead oleate, creates a gelatinous plaster that is readily adhesive to the human skin and it doesn't run or soften. When exposed to intense heat, the entire mixture melts away. Depending on the strength of the adhesive property of the plaster, it can rip the skin clean off a person's body as it melts. The wax-like clumps on Amanda Reilly's face were actually a mixture of her torn-off skin and the melted rubber petrolatum combination used by the killer.

'Where would the killer get hold of that stuff?' Garcia asked after Hunter read the printout out loud.

'Petrolatum is really just petroleum jelly,' Hunter explained. 'It can be bought over the counter at any drugstore. Lead oleate can be easily ordered over the internet, and the killer could've gotten the rubber simply by melting a common Halloween mask. The amount needed to create enough jelly to cover Amanda's face would've been distinctively small.'

Garcia accepted it but still looked unsettled.

'What's bothering you?' Hunter asked, placing the printout on his desk.

Garcia pulled his hair into a ponytail. 'The conversation we had with Mollie this morning and everything she told us. It's like she was there when it happened.'

'And what do you think?' Hunter pushed for an opinion.

Garcia paced the room. 'She knew too many details about both crime scenes for her to be a hoax. She knew about the numbering. Her whereabouts on both nights checked out.' He lifted his hands as if giving up. 'I'm gonna be straight with you, Robert. I never really believed in any of this psychic crap. But unless she knows who the killer is and he's been telling her stories, I think you're right. She's the real deal. And if so, she's told us something we didn't know.'

'The killer showed the victims a piece of paper,' Hunter admitted.

Garcia nodded. 'And as you suggested before, it could easily have been a drawing or a picture of somewhere or someone.'

'Whatever it is,' Hunter said, his eyes fixed on Garcia, 'if Mollie is right, that piece of paper links the victims together.'

Seventy

A muffled, single click sound from Hunter's computer announced the arrival of a new email. This time, Mike Brindle had sent them the blood test results from the photographs they found on the fireplace. Hunter read it first before handing the printout to his partner.

'The killer used the same blood on both pictures?' Garcia sounded unsure.

Hunter nodded and rubbed his eyes.

'Doesn't that do away with your theory that the killer uses the blood of the previous victim to mark his next one?'

'Not at all.' Hunter went back to his seat and reached for his mouse. *Click, scroll, click.*

Garcia waited a few seconds but got nothing. 'Do you wanna elaborate on that?'

'Those weren't the real victims; they were pictures of the victims. Suppose the killer kills a victim and goes away with just enough blood to be able to number his next one. He's not counting on the number washing off or somehow disappearing and having to redraw it.' He pressed a few keys on his keyboard. 'So when the killer finds himself in a situation where he has to use photographs to reclaim victims one and two, he's fresh out of victims' blood.'

Garcia considered this. 'So he adapts and has to use the same blood to mark both photos.'

Hunter stopped dead and faced Garcia. 'He didn't use their blood,' he murmured.

'What?'

'The killer was at a crime scene when he left both pictures on the mantelpiece.'

'Yeah, so?'

'So he could've used Amanda's blood. She was right there and he wouldn't even have needed that much to draw two small numbers on the back of the photos. Why didn't he use her blood?'

Garcia shook his head slowly.

'He also could've used Father Fabian's blood,' Hunter carried on. 'He obviously had some with him to draw the number four on Amanda's back. He wouldn't have needed any more than a small dab for each number.'

Garcia chewed on his bottom lip as he thought about it. 'Maybe he drew the numbers on the back of the pictures before getting to the house in Malibu,' he suggested.

'OK, so why not use Father Fabian's blood? As I said, he had some with him since the Seven Saints murder.'

'Maybe he had some blood left from the previous victims.'

'According to the test results, it's not Amanda's blood, it's not Father Fabian's blood and it's not the same blood as the one the killer used on the priest, the pregnant woman's.'

'So if your assumptions are correct and the killer really is using the blood of a previous victim to mark his next one, the blood used on the pictures wouldn't have come from victims two, three or four.'

'That's right.'

Garcia leaned against his desk. His eyes studied Hunter for a brief moment. 'I can see from the look on your face that you don't believe the blood belongs to the first victim either.'

'I think the killer keeps only a small amount of victim's blood so he can number the next one. After that, my guess is that he disposes of what he has left.'

Garcia pinched his chin, his brow creased with worry. 'If your theory is right, why is he doing it? Why is the killer using the blood of a previous victim to mark the next one?'

Hunter's eyes widened and he felt his pulse race. 'He's linking them together.'

'The killer's linking them?'

Hunter nodded. 'By using their blood on each other, he's linking victims one and two together, victims two and three and victims three and four. Maybe they were all connected, we don't know yet. But the killer's telling us that there is a connection.'

Garcia paused for an instant as a new thought entered his mind. 'OK, then I've got two questions for you. If your theory is correct, then whose blood did the killer use to number the first victim, since there was no previous one? And if you don't think the killer used the blood of any of the victims to write the number on the back of those two photographs, where do you think the blood came from?'

Hunter stopped by the window and watched the hectic traffic outside for a moment. 'Maybe the answer to both questions is the same.'

Garcia's left eyebrow lifted in expectation.

'The killer used his own blood.'

Seventy-One

Two days before the first murder

He rang the bell and stood waiting at the reception window of an old and derelict hotel in Lynwood, south Los Angeles. It was one of those hotels that rented their rooms by the hour, day, week or month. Any kind of arrangement could be reached, as long as you had the money. No questions asked.

The entry lobby was small and neglected. In fact, it looked like it hadn't been cleaned in years. There were water infiltration stains on the ceiling, cigarette burn marks on the carpet, cobwebs in every corner and the wallpaper was peeling off the walls. He thought places like this existed only in police movies, but this was exactly what he was looking for. A place where no one would notice him.

He rang the desk bell a few more times.

'OK, OK. Keep your fucking pants on.' The heavy, southern-accented voice came from behind the wooden partition at the back of the reception office. A few seconds later, a black girl, who couldn't have been older than eighteen, appeared, followed by a massively overweight man. She was wearing tight blue jeans and a sleeveless yellow cotton blouse and seemed to be in a hurry to get out of there. As she unlocked the door and stepped out into the small lobby, the fat man gave her a sleazy wink while adjusting his elasticated trousers around his balloon waist.

'Now next week you bring me the rent on time, you hear.'

The girl kept her eyes low, embarrassed, and disappeared up the narrow stairs.

'What can I do you for?' the fat man asked, finally coming up to the reception window. He smelled of garlic, and his greasy and thinning hair was in desperate need of a wash and cut.

'I need a room.'

The fat man stretched his neck out of the reception window and checked the lobby – empty, except for a small suitcase by the man's feet. When people came looking for a room in his hotel, they usually had a hooker or two hanging from their arms.

'It's five bucks an hour, or if you're feeling like a stag you can get six hours for twenty dollars.' He used his right index finger's nail to scrape something off his front teeth.

'I need the room for a few days. Maybe longer.'

The fat man frowned and looked at the six-foot-two guest skeptically.

'I'll pay cash.'

The worried look vanished as the fat man saw an opportunity presenting itself. 'You know, Christmas is just around the corner and we're quite busy in here, but I might be able to get you something.'

The guest waited patiently for the fat man to carry on.

'If you wanna stay for a whole week, I can give you the room for . . .' He paused, pretending he was calculating the correct amount. 'Two hundred bucks.'

The guest let out a bizarre laugh, picked his suitcase up and silently made for the door.

'Wait, wait,' the fat man called in an urgent voice. 'OK, I can see you drive a hard bargain. A whole week for one hundred and fifty bucks, what do you say?'

The man thought about it for a moment before pulling four hundred and fifty dollars out of his wallet.

'I'll take three weeks. Until New Year's Day.'

The fat man took the money and counted it eagerly. 'If you wanna get a real good deal, I can give you a whole month for five hundred bucks. That's a great price.'

The man calmly returned his wallet to his back pocket and stared at the fat man.

'OK, OK.' He lifted his hands in surrender before pushing a guestbook through the window. 'Just sign your name there and we're all set.'

The man didn't move.

Several silent uncomfortable seconds rolled past.

'OK,' the receptionist said, picking up on the man's look. 'I'll sign you in as Jim Bob, how's that? You'll be the third Jim Bob we have staying here.' He scribbled something down, threw the guestbook onto his messy desk and grabbed a key. 'Room 34B,' he said, handing the key over. 'Third floor, facing the street. It's a good room. One of the best we have.' He let his mouth stretch into a smile, showing stained and dirty teeth. 'If you need any entertainment.' He gave the guest the same sleazy wink he'd given the black girl just a few minutes ago. 'Girls, boys . . . you know what I mean. Just give me a shout. I can hook you up.'

The man wasn't paying attention to the receptionist any-more. He needed nothing else from the fat man.

Seventy-Two

Garcia quickly checked his watch as he parked in front of the old apartment block in Montebello, east LA. He rested his head on his seat's headrest and looked up at the many flickering Christmas lights hanging from several windows. They certainly added a lively touch to the otherwise nondescript brick building. Anna had decorated their first-floor apartment window with fake snow, glowing blue lights and an old Rudolph the Red-Nosed Reindeer stuffed toy whose nose was more pale pink than red. But it was her favorite childhood memento. She'd had it since she was four.

Garcia had called her from the office to let her know he'd be home in time for dinner tonight, something that'd become a luxury lately. They've been together since their senior year in high school, and Garcia couldn't have asked for a more supportive wife. She knew how much he loved being a detective. She'd seen how hard he'd worked for it and how dedicated he was. She understood the commitment and the sacrifices that came with the job, and she'd accepted them as if they were her own. But despite her strength and everything Garcia had told her, Anna sometimes felt scared. Scared that one day she'd get that phone call in the middle of the night telling her that her husband wouldn't be coming home. Scared that the things Garcia saw on a day-to-day basis were changing him inside. No matter how mentally fit anyone is, there's only so much savagery one can stomach. There's only so much psychological abuse one can take before becoming detached. She'd read that somewhere, and she believed every word of it.

Anna was sitting comfortably on their blue fabric sofa when Garcia came into the living room carrying a nicely arranged bouquet of red roses and a bottle of white wine. She looked up from the book she was reading and gave him the same welcoming smile that made his heart beat faster and turned his legs to jelly every time.

He smiled back.

Anna had an unconventional but mesmerizing kind of beauty. Her short black hair complemented her striking hazel eyes and her heart-shaped face perfectly. Her skin was creamy smooth, her features delicate, and she had the firm figure of a high school cheerleader.

'Flowers?' She placed her book on the coffee table and stood up. 'What's the occasion?'

Garcia looked at her, and Anna saw a glimpse of something sad in his eyes. 'No special occasion. I just realized that it's been a while since I brought you flowers. I know how much you like them.'

Anna took the bouquet from his hands and kissed him softly. She thought about asking if everything was really OK, but she knew she'd just get the same answer. Garcia was always OK. No matter what was going on in his mind, no matter how tough his day had been, he'd never worry her.

Because of Garcia's new aversion to grilled steak, Anna had prepared her grandmother's famous lasagne al forno, and the meal was nicely complemented by the Pinot Grigio Garcia had bought. They had fruit salad and vanilla ice cream for dessert, and he helped her clear the table when they were done. In the kitchen, he turned on the hot tap and started washing the dishes while Anna sat at the small breakfast table finishing her wine.

'Can I ask you something, babe?' he said casually, without locking eyes with her.

'Sure.'

'Do you believe a person can see things that happened to other people without being there?'

She frowned at the question. 'What? I don't follow.'

Garcia finished washing the last plate, dried his hands on the flowery dish cloth and turned towards his wife. 'You know, some people say they can see things. Things that happened to other people. Sometimes people they don't even know.'

'Like a vision?' She said the words slowly.

'Yeah, something like that, or a dream of some sort.'

Anna had another sip of her wine. 'Well, that's definitely a very strange question, coming from you. I know you don't believe in things like that. Are we talking psychic people here?'

Garcia took a seat next to Anna and poured them both a little more wine. 'Do you believe in things like that?'

Seventy-Three

Anna stared at her husband, trying to read his expression. They had a very healthy relationship with very few arguments and plenty of frank conversations about most things, but Garcia never offered anything about his job or any of the investigations he worked on. Even without him saying so, she knew the question he'd just asked was much more than simple curiosity.

'Do you remember a girl called Martha?' she asked, leaning back on her chair.

Garcia squinted.

'Strange girl from high school. Short chestnut hair, thick rimmed glasses, awful dress sense. She was a bit of a loner, always sat by herself right at the far end of the canteen.'

'Doesn't ring a bell,' Garcia admitted.

'She was one year below us.' Anna snapped her fingers as she remembered something. 'She was that junior girl who got bathed in ketchup and mustard by those stuck-up bitches from our class, remember? During that barbecue party in the football field?'

'Damn, I remember that,' Garcia said, widening his eyes. 'Poor girl. She was covered from head to toe.' He hesitated for a second. 'Didn't you help her out that day?'

Anna nodded. 'Yeah, I helped her clean up. I lent her some

clothes and took her to a Laundromat. She made me promise not to tell her parents – ever. We talked a few times after that, but she was very shy. Very hard to be friends with.'

'Anyway,' Garcia urged Anna. 'What about her?'

Anna's eyes focused on her glass of Italian wine.

'This is April 1994, two days before our girls' basketball team was due to play the quarterfinals of the California High School Tournament.'

Garcia felt a knot rise in his throat. 'Against Oakland?' he asked tentatively.

Anna nodded slowly. Her eyes still on her glass. 'It was lunch break and Martha was sitting right at the end of the canteen, as she always did. I walked over just to say hi, but she seemed even more distant than usual. As small talk I asked her if she was coming to the game on Saturday. We were the underdogs and the team could do with all the support we could get.'

Garcia leaned forward, his interest growing.

'Martha looked at me and freaked me out. Her eyes were different – cold, emotionless, like two black pits filled with nothing.' Anna ran her fingers over her lips nervously. 'Almost catatonically she said, "There will be no game."'

Garcia saw Anna's arms come up in goose bumps and he held her hand. She gave him a weak smile before carrying on.

'I asked her what she was talking about. The game was advertised everywhere. You couldn't walk five steps in our school without seeing a poster. We had the best girls' basketball team our school had had in years, and that was our big chance.' Anna paused again and with glassy eyes stared at Garcia. 'Martha said, "Oakland's not gonna make it. The bus's not gonna make it."'

This time the goose bumps were on Garcia. He remembered that year very well. The Oakland girls' basketball team was supposed to arrive one day before the game. Their driver fell asleep at the wheel somewhere on Westside Freeway. The bus was involved in a head-on collision with an eighteen-wheeler. No one made it out alive.

'Jesus,' Garcia whispered, squeezing Anna's hand. 'What day was that again?'

'The day before it happened.'

'You're kidding?'

The temperature in their kitchen seemed to have dropped all of a sudden.

'That's why you quit the team,' Garcia said, finally realizing it. 'It wasn't because of the accident itself. It was because of what this Martha girl told you.'

Anna didn't admit to it, but Garcia knew he was right. 'I never talked to Martha again. A few weeks later she left school.'

'You never told me that.'

'I never told anyone.' She had another sip of her wine. 'Somehow Martha knew it before it happened, Carlos. A whole day before it happened. I don't know if she dreamed it or saw it in a vision or what. The fact is, she couldn't have guessed it. No one could.'

Garcia let go of Anna's hand and finished the rest of his wine in silence.

'In answer to your question,' she said, softly touching his arm. 'I do believe there are some people out there who can see or sense things that the vast majority of us can't. But not the ones you see advertised in the back of some magazines. People promising to tell you your future for a few hundred bucks. Those are just conmen. If they really could see the future, they'd all be living in Vegas making a killing at the casinos.'

Garcia smiled. 'You do have a point there.'

'What's this about, babe?'

Garcia shook his head, his eyes averting hers. 'It's nothing really.'

Somehow, she knew that was all the answer she'd ever get.

Seventy-Four

Hunter rolled over in bed uncomfortably. No position was a good one. His eyes grazed the digital clock on the bedside table and he cursed under his breath. It was 4:55 a.m. and he'd managed less than two hours' sleep. It was already hard enough falling asleep in his own bed; in a stranger's bed it was damn near impossible.

He stretched his body and massaged his gritty eyes, but the sandy feeling just wouldn't go away. The darkness of the room was spoiled by the weak light that came in from the corridor, courtesy of a small glass lamp on the telephone table.

Hunter had left his office late last night and hadn't felt like going home straight away. He drove around for a while, welcoming the soothing effect the city's Christmas lights and decorations had on him. On Hollywood Boulevard, where the decorations were certainly the most extravagant he'd seen so far, Hunter ended up in the L'Scorpion, a red and black gothic-themed bar with an impressive selection of tequilas and Scotch whiskeys. He didn't intend to stay long, and that decision had been expedited when the tall, short-haired blond with incredibly seductive lips and an eye-grabbing figure bumped into him, spilling his and her drink all over his shirt. She couldn't apologize enough, and after buying Hunter a new drink, one thing led to another and he was now lying next to her in her bed.

Hunter eased himself from under the covers and out of bed as quietly as he could. His clothes were scattered all over the floor, and he gathered them together in a messy bunch. His shoes, though, were nowhere to be seen. He smiled as he remembered the urgency they'd both had in getting their clothes off. She'd ripped a couple of buttons off his shirt as she franticly pulled it over his head. Their time in bed had been wild and loud – very loud. Hunter figured that if the blond woman's apartment didn't have thick walls, she couldn't be very popular with her neighbors.

He got down on his hands and knees and checked under the bed for his shoes, but it was too dark for him to see anything.

'Did you lose something?' Even though her voice was soft and sexy, it caught Hunter by surprise.

'Sorry if I woke you,' he whispered. 'I was just looking for my shoes.'

She smiled and sat up, placing her back against the headboard. 'They're on this side.' Her head tilted slightly to her right.

Hunter got back on his feet, and her eyes sparkled as they ran the length of his naked body. He circled the bed and as he bent down to collect his shoes, she slipped her right leg from under the covers and softly ran her small, delicate and perfectly pedicured foot against his arm. He looked up and they locked eyes.

'You don't really have to go right this minute, do you?'

Most of her makeup had rubbed off, but she was still stunningly attractive. Her eyes were as blue as Hunter's. Her petite nose was sprinkled with a handful of charming freckles, most of them hidden under her perfect tan. She noticed Hunter furtively checking the digital clock.

'It's still early. The sun isn't even out yet,' she whispered and smiled.

Hunter thought about it for a split second before leaning forward and kissing her softly. She moaned seductively and he kissed her again, a little harder and for a little longer. She pushed the covers off the bed and pulled Hunter onto her, her moans getting louder by the second.

Seventy-Five

Captain Blake had to postpone their daily meeting until later that afternoon. She was tied up in a press conference on another case. This time regarding the Slasher investigation.

Hunter decided to go back to the Seven Saints church and the house in Malibu. He hoped that being alone at the murder scenes for a while would help him understand some of the reasons behind the brutality, behind the rage and anger. Most crime scenes, if you know how to read them, are like witnesses, revealing secrets about the victim, the perpetrator and what really happened. Hunter was in a class of his own when it came to understanding murder scenes. He could sense things and read signs most detectives couldn't. But these crime scenes were silent, with the exception of one word, and they shouted it – FEAR.

Hunter also took some time to go over Amanda Reilly's apartment on Sunset Strip one more time. He went through all three bedrooms, the living room, the kitchen and the reception room. He looked in every drawer, every storage box, every cupboard and wardrobe in the apartment. He wasn't sure of what he was hoping to find. Maybe a diary or old pictures of her and her friends, but Amanda kept nothing. A beautifully decorated apartment with delicate furniture, stylish paintings on the walls and expensive-looking rugs, but devoid of any memories. Not even a single family portrait. The only knowledge Hunter came away with was that Amanda Reilly was very proud, very organized and she'd rather not be reminded of her past.

It was mid-afternoon by the time Hunter made it back to the RHD. The Investigative Analysis Unit (IAS) of the LAPD is confined to a large basement room in Parker Center. Hopkins was gathering a few printouts together when Hunter and Garcia entered the room.

'I was just about to go up and see you guys,' Hopkins said, waving the sheets in his hands.

'I guess we beat you to it,' Hunter said, looking around the young officer's working space.

Hopkins's tiny desk was in the far corner of the room. It was just big enough to hold his keyboard, computer monitor and a telephone.

'I can see they gave you the child's desk.' Hunter's gaze fell on Jack Kerley, the IT Unit supervisor.

'Hey, it's the best we could do with such short notice,' Jack replied, getting up and firmly shaking Hunter and Garcia's hands. His shaved head shone as if it had been waxed just moments ago. 'How're you doing, Robert?'

Hunter nodded but didn't voice a reply.

Jack placed a hand on Hopkins's left shoulder. 'He's a good kid. Fast learner. We could do with more like him down here. We've got work coming out of our fucking asses.'

The phone on his desk rang.

'See what I mean? That'll certainly be a new request.' He returned to his desk.

'Did we get anything on Father Fabian and Amanda Reilly's backgrounds?' Hunter faced Hopkins, who was already flipping through the printouts.

'Father Fabian's charity work involved only his parish community. He didn't do anything on a citywide level. Amanda Reilly has no record of being a charitable person. I found nothing where their paths could've crossed in the last fifteen to twenty years.'

'How about earlier than that?' Hunter leaned against the wall.

Hopkins paused to organize his notes for a moment. 'Brett Stewart Nichols, aka Father Fabian, grew up in Compton where he lived his whole life. He attended Compton High in South Acacia Avenue. He wasn't what you'd call an exemplary student. His grades were quite poor, really. He scraped through most of his classes with a D, barely managing to graduate. He wasn't only a bad student; he was a baaad student, if you know what I mean. A detention's expert.' Hopkins searched for a printout. 'I've got taunting students, destruction of school and private property, cheating, stealing exams, you name it. Hard to believe a kid with this kind of history became a priest.'

'When did he apply for seminary?' Hunter asked.

'A year and a half after graduating. For someone who was such a bad boy, something certainly changed his mind.'

'Did he go to seminary here in LA?'

Hopkins checked his sheet. 'Nope, he went to St John's Seminary College in Camarillo. I called them, but without a warrant they won't disclose a thing.'

'I don't think we'll need his seminary records. What was his high school attendance like?' Hunter queried.

'Funny you asked.' Hopkins chuckled. 'Abysmal, really. He certainly liked skipping classes.'

'Let me see that sheet,' Hunter said, extending his hand. 'How about Amanda Reilly?'

'She didn't go to the same school; she didn't live in Compton. She went to Gardena Senior High.'

'That school is massive,' Garcia commented.

'She lived in Gardena?' Hunter asked, lifting his eyes from the sheet in his hands.

Hopkins nodded. 'That's right, until she dropped out of school and got involved with real estate.'

'Hold on.' Hunter lifted his hand. 'Gardena isn't very far from Compton. What was Amanda's attendance like when she was in school?'

'Not great either. Just like Brett, she skipped a lot of classes.'

'How old was she when she dropped out?'

'Because she flunked tenth grade twice . . . eighteen.'

'Around the same age as Father Fabian,' Hunter announced. 'Where did she live?' Hunter walked over to the large LA neighborhood map on the east wall.

Hopkins checked his sheet. 'South Ainsworth Street in Gardena.'

Hunter found the street and placed a red pin on the map before checking the sheet with Father Fabian's information. He used a blue pin to mark the street where the priest lived when young. They all paused and stared at the map.

'Shit,' Garcia noted, 'they were only six blocks away from each other.'

Seventy-Six

Garcia and Hopkins moved closer to study the map.

'Same-age kids like to hang out together. They could've been part of the same street group,' Hopkins suggested.

'Not many LA neighborhoods mix well,' Garcia countered, 'and Compton is certainly one of those that don't. Especially with Gardena.'

Hunter responded with a head tilt. 'Yeah, but we're talking twenty-five years ago. Things weren't so bad then. We didn't have as big a gang problem as we have today. Neighborhoods mixed a lot better in those days.'

'That's true,' Hopkins admitted.

Hunter kept his eyes on the map for a while longer before checking his watch. 'This is the best we've got, so let's drop by their old schools and see what else we can find out, ask around a little, check their archives,' he said, gesturing for Hopkins to hand him the sheet with Amanda's information.

'Would you like me to call the schools?' Hopkins asked.

'They'll just bounce you around from person to person. Plus, I'm sure they'll have some photographs that we'll need to look at.' Hunter turned and faced Garcia. 'I'll take the priest's old school in Compton; you check Amanda's one in Gardena.'

Garcia nodded.

'I'm still running the two photographs you got from the house in Malibu against the MUPU and the Homicide databases.' Hopkins turned to his computer and clicked his mouse a few times. Both photographs filled his screen. 'No matches as of yet with any.'

'Keep trying,' Hunter said confidently and noticed a doubtful look about Hopkins. 'Something wrong?'

'I've been thinking about this. What if these two were killed a while ago? Maybe even years?' Hopkins offered cautiously, his eyes on the photographs. 'That'd explain why we haven't found them yet and why there's been no link. Maybe the killer started killing sometime ago and had to stop for some reason. Now he's back.' He checked his watch absentmindedly.

'Sonofabitch,' Hunter said. His wide-opened eyes moved from Hopkins to the computer screen a couple of times.

'What did I do?' Hopkins asked nervously.

'Those two weren't killed a long time ago,' Hunter said firmly. 'They were killed within the last five months.'

Garcia frowned, struggling to keep up with his partner. 'And how do you know that?'

'His watch,' Hunter said, tapping the screen.

Garcia and Hopkins leaned forward and squinted as they tried to make out the partially obscured timekeeper on the man's left wrist. Garcia gave up after a few seconds.

'You can't really see the entire watch,' he said, returning to an upright position. 'Half of it is cut off by the edge of the picture.'

'Sonofabitch.' Hopkins this time. 'It's an LA Lakers commemorative NBA final champion's watch. It was only released in July, after the NBA finals in June.'

'How the hell do you know that?' Garcia asked.

'Because he's got the same watch,' Hunter said, and all eyes focused on Hopkins's wrist. 'Contact the morgues. Get a personal possessions' inventory for every male body they've received in the past eight weeks. We find the watch, we find victim number one.'

Seventy-Seven

Earlier the same morning

Despite feeling tired, he had almost no sleep during the night. The loud and constant noises that came from the adjacent room jolted him awake every time he dozed off. He should be used to them by now. Strangled male voices roaring like wounded animals accompanied by squeaky female ones screaming, 'Harder, baby, harder.' Those sounds invaded his room every night. At times he'd be forgiven for thinking he'd woken up during a typical Californian earthquake. The thunderous banging against his walls shook the entire room. For some reason last night's screams sounded louder, the banging more urgent, almost violent. And it didn't stop until way past five in the morning.

He left the seedy hotel early, as he did every day. His first stop was always the small Catholic church just a couple of blocks from where he was staying. He found it insulting that such a dirty and sleazy hotel used by prostitutes and drug pushers could be so close to a place of worship. Once he'd found what he was looking for, he'd never set foot in this city again. This was no city of angels; this was the city of sins. The city of devils.

By nine in the morning the temperature was no higher than

fifty-three. Most of the people on the streets were wearing coats with their collars high around their necks. An unshaven man in a stained T-shirt and ripped jacket was sitting by the entrance to a disused shop trying to hide from the wind. He scratched his expanding stomach and drank from a bottle in a brown paper bag. Their eyes met and the tramp extended his hand, hoping for some charity. The man felt a surge of anger crawl up his spine, and he wrapped his fingers tightly around the oddly shaped metal crucifix in his pocket, fighting the urge to punch and kick the beggar until he bled. They must've stared at each other for half a minute. The man felt the skin on the palm of his hand rupture as the edges of the crucifix dug into his flesh. His hand became sticky with blood.

'Thank you, Lord,' he whispered to himself before finally breaking eye contact with the drunken man and forcing himself to carry on walking.

He stood by the side of the road waiting for the lights to turn red. Traffic was urgent. His throat felt dry and he massaged his neck, rotating his head from left to right. He caught a glimpse of something on the newspaper stand and went rigid. His eyes widened and his jaw dropped open. He couldn't believe what he was seeing. He felt his whole body shiver and his heart hammer the inside of his chest with incredible ferocity. God was on his side, he was now certain of it.

Seventy-Eight

High schools don't come much larger than Gardena Senior High. Its grounds occupied half a city block. Sports were clearly encouraged. There were thirty playing courts divided among tennis, basketball and volleyball, not to mention the two baseball fields and the regulation football one that doubled as a soccer pitch. Thirty buildings hosted over a hundred student classes, and the library housed enough books to give City Hall a run for its money.

Garcia parked in one of the three large car parks inside the grounds and made his presence known at the reception desk. A thirtysomething, exotic-looking receptionist of mixed race scrutinized his badge while ignoring the ringing phone line. She peeled her eyes away from his shield, flipped a sheet of black hair over her shoulders and looked at Garcia's face before checking her log. 'Principal Kennedy's very busy today.'

'Well, so am I, honey,' Garcia replied. 'I won't take much of his time, but I do need to speak to him.'

She flicked her hair once again. 'He's with a student's parents, but he's supposed to be finished in about five minutes.'

'Five minutes I can wait.'

Six minutes later, Principal Kevin Kennedy welcomed Garcia into his office. He was a serious-looking man in his late forties, as tall as Garcia but better built, with dark hair combed back Dracula-style. His face looked honest and trustworthy. The kind of face high school students would respect. He wore stylish thin-rimmed glasses and a crisp and well-fitting light gray suit. He welcomed Garcia with a warmish smile and a firm handshake.

'Please have a seat, detective,' Principal Kennedy said, indicating one of the black leather chairs in front of his large rosewood desk. Garcia scanned the spacious office. There were pretty paintings and framed degrees on the walls. Dozens of tiny primitive figures adorned several wooden shelves. Two metal filing cabinets sat to the left of the principal's desk. The large window on the east wall overlooked the main students' playing area outside. Kennedy stood by it.

'I'm sorry about keeping you waiting,' he said, giving Garcia a sympathetic smile with a nervous edge. 'Even though the students broke for Christmas vacation five days ago, things are still a little crazy, made more hectic by the fact that today is the last day of the faculty. You're lucky that you came in today; tomorrow you would've found nobody here. So, how can I help you, detective?'

Garcia explained about Amanda Reilly and how keen they were to find any information concerning the people she used to hang out with when she was a student at Gardena High. Principal Kennedy pressed a few keys on his computer keyboard and repositioned his monitor so Garcia could have a better look.

'We've migrated many of our past students' records into an electronic database,' he explained, 'but not all. At least not yet. It's a slow, expensive and lengthy process and it requires manpower, something that at the moment we're experiencing a shortage of.' Another edgy smile. 'Anyway, our records wouldn't mention her friends. This is pretty much all I have on this Amanda Reilly.'

Garcia read the information on Kennedy's computer screen. It revealed nothing that Hopkins hadn't yet found out. 'How about yearbooks?' he asked.

Principal Kennedy pushed his glasses up his nose. His expression didn't fill Garcia with hope. 'We used to have a section in our library dedicated to yearbooks,' he explained. 'We had a copy from every year, but a few years ago they started disappearing.'

'Stolen?'

'That's what we figured. The problem is some kids steal out of habit. It's not because they really want or need the particular item they're stealing.'

Garcia smiled.

'I'm sorry,' Kennedy said half embarrassed, remembering he was talking to a detective. 'I guess you know all this already. Anyway, most of our old yearbooks were taken.'

'You didn't order new copies?'

'Yes, once.'

Garcia leaned back in his chair. 'Stolen again?'

Kennedy nodded. 'We thought about reordering them one more time, but the printing company we used for several of our early yearbooks burned down a few years ago.'

Garcia let out a defeated sigh.

'A lot of them were stolen, but not all. Let me check if we're in luck.' Kennedy reached for the phone on his desk and dialed the library internal line, replacing the receiver on its cradle after a quick conversation. 'Mrs. Adams, our librarian, will check and let us know. Can I offer you a drink in the meantime? Coffee, water?'

Garcia declined with a quick head shake.

The phone on Principal Kennedy's desk rang and he answered it promptly. His conversation was restricted to – 'OK' and 'I see'.

'I'm sorry.' He shook his head sadly. 'That whole decade is gone, not a single yearbook left.'

Garcia pinched the bridge of his nose as he wondered what to do next.

The phone rang again. Kennedy excused himself and answered it. He looked at Garcia and lifted both eyebrows. 'That's a good idea, Mrs. Adams. Thank you.'

'Some hope?' Garcia asked.

'Mrs. Adams suggested you take a look at the basement storage rooms in the main building. I forgot about them. We keep a lot of very old stuff there. Mrs. Adams reminded me that there are boxes and boxes of old photographs taken by the photography clubs. The ones that didn't make the yearbooks.' He smiled confidently. 'I'd say that's your best bet.'

Garcia's eyes lit up. 'How do I gain access to them?'

'You need to talk to old Mr. Davis. He might even help you look through them. He's been the janitor here at Gardena High for over forty years. He still takes care of the gardens. He's the only one who'll have the keys to the old storage rooms.'

'Where can I find him?' Garcia asked, standing up.

'He lives in the staff quarters, number 3C if I'm not mistaken.' Kennedy intuitively gestured towards the large window. 'You can try his door, but today is his day off. If he's not around, try the Roosevelt Memorial Park. It's about a five-minute walk from here.'

Garcia's brow creased. 'Memorial Park?'

Kennedy nodded. 'His wife is buried there. He spends most of his free time talking to her.' He shrugged as if that was a crazy thing to do.

Seventy-Nine

Darnell Douglas observed the man checking out the raven-black Cadillac Escalade in the lot with eager eyes. He'd been a cars salesman for fifteen years, and if there was one thing he was proud of, it was his ability to split the real buyers from the bull-shitters just by looking at them. And the tall gentleman wearing the dark, expensive-looking overcoat was as real as they got.

Darnell quickly checked his reflection against the shop window. He was a good-looking black man with a shaved head and a perfectly trimmed goatee over a squared jaw. He centered his blue and white checked tie and made his way towards the customer.

This one is all mine. 'It's a beauty, isn't it?' he said, giving the customer a welcoming but not overenthusiastic smile.

The man nodded and walked around to the front of the car.

'It's only got four thousand miles on the clock. The owner had to get rid of it. Financial problems.'

The customer walked over to the driver's door and pulled it open. Both the exterior and interior were in pristine condition.

'It still has that new car smell, doesn't it?' Darnell said, but kept his distance. He knew good buyers didn't like to be crowded. He waited a few more seconds before offering a new piece of information. 'The great thing is that this is a new car with a used-car price tag.'

'OK to sit inside?' the man finally asked in a Texan twang.

'Of course.' Darnell nodded. 'You won't find a more comfortable car. Cadillacs are the American Rolls-Royces.'

The man took a seat and held the steering wheel with both hands just like a kid in a playground. A pleased smile graced his lips for a split of a second and Darnell knew he had him.

'What kind of mileage do I get with this?' the man asked, his hands still on the wheel.

'Twelve miles per gallon in the city, nineteen on the highway.'

'Really?'

'I'm telling you, this bad boy rocks.'

The smile returned to the man's lips.

'I'll tell you what,' Darnell said, coming up to the open driver's door. 'I'll go get the keys and we can take this baby for a spin. What do you say?'

The man paused for a moment, considering it. 'OK.' He nodded.

'Great, I'll be right back, Mr . . .?'

'Turner.' The man extended his hand. 'Ryan Turner.'

Eighty

Garcia knocked on the door numbered 3C for a whole minute without a response. Roosevelt Memorial Park was literally across the road from Gardena Senior High. With the description of Mr. Davis Principal Kennedy had given him, it didn't take long for Garcia to find the kind-looking man in his late sixties sitting alone on a stone bench in front of a very peaceful rose garden. He wore a flop-brim hat that reminded Garcia of his grandfather. His wrinkled lips were moving, murmuring something only he could hear.

'Mr. Davis?' Garcia asked, coming up to the bench.

The old man looked up, startled at hearing his name. He saw Garcia towering over him and squinted as if looking directly into the sun, searching the thousands of faces in his memory for a match.

'My name's Carlos Garcia.'

The squinting intensified. The old man's memory now searching for the name.

'You don't know me,' Garcia said, displaying his badge and ending the old man's struggle to remember. 'I'm a detective with the LAPD.' For the moment he thought it was better not to mention he was with Homicide Special. Those two words together tend to make most regular citizens nervous.

'Is there a problem?' Mr. Davis asked in a frail and worried voice. 'Has there been an accident in the school?' The concern in his eyes was touching.

Garcia smiled gently and told him that there was no need for alarm. He explained the reason for his surprise visit but was careful not to mention that Amanda Reilly had been murdered.

'Principal Kennedy said you could allow me access to the storage rooms and maybe even help me look through the pictures.'

'I'd love to help if I can.' The old man nodded before forcing his tired body to stand up. His gaze went back to the rose garden, and he raised a liver-spotted hand in a half wave. 'Goodbye, Bella. I'll be back in two days.'

The large rose garden at the Roosevelt Memorial Park is where cremated remains are scattered. In a respectful gesture, Garcia nodded at it as if also saying goodbye.

The storage rooms were at the end of the long, dimly lit, brick-walled basement corridor of the main building in Gardena Senior High. The cobwebs and the heavy stale smell were a clear indication that not many people ventured down here.

Mr. Davis unlocked the door of the main storage room and pushed it open. 'Most of the old photograph boxes are stored in here,' he said, flicking on the light switch.

They stood at the entrance of a large room cluttered with old desks and chairs, disused gym equipment and hundreds of cardboard boxes stacked on wooden shelves that covered three of the four walls. Dust was everywhere, and the corridor's stale smell had intensified five-fold inside the room. The light bulbs that hung from the ceiling on thin wires were old and dim.

Garcia coughed a couple of times and waved his hand in front of his face like a fan, but that just circulated the dust even more. 'Jesus!' he said as his eyes scanned the disheartening number of boxes. 'Where do we start?'

Mr. Davis gave him an encouraging smile. 'It's not so bad. I spent many of my free days in these rooms, trying to organize what we have.'

Garcia arched an eyebrow.

'I hate not having anything to do.' He started moving around the many broken, old-fashioned wooden desks. 'It's a way of keeping busy.' He shrugged.

The damp and cold room made Garcia's fingers hurt, and he rubbed the scars on the palms of his hands for a few seconds.

'What year are we looking for?' Mr. Davis asked, approaching the boxes stacked on the east wall.

'She dropped out of school in '85.'

Mr. Davis's eyes scanned the boxes in front of him. 'It should be right at that end.' He pointed to the opposite wall.

It didn't take Garcia long to find four large boxes marked '1985'. 'Here we go.' He pulled them out of the shelves and placed them on the floor. From his pocket he retrieved a photograph of Amanda Reilly they'd gotten from Tania Riggs. 'This is the only picture I have of Amanda. It was taken just a year ago. Let's hope she hasn't changed much.'

The old man took it from Garcia's hand and studied it for a few seconds. 'She does look familiar,' he said, nodding at the picture.

There must've been over two thousand photographs inside the four boxes. Individual ones, group pictures, whole classes together, students having fun and goofing around, playing sports, studying and eating lunch. Some were clearly posed and some captured the students naturally – laughing, angry, crying. Garcia and Mr. Davis started the lengthy process of going through them and trying to identify someone they'd never really met. The school janitor would stop every once in a while as flashes of memory came back to him and he'd tell Garcia a quick story concerning the students in the picture. They'd been flipping through photographs for hours when Mr. Davis stopped and squinted at one, bringing it up closer to his face.

'Let me see that picture you have of this Amanda girl again,' he said, extending his hand.

Garcia handed him the photo and waited impatiently.

'Here she is,' Mr. Davis said with a pleased smile after just a few seconds. He handed Garcia both photos. The picture in question was of a group of four girls dressed in what looked to be expensive, designer clothes. All of them in full makeup. Two of them were laughing, one had an amused look on her face and the last one was sideways, looking down. They were standing by one of the school's basketball courts where several kids were bouncing a ball behind them. Garcia didn't have to ask. She had certainly changed, but there was no doubt the second girl from the left was Amanda Reilly. They were all stunning in their own right, but Amanda certainly stood out. She was drop-dead gorgeous. A light wind was blowing her shoulder-length blond hair away from her face. She was one of the girls who were laughing, and even frozen in time her laughter seemed contagious.

'I remember that group of girls,' Mr. Davis said with a melancholic grin. 'They were always together, and all the boys—' he shook his head and the grin widened as he remembered '—they were crazy for them. But these girls, they didn't wanna know.'

'What do you mean? Didn't they have boyfriends?'

'Oh yeah, but if my memory serves me right, they weren't boys from this school. They were older, I think.'

'Do you remember any of these girls' names?'

Mr. Davis laughed. 'My memory is good, detective, but not that good.'

Garcia nodded and returned his attention to the picture. 'No way,' he murmured after a few seconds, squinting at the photograph.

'What? Something the matter?' Mr. Davis asked, craning his neck.

'Do you have a magnifying glass or something like that?' Garcia asked without taking his eyes off the picture.

The old man smiled and pulled an old-fashioned Swiss army knife from his belt. It contained everything, from pliers to a screwdriver, a bottle opener and a small magnifying lens. 'I knew this would come in handy someday.' He handed it to Garcia, who quickly brought it to his eye, scrutinizing the picture for what seemed like an eternity. His mouth went dry.

'I'll be goddamned.'

Eighty-One

They drove down Yukon Avenue and turned left into Artesia Boulevard. Darnell Douglas was at the wheel. Ryan Turner sat comfortably in the passenger's seat, his eyes studying the car's interior.

'It feels like a very smooth ride,' Ryan said casually.

'Oh, it is. This is a V8, 6.2-liter engine as smooth as aged whiskey.' Darnell's eyes stole a peek at Ryan. 'Do you drink, Ryan?'

'I occasionally enjoy a good whiskey, yeah.'

'Oh, you'll enjoy this more, believe me.'

'I'm sure.'

Darnell knew it was time to play the cool salesman. 'I'll tell you what, Ryan.' He pulled over to the side of the road. 'I'm not supposed to do this, because we haven't properly filled in a form back at the office, but you need to drive this puppy to really get a feel for it.'

Ryan's eyebrows lifted in surprise.

The 'nice salesman who breaks the rules' routine always worked for Darnell. It was a buddy-bonding thing. Give and take trust.

'We can hook onto San Diego Freeway and you can let it rip for a while.'

'You sure?' Ryan looked uncertain.

'Yeah, why not? You look like a pretty decent and responsible guy. I think I can trust you.'

Ryan held Darnell's gaze for a few seconds.

'Seriously, if this car doesn't blow your mind, no car will.'

'OK.' Ryan nodded before unlocking the passenger's door and walking the longest way around, buying himself a few seconds.

'*This one's in the bag,*' Darnell thought.

'So what do you do, Ryan?' he asked as Ryan took his seat behind the wheel.

'I'm a doctor.' He buckled up.

'Wow.'

'I'm an anesthetist.'

'Ooh.' Darnell shook his whole body in a shiver.

'Something wrong?'

Darnell made a bitter face. 'I really don't like needles, you know? They freak the fuck out of me.'

Ryan's hand wrapped around the syringe in his pocket and he smiled.

'Yeah . . .' He stared into Darnell's eyes. His voice guttural. 'I already knew that.'

They say that when it comes to danger and fear, human beings are just like any other animal. We can sense it. Some primitive instinct inside alerts us. And something inside Darnell was screaming for him to get the hell out of that car.

Ryan pressed the central locking button and smiled. 'Guess what?' he whispered. 'I know what scares you to death.'

Eighty-Two

In Compton High, Hunter got his hands on a 1985 students'
yearbook – Father Fabian's graduating year. He also managed
to dig up some of his old report cards and records. The young
priest had been suspended seven times during his junior year.
The interesting fact was that all seven suspensions had been
requested by the same teacher – Mrs. Patricia Reed, who taught
algebra 2, the priest's weakest subject, according to his grades.
Teachers tend to remember their worst students better than
their best ones. If anybody would remember Brett Stewart
Nichols, Patricia Reed would, Hunter was certain of that.

The day was sliding from pale blue to dark night when
Hunter walked into his office. Garcia had arrived only a couple
of minutes before him and was standing in front of the picture
board, attentively studying one of the photos. He turned and
faced Hunter.

'You won't believe what I found.' Excitement coated his
words as he wiggled a six by twelve photo in his hand.

Hunter arched an eyebrow and took a few steps towards his
partner.

'I got this from an old storage room in Gardena High.' He
handed Hunter the photo.

'Storage room?'

Garcia quickly summarized his day at Gardena High before

stabbing at the picture with his index finger. 'Second girl from the left.'

Hunter studied the girl Garcia had indicated. It didn't take him long. 'Amanda Reilly,' he said confidently.

'That's right.' Garcia retrieved an old-fashioned, Sherlock Holmes-style magnifying glass from his desk and handed it to Hunter. 'But that's not all. Take a look at the last girl on the right, the one who has a sort of amused look on her face.'

Hunter analyzed the picture once again, this time for a while longer. There was nothing peculiar about the girl, and he was about to ask Garcia 'What about her?' when he saw it and stopped.

'You're kidding me?'

'Looks familiar?' Garcia said, arching his eyebrows.

Hunter turned to the picture board and unpinned the woman's photo they'd found on the fireplace inside the Malibu mansion. The one with the number two written on the back. He brought it back to his desk and sat it next to the schoolgirls' photo. His eyes jumped from one picture to the other several times before he looked at Garcia. 'It's her.'

Garcia nodded slowly. 'That's what I thought, but I didn't have that photo with me.' He pointed to the woman's picture on Hunter's desk. 'I needed to come back here to confirm it. Now I'm positive. They went to the same school, Robert. Amanda and the alleged second victim hung out together.'

'What's her name? Who is she?'

'That, I still don't know.'

'Did you get a yearbook?'

Garcia told him about the stolen yearbooks and the burned down printer. 'The school might have a graduating picture, but I'm not sure. As I said, I needed to first confirm my suspicion, and by the time I got out of the storage room everyone was gone. Today was the last day for the faculty. The school is closed for the holidays.' Garcia returned to his desk. 'If they have a graduating picture and it hasn't been stolen, it will probably be in the library.'

'Won't this Mr. Davis have the keys?'

'Probably, but I wouldn't know where to start. Their library is massive. I would've ended up just wasting time. We need the librarian or someone who works there, and as of today they're all on vacation.'

Hunter thought it over. 'OK, let's try and get back in contact with the school principal or anyone who might know where to find these graduating pictures.' He glanced at the girls' photograph. 'Two out of four girls on that picture are dead. The other two are probably in great danger. We need to find them, and we need to find them fast.'

Clang. The office door slammed shut with a thundering noise, making both detectives turn around. Captain Blake was standing inside the room. She looked furious.

'What the fuck do you two think you're doing?' The question was spat out between clenched teeth.

Eighty-Three

Both detectives frowned as they exchanged puzzled looks before facing the captain.

'Are you sure you're yelling at the *right* detectives, captain?' Hunter answered, cocking his eyebrows.

Captain Blake's piercing gaze focused on him. 'Are you sure you wanna get cute with me today, Robert?'

Hunter straightened his body. 'Captain, we were out all day. I have no idea what you're talking about.' He looked at Garcia.

'Me neither.' Garcia shook his head, his stare jumping from Hunter to Captain Blake.

'Would you care to explain?' Hunter said calmly.

'I thought I'd made myself clear about you going after that psychic girl, if that's what she is.'

Hunter's confused look intensified. 'Did she call?'

'How the hell would I know that? Do I look like your personal answering service?'

Hunter glanced at Garcia, who was staring at the captain wide-eyed. 'Maybe you should get to the point before that bulging vein on your forehead pops, captain. We still don't know what this is all about.'

'Did you see the paper today?'

Garcia shook his head. Hunter held a blank stare.

'Oh, I forgot. You don't read the paper 'cos it depresses you, isn't that what you said?'

Hunter was in no mood to carry on with the irony game. 'What's in the paper, captain?'

'The two of you – front page.' Captain Blake slammed the copy of the *LA Times* she had with her on Hunter's desk. The paper was folded in half. A black and white photograph of Hunter and Garcia sitting at an outside table in the company of a young woman occupied a quarter of the page. Hunter snatched the paper. Garcia joined him by his desk, trying to read the article over Hunter's shoulder. The girl in the picture was Mollie Woods.

Hunter read the small article in silence. It went on to explain how detectives Robert Hunter and Carlos Garcia of the HSS were so stuck for leads in their investigation into the murders of Father Fabian and Amanda Reilly that they had to resort to asking for the help of a psychic girl. The article had been written by Claire Anderson.

'Bitch,' Hunter murmured.

Garcia grabbed the paper from Hunter when he was done.

'You went behind my back on this,' the captain said angrily.

'We were just talking to her, captain, listening to what she had to say. That's what we do in investigations, remember? We talk to people, we ask around.'

'According to that article, you asked her to help with the investigation. Did you do that?'

No reply.

'Without clearing it with your superior officer? In this case, me.' The captain stood with her hands on her hips.

Hunter ran a hand over his face and breathed out. 'It's psychology, captain.'

'What?'

'She was nervous, hesitant. I had to make her feel at ease and unthreatened. By telling her that we *needed* her help I shifted the power balance.'

'So you *did* ask her for her help?' the captain pressed.

'It was a play on words to get her to talk to us, captain. I'm the lead detective in this investigation. I did what I thought I should do. That's how I work.'

'Hold on.' Captain Blake lifted a hand, stopping Hunter and glaring at him. 'Did you just throw a title at me? You're the lead detective in this investigation because I said so, a decision I'm starting to regret. We've now become the laughing stock of LA's law-enforcement agencies. The article called us the *mystic police*, Robert. The *tarot cops*.' She paused, and her stare bounced between Hunter and Garcia for a while. 'No surprise the mayor's been on the phone screaming like a lunatic, and he's now accusing me of being unable to run this department properly. He said I lack authority, unlike my predecessor. Do you know how much that pissed me off?' She didn't wait for a reply. 'He's on a crusade to get you busted down to traffic duty if not off the force for good, and let me tell you, he's gaining momentum.' She started pacing the room. 'I told you I wanted this to go by the book. That if you found this girl, you were to bring her here. She needed to be interviewed under caution and I wanted to observe.'

Hunter rubbed his eyes and leaned against his desk. 'She was *scared*, captain,' he said slowly. 'She wanted to talk, but not here. She felt nervous in the interrogation room. She wanted to meet in a public place.'

'So you disobeyed my order because that's what she wanted?'

'I had to make a decision, captain,' he replied firmly. 'Go by the book or hear what she had to say. We couldn't have both.'

'How the fuck did the paper get to know what we talked about?' Garcia asked. 'High-powered directional mikes?'

Hunter shook his head. 'Eavesdropping could lead to prosecution. Claire Anderson can be a bitch, but she ain't stupid, she wouldn't risk it. Plus, if she had eavesdropped, she would've published everything Mollie told us about what she saw.'

'And what exactly is it that this girl told you?' The annoyance in the captain's voice was now reaching new heights.

Hunter related the whole conversation he and Garcia had had with Mollie Woods the day before. The captain listened without interrupting, her perfectly threaded eyebrows lifting slightly at times, showing surprise.

'She knew about the numbering?' the captain asked, her eyes fixed on Hunter, who nodded in silence.

'I've always been skeptical about this whole extrasensory perception thing, captain,' Garcia interrupted. 'But after yesterday, I think this girl's the real deal.'

'Even if she is, the fact of the matter is that you disobeyed my orders. You made me and this whole department look stupid.' She paused for a moment, considering what to do. 'It's obvious that your reporter friend has talked to this Mollie girl. Now, she's gonna have a ton of reporters descending on her. Where is she?'

Silence.

'Don't fucking tell me you don't know.'

'I told her we needed to keep in touch. She said she'd call me today. She hasn't yet.'

'Why don't you call her?'

'She doesn't have a cell phone.'

The captain let out a deep breath. 'Did she tell you where she lives?'

'No, and I couldn't force her.' Hunter took a seat behind his desk.

'We won't be able to find out either, will we?' The captain massaged her neck, trying to relax her tense shoulder muscles. 'She's too young to have a proper tenant agreement, and I'll be very surprised if she used her real name to rent a room anywhere. If she saw the papers, and my guess is that she did, she's running scared. The problem is, vision or not, she knows details about this investigation that can't be leaked. Do you understand what I'm saying, Robert?' Her voice calm and authoritative. 'You're not the only one who knows psychology. If some of these reporters catch up with her, they'll persuade her to talk, I can guarantee you that. Find her.' She opened the door but spun around before leaving to face both detectives. 'If you ever pull another stunt like this or disobey a direct order from me again, I swear to God the next job you'll be doing will involve touching shit with your hands.' The door slammed behind her hard enough to make the room shake.

Garcia punctured the silence that followed with a nervous sigh. 'Do you have any idea where Mollie could be?'

'I'll find her,' Hunter replied. 'Trust me.'

Eighty-Four

The luxurious Hilton Hotel in Beverly Hills – known as the Beverly Hilton – stands imposingly at number 9876 Wilshire Boulevard. Just a short walk away from the famous Rodeo Drive and Century City, the hotel is a favorite retreat for stars and for those who appreciate being treated like one.

At 8:30 p.m. Hunter sat alone at a corner table near the entrance to the busy and stylish lobby bar. Other than the small saucer filled with assorted peanuts, the only other object on the table was an empty whiskey tumbler. His eyes followed a well-dressed thirtysomething man as he walked in and grabbed the attention of the absurdly tanned barman. Hunter waited a few seconds before approaching him. They talked for less than a minute.

Trader Vic's Lounge, a meticulously decorated Polynesian-themed indoor/outdoor restaurant and cocktail bar, is one of two gourmet restaurants inside the Beverly Hilton. That's where the well-dressed man had come from. That's where Hunter was heading.

She was sitting alone, sipping champagne at a candlelit table by the east wall.

'Have you seen any famous people yet?' he asked, standing in front of her table. 'I heard this place is a must if you wanna play spot the celebrity, but I haven't seen any.' He smiled. 'I probably wouldn't recognize them anyway. I don't watch much TV and I barely go to the movies.'

She put her glass down and stared at him, surprised. It took her a few seconds to overcome the shock and string a sentence together. 'What the hell are you doing here?'

'What, are you kidding? This is one of my favorite hang-outs.'

Claire Anderson chuckled cynically. 'Somehow I doubt that very much, Detective Hunter. But the blazer and tie suit you.'

Hunter adjusted his tie. 'Thanks. I thought we were past the Detective Hunter and Miss Anderson phase.'

'How in the world did you know I'd be here tonight, *Robert*?'

Hunter frowned. 'Is that a serious question? Maybe the hint is in what I do for a living.'

'Oh yes, I forgot. The mighty Robert Hunter. Shouldn't you be using your powers to look for a sadistic serial killer instead of stalking me?'

'You should talk about stalking.' He took the empty seat directly in front of her. 'You wrote the book on it.'

'What're you doing? You can't sit there. I'm with someone.'

'You mean the married guy in the shiny new dark gray suit, short black hair with a cleft chin?' Hunter nodded and screwed up his face at the same time. 'He left.'

'What?' Her face dropped in realization. 'That was you, wasn't it?'

Hunter's expression indicated he didn't know what she was talking about.

'The maître d' came over a moment ago and whispered something into Sean's ear. He excused himself and said he'd be right back. That was you.'

Hunter didn't answer.

'Who told you Sean was married?'

Hunter leaned back and crossed his legs. 'I didn't really come here to talk about your date, Claire.'

The maître d' came over to announce that their starter was ready. Claire was about to send it back, but Hunter got in before her.

'It's OK, you can serve it.' He turned to Claire. 'You ordered it, we might as well eat it.'

'You're an asshole.' She ran her hand through her shiny hair, which she had straightened to perfection.

'Your hair looks nice that way,' Hunter said, disarming her for an instant.

A tall waiter returned with their starters. 'Excuse me. What's this?' Hunter asked, pointing to the plate in front of him.

'Crab Rangoon folded in a wonton skin with cream cheese,' the waiter answered with a polite smile. 'Anything wrong, sir?'

'No, no. That's fine.'

'I guess you're upset about the article today?' Claire said after the waiter left.

'The article didn't bother me in the least.' Hunter pointed to the jug of iced water on the table. 'Is it OK if I have some water?'

'Knock yourself out.'

He poured himself a glass and had a sip. 'What did piss me off no end was the picture.'

'Why? I thought you looked quite cute,' she teased.

'She's just a girl, Claire.' Hunter's tone went from playful to morbidly serious. 'You put her life at risk.'

'What the hell are you talking about?' Claire shot back.

'You think psychopathic killers don't read the papers?'

'So?'

Hunter shook his head. 'You didn't do your homework

properly, did you? Many killers have an agenda, which they'll do *anything* to complete. If they feel that agenda is threatened in any way by someone or something, they tend to try and eliminate that threat. In your article you not only made it clear that she was a threat to the killer, but you also gave him her picture. He now knows what she looks like.'

Eighty-Five

Claire stopped picking at the fancy food and stared at Hunter uncomfortably. Her smile vanished. 'Do you think she's in danger?'

'It's a little too late to be asking that question, don't you think? If you wanna be a crime reporter, it stands to reason that you maintain a good relationship with the people in the force, especially detectives.' He stopped and waved his hand. 'Oh, that's me.' His irony was back. 'You could've called and run the story by me before going to press. It's actually common practice. That way you don't piss us off, we get to have a first look at what kind of bullshit you're about to print, and if there's anything we judge detrimental to the investigation we can ask you to omit it. By doing that, you keep us sweet and – who knows? – we might even share some information.'

'I tried calling,' she shot back with irritation. 'But you didn't return any of my calls. Do you even check your messages?'

Hunter ran his hand over his mouth. 'How did you get her to talk to you?'

'I've got my methods.'

'You just sounded like a torturer.'

'There was no torture.' Claire shook her head and smiled.

Hunter glared. 'You lied to her, didn't you? What did you

say? That you worked with me and you needed a few more details?'

Another enigmatic smile.

'You bitch.'

'Fuck you, Robert. I tried talking to you, but you didn't wanna know.' Her voice got louder, and some of the neighboring tables sent a disapproving look their way.

'You tried taking me back to your place. You call that talking?'

'Fuck you. Don't come telling me how I should do my job.'

'Someone should, 'cos you're obviously fucking it up.'

'Only an arrogant bastard like you could call getting a story on the front page of the *LA Times* "fucking it up".'

'It's not a story, Claire; it's a case, and people's lives are at stake.' Hunter paused for a deep breath. 'You scared her away. I need to find her before something happens.'

Claire narrowed her eyes. 'You want my help, don't you?'

'Do you know where she is?'

'Wait a second. You did all this, played the macho detective, scared my date away, called me incompetent and now you ask me for my help?' She leaned back on her chair and put on a snobbish face. 'Oh, this is rich. No wonder you have no wife or girlfriend. You have no tact with women.'

Hunter kept silent, his eyes holding Claire's.

'If I tell you where to find her, what information will you send my way?'

Hunter's eyes narrowed. 'Are you serious?'

She studied him for a second. 'Dead serious.'

'Have some decency, Claire. She's just a girl, and she's probably scared shitless. I'm just asking you to do the right thing.'

'If you rub my back, I'll rub yours.' A whisper of seduction in her voice. 'Nothing in this world is free. At least not the good things.' She gave Hunter the same inviting wink she'd given him the first time they met.

'Her life could be in danger.'

No reaction.

'You don't give a shit, do you?'

'A lot of people die every day in this city, Robert. It's a fact of life. We can't save everyone.'

'But we *can* help this girl. That's all I'm asking.'

'And all I'm asking is for something in return.'

Hunter's cell phone went off. He held Claire's gaze for a tense moment.

'Aren't you gonna answer that?' she asked, conscious that heads were starting to turn.

Hunter reached into his jacket pocket. 'Detective Hunter.'

'Detective, it's Monica.' A quick pause. 'I mean, Mollie.' She sounded like she was crying.

Hunter turned away from Claire. 'Are you OK? Where are you?' he asked, but the only reply he got was static noise. He quickly covered the mouthpiece with his hand and looked back at the reporter. 'You're wrong, Claire—' getting up, he placed five twenty-dollar bills on the table '—there're a lot of good things in this world that are free.'

Eighty-Six

Hunter covered the twenty-five miles between Beverly Hills and South Gate in record time. Mollie had told him she'd be waiting in a coffee shop called Café Kashmir in Tweedy Boulevard. Hunter didn't need the address; he knew the place.

After parking his Buick just outside, Hunter entered the café. At 10:35 p.m., it surprised him how busy it was. Even more surprising was that all of the customers seemed to be younger than twenty-five. Mollie was sitting at a round table by a terracotta-brick wall adorned with several oil paintings – a young artist's exposition. A small rucksack sat by her feet.

'Hello,' he said, smiling as he joined her. She tried to mirror it but failed. The sleepless night and apprehension showed on her face. Telltale dark circles. Bloodshot eyes. Flushed cheeks. She closed the notebook she was scribbling on and put it away.

'You write?'

Mollie looked embarrassed. 'Ah, it's nothing. Children's stories.'

Hunter sat down. 'When I was young I dreamed of becoming a writer someday.'

'Really?'

'I loved reading so much that it seemed only natural.'

Mollie looked at her rucksack where she'd just stuffed her notebook. 'Me too.'

'Were you thinking of going away?'

'I made a mistake coming to Los Angeles.' Her voice was firm, but it lacked conviction.

'Do you think if you'd gone someplace else you would've avoided the visions?' Hunter asked.

No answer. No eye contact.

Hunter let the moment pass. 'I'm hungry,' he said, turning to look at the cake display on the counter. 'I'd love some cheesecake or something. How about you?'

Mollie looked unsure.

'C'mon. I feel really guilty eating cake by myself. Just to keep me company. What do you say? How about a slice of that chocolate one?' He pointed to a chocolate gateau on the top shelf of the display.

She hesitated for an instant before nodding. 'OK.'

'Hot chocolate?' He gestured towards the empty mug on the table.

'Yes.'

A minute later Hunter returned with two slices of cake, a coffee and a hot chocolate. As Mollie stirred her drink, Hunter noticed that her fingernails had been chewed to the nail beds.

'I'm sorry,' she said, fidgeting with her teaspoon.

'You've got nothing to be sorry about.'

'The woman I talked to. I didn't know she was a reporter. She said she was working with you. I never told her I was a psychic. You've gotta believe me.'

'I believe you, and it's not your fault,' he replied in a serene tone. 'Unfortunately, this city is full of people who will do anything to try and get ahead. I'm the one who's sorry for exposing you like that. I should've known better.'

Hunter retrieved a brand-new cell phone from his pocket and handed it to Mollie. He explained that his and Garcia's number were already programmed into it and the phone had the latest GPS chip. It was the easiest way for them to keep in contact. She promised never to turn it off.

'The photo in the paper,' she said after a short silence. 'I'm scared someone might recognize me.'

Hunter picked up on her fear. 'And maybe tell your father?'

Unconsciously, she ran her right hand over her left arm.

'Did he do that to you?'

She looked up with questioning eyes.

'The broken arm?' Hunter nodded at her arm.

'How did you know?'

'Just observation, really,' he said with a subtle head shake.

She looked at her arm and at the minor irregular curvature just past her elbow. When she spoke, her voice carried a mixture of anger and sadness. 'He beat me up almost every day.'

Hunter listened while Mollie told him about the beatings. The broken arm and fingers. And the never-ending hate her father had for her, simply because she was born a girl. She told him how much she missed her mother and how her father blamed her for her death. She still never told Hunter about the sexual abuse. She didn't have to.

Hunter clenched his hands as he thought of the many psychological scars and how they'd affect Mollie for the rest of her life.

'I know you're scared, Mollie. But running away isn't the answer. It never is.'

'It's the only answer I have,' she shot back. 'You don't know what it's like. You don't know what it's been like.' Her voice urgent. 'My father will never give up.'

'I'm not trying to tell you what to do, Mollie,' Hunter said in an even voice.

'So don't.'

Hunter regarded her. Her reaction had been generated by fear, not anger. The same fear that made her run away and kept her running. The same fear that seemed to fuel her existence.

'I'm sorry. I didn't mean to make you angry.'

Mollie took a deep breath and looked down at her mug. A whole minute passed before Hunter spoke.

'You sounded very worried on the phone, Mollie. Did something happen?'

'I had another vision,' she announced quickly and in a steady voice.

Hunter leaned forward.

'After I saw my picture in the paper this morning I panicked. I wanted to run away again.' She pointed to the rucksack at her feet. 'I made it all the way to the Greyhound Bus Station.'

'Where would you go?'

Mollie coughed a laugh. 'Anywhere the little money I had could take me. I didn't care. I just wanted to get away from here.'

'And the vision changed your mind?' Hunter asked.

Mollie nodded and started fidgeting with the teaspoon again. 'It happened while I was at the station, trying to decide where to go.'

'What did you see?'

Her eyes met his and Hunter saw fear.

'The visions, since they came back, are very different from the ones I had when I was younger.'

'You said they're now in the first person and sometimes they aren't silent anymore.' Hunter nodded.

'What I saw today wasn't a person or a place or anything

like that. It didn't play like a film. But I know it was something very important to the killer.'

Hunter waited.

'I saw a date.'

He craned his neck. 'What date?'

Mollie took a deep breath and shuddered. 'New Year's Day.'

Eighty-Seven

Garcia picked Hunter up at 7:00 a.m.

After a marathon of phone calls the night before, Mrs. Adams, Gardena High School's librarian, had agreed to meet them at the school at 7:30.

'I found Mollie,' Hunter said as Garcia joined Hollywood Freeway heading northwest.

The statement caught Garcia by surprise, and he glanced at Hunter. 'What, really? How?'

'Actually, she found me. She called me last night.'

'What did she say? Where is she?'

'It took some convincing, but I booked her a room at the Travel Inn just a few blocks from my apartment.'

'You booked her a room? Is she OK?' Garcia asked, concerned.

'She's scared. She was about to run away.'

'Where to?'

Hunter tilted his head. 'Anywhere but here.'

Garcia thought about it for a moment. 'Because of the newspaper article?'

Hunter nodded. 'She told me a little bit more about herself last night. She was abused in every possible way. She's terrified her father will find her.'

'How can you guarantee she won't run away from us again?'

'I can't. But I'm earning her trust.'

Garcia knew no one who inspired trust more than Hunter.

'I gave her a prepaid cell phone. Our numbers are pro-grammed in and it's equipped with GPS. I told her never to turn it off.'

They hit heavy traffic as they merged into Harbor Freeway.

'She had another vision.'

Garcia stared at Hunter in anticipation. 'A new victim?'

A quick head shake and Garcia let out a relieved breath. 'What did she see this time?'

Hunter ran through everything Mollie had told him the night before. Traffic started to ooze through, but Garcia didn't notice.

'New Year's Day? What does it mean?'

'I'm not sure, but Mollie was certain it meant something to the killer. Something important.'

'Maybe it's when the killer plans to strike again,' Garcia ventured.

Hunter closed his eyes and massaged his forehead. 'Or the day he plans to end it. Maybe it means that they'll all be dead by New Year's Day.'

'All? How many is all?'

'I'm not sure, but whatever she meant by New Year's Day, it doesn't give us much time.'

'Nine days, to be exact.'

Hunter understood and shared Garcia's frustration. So far they had nothing concrete, no real leads, just suppositions based on the little they knew and the visions of a seventeen-year-old girl.

Angry drivers sounded their horns. Garcia inched his car forward.

'Did she see any reasoning behind any of this? Why the killer is going after these people? Anything to do with the schools or the students at all?'

A quick head shake.

They drove the rest of the way in silence.

Eighty-Eight

Hunter and Garcia arrived at Gardena High fifteen minutes late.

Mrs. Adams was a plump, cheery-looking woman of almost sixty with perfectly coiffed silver hair and a heartwarming smile. She was glad to help and directed both detectives to an archives room filled with storage boxes at the back of the library.

'The boxes are all labeled by year.' Mrs. Adams's voice was as sweet as her pale green eyes.

Hunter turned to her. She was almost a foot shorter than him. 'Thank you very much for your kindness, Mrs. Adams. We'll be OK now.'

She hesitated at the door.

'We won't make a mess.' Hunter smiled. 'I promise.'

'If you need me, I'll be in the main library floor.' She closed the door behind her.

From a folder he'd brought with him, Hunter retrieved the picture of the four girls Garcia had gotten from the old storage room the day before. He placed it on a large table in the center of the room. He also retrieved the male photograph they'd found on the fireplace in the house in Malibu. If the second victim had been a student in Gardena High, there was a chance so had the first one.

'This was taken in 1985.' Hunter pointed to the girls' photo. 'Let's include that year and go two above and one below – from '84 to '87.'

Garcia frowned.

'Just because these girls hung out together doesn't necessarily mean they were in the same class,' Hunter explained.

They pulled the relevant boxes out of the shelves and it didn't take them long to find four black and white thirty-six- by twenty-four-millimeter photographs of the graduating classes. Hunter started at the top, class of '87, the year Amanda Reilly would've graduated if she hadn't dropped out of school. There were a hundred and twenty-six tightly packed students in the photo.

Using a magnifying glass, he took his time jumping from the graduating photo to the girls and the unidentified first victim one, comparing every face until he was sure.

Nothing.

He moved on to the next picture, and the slow, comparing process started again. Twenty-five frustrating minutes later, Hunter struck gold.

'I found her.'

'Who?' Garcia looked up excitedly.

'Our victim number two.' Hunter turned the picture around and pointed to a girl hidden behind two quarterback-looking boys on the second to last line of students. Only her face was visible.

Garcia used his magnifying glass, his eyes bouncing between pictures. 'It's her alright.'

Hunter consulted the name sheet attached to the back of the photo. 'Her name's Debbie Howard.' He quickly got on the phone to Hopkins with the news, asking him to dig out everything he could on Miss Howard.

It took Garcia another twenty-five minutes to find the first of the remaining two girls – Emily Wells, class of '84. Fifteen minutes later Hunter spotted the last one – Jessica Pierce, class of '85. They'd been through all the pictures as thoroughly as they could. Victim number one wasn't in any of them. They were both very sure of it.

Emily Wells and Jessica Pierce's names were immediately passed on to Hopkins and the Investigative Analysis Unit.

'Find them,' was all Hunter said.

Eighty-Nine

The address they had for Patricia Reed, Father Fabian's old algebra 2 teacher, was in Pomona, the fifth-largest city in Los Angeles County and home to the famous California State Polytechnic University (Cal Poly). In stop-and-go traffic, the drive from Gardena Senior High took them an hour and a half.

Minnequa Drive was a quiet street about ten minutes away from Cal Poly, and they had no problem finding the building they were looking for. Modern in style and set back from the street, the large two-story house was fronted by several perfectly trimmed hedges, a small patch of grass to the left and a two-car garage to the right. A black Dodge Journey was parked in the lavish black-and-white-checked paved driveway.

'Wow, this is quite a nice retirement home,' Garcia said, parking on the street in front of the house. 'Nice ride too.'

They climbed the railed granite steps that led to the front door and rang the bell. After a few moments it was answered by a diminutive, wiry Mexican woman in her thirties dressed in a uniform like a hotel maid's. Her black hair was bundled tightly under a hairnet.

'Good morning,' Hunter said with a pleasant smile, quickly returning his badge to his pocket. He knew from experience that many private house workers in LA were illegal immigrants.

A police badge only causes them to panic. 'We're looking for Mrs. Reed.'

'Mista Reed?' the maid replied in heavy accented English, returning the smile.

'No, no. Mrs. Reed. Patricia Reed.'

'Ah. *No hay*. No Mrs. Reed.'

'What do you mean, no Mrs. Reed? She isn't home?'

'No. *Ella se ha ido para siempre*.'

Hunter frowned. 'She's gone forever?'

'What's the problem, Emilia?' A man in his early forties dressed in a gray pinstripe wool suit with a light blue tab-collar shirt and a blue-on-blue striped tie appeared at the end of the entrance hall. He was tall, well built and movie-star handsome, with dark blue eyes and a strong, squared jaw.

The maid turned to face him. '*Creo que estos señores están en busca de su madre*, Mr. Reed.'

'*Esta bien*, Emilia, *tranquilo*. I'll talk to them.' He motioned her to go back to her duties.

'Good morning, gentlemen. I'm James Reed,' the man said as he got to the door. 'Can I help you?'

'I understand by what Emilia said that Patricia Reed is your mother?' Hunter asked in a polite tone.

'I thought you said you didn't understand Spanish,' Garcia said under his breath.

'Patricia Reed was my mother. She passed away five months ago.'

'We're sorry to hear that. We didn't know.'

'What's this about, gentlemen?'

Hunter and Garcia introduced themselves, going over the customary badge-displaying ritual.

'We were hoping to ask her a few questions about one of her old students from Compton High,' Hunter said.

A look of interest came over Reed's face. 'What year are you talking about?'

'1984, 1985?'

'I was a student at Compton High in '84. It was my freshman year. I graduated in 1987.'

'Really?' Hunter's interest grew. 'Would you mind looking at some pictures for us? Maybe you might remember them.'

Reed checked his watch and screwed up his face. 'I'm a professor at Cal Poly. I'm due in class soon. I've got only about an hour before I have to leave. Could you come back later this evening, maybe?'

'It shouldn't take more than ten, fifteen minutes max,' Hunter pressed.

'I've got some papers I still have to go over. I have very little time.'

'It's very important, Mr. Reed,' Hunter stated.

Reed studied both men before relenting. 'Please come in,' he said, showing them inside.

Ninety

James Reed's living room had a hardwood floor and an L-shaped sofa that faced a large wall-mounted flat-screen TV. The curtains were drawn shut. The only light came from a single pedestal lamp in a corner, positioned to illuminate a large round table. On it, thousands of pieces of an unfinished jigsaw puzzle were perfectly separated into color groups. All the border pieces had already been assembled, forming a large rectangular frame. Reed was an aficionado and very organized, Hunter noted.

'Seven and a half thousand pieces,' Reed confirmed, following Hunter's gaze. 'It won't take me long to finish it,' he admitted proudly. 'I only started it yesterday. Do you like jigsaw puzzles, detective?'

Hunter looked up from the pieces on the table. 'I do.'

'There's no better exercise for a human's analytical and visual mind.' Reed paused by the table. His eyes studied the pieces and he picked one up, slotting it into place at the top right-hand corner. 'It's also very therapeutic,' he said before motioning both detectives to the seating area.

Hunter and Garcia sat on the sofa while Reed took the antique-looking chair facing them.

'Is it a particular student you're after?' Read asked, crossing his legs and resting his hands on his knees.

'Yes,' Hunter replied, placing the old Compton High year-book on the glass coffee table in front of them and flipping it open. 'He wasn't from your year. Three years your senior. His name's Brett Stewart Nichols.'

James Reed tensed and shuffled on his seat.

'This is him.' Hunter pointed to the photograph in the center of the page – a skinny kid with wild black hair and energetic dark brown eyes.

Reed made no effort to look at it. His unflinching eyes stayed on Hunter. 'I don't need to look at the picture. I remember him.'

'What do you remember about him?'

Reed ran a hand over his mouth a couple of times as he searched for the right words. 'He . . . wasn't a very nice person.'

'What do you mean?'

'What did he do, detective? Did he kill someone? That wouldn't surprise me. In school he could easily have been classed as a psychopath in the making.'

Neither detectives were expecting that statement.

'Why do you say that? Can you tell us a little more about him?'

Reed leaned back, his shoulders tense. 'He was a bully. He didn't go to school to learn. School was just a place full of weaker kids he and his friends could push around.'

'Did he push you around?' Hunter watched every subtle movement and reaction.

Reed chuckled nervously before retrieving a cherry ChapStick from his pocket and running it over his lips. 'They pushed everyone around. It didn't matter what grade you were in. They didn't care. People were scared of them.'

'Scared?'

'You know, when the word bully was used back then, people

just imagined a foul-mouthed pupil calling other students names. Maybe teasing them because they were a little over-weight or dressed funny or weren't very good at sports, but not Brett and his friends. If you could imagine a modern-day street gangster with a severe attitude problem being taken back in time, then you'd probably come close to what kind of person Brett was.' Reed paused and scratched his chin apprehensively. 'There was this girl I remember. Katherine, I think her name was. She wasn't in my class. I was a freshman, she was a junior, but I remember she was quite shy, very chubby, always by her-self. She wasn't an attractive girl – strange, hawk-like nose, unaligned teeth, bad hair and deep-set eyes behind big thick glasses. Brett and his friends loved tormenting her. Every time they saw her they'd make loud pig noises and call her names. Anyway, one day, I think it was during fifth period, they fol-lowed her into a bathroom and while she was in her cubicle, from over the partition of the adjacent one, they poured a bucket of human excrement over her.'

Garcia grimaced.

'Did anyone see Brett doing it?' Hunter asked.

'No, but everyone knew no one else in Compton High would've been capable of something like that.'

'Nobody ever notified the authorities or the school princi-pal?' Garcia asked.

'I don't think there were any witnesses to that specific incident.'

'How about bullying in general?' Hunter asked. 'Did they simply get away with it all the time?'

Reed looked at Hunter. 'Do you understand how bullying works, detective?'

Hunter met his stare. 'Yes. Intimidation.'

'That's right, intimidation, and they were very good at it. In and out of school. They'd do things like what they did to this Katherine girl just for fun. No reason, no major grudge against anyone, just because they liked pushing people around and it made them laugh. Imagine what they'd do if you crossed them and they wanted to get back at you.'

'This gang you refer to, how many were there? Could you point them out to us?' Hunter pushed the yearbook towards Reed.

'I can't really remember.' Reed shrugged, ignoring the book. 'It was twenty-five years ago. I was a freshman, Brett was a senior. I tried my best to keep out of their way, as did everyone else. But Brett wasn't the worst one. He wasn't the—' he drew quotation marks in the air '—leader.'

Hunter exchanged a quick look with Garcia. 'So who was?'

Reed pinched his lip for a moment. 'You still haven't told me what this is about, detective. Is he wanted for questioning?'

'Not exactly,' Hunter replied.

Reed studied Hunter and Garcia. 'Wait a minute. You guys are homicide, right? Did someone finally kill Brett?' A thin smile played on his lips.

'Do you think someone would have reason to?'

'Did you listen to anything I said?' Reed frowned. 'They terrorized everyone in that school. Some students and at least one teacher quit Compton High because of them. It wouldn't surprise me at all if they became hardened criminals after they left school.'

Hunter leaned forward, resting his elbows on his knees. 'Would it surprise you if I told you Brett Stewart Nichols became a Catholic priest?'

Reed stared at both detectives. 'Are you serious?'

No reply.

'They say redemption isn't beyond anyone, but yes, that would surprise me immensely.'

'The leader,' Garcia questioned again, pushing the open year-book closer to Reed. 'Who was he?'

Reed's eyes finally drifted towards the book. For a minute he flipped through the pages before pausing and glaring at a picture on the bottom left-hand corner for a long while. A nervous muscle flexed on his jaw as he tapped the photo with his right index finger.

'Him.'

Ninety-One

The picture Reed had pointed out showed a pale-faced boy with full lips, cat-like menacing dark eyes and shoulder-length black hair. The name under the picture read Peter Elder.

Hunter wrote the name down in his black notebook. 'What do you remember about him?'

'I already told you. They were bullies and I stayed out of their way. There's nothing else I can say.'

'Anyone else you recognize?' Garcia pressed. 'The rest of their gang, maybe?'

'No,' Reed said curtly, closing the yearbook with a thump and pushing it back in Hunter's direction.

'How about any of these girls?' Hunter showed Reed the photograph of Amanda Reilly's girl group.

Reed looked at it attentively for almost a minute before shaking his head. 'No, I never saw them in school.' His eyes stayed on the picture.

'They weren't students at Compton High. I was wondering if you might've seen them hanging around outside school, maybe with Brett and Peter's gang?'

'We're talking twentysomething years ago, detective. Unfortunately, I don't have a photographic memory. And as I said, I did everything I could to stay out of their way.' Reed checked his watch. 'This has gone way over fifteen minutes, detective. I really have to get going.'

'As a teacher, your mother suspended Brett seven times, didn't she?' Hunter pushed.

'That's right.' The answer came with a hint of indignation. 'My mother was a very good and proud teacher. She always did what she thought should be done in any given situation. She refused to be intimidated by anyone, never mind a pushy student.'

'Did he threaten her after he was suspended?'

'Brett and Peter didn't threat. They acted.' The muscle in his jaw flexed again.

'What did he do?'

The question made Reed edgy. 'Gentlemen, I really have to go. I have a class to teach.' He sprang to his feet, and both detectives stood. Reed motioned his guests towards the door.

As Hunter walked past the large table with the jigsaw puzzle he paused, studied the pieces for a few seconds, reached for one and slotted it in place.

Reed glared at him.

'Lucky guess,' Hunter said, shrugging.

At the door Reed's eyes narrowed and a look of recognition came over his face. 'Wait a second. Now I remember where I've seen you two before. You were in the paper yesterday. The Tarot Cops, right? Something to do with enlisting the help of a young girl who claims to be psychic.'

'You shouldn't believe everything you read in the papers,' Garcia shot back.

'A priest was killed, isn't that right?' Reed continued. 'Decapitated? The papers are calling the killer the Executioner. You said Brett became a Catholic priest. Was he the one who was killed?' A flicker of satisfaction flashed in his eyes.

Hunter zipped up his jacket and nodded. 'Yes, Brett Stewart Nichols was savagely murdered.' He waited for a reaction from Reed but got none. 'Thanks for your time and help, Mr. Reed.'

'All the best with your investigation, detective.' Reed closed the door calmly. A satisfied smile spread across his thin, ascetic face.

Outside, Hunter reached for his phone and called Hopkins again. 'Ian, listen, there's one more thing I need you to investigate . . .'

Ninety-Two

Today was an important and proud day for young police officer Shauna Williams. It was her first-ever solo patrol.

Shauna was born in Inglewood, a tough neighborhood in southwestern LA. The youngest of four siblings, she was also the only girl. In school, contrary to all her brothers, she was dedicated and studious. Her grades only occasionally fell under B+. Tall and athletic, Shauna played shooting guard for the basketball team and third base in varsity softball. She was the first and only of all four Williams to ever graduate from high school. Maybe, if things had turned out differently, she would've also been the first in her family to have ever gone to university.

Shauna knew her brothers were involved in bad things, she just didn't know how bad. It's hard to grow up in an underprivileged neighborhood in a city like Los Angeles and not be affected by the crazy gang culture that rules the streets. Being African-American, for some reason, seemed to make it even harder. She'll never forget the night she opened the door to a couple of police officers who'd come to give her parents the worst news any parent can ever get. All three of her brothers had been gunned down inside a stolen vehicle in what looked to be a gang retaliation hit. She had just turned nineteen.

Shauna gave up her dream of university and months later, after passing the recruitment tests, she joined the LAPD academy.

The six months of rigorous training that followed didn't bother her and Shauna graduated top of her class. Her ambition was to make detective or the SWAT team.

Shauna was assigned to the West Bureau Pacific Division and paired up with a more experienced officer, twelve years her senior. She's been out of the academy for only five months, but she was a quick learner, very intelligent and extremely focused. Lieutenant Cooper thought it was time Shauna did a few rounds by herself, and when her partner called in sick this morning, Cooper saw it as the perfect opportunity.

Shauna received a call from dispatch about a teenage disturbance near Marina Del Rey, just a few blocks away from where she was. The disturbance turned out to be nothing more than a couple of drunken kids making a mess and burning off steam near an abandoned construction site. Shauna was able to tactfully and quickly de-escalate the situation. As she returned to her vehicle, something caught her eye. A black Cadillac Escalade half hidden behind the unfinished building. She remembered an All Points Bulletin that circulated the day before about a black Cadillac car that'd been taken out from a dealer's in West Hollywood for a test drive and never went back. She checked her in-car computer – the plates matched.

Shauna called dispatch requesting more information and was told that the salesman, an African-American citizen named Darnell Douglas, had taken the car out for a quick test drive with a potential buyer. They had no information on who the customer was. No dangerous warnings had been issued. Shauna told dispatch that she was going to investigate.

The car's bodywork was intact – no bumps, no scratches. It didn't look to have been involved in any sort of accident. The doors were all locked. Shauna used her flashlight to illuminate the car's interior through the tinted windows – nothing suspect. The car was parked on a cemented area. No footprints showed around the vehicle.

Calling dispatch again, Shauna told them she was going into the building to make sure neither Darnell nor the unidentified customer were inside and in need of assistance. She'd call them back if she found anything.

The first room was large and full of construction debris. The air inside was heavy with the pungent fragrance of urine.

'Hello?' she called in a loud and firm voice. 'Anyone in here?'

No sound. Thick, once-clear plastic sheets had been used as a cheap substitute for doors. Shauna used her flashlight to push the ugly drapes aside and moved into the next room.

'Darnell, are you in here? LAPD. Anyone in need of assistance?'

Nothing.

Shauna cautiously moved deeper into the abandoned building. The further she went, the darker it got, the staler the air became – another empty room, and then another, and then another. Everything was quiet, but instinct told her something was wrong. She was about to go back when a gust of wind shifted a dirty plastic sheet door at the entrance to a room on the south wall. She caught a glimpse of something and her skin crawled.

Cop training took over, and Shauna reached for her gun before nervously moving towards the door in baby steps.

'Hello, Darnell?'

No reply.

'LAPD. Anyone in there?'

Silence.

Using her flashlight, she lifted the plastic sheet and stepped inside.

Shauna vomited five seconds later.

Ninety-Three

Debbie Howard, Amanda Reilly's old school friend and the possible second victim of the Executioner Killer, was an only child. She was brought up by her mother after her father left when she was eight years old. Her mother never remarried and now lives in an old people's home dedicated to dementia sufferers.

Just like Amanda Reilly, Debbie grew up in Gardena. She finished high school in 1986 and moved to Seattle shortly afterwards to study at Washington State University – School of Law. She graduated with honors and immediately landed a job with Foster Harvey, one of the largest law firms in the Pacific Northwest. Five years after joining the firm she married William Clark, an attorney and associate of Foster Harvey. Their marriage lasted only three and a half years. After her quick divorce, Debbie decided to leave the company and Seattle behind and head back to Los Angeles. Her record as a lawyer spoke for itself, and after passing the California bar exam she was offered a job with the Los Angeles District Attorney's office – Antelope Valley branch.

Debbie was intelligent, ambitious, pushy and a fierce opponent in a court of law. Since moving back to California, she tried and convicted over five hundred criminals, their offences ranging from misdemeanors to felonies and capital crimes. Two years ago she met, fell in love and married Jonathan Hale, a very successful architect. She was found dead in their home in the city of Lancaster two weeks ago. There was no mention of a number drawn onto her body.

By the time Hunter and Garcia got back to their office, Hopkins had already gathered all the information into a neatly typed two-page report.

'How did she die?' Hunter asked, checking the report.

'According to the detective I spoke to from the LA County Sheriff's Department, she was found dead inside her bathroom. Because the case is still open and the victim is a prosecutor from the LA DA's office, they wouldn't disclose any more information. I talked to Captain Blake and she got on the phone to them with an urgent and very demanding request.' Hopkins nodded. 'They'll share.'

'So where are the files?' Hunter pressed.

'On their way here. Detective Ross from the Sheriff's Department in Lancaster is making copies of everything they have on Debbie Howard's death. Captain Blake told them to send us whatever they could get their hands on, immediately. That was just half an hour ago. They should be here soon.'

'Good. What else you got?'

Information on Peter Elder, Father Fabian's high school buddy James Reed identified via the yearbook, was a lot easier to come by. He never graduated, and, unlike Brett, Peter never reformed. He escalated from bullying to shoplifting, muggings, armed robbery and finally homicide.

Hopkins handed the detectives Elder's shorter report.

'He's in CCI State Prison?' Garcia asked, surprised.

The California Correctional Institution State Prison in

Tehachapi is one of only three Californian prisons with a Security Housing Unit. The most secure area within a Level IV prison, designed to provide isolation and the highest possible coverage to maximum-security inmates.

'He was found at the scene of the crime covered in blood with a body at his feet – a shop owner,' Hopkins explained. 'The only reason he isn't sitting in death row is because of some technicality. The cops screwed up at the crime scene. He got life, with no possibility of parole.'

'How about the two other girls in the Gardena High photo?' Hunter stood up. 'Emily Wells and Jessica Pierce. Have we found them yet?'

A quick head shake. 'I've got several searches running at the same time, but so far nothing. You gotta give me a little more time.'

'Time is something we seem to be running out of very quickly,' Garcia said, glancing at Hunter. They didn't want to reveal Mollie's latest vision about New Year's Day.

'I was lucky with Debbie Howard's search,' Hopkins said. 'She opted for keeping her maiden name instead of taking on her husband's. That and the fact that she worked for the District Attorney's office made things a lot easier. Her name popped up almost instantly in the Homicide database query. Emily Wells and Jessica Pierce are probably married. I'll have to track down old records and possibly their parents. I'm working as fast as I can. I'll get there, but I need a few more hours.' He ran a hand over his tired-looking face.

'How about our possible first victim, the unidentified male and the watch search?' Garcia asked. 'Any luck?'

'Nothing so far from the personal possessions' inventories, but believe it or not, in this day and age, those inventories aren't entered into a database.' Hopkins shrugged as if he didn't get it. 'They are handwritten forms.'

Hunter threw his head back and let out a tired sigh while running both hands over his face. 'I'll get some people over to the morgues to go through those forms. We've gotta find this guy.'

Ninety-Four

Captain Blake entered the room without knocking. Her makeup seemed a little heavier than normal, and Hunter deducted it was to hide the dark circles under her eyes.

'Is this for real, Robert? Is Debbie Howard the second victim?' She tilted her head towards the pictures on the corkboard.

'There's a good possibility, yes. But I need the case files before I'm able to say for sure.'

'They'll be here soon,' the captain confirmed. 'A prosecutor with the DA's office?' she shook her head disapprovingly. 'The shit will certainly hit the fan once the chief of police and the mayor hear about this.'

'For now we're only checking leads, captain,' Hunter said calmly. 'No one has to hear about anything.'

'Since you made the front page of the *Times* yesterday, the chief wants a daily report from me on this investigation. He wants to keep an eye on us, the "Mystic Cops", as I'm sure so does the mayor.'

'So give him a report. Does anyone know you requested the files in connection with our investigation?'

The captain shot Hunter an arctic look. 'I'm not that dumb, Robert.'

'So we don't have to tell them, at least not yet.'

'Are you asking me to lie to the chief of police, Robert?'

'No, captain, just to manipulate the truth for a day or two.'

The captain glared at Hunter and then Garcia. 'What's your problem with authority and following rules, detective? Have you forgotten that we answer to the chief of police and the mayor? I'm not sure how William Bolter used to run this department, but lying and disobeying your superior's orders will no longer be officially sanctioned. Not as long as I'm captain. If we get confirmation that Debbie Howard really was our killer's second victim, it will make the report.' She paused. 'So what have we got so far?'

Hunter told her about the graduating pictures from Gardena Senior High and their meeting with James Reed.

'And this Peter Elder, the priest's old high school buddy, he's in CCI in Tehachapi?' she asked.

'A homicide crime scene that the cops messed up,' Hopkins confirmed. 'He should've been in San Quentin.'

'I'd like to talk to him ASAP, captain.' Hunter consulted his watch. 'How fast do you think we can get a prisoner's interview request?'

The captain sighed, looking at Peter Elder's file. 'Elder is in a maximum-security prison – Secure Housing Unit, Robert. Visitation privileges are few, if any. I'll need to send a formal request to the warden. Even if I overstress the urgency of it, it'd still probably take at least twenty-four hours.' She returned the file to Hunter's desk. 'I have a very good friend in the California Department of Corrections and Rehabilitation board, who might be able to speed things up. But how do you think this Peter Elder can help? He's been in prison for—' She made quick eye contact with Hopkins.

'Fourteen years,' he confirmed.

'My guess is that he hasn't seen his old school friend for at least that long.'

Hopkins checked his report. 'That's right, captain. His visitation records show only one name, his mother, and that stopped five years ago when she passed away.'

Hunter rubbed his eyes with the heels of his hands. 'We already know that Amanda Reilly and Debbie Howard were school friends,' Hunter pointed to the picture of the four girls together. 'But we've still to make a connection between the girls and a young Father Fabian. We know they didn't know each other from school, but look at this, captain.' Hunter called her attention to the large LA neighborhood map on the wall. 'Those pins indicate where Amanda and the young priest lived when they were teenagers, not that far from each other.' He picked Debbie Howard's report from his desk. 'Debbie lived in the same street as Amanda.'

'You think they were a gang?' the captain asked.

'Something like that.' Hunter nodded and leaned against the edge of his desk. 'But the only way I can confirm that is if we find someone who knew them when they were young. Someone who was a good friend, maybe part of the gang.' He pointed to Compton High's yearbook. 'Peter Elder is that someone.'

'And if he confirms your assumption, what do you get?'

'Motive.'

Everyone stood still. All eyes on Hunter.

Ninety-Five

'I'm listening, Robert,' the captain urged Hunter.

'Bullying.'

'Bullying? You mean school bullying?' the captain asked doubtfully.

'We found out today that in school Father Fabian was a bully, and a nasty one at that. He and his little gang of friends pushed students and teachers to their limits. Peter Elder was not only part of that gang, but according to James Reed he was the leader.'

'The priest was a bad bully in school?'

'Hard to believe, isn't it?' Garcia commented.

'Wait a second. Amanda and Debbie didn't go to their school.'

Hunter searched his desk. 'Have a look at this.' He handed the captain Amanda Reilly's high school records.

Her eyes scanned the sheet for a moment. 'Bad grades, a few detentions and poor attendance.' She shrugged. 'Half the students in LA have a record similar to this one. So she wasn't an exemplary student, and . . .?'

'Most bullies aren't.'

The captain's eyes widened. 'Are you saying she was a bully simply because her grades weren't good? That's quite a harsh conclusion, Robert.'

'No.' Hunter shook his head calmly. 'Look at the number of detentions she got.'

Another quick look at the sheet. 'Quite a few . . . your point is?'

'No student gets a load of detentions because of bad grades, captain. They've gotta be disruptive, argumentative, even aggressive. All I'm saying is that there's a good chance Amanda Reilly was also a bully. If she wasn't, she still might've hung out with Brett and Peter's gang.'

The captain considered this. 'You think this killer is going after the people who bullied him when he was young?'

'I think so.' Hunter nodded.

'That's over twenty years ago,' Hopkins commented. 'You think someone could hold a grudge for that long?'

'People can hold a grudge indefinitely,' Hunter answered. 'But I wouldn't call it a grudge in this case.'

The captain tucked a loose strand of hair behind her ear. 'Carry on.'

'Young people are very susceptible to psychological traumas. Teenagers are insecure by nature, no matter how tough they might want to appear. At that age the doors to those insecurities are wide open, and nothing is stopping a bully from going in and making a mess of their subconscious without them even knowing.'

'A mess strong enough that it'd make someone wanna do this?' the captain asked, pointing to the gruesome pictures of both murders.

'Bullying can be extremely destructive, leaving behind psychological scars that can take years to heal, if they ever do.'

'But why come after these people twentysomething years later, when their bullying days are well and truly over? You're not gonna tell me that Father Fabian and Amanda Reilly were still bullies, are you?'

'Psychological traumas can sit in someone's subconscious for years just waiting to come out.' Hunter approached the window and stared at the busy street down below. 'Haven't you ever wondered about homeless people?'

Everyone in the room frowned.

'Are you on medication? What the hell does that have to do with anything, Robert?' the captain asked, shaking her head.

'Sometimes, when I see a homeless person sitting in a corner, cold and hungry, I wonder how far back I'd have to trace that person's life to find the exact moment in time that broke him.' Hunter watched an old man cross the street below. 'It could be the moment he lost his job, or his wife, or his kid. It could be anything. But there's always something, captain. The proverbial "last straw". Everyone has a breaking point.' He faced the room. 'Now imagine if this killer was desperately bullied when he was a kid. His subconscious is full of rage and anger that not even he's aware of. Twenty-five years later, his life isn't going that well. He lost his job or his wife is about to leave him or whatever. He's at boiling point. Then finally the "last straw" happens. Something pulls the trigger inside his head and reopens the wound. All of a sudden, all that rage and anger isn't hidden in his subconscious anymore.'

'And he goes back to what he considers to be the root of everything bad. The bullying when he was a kid,' Garcia said, following Hunter's line of thought.

Hunter nodded. 'Whatever that "last straw" was, it's awakened a monster.'

'I can see that.' Captain Blake nodded at the picture board.

'In one of his journals,' Hunter continued, returning to his desk, 'Father Fabian mentions a group of street kids he used to hang out with, and from what we gathered those kids were bad news.'

'And you think maybe Amanda Reilly, Debbie Howard and Peter Elder were part of that group,' the captain commented.

'It's very possible.'

'So we aren't talking about school bullying,' the captain concluded. 'We're talking about street bullying.'

'Most students live close to the school they attend,' Hunter said evenly.

'Shit!' Captain Blake closed her eyes as she realized what Hunter meant. 'Double bullying. In and out of school. Double the possibility of a severe psychological trauma.'

'Bullies have favorite targets,' Hunter continued. 'Maybe, if I'm persuasive enough, I can get Peter Elder to identify them.'

'Why would he cooperate?' she challenged.

'Because he's got nothing to lose.'

Captain Blake let out a deep breath, but she was convinced. 'I'll put in a CCI prisoner interview request straight away and contact Clayton on the rehabilitations board. If we're lucky, we might get you in tomorrow.'

'That works.' Hunter nodded. 'I can drive. Tehachapi is less than two hours away.'

The captain retrieved Debbie Howard's file from Garcia's desk and read through the little information they had. 'How about Jonathan Hale, Debbie's husband?'

'I can't interview him without having read the case files. We don't even know exactly how she died.'

'I'll call Lancaster again,' the captain said resolutely, 'check where the hell these files are. They should've been here by now.'

The phone on Hunter's desk rang.

'Detective Hunter.' He listened for a few seconds before putting the phone down and facing everyone in the room. Even before he said a word, they all knew.

Ninety-Six

This time, Captain Blake wanted to see for herself the brutality the Executioner was capable of. They arrived at the derelict construction site in Marina Del Rey thirty-five minutes later. Several police vehicles were already at the scene. Hunter recognized Doctor Winston's silver convertible BMW parked next to the crime-lab van. A tall black female police officer was leaning against a black and white unit, being attended to by a paramedic.

'What have we got?' Hunter asked, approaching the officer who was standing by the yellow crime-scene tape at the building's entry point.

'I know very little, sir,' he replied, worried, and proceeded to explain about the APB put out on the black Cadillac the day before. 'Officer Williams—' he nodded in the direction of the tall officer with the paramedics '—located the vehicle about two hours ago. No occupants, so she decided to check in here.' He lifted his thumb over his shoulder. His gaze met Hunter's and he shook his head. 'God only knows what's in there.' He crossed himself.

Garcia popped a couple of anti-acids in his mouth, and Captain Blake frowned at him. They put on their Tyvek coveralls in silence. The expectation of what this new murder scene would bring seemed to electrify the air.

They stepped into the first room clattered with debris. The air was cold and pungent, laden with the sharp smell of urine and feces. The captain screwed up her face and cupped a hand over her nose. Moving through the plastic door drape at the far end of the squared structure, they delved deeper into the building. The uncomfortable cold intensified and the light got weaker the further they went. After clearing the fourth room, they saw the powerful brilliance of the forensic lights shining through the dirty plastic curtains at the door to a new area. A crime-lab agent was standing outside the door frame, his eyes gazing at a distant nothing. He didn't register the three new arrivals.

Hunter, Garcia and Captain Blake stepped into the brightly lit room together. The cold that'd accompanied them throughout the building evaporated from Hunter's body. Not because of the heat produced by the powerlights, but because of the extra blood his heart was pumping into his veins. It was beating twice as fast as moments ago. All three pairs of eyes stared at what occupied the center of the room.

'Sweet Jesus!' the captain whispered, bringing a trembling hand to her mouth.

Ninety-Seven

A naked black man was sitting in a high-back metal chair. His skin was a dull shade of gray. His head was slightly tilted back. Protruding from his open mouth was a thin, clear plastic tube. But what was causing Captain Blake to shiver wasn't the tube shoved deep down the man's throat. It was the two hundred and fifty ten-milliliter syringes filled with blood that had been plunged all over the man's body. From his eyes to his ears, head, torso, genitals, legs and feet.

Doctor Winston was standing to the right of the victim. He slowly approached both detectives and the RHD captain. Hunter had never seen him look so distressed. All four of them stood in silence. Captain Blake was the first to speak. Her usually calm and authoritative voice had a nervous quiver to it.

'The killer made the victim into a blood-filled pincushion?'

'In a way.' A small pause. 'Those syringes contain about fifty percent of all his blood.'

The captain's questioning stare moved from the doctor to Hunter.

'Without help, human beings won't survive if they lose over forty percent of their blood,' Hunter stated.

Garcia let out a constricted sigh.

'Are you telling me that the killer literally sucked the life out of the victim?' the captain asked.

'Ten milliliters at a time,' the doctor confirmed.

The scene was as abhorrent as it was hypnotic. Disgusting, but they couldn't peel their eyes away from it.

Gingerly, they approached the victim.

The sight of the two blood-filled syringes plunged into the man's open eyes were starting to churn Captain Blake's stomach. She forced herself to look away.

'The number?' Hunter asked.

In silence, Doctor Winston directed their attention to the victim's back. Centered between his shoulder blades and six inches long, the number five had been drawn in blood.

Hunter walked around to the front of the chair. 'What do we know of the victim?'

'His name was Darnell Douglas. Forty-one years old. Lived in West Hollywood with his wife of seven years.'

Hunter looked up.

'She hasn't been told yet,' the doctor confirmed with a sad head shake. 'He was a car salesman for Princeton Cars, also located in West Hollywood. You probably already heard how he disappeared yesterday after taking one of the vehicles from his shop out for a test drive.'

Hunter nodded.

'My team is dusting the entire car as we speak. If the killer left anything behind, we'll find it.'

'How did the killer manage to extract so much blood?' Garcia asked, cringing as he studied the syringes.

'Very good question,' the doctor agreed, 'and the answer is – very slowly.' He pointed to the internal midsection of the victim's right arm. 'As you all know, given its high-pressure blood flow, the arm's basilic vein is the preferred vein for venipuncture – taking blood. If you move a little closer, you'll notice that the basilic vein region in both arms have been pricked to exhaustion.'

Due to the victim's skin color, hematomas were hard to spot, but Hunter had already noticed the exaggerated number of needle pricks on the midsection of the victim's arms.

'If you try to extract blood from someone's leg or chest or anywhere but a venipuncture site using a syringe,' the doctor continued, 'unless you were lucky enough to have hit a vein, you'll get little, if any blood at all.'

Hunter thought about this for a second. 'So the killer extracted ten millileters of blood at a time from the victim's arms and then . . .' His words trailed off.

Doctor Winston nodded and pointed to the victim's neck, where tens of closely set pinpricks were visible on both sides. 'Not only the arms. He also used the neck veins. Every time he filled a syringe up, the killer needed a place to store it before moving to the next one.' He looked at Barbara Blake, who was now staring at him – mouth half open, eyes wide. 'So he didn't use the victim's body as a pincushion, Barbara. More of a storage unit.'

Oh God!

'The killer could've dragged this out for hours,' the doctor proceeded, 'and judging by what we've seen from the previous victims, I'm certain he did.'

'And he made him suffer,' Hunter noted.

'Immensely,' the doctor agreed. 'Every new syringe filled with blood was stabbed into the victim's body as opposed to inserted.' He pointed to each body part as he mentioned them. 'Eardrums, testicles, nipples and eyes were most likely the first to be stabbed, as they'd be the ones to cause the greatest amount of pain. In the less fleshy body parts like the face, shins, knees and so on, the needles hit bone.'

'The killer wouldn't have gone for the eyes early.' Hunter disagreed, having a closer look at the victim's face.

Doctor Winston and Captain Blake frowned.

'He would've wanted the victim to see the needles being plunged into him,' Hunter explained.

'Why?' The captain this time.

'Oh my God!' Garcia whispered, realizing what Hunter meant. 'The killer always goes after the victim's fear.' All eyes moved to him. 'Darnell Douglas was scared of needles.'

Ninety-Eight

The huge open-plan floor was a labyrinth of large and small desks. All of them piled high with books and cluttered with stacks of papers and photographs. Oversized computer monitors, telephones, framed family pictures and cuddly toys occupied whatever worktop space was left. There were no placards hanging from the ceilings. No names anywhere. No way of knowing who was who or who did what. The place sounded like a beehive, bustling with phone talk and keyboard clacks. Over two hundred people in total putting the final touches to the stories that would make the next morning's edition of the *LA Times*.

Claire Anderson sat at the far corner, facing a desk that looked more like a coffee table than a reporter's workstation. Even though she'd made the front page of yesterday's edition with her *serial killer/psychic girl* story, she was still on her trial period. Sure, yesterday's story had certainly won her a few Brownie points, but she knew that in this game there were no certainties. Yesterday's front page could easily become today's old news. She had to follow it up; she had to keep the buzz going. Instinct was telling her that she'd stumble onto something different.

A killer like no one had ever seen before, but she needed more information. Unfortunately, she was well aware that she'd pissed off the lead detective in the case. She couldn't allow this story to run away from her. She had to explore the angle that only she and no other reporter had found out – the psychic girl.

Last night at Trader Vic's Lounge, Claire had a feeling the phone call Hunter received at their table had something to do with the girl. But by the time she collected her coat and made it outside Hunter had gone. Not wanting to waste any time, Claire jumped into a cab and made her way back to the same old and squalid hotel in Lynwood where she'd followed the girl after her coffee shop meeting with Hunter and Garcia. But she was also gone. The tall, bald landlord at reception told Claire he hadn't seen the girl he called Monica since the previous night.

'You her friend?' he asked in an unrecognizable foreign accent. His breath stunk of booze. 'If you good friend you pay me the money she owes, huh? She no pay no rent for three weeks.' He lifted three long, bony fingers. Their nails crusted with dirt.

'I'm not that good a friend,' Claire replied, subtly covering her nose with her right hand. 'But I'll tell you what Mr . . .?'

'Petrosky. Pat Petrosky.'

'I'll tell you what, Pat.' She scribbled her name and number on a piece of paper and placed it on the counter. 'If you call me as soon as you see her again, and I mean the very same second, you can make yourself a hundred bucks. How does that sound?'

Pat read the note without picking it up. When he looked up, his eyes stopped at Claire's cleavage. 'OK, Claire. You got deal.'

Claire still hadn't heard a word from 'smelly-man'. She sat staring at her laptop screen, tapping a ballpoint pen against her teeth. She still had one trump card to play. By chance, she'd managed to track down one of Mollie's friends. A twenty-three-year-old waitress named Susan who used to work with her.

Claire's cell phone vibrated on the desk. She snatched it up. 'Claire Anderson here.'

It was the newspaper's phone operator. Claire didn't have a direct line. Reporters on trial periods never did, so any calls that came into the *LA Times* main switchboard asking for her were diverted to her cell phone.

'Miss Anderson, I've got someone on the phone for you,' the operator said.

'Someone, who?'

'He doesn't wanna give me his name. He called several times yesterday and a few this morning. I recognize the voice.'

'OK, put him through.' She heard a click. 'This is Claire Anderson.'

'*The reporter?*'

'Yes,' she chuckled, 'the reporter. What shall I call you?'

'*You can call me friend.*'

Claire squeezed her eyes and shook her head slowly as the term 'crackpot' entered her head. 'How can I help you, Mr. Friend?'

'*I was wondering if we could meet. Maybe we can help each other.*'

'And what would you like to meet about?'

No reply, only heavy breathing.

'Hello . . .? Are you still there?'

'*I'm here.*'

'So what would you like to meet about?'

'*Someone who in your article you called "the psychic girl".*'

Claire straightened her body and sat up. Something in his voice made her shiver.

'*She's not who you think she is.*'

Ninety-Nine

No one spoke for an entire minute. Captain Blake shifted from foot to foot. Garcia's suggestion that Darnell Douglas was scared of needles struck a chord on her. She didn't like them either.

'If he was scared of needles, what the hell is that tube coming out of his mouth?' Captain Blake finally asked pointing at Darnell. 'Did the killer force-feed him something?'

Doctor Winston rubbed his face, taking his time. 'I won't know for sure until I get the victim into my autopsy room, but I don't think so. This is an intubation tube.'

A new shiver kissed the back of the captain's neck. 'The killer intubated the victim? Why?'

'Look closely. What's missing?' The doctor's keen eyes challenged them.

Their stare moved back to the grotesque image of a man adorned with two hundred and fifty blood-filled syringes.

'I give up and I'm in no mood to play games, Jonathan,' the captain said firmly. 'What *is* missing?'

'Restraints,' Hunter said, moving closer. 'The victim ain't tied to the chair. He's just sitting there as if of his own free will.'

'Bingo.' Doctor Winston acknowledged it. 'Restraints wouldn't serve the purpose of this murder.'

'I don't get it.' Captain Blake shook her head. 'What do restraints have to do with the victim being intubated?'

'A tied-down victim wouldn't be able to move, but he'd certainly be able to wiggle his body about,' the doctor explained.

'Yeah, well, that ain't much of a fight, is it?' the captain countered, still looking puzzled.

'It is if you're trying to prick a vein,' Hunter offered.

'Correct again,' the doctor confirmed. 'All Mr. Douglas would've needed was a quick body wiggle and the killer's plan to catch a venipuncture site with a needle would've been fumbled. Knocking the victim unconscious would've given the killer no satisfaction either. He wanted the victim to be awake.'

'So the killer would've needed to completely immobilize the victim?' Garcia asked.

Doctor Winston took a deep breath. 'The killer would've needed to paralyze the victim.'

'Drugged?' Captain Blake asked.

'Most probably,' the doctor agreed. 'I'll need the lab results to confirm it, though.'

'A paralyzing agent that would've kept the subject conscious?' Hunter glanced at the doctor meaningfully.

'Not only conscious. I'm sure the killer wanted the victim to also retain feeling.'

'Oh man!' Garcia folded his arms tightly, as if the doctor's words had intensified the cold inside the room. 'Is there such a drug? A paralyzing agent that allows the subject to still feel everything?'

'Oh yes.' A quick nod. 'Quite a few, actually. And with the internet and the hundreds of clandestine drug sites, very easy to obtain.'

'Still—' Captain Blake cut in, shaking her head '—why intubate him?'

'Because whatever the killer used probably also paralyzed his diaphragm,' Hunter deducted. 'He would've suffocated because he wouldn't have been able to breathe. The killer needed him alive.'

'That's exactly what I was thinking,' Doctor Winston concurred. 'The tube fed him oxygen and kept him alive while the killer inflicted as much pain as anybody could possibly take.'

Captain Blake's cell phone rang and they all tensed. She moved to a corner of the room, and her conversation didn't last longer than a few seconds.

'You're in,' she said to Hunter as she rejoined the group. 'Clayton pulled a few strings and got you a prisoner's interview with Peter Elder in CCI first thing tomorrow morning, seven o'clock.' Her gaze returned to Darnell Douglas's body. 'We've gotta find the motherfucker who did this, and fast.'

After spending most of the night at the new crime scene with Doctor Winston, Hunter left for the California Correctional Institution State Prison in Tehachapi at 4:30 a.m. Garcia, on the other hand, had headed back to Parker Center at around 10:00 p.m. Hunter had asked him to come up with everything he could on Darnell Douglas, their new victim.

The information Garcia had gathered was patchy, but good enough to supply Hunter with what he was looking for.

Darnell hadn't gone to Compton or Gardena High, but as a teenager he'd lived just two streets away from Brett Stewart Nichols. That information flooded Hunter with excitement. His street gang theory was starting to come together.

Hunter had watched as Doctor Winston and two other crime-lab agents went through the laborious and painstaking process of extracting the two hundred and fifty blood-filled syringes from Darnell's body. Even though he wasn't expecting any results, Hunter knew that each syringe had to be tested for fingerprints. The doctor told him that he'd have the autopsy results by the time Hunter was done with his interview in CCI.

Hundred

The evening had started slowly and, as it progressed, all hope of it picking up was evaporating fast. Honey had been walking her beat in West Hollywood for the best part of three hours. So far, she'd managed to make only twenty-five measly bucks by blowing a hairy, curry-stinking driver on the backseat of his cab. Customers were getting harder to find. Street prostitution was risky and it paid badly, but for some older girls, or the ones who were too hooked on something to join one of the many escort services, massage parlors or named pimps scattered all over Los Angeles, there was no other alternative.

At twenty-one, Honey couldn't really be considered too old, but seven years of heavy heroin abuse had destroyed her once-beautiful features. She was too skinny, with sunken eyes, pitted skin, cracked lips and a distant, dozy gaze.

Honey was born Aisha Kemp in South Pasadena. Her beautiful golden-brown skin earned her the nickname 'Honey' even before she was able to walk. But if it's true that children learn by copying what they see, her fate had been sealed very early in her life.

Her father was an alcoholic who'd smoke crack cocaine in their living room while rocking baby Honey to sleep. Her absent mother was a street hooker who'd do anything for her next fix. The rows in their house were violent and constant and no one cared when hungry Honey cried. Honey experienced her first hangover before her tenth birthday, and got high for the first time just after it. At thirteen she lost her virginity to a group of street kids, and by the age of fourteen needles had become her new best friends.

Just like her mother, Honey quickly found out that her habit was an expensive one. When she told him she had no money, her street dealer offered her a hit in exchange for her spreading her legs for him and his friends. She simply smiled and nodded.

Suddenly, at the age of fifteen, Honey was propelled into a whole different world. A world where people were prepared to pay for the pleasures she could give them. She was a fast learner, and one of the first things she learned was that the fewer limits she had, the more customers and money she could get. Honey soon gained a reputation for being game for just about anything – pain, filth, submission, domination, abuse, humiliation, nothing was ever too bizarre. But that lifestyle, together with her excessive drinking and daily hits, took its toll on her body in just six years.

By the age of twenty, her skin had lost its smoothness and glow; her weight had plummeted into an almost anorexic state and her hair was so thin she couldn't go anywhere without a wig. Even with all the makeup she applied, no one would really consider her an attractive woman. The big payers didn't search the streets for company. They called agencies and sex dealers from the comfort of their hotel rooms or the back of their limousines. At twenty-one, Honey was left with only the drunk, dirty and stingy street sex seekers.

The drizzling rain only made matters worse, and Honey was already accepting that twenty-five dollars was all she'd be taking home today. Not enough for her daily fix, but she was hoping maybe Cliff would be willing to work something out. She knew exactly what he liked.

She had just re-applied her red lipstick and kissed the excess onto a paper tissue when she noticed a man in his forties checking her out from across the street. She smiled but got no reply. The man looked away timidly. Money bells started ringing in Honey's ears as she recognized the man for what he was – an out-of-town tourist. She waited for him to make eye contact with her again, which he did in five seconds flat. Honey was an expert at the flirting game, and within a minute she'd gotten the inviting smile she was looking for. She took off her coat, perked up her perfectly round breasts and checked her cleavage before crossing the road.

'Hello,' she said in her lilting twang as she approached the tourist. 'I'm Honey.' She offered her hand.

'Hello, Honey.'

'Wow, you have fantastically strong hands,' she said in an overly seductive voice. 'I bet you're all muscular under those clothes, aren't you?'

He tilted his head sideways gently, too shy to agree.

'I'd love it if you showed it to me.' A sexy wink. 'Maybe I can show you what I have under my clothes too.' She gave him a little twirl. 'Would you like that?'

'I think so.' He smiled, crinkles appearing in the corners of his eyes. 'I've only got a hundred dollars.' He looked embarrassed.

Yes. She reached for his hand. 'A hundred dollars can buy you a lotta pleasure with Honey, babe.'

Hundred and One

The room was illuminated only by a tacky, pink-neon *Playboy* bunny lamp, and everything about it was cheap. The flowery wallpaper, the dark chocolate carpet, the tasteless prints on the walls, the dirty drapes that hung from the windows and the bed that looked like it'd cave in if one more couple had sex on it.

'I'm just gonna go into the bathroom and get cleaned up, babe,' Honey said, running a hand softly over the tourist's cheek. 'When I come out, I hope you won't be wearing these many clothes. I know I won't be.'

Honey counted her money again. She knew better than to get paid at the end of it all. She made that mistake once, and all she got for her troubles was a black eye and a bloody lip.

She fixed her wig, checked her makeup and got rid of her clothes. Her underwear wasn't new. She couldn't even remember the last time she bought new underwear, but it was clean and she knew she wouldn't have it on for much longer. 'Let's go to work, girl,' she said to her reflection, pouting her lips.

The tourist was sitting at the edge of the bed still fully dressed. His hands between his knees, his chin against his chest.

'What's the matter, babe?' Honey knelt down in front of him.

He kept his eyes on the floor, too embarrassed to look at her. 'I . . . I've never done this before.'

Honey smiled and placed a hand on his leg, caressing it gently. 'Don't worry, babe. I have all the experience you need.'

'Do you mind if I go get cleaned up a little?'

'Of course not, hun. Take your time. I'll wait for you out here.' She shot him a sensual wink. 'With nothing on.'

Honey was in bed, naked, with her back against the uncomfortable metal headboard when the man came out of the bathroom. She had already rubbed and pinched her nipples so they were hard and pointing up. She always thought they were one of her best features. But her expression changed as the tourist stepped back into the room. He was wearing what to her seemed like a long, clear-plastic raincoat, and nothing else. She also noticed his massive erection.

'Wow, babe. That's quite kinky.' She sat up. 'I like kinky.'

'I'm here for you, Honey.' The man's shy voice and demeanor had vanished. His new tone covered Honey's whole body in goose bumps. She got out of bed and he took a step towards her. As he moved, the pink-neon light reflected on something in his right hand, and she froze. She'd seen that kind of glint before. She tried to scream, but he was too fast for her, bridging the space between them in a flash and covering her mouth with a powerful hand. He pressed his body hard against hers, and she felt his excitement brushing her thigh. Her terrified eyes found his, and the evil she saw in them made her wet herself.

'You'll have to kneel and pray,' he murmured, and she shivered in his arms. Only this morning she'd read about him in the paper. They called him 'The Slasher'.

He licked his lips slowly as he raised the blade to her neck and whispered in her ear. 'I'm your salvation, Honey.'

Hundred and Two

Hunter sat patiently at the metal table inside the small, all-white, private visiting room in the California Correctional Institution State Prison in Tehachapi. He heard the shuffle of chains being dragged across the corridor floor outside before the door to the room opened. The first person to walk in was a Hulk of a guard. His muscles about to rip through the fabric of his tightly stretched XXL uniform. His size dwarfing the person behind him, a pale-skinned, average-height man dressed all in white.

The same piece of chain that bound the man's hands together in front of his body ran a loop around his waist and continued down to his ankles, giving him just enough length to perform a geisha step. His hair was cut short, but Hunter noticed it was graying at the temples. His lips weren't as full as they were on the yearbook picture. A badly healed scar graced his left cheek. His eyes were still cat-like, but they'd lost all the menace in them. He stopped at the door and frowned as he saw Hunter.

'Who the fuck is this cherry, Dubal?' he asked Hulk guard, who shrugged indifferently before ushering the prisoner inside and sitting him across the table from his visitor.

'If you need anything, I'll be right outside,' Dubal said before allowing the thick door to slam shut behind him.

Peter Elder sat with his hands on his lap, his chin low and his shoulders slumped forward, but his eyes studied Hunter like a predator studied its prey.

'You must be a very important cop,' he said in a low voice.

Hunter was leaning back on his chair. His posture relaxed. 'Why's that?'

Elder smiled, revealing badly cared-for teeth. 'This ain't normal visitation hours; this ain't the normal visitation room. That's why I'm all chained up. Usually they just cuff my hands behind my back, but it's a long walk from the Security Housing Unit and they don't take any chances in here. You've gotta be somebody with weight and want something from me real bad to pull this room.'

'My name's Robert Hunter. I'm a detective with the Los Angeles Homicide Special Section.' Hunter showed him his badge.

'I don't give a shit about who you are or where you come from, cop. What I wanna know is what the fuck you want with me?'

Hunter studied the man in front of him for several silent seconds. 'Your help,' he said calmly.

Peter laughed loudly and placed his hands on the table. His chain rattling loudly against the metal. 'Why the fuck would I wanna help you, cop?'

Hunter understood that among inmates there was an unwritten rule that they should never help a cop. To them it was like betraying a brotherhood, snitching, jumping sides, and if other inmates found out, the consequences would be lethal. If Hunter wanted Peter Elder's help, he had to play his cards just right.

'Not help me. Help your friends.'

Elder's eyebrows arched. 'Friends?' He chuckled. 'Have you been smoking, cop? I've been in here for fourteen years, all of them spent in SHU.' He talked with no modulation. Every word was delivered in the same monotone as the last. 'I don't social-ize. I'm isolated from everything and everyone. Even my mail is restricted. All the friends I have live inside my head, cop.'

'The friends I'm talking about go way back. Way before you got in here.'

Elder looked up, interested.

'Do you remember a kid from Compton High called Brett Stewart Nichols?'

Elder leaned back in his chair with a hint of a smile. For an instant his gaze became distant, as if the past was playing before his eyes. When he spoke, there was a certain lift in his tone. 'This is about Brett?'

'Partially.'

'And that means what, exactly?'

Hunter took his time as he told Elder a slightly modified ver-sion of what had happened. 'We believe this killer is after your old group of friends.'

'From Compton High?'

'Not necessarily.'

'Would you fucking stop talking in riddles, cop. It's messing with my head. What does "not necessarily" mean?'

From a plastic folder Hunter produced the Gardena High photo with the four girls. 'These girls weren't students at Compton High.' He pushed the picture across the table. 'Do you recognize any of them?'

Elder stared at the photo for a long while before shaking his head. 'Nope,' he said coldly.

Hunter knew he was lying, but played along. 'I thought maybe some of these girls used to hang out with you and Brett after school.' He pulled the picture back and observed as Elder's eyes reluctantly broke away from it. 'The killer's killed two of them.'

'Which two?' The question came automatically. A nervous reflex from a concerned person.

'It doesn't matter,' Hunter shook his head. 'If these girls didn't hang out with you, then it doesn't matter. We're done here.' He made as if he was getting up.

'Wait a second.' Elder leaned forward. His voice a touch more urgent. 'Let me see that picture again.'

'Why?'

'It was a long time ago, cop. My brain has forgotten a lot. Maybe if I look at it again . . .'

Hunter slowly pushed the picture back towards Elder. This time the inmate held it with his chained hands. Hunter observed Elder. The way his eyes moved from one girl to another. There was no doubt his gaze concentrated mostly on the girl who was second from the left – Amanda Reilly.

Hundred and Three

'Which two have been killed?' Elder's cold voice had softened a touch.

'Do you remember any of them?' Hunter pressed.

Elder looked up, and his piercing eyes rested on Hunter. He blinked quickly a couple of times as if to clear his vision. The edges of his mouth curled up. 'You're the one who's on a tight schedule, cop.' The monotone was back. 'Trying to catch a killer and all. I already know my fate. I ain't ever coming out of here. You can play games all you like, it doesn't bother me. Maybe I do remember them, but first I wanna know which two have been killed.'

Peter Elder needed a reason to help. From the way he stared at Amanda Reilly, it was clear he was struggling with an emotion he hadn't felt in too many years. And the picture had certainly stirred some of it back to life. Hunter decided to gamble. 'The last two girls on the right – Debbie Howard and Jessica Pierce.'

Elder's face relaxed a fraction with relief. Hunter was certain he'd gambled correctly – time to roll the dice one more time. 'The others are all in danger, as is everyone who was part of your street group. We have reason to believe the next one on the killer's list will be the second girl from the left – Amanda Reilly. Do you know her?'

Peter Elder tensed. 'If you believe she's gonna be the next victim, why don't you protect her?'

'We can't find her. We think she's running scared. Our best chance is to catch the killer before he strikes again. We know those girls knew each other, but we still don't have a link between them and Brett.'

'And how will that help?'

Hunter leaned forward. 'Look, I know you guys bullied a few kids when you were young; it happens in every school in America. From what we have so far, it looks like that for some reason one of the kids you pushed around back then decided it's payback time.'

Elder frowned. 'That was about twenty-five years ago.'

'Some people don't ever forget.'

'But these girls weren't Compton High students. Why would the killer go after them?'

Hunter explained his street gang theory.

Elder used both hands to scratch his forehead. 'So you need me to confirm if you got it right. A pushed-around kid who decided to get his own back on our little gang.'

Hunter nodded.

'You didn't.'

'What do you mean?'

'Your theory is bullshit, cop.' Elder allowed his eyes to study the picture again and they mellowed. 'Some of us did hang out together.' He pointed to the last girl on the right. 'Debbs, one of the girls you said was killed, was one of them, and so was Mandy.' He pointed to Amanda Reilly. 'But this other girl who died, what did you say her name was?'

'Jessica Pierce.'

'I've never even seen her before. She didn't hang out with us; neither did the other one. So this killer of yours can't be going after my old street gang.'

'Your old gang – how many were you?'

Elder thought about it for a moment. 'Eight, counting me.'

Hunter pulled a new picture from his folder and slid it across the table. Elder switched his gaze from the girls' photo to the new one – a slender man with neatly trimmed fair hair leaning casually against a white wall. The one they got from the house in Malibu – the still unidentified first victim. Hunter observed Elder's eyes and expression. The recognition came within five seconds.

'He was the first victim,' Hunter announced.

Elder remained silent.

'Was he part of your street gang?'

Elder returned his clasped hands to his lap and considered what to say. 'Strutter was the craziest motherfucker I'd ever met.'

Hundred and Four

Hunter's brow creased slightly. 'Strutter?' he asked.

'That's what we called him. He was a huge Kiss fan and "Strutter" was his favorite song.'

'Good song,' Hunter agreed.

The smile that came to Elder's lips was genuine. 'He was a bad motherfucker, but a very cool guy. If there was a leader in the group, he'd be it. Strutter wasn't scared of shit, except wasps. He was very allergic to them. If one came flying around, Strutter was out of there like lightning.'

'Was he a student at Compton High?'

The smile turned into a laugh. 'Strutter wouldn't be caught dead inside a school. He hated the whole education thing. He used to say he could learn everything he'd ever need from the streets.' He studied the picture once again and shook his head almost sadly.

'What was his real name?'

'Fucked if I know, cop.' Elder chuckled. 'We just knew each other from the streets. I knew Brett's name because we were in school together. In the streets we called everyone by their nick-names – Strutter.' He pointed to the picture before moving to the girls' one. 'Mandy, Debbs. Brett was BS, and that didn't mean Brett Stewart. I was Kicker and then there were JayJay, Double D and Lipz.' Elder noticed Hunter's intrigued look and clarified. 'JayJay was a crazy, skinny fucker, Double D an all-dancing, all-jiving black dude and Lipz a very hot Puerto Rican girl. She had the sexiest lips I've ever seen or kissed.' He smiled as he remembered.

'And you never called them by their real names?'

'Not really,' he replied coolly. 'I don't think I ever knew Strutter or JayJay's real name. Lipz's one was too strange for me to pronounce. Double D's was something like Darnell or Darrell or something like that.'

Double D – Darnell Douglas. Hunter chose not to mention anything for now. His urgency was in identifying the two remaining members of Elder's old gang. 'How about JayJay and Lipz? Were they students at Compton High?'

'Nope.'

'Were they like Strutter, street kids?'

'No, they did go to school somewhere, but it wasn't Compton High. I didn't fucking know and I didn't fucking care. We all hated school anyway. I think they both flunked out of it just like me.'

Hunter pulled one last item from his file, the Compton High yearbook. 'Could I ask you just one more thing?' He placed the book in front of Elder, who arched an eyebrow. 'Could you have a look at this yearbook and point out the students you guys pushed around the most?'

'Why? I already told you your theory is shit. Your killer killed a girl who wasn't part of the gang.'

Time to play the last card. Hunter retrieved a photograph of Darnell Douglas and placed it on the table. 'Do you recognize him?'

From his leaned-back position Elder lowered his eyes to the picture, studying it for a moment. A few seconds later his relaxed expression morphed into a frown. He craned his body forward and picked the picture up with both hands.

'Motherfucker. It's Double D,' he said with a chuckle. 'He put on some weight.'

Hunter took a deep breath. 'He was found murdered yesterday.'

Elder's head snapped up.

'It was the same killer.' Hunter had to think quickly. 'Maybe Jessica Pierce wasn't part of your gang, but she might've pushed him around anyway. Maybe the killer had a crush on her and she made fun of him, embarrassed him in front of others.' Hunter pointed to the pictures again. 'Brett, Strutter, Double D and the girls' paths never crossed in their adult lives. You all went your different ways. Nothing connects the five victims except their school days and your old gang. That's no coincidence.'

Elder's left eye twitched slightly.

'We can still save them.' Hunter tapped the girls' picture, making sure his finger landed on Amanda Reilly. 'But they need your help.' He extended his hand offering the convict a blue crayon.

Elder paused for a long instant before taking the crayon and drawing a circle on the table around the yearbook. 'There you go. We messed with just about everyone in that school.'

'OK, how about if you narrow it down to the ones you messed with not only in but outside school as well? Just the ones your gang pushed around.'

'Why should I give a shit? None of them ever came to visit me. They didn't give a fuck for how I was doing. Not even BS came to see me. He was my best friend.'

Hunter tried to think of something he could say. He could lie and tell Elder that it wasn't true. That Brett and Amanda had requested visitation rights but were denied. But that would play in Elder's mind until his last days, and no one deserved that kind of psychological torture. 'I can't answer that question,' he finally said. 'Only you can find a reason why you should care.'

The silence that followed as they stared at each other seemed interminable.

'This could take a fucking long while, cop,' Elder said, flipping open the yearbook and reaching for the crayon.

Hundred and Five

Hunter was on the phone to Doctor Winston as soon as he left CCI. The autopsy had confirmed their suspicions. Darnell Douglas had died of severe blood loss. Toxicology showed he'd been injected with succinylcholine, a paralyzing agent used for surgery that doesn't affect the nervous system. The subject wouldn't be able to move, but he'd still feel everything. The black Cadillac found outside the crime scene gave the forensic team nothing; not even Darnell's prints were found. The killer had done a thorough job of wiping the car clean.

It took Hunter just short of two hours to drive back to LA. At Parker Center he went straight down to the basement and the Investigative Analysis Unit. Hopkins wasn't at his desk and neither was Jack Kerley. Hunter called the young officer's cell phone.

'Ian, where the fuck are you?'

'I'm at the morgue.'

'What the hell are you doing there?'

'Going over personal possessions' inventories. They're hand-written forms, remember? I can't search them using a computer.'

'Well, get someone else to go over the forms for now. I need you back at the RHD.'

'OK, I'm on my way.'

Garcia was at his desk going over a few files when Hunter entered the office.

'How did it go with Peter Elder?' he asked eagerly.

Hunter quickly summarized his interview while checking the fax Doctor Winston had sent.

'Debbie Howard's case files only got here this morning from Lancaster,' Garcia said, making a face and handing Hunter some of the documents he'd been studying for the past hour.

Hunter took them and sat at his desk, quickly flipping through the crime-scene pictures and frowning several times in the process.

'Do we have an autopsy file?'

'The green folder on your desk.'

Hunter scanned it. 'According to the autopsy report, Debbie Howard drowned.' He arched his eyebrows at his partner. 'The crime-scene pictures show her inside an empty bathtub.'

Garcia handed him a new file. 'Debbie's husband, Jonathan Hale's account of events. He found the body.'

Hunter read his statement in silence.

Jonathan Hale had been out of town for four days on an architects' convention. His flight back from Dallas on 13 December was delayed by three hours, and by the time he made it home from the airport it was past midnight. He didn't manage to get through to Debbie on the phone, but he left her a voice message explaining about the delay. Debbie worked late more nights than not, so finding the house quiet with the lights turned off didn't come as a surprise to Jonathan. The burglar alarm was armed and there was no sign of a break-in. He spent some time in the kitchen preparing a sandwich and a cup of coffee before making his way up to their room. The room looked tidy and unperturbed. No sign of any struggle. He walked into the bathroom to get cleaned up and that's when his life shattered.

Debbie Howard was naked, hanging from her feet upside down over their large bathtub. Only her head and shoulders were submerged in water. Jonathan panicked, jumping into the tub and trying to lift her lifeless body. He cut her down and sat hugging her for what must've been at least an hour before emptying the tub and calling the police.

'By cutting her down and emptying the bathtub, Jonathan Hale completely destroyed most of the evidence from the crime scene,' Garcia said as Hunter reached the end of the file.

'It's understandable, though,' Hunter said, rubbing his eyes. 'You come home to find your wife hanging upside down in your bathroom, her head submerged in water, what do you do?'

Garcia's eyes saddened, and Hunter knew he was thinking of Anna.

'Most people would do what Jonathan did. They'd go to her and hug her . . . and cry . . . and ask why. Preserving the crime scene didn't even enter his mind.'

Garcia let out a deep, heartfelt sigh, and the room went silent for a short moment. 'Check the autopsy report again,' he said. 'At the bottom of the first page.'

Hunter glanced at it. 'She was pregnant.'

Hundred and Six

Garcia used his index finger to rub between his eyebrows. 'Three weeks,' he confirmed.

'Has the lab tested her blood against the one used to draw the number three on Father Fabian's chest?'

'No. This was two weeks ago, and though the investigation is still ongoing, Jonathan Hale, with the support of the DA's office, did everything he could to get the body released. She was cremated two days ago.'

'Fantastic,' Hunter said, running his fingers through his hair.

'It doesn't matter, Robert. She was pregnant just as you said the second victim would be,' Garcia said in a more animated tone. 'Her picture was left in Amanda Reilly's crime scene by the killer, who drew the number two on the back of it. I don't think there's much doubt Debbie Howard was a victim of this same lunatic.'

'It's dismissive to think this killer is a lunatic. Don't make that mistake, Carlos.'

Garcia picked up a new sheet of paper from his desk. 'In a later interview, Jonathan Hale said Debbie was petrified of water. I mean, going into deep water. We live in a tropical weather city where the sun shines almost throughout the year. They were a very well-off family. Their house is massive, but it's the only one in their street without a swimming pool. The reason for it is because Debbie never wanted one. She wouldn't even go close to pools or the beach or anything. Apparently, she came this close to drowning when she was young.' He brought his thumb and index finger close together. 'Just like the other victims, Robert, she was killed in the way that scared her the most. As you said, this guy goes after their fears.'

Hunter thought about it for a second. 'He cut her down,' he whispered. 'That's why no one found the number two on her body.' He stood up, approached the nonmagnetic marker board and started drawing on it.

'Debbie is hanging upside down over her bathtub.' He used a stickman to represent her. 'Her husband comes in and finds her this way. He panics and cuts her down, but the bathtub is still full of water.'

Garcia took a step closer. 'Jonathan allowed her body to splash into the tub.'

'If there was a number drawn on her body, it got washed off.'

'But why not just force her head into the tub and hold it there like we see it in the movies? Why take the time to hang her upside down and all? The drowning effect would've been the same.'

'No, it wouldn't,' Hunter disagreed. 'We have no pictures, but the report says that only her head and shoulders were submerged.'

'That's correct.'

'If this killer goes after his victims' fears, how would he exploit the fact that Debbie Howard was petrified of water? How could he really terrify her?'

Garcia rubbed his face as he stared at the crude stickman drawing. 'Christ . . .' He turned to face Hunter as he realized. 'The tub was empty when he strung Debbie from the wooden beam on the ceiling.'

Hunter nodded. 'I'm sure of it.'

'Shit. Debbie knew her head was way past the bathtub's edge. She could see the water creeping up slowly. She felt it as it wet her hair and forehead and it just kept coming. She had to watch her worst nightmare slowly becoming a reality.'

'The killer could've tortured her even more by stopping the water just as it reached the top of her nose—' Hunter took over again '—forcing her to breathe only through her mouth for a while. But even a calm person in an upright position would've found that hard to do, never mind a terrified woman hanging upside down knowing she was about to die. Her drowning was slow and very painful.'

'That's fucking creepy,' Garcia said, screwing up his face.

'It's what the killer does,' Hunter continued. 'He sat and watched Amanda Reilly cook to death for two days. He slowly and patiently extracted two and a half liters of blood from Darnell Douglas, ten millileters at a time, before stabbing the syringes into his body. I'm sure he watched Debbie Howard drown, and he'd want to make it last. He wanted the torture.'

Garcia shuddered. 'I'm glad I wasn't a bully when I was in school. You never know what kind of freaks people may grow up to be.'

Hunter flipped through the autopsy photographs again but stopped halfway through the pile. 'She had a venipuncture mark on her right arm,' he announced, lifting one of the pictures to show Garcia and checking the coroner's notes. 'Probably acquired on the same day of her death.'

Garcia nodded. 'The killer needed her blood.'

'Exactly. Debbie drowned. No spillage of blood for the killer to collect. And he needed blood to draw the number on his next victim – Father Fabian. We need to talk to Jonathan Hale.'

'Well, that's gonna be a problem,' Garcia admitted.

'Why?'

'He's spending Christmas at his parents' house far away from here.'

'How far away?'

'Tennessee.'

'Damn.'

A knock came to the door.

'Come in,' Garcia called.

Hopkins stepped into the room with his usual blue folder under his arm.

'I found him.'

Hundred and Seven

'Who did you find?' Hunter asked. His and Garcia's stare locked on Hopkins, who frowned as his eyes rested on the stickman drawings on the board.

'You guys playing hangman?'

'Never mind the drawings, Ian,' Hunter answered. 'Who did you find?'

Hopkins smiled. 'Victim number one. Just after you called me at the morgue, I came across the file. White male, six-three, two hundred pounds. Only person we found who had an LA Lakers commemorative NBA final champion's watch. The body was taken in three weeks ago.' He shook his head. 'Not a pretty sight. And you won't believe how he died.'

'Let me guess,' Hunter cut him short. 'Wasp stings.'

Hopkins and Garcia stared at Hunter. 'How the hell did you know that?'

Hunter explained about Peter Elder identifying Strutter, him being the leader of their street gang and the fact that he was allergic to wasps' venom and very scared of them.

'Well, the killer did a great job. This is what he looked like when they found him chained to a wall in his own basement in Culver City.'

Hopkins handed Hunter a photograph, and he cringed as he stared at it.

Seated on the floor, naked, with his back against a brick wall, his arms chained by the wrists and extended high above his head, was the badly deformed body of a man. His face had puffed up grotesquely, with both of his eyes swollen shut. His lips had inflamed so severely they'd cracked where the skin could stretch no more. His nose was an undistinguishable red ball, so large the nostrils had sealed. The brutal swelling extended to his arms and the rest of his body where small, pin-prick-like black dots were visible just about everywhere. He looked like an over-inflated rubber doll. His right ankle had been broken, the bone protruding through the skin. Three nails had been hammered into his right knee. On his chest, a long, vertical splash of blood.

'There's our number one,' Hunter said, showing Garcia the photo.

'No wonder no one recognized it as important,' Garcia commented. 'It looks more like the victim hemorrhaged from the mouth and it dripped onto his chest.'

'The autopsy report says the subject had a systemic reaction and died from anaphylactic shock induced by his severe allergy to wasps' venom,' Hopkins explained. 'The killer chained him to the wall and locked him in his basement, but not before retrieving a large wasps' nest from a wooden box and exploding it on the floor next to him. He was stung over five hundred times. They found wasps in his mouth, down his throat and even in his stomach.'

Garcia rubbed his face as if in agony. 'I hate wasps.'

'Do we have a name?'

Hopkins nodded. 'Gregory Carlson. I just found him, so I haven't had time to gather a file on him, but I don't think it'll take me long,' he announced before Hunter asked.

'Good. Find whatever you can as soon as you can.'

'I need to know,' Hopkins said curiously. 'What are the stickman drawings for?'

Garcia quickly explained how they figured out why no one had found the number two drawn on Debbie Howard's body.

'It makes sense,' Hopkins agreed and flipped a page in his notebook. 'I'm trying, but I still haven't found the two remaining girls from that Gardena High picture—'

'We can probably put them on the back burner for now,' Hunter interrupted him. 'The killer won't be going after them.'

'Why not?'

Hunter told them how his bluff with Peter Elder had almost turned sour.

'So they weren't part of the gang?'

'Out of that picture, only Amanda and Debbie. And unfortunately we're too late for them.'

'Yeah, but that confirms your theory,' Hopkins said excitedly. 'The killer is definitely going after the members of this street gang.'

'It looks that way. And that leaves us with three remaining members. Peter Elder, who's in CCI and a very hard target to get to.'

'He got life,' Hopkins said. 'The killer doesn't have to get to him. His fate is already sealed.'

'We also have a Caucasian male they used to call JayJay,' Hunter continued. 'And a Puerto Rican woman they called Lipz.'

Garcia stretched his body. 'If that's all we have on them, they'll be hard to find. Even if they're still on the streets, their nicknames are too common.'

'I understand,' Hunter agreed. 'But we've got something else to go on.' He handed Hopkins the Compton High yearbook. 'This is why I needed you back here. Peter Elder has highlighted a few pictures in there. Those were the students they bullied the most. The ones bullied by their gang.'

Hopkins started flipping through the pages.

'I want you to scan all the pictures Elder's highlighted. Let's find out who those people are, what they've been doing since they left school and, most important, where they've been for the past three weeks. Get everybody you can on it. If you need more help, let me know and I'll talk to Captain Blake. We don't have much time left.'

'No problem. I'll get right . . .' Hopkins stopped flipping the pages and squinted at something in the book. 'Have you looked through these pictures?'

'Not yet. I came straight out of CCI, got in the car and drove here. I can multitask but not *that* well. Why?'

Hopkins turned the opened yearbook towards Hunter and Garcia. There were three highlighted pictures on the two displayed pages.

'The second picture,' he said. 'Read the name under it.'

'No fucking way,' Garcia said, running his hand through his hair.

Hundred and Eight

He took a deep breath before studying the photographs taped to the brick wall inside the candlelit basement room. The faces that stared back at him each had their own different history – told their own different story. A wave of excitement rushed through his body at the thought of what he'd already accomplished and what was still to come.

'*It won't be long now.*' He smiled before running his tongue over his cracked lips. '*Five are gone; only two more to go.*' He consulted the large calendar hanging from a rusty nail. '*Plenty of time to achieve it.*'

His eyes rested on the sketches and plans on the oversized metal table and he laughed. He'd decided to leave the best for last. He knew exactly what scared them to death – one was petrified of spiders and the other of rats. That knowledge filled him with a mind-boggling feeling of power. What he had in store for them was a masterpiece – a whole new dimension of panic and pain. He couldn't wait to be face to face with them. To see the fear in their eyes. To taste their blood. To make them suffer. But he knew the importance of being patient.

He opened the miniature fridge at the corner of the room, and carefully ran his fingers over the small glass vial of blood he'd extracted from his last victim.

So far everything had gone to plan, but something unexpected had come into play. He glared at the photograph on the front page of the *LA Times*. This was something he could've never foreseen. But this was also something he could easily deal with. Nothing and nobody would keep him from achieving his goal.

Hundred and Nine

'Motherfucker! He lied to us,' Garcia whispered, staring at the picture Hopkins had showed them.

'I asked you to run a check on him. Did you find anything out?' Hunter asked Hopkins.

The officer nodded, searching his folder. 'Unlike Brett, James Reed was an exemplary everything – student, citizen, you name it. He maintained a 4.0 average all throughout high school and graduated with honors in '87. He didn't lose any time either, starting university the same year – UCLA. Two majors, mathematics and physics, and again his grades were outstanding. He got involved with computer software design right after university and for several years worked for a games company right here in LA named Konami. They're one of the big boys. He made a lot of money using his math and physics knowledge to develop 'shoot 'em up' game engines. His mother, who used to be Father Fabian's algebra 2 teacher in Compton High, fell ill about three years ago, and that's when he quit the company.' He looked at Hunter. 'You asked me to also check where he lived when young. Guess what?' He smiled. 'When he was in high school, they used to live just a few houses from our young priest.'

'And that's why Elder has highlighted him. If they lived on the same street as Brett, Strutter's gang must've picked on him no end.'

'Funny how he failed to mention that when we talked to him yesterday,' Garcia commented with irritation. 'I think we should pay him a less cordial visit this time.'

'You were right on the money again when you suggested I check everything about him, including who his neighbors were and if they had kids the same age,' Hopkins said, nodding at Hunter. 'I would've never thought of that.'

'What did you get?'

'One of their neighbors had two kids, a boy and a girl, both around James Reed's age. Neither of them went to Compton or Gardena High. They went to Centennial High on North Central Avenue. The boy's called Keyon Powell. He's now a doctor and lives in Colorado, but his sister, Kelly Powell, now Kelly Sanchez, is an attorney at law and lives in Santa Monica with her husband and two children.' Hopkins handed Hunter his sheet.

He studied it for a moment before checking his watch.

'Maybe we should talk to her first – like now.'

'Sounds good to me,' Garcia said, reaching for his jacket.

Hundred and Ten

Hardgrave and Mortimer Law Firm occupied the third, fourth and fifth floor of the large, all tinted-window modern office building on the corner of Sixth and Broadway in Santa Monica. Hunter had called from the car just to make sure Kelly Sanchez was in her office and not in court this afternoon.

At the reception, a young and immensely attractive red-haired woman told them that without an appointment it was very doubtful Mrs. Sanchez would be able to see them today, but the magic of Hunter's detective badge created a last-minute opening in her schedule.

They still had to wait a few minutes before the receptionist was given the all clear to guide them inside. They tailed her down a corridor where photographs and framed newspaper articles hung on the walls, passing a display case filled with golf trophies and into a second corridor. Kelly Sanchez's office was the second to last on the right. The red-haired receptionist knocked gently and waited precisely three seconds before opening the door and showing them into a spacious and luxurious office. Delicate furniture, oil paintings on the walls, a broad window behind an imposing Victorian mahogany desk and an entire wall covered in books. An office certainly decorated to impress clients.

Kelly Sanchez came to meet them at the door. A statuesque

black woman in her late thirties with lush, straight shoulder-length hair and razor-sharp hazel eyes. They shook hands and Kelly scrutinized their credentials before offering them a seat.

'How can I assist you, gentlemen?' she asked, taking her place behind her desk.

Without giving too much away, Hunter explained the purpose of their unannounced visit.

'James Reed? Wow, that's a blast from the past.'

'You were neighbors, is that correct?'

Kelly nodded skeptically. 'Many years ago.'

'Do you remember a boy they used to call Strutter and the group of kids he used to hang out with?'

Kelly's sweet demeanor hardened, and she leaned back on her chair, clinically studying both detectives. 'Yes, I remember them.'

'Did you or your brother know any of them? Did you know their names?'

She shook her head. 'The only name that was ever mentioned was Strutter's, and that's a nickname. I knew who they were if I saw them on the street. Every time I did I went the other way.'

'In Strutter's gang there was a girl they called Lipz and a skinny boy they called JayJay. Did you know them at all?' Garcia pressed.

She frowned. 'I just told you I didn't know any of them.' Her stare moved from Garcia to Hunter. 'What's this really about, detective? James was never part of that gang.'

'Yes, we know. Were you and your brother friends with James Reed? Did you know him well?'

'We were friends, but I wouldn't say we knew him well.'

'Do you remember if he got along with Strutter and his gang?'

Kelly chuckled. 'Nobody got along with Strutter's gang. In fact, everyone did their best to avoid them.'

'Including James?'

'Especially James, but it was harder for him.'

'How's that?' His leather seat squeaked as Hunter leaned forward.

Kelly gave them a subtle shrug. 'James went to Compton High. His mother was a teacher there, and I think some of Strutter's gang members were students of hers. James paid the bill every time they got bad grades or detentions in her class.'

'Or suspensions,' Garcia noted quietly.

'Strutter's gang sought him out. He got more heat than most.'

'How about you and your brother?'

'We went to a different school, Centennial High. None of Strutter's gang were students there. It was easier for us to avoid them.' Kelly rested her elbow on the arm of her luxurious leather chair and her chin on her closed fist. 'We got pushed around every now and then, but nothing extreme, mainly just name-calling.'

'And that wasn't the kind of *pushed around* James got?' Garcia asked.

She shook her head. 'James was very timid, very insecure. I'm not sure if that was the reason or if it was because his mother was a teacher, but Strutter's gang made his life hell.' Kelly tucked her hair behind her ears. Her eyes moved slightly up and to the right. 'James used to have this little white dog. It was very cute and tiny and it was always running around, full of energy. Even my mom liked that dog, and she definitely wasn't a dog person.' Her expression saddened at the memory. 'The dog went missing one day and James went absolutely nuts. He probably knocked on every door in our neighbor-hood, but no one had seen it. I don't think he got any sleep that night. I'm not sure of all the details, but the next morning a cardboard box was left at his door. Inside was the little dog. Its head was missing.'

Garcia shifted uncomfortably in his chair and glanced at Hunter, who kept a steady face.

'James buried its body in the park. He cried for weeks.'

The room fell silent for a long moment. 'James blamed Strutter's gang.' Hunter concluded.

Kelly nodded. 'Poor little Numberz,' she said sadly.

'What did you say?' Hunter frowned.

'James's tiny white dog.' She nodded. 'It was called Numberz, with a "z" at the end.'

Hundred and Eleven

One of the busiest freeways in the state, busiest time of the day. From Santa Monica to Pomona they moved at a snail's pace, averaging twenty-five miles an hour. On their way they encountered gridlocks, foul tempers, compulsive horn blowers and some frightening risk-takers.

'We should just take him in and put him under pressure in an interrogation room, I'm sure he'll crack. Especially if you interrogate him.' Garcia said as they slowed down behind a truck.

'You wanna arrest him on what charge? Being bullied by a street gang over twenty years ago and having a dog called Numberz? At the moment we've got nothing.'

'We've got motive.'

'*Probable*. You have to work that word into your vocabulary, Carlos.'

'OK, so we've got probable motive. James Reed was severely bullied when young and he blamed Strutter's gang for what happened to his dog, whether they did it or not. A dog called Numberz that was beheaded. The killer numbers his victims, Robert. Father Fabian was decapitated and his head replaced by a dog's one. Coincidence? And did you notice that he's—'

'Your height, six-two,' Hunter interrupted, nodding.

'The man we're looking for is six-two.'

'I know.' Hunter leaned against the passenger door and

pinched his chin. 'Look, all I'm saying is that we can't panic. If we do, this killer will get away. The only thing we have that can tie anyone to one of the crime scenes is a partial fingerprint found in the mansion in Malibu. That's good, but it's not enough and you know it. Even if we take him in and match his fingerprint to the one we have, he could easily beat it in a court of law. The house was on the market for quite a while, remember? Anyone could have gone for a viewing. If that's all we've got, no jury in the country will convict. There are still two members of Strutter's gang out there, and I know the killer will be going after them. We've gotta play this tactfully. If James Reed's our guy, he knows we're closing the circle. We knocked on his door yesterday, and we're about to do it again.'

'And that might make him nervous,' Garcia concluded.

'With nervousness comes mistakes. One mistake is all we need.'

The short winter LA afternoon was sliding to an end when they finally reached Pomona. Hunter consulted his watch and decided to go straight to Cal Poly University.

The main campus of the California State Polytechnic University sits on almost fifteen hundred acres of suburban district, making it the second-largest campus in the California State University system. Once inside the grounds, it didn't take them long to spot the famous CLA building – Classroom/Laboratory/Administration. Its daring futuristic architecture has earned the structure a place in several sci-fi Hollywood productions as well as numerous TV commercials. But the building also sits directly above the San Jose Hills Fault. It has a very high seismic risk, and its connections and beams don't meet California earthquake safety standards.

'Cool building,' Garcia commented as he parked his car.

'Let's just hope we don't get a quake in the next few minutes.'

'Huh?'

Hunter shook his head dismissively. 'Don't worry about it. Useless information, really.'

Garcia's brow furrowed and he doubled his step, following Hunter into the building.

The reception area wasn't busy. A heavyset man with friendly eyes and long dark hair tied back in a ponytail smiled with bright white teeth as they approached his desk. 'How can I help you, gentlemen?' he asked giddily.

'We're looking for Professor Reed, James Reed.' Hunter returned the smile.

'Do you know what subject he teaches?'

'I'm not sure. Is there a way you can find out for us?'

'Sure, give me a minute.'

'Computer Science and Software Engineering.' The answer came from a tall angular woman with a delicate and attractive face framed by ash-blond hair. She was standing next to the receptionist's desk, reading through some sort of report. Both detectives turned to face her. 'Professor Reed teaches Computer Science and Software Engineering,' she confirmed. 'But he's not around.'

'Oh.' Hunter nodded disappointedly. 'You are?'

'Doctor Nicola Pate.' She offered her hand. 'I run the computer science department. Are you looking to enroll?'

Garcia coughed and Hunter's smile widened. 'Wow, do we look that young?'

'You look old enough to me,' the receptionist said, flashing Hunter a new smile followed by a discreet wink, which made Garcia almost choke.

Doctor Pate chuckled comfortingly. 'You don't have to be a teenager to enroll in university.'

'Does that mean we don't look like teenagers?' Hunter teased and got a 'don't push it' look from Doctor Pate.

'I'm at a loss here,' she said, running her hand through her hair. 'I know you're not looking to enroll as students, but I still don't know who you are.'

They stepped away from the receptionist's desk and Hunter went through the proper introductions.

Doctor Pate's aura changed as she checked their badges. 'Homicide?'

'Don't be alarmed,' Hunter reassured her. 'James Reed is just helping us.'

'Is there a problem with one of his students?'

'No, nothing like that. An investigation we're conducting might involve someone James Reed knew a very long time ago. He might be able to help us obtain a better insight.'

The doctor's gaze bounced between both detectives for a moment and her worried expression relaxed.

'Do you know where we can find him?'

A gentle head tilt. 'You're a day too late.'

'I'm sorry?'

'We're three days away from Christmas, detective. Classes have been dying down for the past week. Professor Reed finished his last scheduled class yesterday afternoon. He told me he was going away for a few days.'

'Did he tell you where?'

Doctor Pate shook her head. 'Reed's a very introvert person. A great professor, but he keeps himself to himself. He said he needed a change of scenery, at least for a few days, and I don't blame him. Life as a university professor can be very demanding. I think he likes going to the mountains somewhere, but don't quote me on that. I didn't even know he was going away. The first I heard of it was yesterday.'

Garcia glanced at Hunter.

'If you leave me your number, I'll give you a call if I hear from him.' This time her smile was more than friendly.

Hundred and Twelve

Night had already descended over LA by the time Garcia pulled up in front of James Reed's house. The black Dodge Journey they saw parked in his driveway the day before was gone. From outside, the house looked deserted. The curtains were drawn shut and the lights were all off. They insistently rang the doorbell, knocked on the door and called his name, but after a few minutes they knew they'd be getting no reply.

'He's fled,' Garcia said curtly.

'We don't know that yet. He might not be our guy and he's really just off on a break to clear his head.'

'Or the panic is already starting to set in. As you said, he knows we're closing in on him.'

The neighbors confirmed Doctor Pate's allegations that Reed was an introvert man who liked to keep himself to himself. The woman directly across the road from him said she was watering the flowers in her garden when she saw Reed loading his car with a backpack and what looked to be a few supplies before setting off in the middle of the afternoon.

From the car, on their way back to their office, Hunter called Hopkins and asked him to find out Reed's license plate number and put a citywide sighting call out on the car. They had no grounds to detain him yet, but Hunter needed to know his location.

'What if he's left LA or crossed state lines?' Garcia asked.

'Then that's a good sign,' Hunter replied, returning his cell phone to his pocket.

'What?'

'Doctor Pate said he finished his last scheduled class yesterday afternoon. His neighbor said he set off today in the middle of the day. You know Los Angeles traffic. If you were setting off on an interstate trip this close to Christmas, would you leave in the middle of the afternoon?'

'Are you kidding? If I had a choice I wouldn't go from West Hollywood to Long Beach in the middle of the afternoon. You saw how long it took us to get here from Santa Monica. Gridlocked all the way.'

'Reed is a computer science professor and a jigsaw puzzle aficionado. His brain is conditioned to think logically. If he had this trip planned beforehand, he would've been ready to leave last night or early this morning, when traffic wasn't so busy.'

'But he didn't.' Garcia smiled. 'I'm telling you, he's panicking.'

'When we were in his house yesterday, did you see any signs of a person who was about to leave on a long car trip?'

Garcia shook his head. 'And if he was, he also failed to mention it when we told him that we might need to talk to him again.'

'Peter Elder also told me that the two remaining members of their gang, JayJay and Lipz, hated school as much as he did,' Hunter explained. 'They flunked out of it as well. Statistically, street kids without a high school diploma don't move around much. I'm certain they're still in LA. If James Reed is our man, he hasn't left this city.'

Hundred and Thirteen

By the time they got back to their office, Hopkins had already covered a new corkboard with photographs.

'I scanned all the pictures Peter Elder highlighted in the Compton High yearbook and left copies on both of your desks.' He nodded towards two piles of photographs on both detectives' desks and chuckled at their surprise. 'Don't be alarmed – that's the whole lot.' He fumbled for his notes. 'Out of those, three have passed away, seven aren't US residents any-more, three are serving time, six are in the military and stationed somewhere else and five are either confined to wheel-chairs or have some debilitating physical condition.' Hopkins pointed to the new corkboard. 'These are the ones we must concentrate on. Twenty-one in total.'

'Fuck!' Garcia looked surprised. 'How many people did they bully?'

'A hell of a lot,' Hopkins confirmed.

The first picture on the board was of James Reed.

'No feedback from anyone yet on Reed's car being sighted?' Hunter asked.

'Not yet, but I did get more information on our first victim, Gregory Carlson, aka Strutter.'

'I'm listening,' Hunter said while his eyes studied the new photo board. Typical yearbook portraits – dated haircuts, fake smiles and acne-covered cheeks. All of the kids would be in their forties now.

Hopkins cleared his throat. 'Apparently, Greg was a bona fide badass. He dropped out of high school in Rancho Dominguez before completing his freshman year and disappeared under the radar for several years. No job, no social security contribution, nothing. Quite a violent person too. Looks like he beat up every girlfriend he ever had. He was arrested several times, the charges ranging from violent assault to possession of illegal substances. Greg wasn't a dealer, though. He never made money out of drugs. Instead, he became a technology crook, creating internet companies and conning people out of their cash. Allegedly, he was also involved in several email scams. Due to his background, the LAPD is treating his death as revenge kill. They think Greg finally conned the wrong person out of his money.' Hopkins flipped a page on his report. 'Strangely, it looks like he was a good father.'

'He had a son?' Garcia questioned.

Hopkins shook his head and faced him. 'A daughter, Beth, whom he visited four times a week. She suffers from multiple sclerosis. Her mother left as soon as Beth started showing symptoms of the disease. Her present location is unknown.' He handed Garcia his report.

Hunter kept his attention on the photos.

'A preliminary list with all their names and locations is on your desk, on top of the photographs,' Hopkins confirmed. 'We've got addresses, but we haven't had time to establish the whereabouts of these twenty-one for the past three weeks yet.'

Hunter nodded. 'Let's each pick seven and see what we can come up with in the next hour.'

Hundred and Fourteen

Mollie had spent the day in a cloud of worry. Something wasn't adding up. She kept having residual flashes, but they were getting stranger and more confusing. It looked like everything was doubling up, as if there were two killers, two sets of victims. She couldn't make sense of anything anymore, and it was scaring her like never before.

She'd woken up in the middle of the night feeling claustrophobic. Her room was spacious enough, but the air inside felt stale. As she opened her window and allowed the cold and humid Los Angeles winter breeze to caress her face, an uncomfortable feeling made the hairs on the back of her neck stand on end. She felt as if she was being watched. Craning her upper body out of the window, she allowed her eyes to scan the portion of the street she could see from her room. The street was deserted.

Mollie went back to bed, but her mind kept playing tricks on her, keeping her awake for the rest of the night. The sun rose at 6:53 a.m. and finally Mollie was able to relax a little. Nighttime was always harder. For some reason the images came stronger then – more real, more painful.

She finally left her room as the afternoon was coming to an end. Hunger was stinging at her growling stomach. Just down the road, Mollie found a sandwich shop which also sold cakes, sweets and creamed-topped coffees. She ordered a salami and cheese sandwich, a slice of apple pie with ice cream and a hot chocolate before taking a seat at a table close to the shop's front window.

Hunter had told her that maybe tonight he'd be moving her to another location – a friend's house, he said, but he still hadn't called. She finished her pie and was distracted by a short and stout man standing across the road dressed in a Santa Claus outfit. He enthusiastically dangled his oversized golden bell, trying to collect money for some charity. Mollie watched him for at least five minutes. No passerby made a contribution.

'No one seems to care these days, do they?' A tall man sitting on the next table commented, noticing Mollie's attention on Santa Claus.

'Not really,' she replied with a sad head shake.

The man was wearing a long black overcoat and a dark, old-fashioned mobster hat. 'It's a sad world when people have no heart for charity anymore,' he said before running his tongue over his cracked lips.

Mollie didn't know how to reply, so she just smiled and had a sip of her hot chocolate.

'You're not from LA, are you?'

She looked at him intrigued.

'I can spot a Los Angeles smile a mile away. It has a fake edge to it, but not yours. Yours is—' he paused, searching for the right word '—kind, sincere.'

'Thank you.' She blushed slightly.

The man noticed her uneasiness and stood up, gathering his things. 'I hope you enjoy Los Angeles,' he said, offering his hand.

Mollie shook it with the most delicate of touches. The man's hand felt strong and powerful.

'My name's Ryan, Ryan Turner.'

A new smile blossomed on her lips. 'I'm Monica.'

'Enjoy LA, Monica,' he said again before exiting the shop, approaching Santa Claus and depositing some money into his bucket.

Back at the hotel her bad night's sleep caught up with her and Mollie kept on dozing off in front of the TV. She wasn't sure if she was awake or asleep when the vision came, but it hit her like a knuckleduster punch to the face.

When she opened her eyes she was standing in front of the bathroom mirror, naked and bleeding.

Hundred and Fifteen

If any of the twenty-one faces pinned onto the photograph board had any sort of a police record, their fingerprints would've been on file and they could've compared them to the partial one they had from the house in Malibu, but that wasn't the case. Hunter, Garcia and Hopkins were staring at twenty-one all-regular, all-American model citizens. No convictions, no problems with the IRS or any government organization. No jury services or appearances in court. The worst they could come up with were two unpaid parking tickets.

Twenty-one people, whose lives on paper were as adventurous as a glass of milk. Their professions ranged from a university professor to a scriptwriter, from medical doctors to temporarily unemployed.

Their first step was to eliminate anyone under or over six foot two. That left them with twelve possible suspects. After checking with the airlines and passport control, five more names were crossed from the list.

'We can cut Doctor Pedro Ortiz and Doctor Michael Grifton from our list too,' Garcia said as he got off the phone. 'They were both on night shift on the night Father Fabian was attacked.'

'Jason Lowell was on a camping trip with his students during the weekend Debbie Howard was murdered,' Hopkins said. 'He's off the list as well.'

Hunter rubbed his tired eyes. He'd been up for almost forty-eight hours, and he wasn't sure they'd find much more from phone calls and database searches. They were looking for someone who had certainly been carrying psychological scars hidden in his subconscious for twenty-five years. Hunter had no doubt something had triggered off the killer's rage. Something fairly recent. The 'last straw'.

He knew that identifying what might have pushed the subject over the edge would be hard to do from behind a desk. Things like being dumped, pressure at work, losing your job, big financial difficulties would need detailed investigative work.

'OK,' he said, massaging his stiff shoulders. 'We've only got four names left on the list. We know James Reed is missing. Let's find out where the remaining three are.'

'Maybe you should bring Mollie here and let her have a look at these pictures,' Garcia suggested. 'Maybe she'll be able to sense something.'

Shit! Hunter checked the time. He needed to call her. He wanted to move her to another location tonight.

'That's not a bad idea,' Hopkins agreed.

'That's not what she does,' Hunter said calmly, looking at them both. 'She can't control what she sees. And she only senses pain.'

'Don't you think it's worth a shot?' Garcia insisted. 'We're sort of running out of options and time.'

'No,' Hunter responded. 'She's a seventeen-year-old girl who's been through more crap than most people would face in a lifetime. She's alone and she's scared. And to top it all off, she sees grotesque images of unimaginable suffering.' His eyes focused on Garcia. 'You've been to three of the five crime scenes. In Malibu you had to leave the room to be sick.'

'Really?' Hopkins asked, surprised.

'Don't even go there,' Garcia warned him.

'We are detectives with the HSS,' Hunter continued. 'Special circumstances' crimes are all we do. We're the experts, the real tough guys. We're supposed to be used to it, and it still turns our stomachs inside out. Imagine what being alone and seeing those images – images as real as the ones we saw with our own eyes – could do to a fragile teenage girl. There's no way in hell I'd bring her here, show her these pictures and ask her to deliberately try to force those visions into her mind.'

The silence that followed indicated that everyone understood Hunter's position.

His cell phone rang. The caller display showed Mollie's number. *Spooky*.

'Hello, Mollie.' Hunter moved towards the window. Even through the phone he could feel something wasn't right. Her breathing was labored, as if she'd been running. 'What's wrong?'

Mollie took a deep breath, and Hunter realized she was also crying.

'Mollie, talk to me. What's wrong?'

Garcia and Hopkins tensed.

Another deep breath. Hunter heard a car horn. 'Mollie, are you at the hotel?'

'No.' Her voice trembled.

'Where are you?'

'I don't know.'

'What? What do you mean?'

'I left.'

'You left the hotel?'

'Yes.'

'When?'

'I don't know. Some time ago.' Her words dragged, stalled by her tears and the lump in her throat.

'Calm down, Mollie. Talk to me. What happened? Why did you leave the hotel?'

'I saw it . . .' Her tone was becoming hysterical.

'Take a deep breath, Mollie. What did you see?' Hunter stood up and reached for his coat.

Silence.

'Mollie, stay with me. What did you see?'

'I saw the victim . . .'

'The victim?'

'The killer's next victim. He's going after the next victim tonight.'

Adrenalin pumped through Hunter's blood. 'OK, try to calm down for a sec, Mollie. How do you know it's the next victim? It could've been an earlier one.'

'Earlier?'

Hunter hesitated for a moment. 'The visions you had before. The two people you saw. They weren't the only victims. There were others before them, and there's been another one since.'

'No, no. It's not them. It's the next victim. I know it,' she said in a panic-stricken tone.

Hunter was already at the door. 'How can you be so sure, Mollie?'

'Because it's me.' Her voice faltered. 'He's coming after me.'

Hundred and Sixteen

'Wherever it is that you're going I'm coming with,' Garcia said, reaching for his jacket as Hunter ran past him and out into the corridor. 'What's going on, Robert?'

Hunter didn't answer. He didn't stop or turn around. Garcia only managed to catch up with him when they reached the parking lot.

'You're driving,' Hunter said, pressing the speed dial button on his cell phone. He got the prerecorded message straight away.

'Where am I going?' Garcia asked as he turned on the engine.

'Drive as if you were going to my place. The hotel where Mollie is staying is just three blocks from me.'

'What happened?'

Hunter recounted the conversation he'd had with Mollie.

'Holy shit!' Garcia's eyes widened. 'When did she have the vision?'

'I don't know. I told you word for word what she said.'

'And the connection simply went dead?'

A quick nod. 'As if somebody had snapped the phone shut. I just tried calling her back – voice mail.' Hunter closed his eyes, pinched the bridge of his nose and forced himself to think clearly. Mollie hadn't been exact when she told him that she'd left the hotel. That could've been ten minutes or five hours ago. She could still be in the hotel vicinity, or miles away by now. But where would she go?

Hunter remembered Mollie mentioning a friend she used to work with called Susan, but that was done in passing and he had no address for her.

'Did she have any money?' Garcia asked, eager to help.

Hunter opened his eyes and looked at his partner. 'Not enough for a ticket anywhere,' he replied, already knowing what Garcia was thinking. He tried her cell phone again – pre-recorded message.

They arrived at the Travel Inn in East Florence Avenue in less than twelve minutes. It was a typical two-story, U-shaped travelers' hotel found all across America. No need to go through reception to get to the rooms. Both detectives rushed up to number 219 on the second floor. They knocked on the door, tapped on the window and called her name. Mollie wasn't in.

Hundred and Seventeen

The overweight receptionist at the front desk confirmed that the key to room 219 was in its cubbyhole. That particular Travel Inn hadn't yet upgraded to the now-conventional key cards, still using the old-fashioned key and massive key-ring combination. Guests at the hotel weren't requested to leave the key at reception when they were going out. The receptionist hadn't seen Mollie. The key had been dropped into the express-return box and she had no idea what time that happened.

Hunter flashed his badge, grabbed the key and returned to Mollie's room. The few things she had with her when he took her there two nights ago were gone, and so was her rucksack. Hunter checked the room and the bed while Garcia took care of the bathroom.

'Robert, you better come take a look at this.'

Hunter entered the bathroom and froze as his eyes rested on a few drops of blood in the sink. They looked around but there was no sign of a struggle. Nothing seemed disturbed. Hunter examined the blood.

'What're you thinking?' Garcia asked.

'Nosebleed. Mollie told me she gets them sometimes, mainly after visions.'

'What do you wanna do?'

Hunter dialed a number on his cell phone. The person at the other end answered it on the second ring.

'Trevor, it's Hunter, Robert Hunter. I need you to do me a favor.'

Trevor Tollino was the most senior officer with the Special Operations Bureau of the LAPD, and a close friend.

'What do you need, Robert?' he murmured down the phone. Trevor used to be a field cop, but during a gunfire exchange with a drug gang in south LA he was hit in the neck. The bullet damaged his vocal cords, and after two operations he was left with a soft whispering voice. Hunter was the one who risked his life to pull a bleeding Trevor back to cover.

'I need you to track down the location of a cell phone. It's equipped with the latest GPS chip.'

'Even with GPS, cell phones can be tricky to trace, Robert. If the phone's on, it should take a few minutes. If the phone's been turned off, then we've got a problem.'

'Can you give it a try?' Hunter said, giving Trevor Mollie's number and all the information he'd copied down when he purchased the phone. 'Call me back as soon as you have something.'

There was a pause. 'Is this an official request, Robert?'

'It's a life-or-death request.'

Another short pause. 'No problem. Leave it with me. I'll call you back in a few minutes.'

Hunter paced the room and checked the window a couple of times. From the room he could see a small section of the street below and nothing else.

His phone rang, making Garcia jump on his seat.

'Trevor, talk to me?'

'I've got nothing, Robert. I can't triangulate on it. The phone has either run out of battery or it's been switched off. What I do have is the general location of its last call.'

'I'm listening.'

'The call was made to your phone.'

'And the location?'

'Firestone Boulevard in Downey.'

'What? Downey is about seven miles from here. Can you give me a more specific location?'

'Sorry, Robert. The call didn't last long enough for me to properly close in on it. The best I could do was to narrow its location down to a general area. The phone was last active somewhere around the junction of Firestone and Lakewood.' A brief pause. 'After that it simply vanished.'

Hundred and Eighteen

Hunter took a moment to rearrange his thoughts. There were four possibilities swimming around in his head. One – Mollie had been too spooked by her new vision and was now wandering the streets of LA with no real objective. Two – she'd decided to leave Los Angeles; after all, she'd thought about it before. Three – she'd looked up a friend, possibly the Susan woman she'd mentioned in passing. And four – she'd been abducted.

Mollie didn't have enough cash for an air ticket, and there was no rail or bus station anywhere around Downey. If she was thinking about leaving LA, she had gone to the wrong part of town. Downey was also too far for her to have aimlessly walked there in a panic. There had to be a reason why her call to Hunter had come from a place seven and a half miles away from where the hotel was.

'Robert,' Garcia called again. 'Are you OK? What do you think we should do?'

'We've gotta go to Downey. According to Trevor, that's where she was when we got disconnected.' He instinctively checked his watch. 'That was no more than twenty minutes ago. She wasn't indoors. I heard traffic noise through the phone, and Trevor said the call was made from Firestone Boulevard. She might still be there somewhere.'

'OK, let's go.'

Firestone and Lakewood are two large and very busy boulevards in Downey, southeast Los Angeles. Garcia made the journey in less than twenty minutes.

'Shit!' he whispered as they got to the junction.

They were looking at Stonewood Center mall – a massive shopping complex of over a hundred and seventy stores. But that wasn't all. Moving west from the junction, up Firestone Boulevard, was a carnival of smaller malls and stores – a shopper's paradise.

There was a long line of cars at the entrance to Stonewood Center's parking lot. Garcia slowed down, as if he was about to join the back of it. The streets were heaving with people carrying bags, packets and different-size boxes. Two days of shopping left until Christmas Day – every shop was open late, and the malls looked like an ant house at mealtime. They didn't know what Mollie was wearing and they had no picture of her. Even if they did, who'd they ask? With the number of people Christmas shopping at this hour, they were looking at the proverbial needle in a haystack situation.

Hunter massaged the rough, ugly scar on his nape. Their best shot of finding Mollie at the moment was if she switched her phone back on. He'd asked Trevor to keep trying to pick up a track signal on it. If it came back into the grid, they'd know. But why had it been switched off?

Impulse was telling Hunter to search the crowds, but reason told him it would be a waste of time. There was nothing they could do from there. Hunter told Garcia not to join the line of cars.

'We've gotta go back to the RHD and coordinate from there.'

As Garcia swerved his car away from the parking lot line and rejoined traffic, Hunter closed his eyes. Mollie's last words still echoed in his ears.

'*He's coming after me tonight.*'

Hundred and Nineteen

Captain Blake was standing in front of the new picture board, studying the four suspects' photographs left on it, when Hunter and Garcia arrived back at the RHD. Hopkins had already brought her up to speed with the latest developments.

'There's one thing I forgot to tell you about me when we first met,' Captain Blake said calmly, closing the door once Hunter and Garcia reached their desks. 'I'm not the kind of person who swears easily.' She lifted both hands in an 'I admit' gesture. 'Don't get me wrong. I'm no Miss Goody Two Shoes. Sometimes you need to swear to properly express yourself. In my case that happens only when I'm really pissed off.'

'Are we in any danger of you getting to the point anytime soon, captain?'

'Shut the fuck up and listen, Robert. Does this look like a fucking two-way conversation to you?' Her calm tone had vanished. 'Do you two have shit for brains, or are you both just plain imbeciles? I'm getting goddamn tired of repeating myself to you. What did I fucking tell you two? I told you I wanted to be informed the second you located the psychic girl. Do you wanna know what I just found out?' Her heels clicked as she paced the room. 'I just found out that you not only knew where the girl was, but you transferred her into a hotel, and now you fucking lost her. Shit, Robert.' The captain slammed her closed fist on his desk with an emphatic thump. 'Why the fuck didn't you tell me?'

Hunter kept his voice even. 'Because I know what would've happened, captain. You would've brought her here, stuck her in an interrogation room and bombarded her with questions she wouldn't have been able to answer. Not because she wanted to hide anything, but because she simply doesn't know the answers. I've asked her everything that could be asked. She doesn't know why she sees the things she sees, and she can't control it.' Hunter breathed in sharply. 'If she made it into your report, I'm sure Chief Collins or Mayor Edwards would've requested she'd be interviewed by a psychologist, who'd certainly be looking to discredit her rather than understand.'

'You're a goddamn psychologist,' the captain shot back angrily. 'You could've done the interview yourself.'

'Do you think the mayor would've allowed me to conduct the interview?'

'I told you I'd deal with the mayor. He's my problem, not yours. I always stand behind my detectives, but you don't seem to wanna trust me. I would've listened to you first, Robert.'

Hunter ran his hand through his hair.

'Now, the chief and the mayor will inevitably hear about this, via my report or not. And all of a sudden the pressure that I'm already under will start to reach boiling point. The two of you have undermined my authority twice. If I don't take action, I'm gonna look weak in my position as captain, not only to them, but to everyone in this department and the LAPD.'

'What do you mean by "take action"?' Garcia asked.

'I mean suspend your asses.'

Hundred and Twenty

'Wait a second, captain.' Hunter shot to his feet. 'You can't suspend us. Not now.'

Captain Blake chuckled. 'I can do what the fuck I like, Robert. You're the only two people who don't seem to have noticed that I run this division.'

'Captain, you can't do that.' Hunter tried to calm his voice. 'There's no time for any other detective to hit the ground running with this case.' He paused. 'The killer will strike again tonight.'

The captain's gaze held Hunter motionless. 'You better start talking to me, detective. And you better come as clean as morning rain.'

This time Hunter told Captain Blake everything.

'And this phone you gave her – is it still switched off?'

'Trevor told me he'd call the second it came back on the grid.'

The captain paced the room as she considered what to do. 'We can't even mobilize units, Robert. This girl could be anywhere. And I don't even know if I should believe any of this shit you just told me. All I have to go on are crazy visions from a seventeen-year-old girl who I never really met.'

'You have our opinion to go on, captain.' Hunter shook his head gently. 'She's not a fake.'

'Why should I believe you, Robert? You've been everything but straight with me.'

'OK captain, I admit, I screwed up, but not because I wanted to piss you off or undermine your authority or show disrespect. I did what I did because I wanted to protect a seventeen-year-old girl from the destructive circus she was about to be thrown into. Interrogations, people doubting her, the press, the mockery . . . Most people would crack under much less pressure. Mollie doesn't deserve that. She just wanted to help, and in her heart she believed she could.' Hunter paused for air. 'You can do whatever you like, captain. You can bust me down to traffic duty when this case is over if it pleases you, but you can't pull us off this investigation now. This killer's on a revenge mission. He won't keep on killing. After he gets his revenge, he'll disappear, I'm certain of that. We've only got seven days, captain. And he's only got two more names on his list.'

'Three if he's really going after Mollie tonight,' Garcia noted.

'Exactly, but Mollie wasn't part of his original plan.'

The captain narrowed her eyes as a hint of confusion crossed her face.

'By going after Mollie, the killer's breaking away from his own schedule, his own rules,' Hunter clarified.

'And when they deviate from their original plan, that's when they make mistakes,' Garcia complemented.

The captain looked unsure. 'We've got protocols to follow, Robert.'

'With all due respect, captain, fuck protocol. I'm not putting a set of bullshit, bureaucratic rules over anyone's life,' Hunter said firmly, to Barbara Blake's surprise. 'Captain Bolter told me you were a great cop. You had great instincts. You always followed your gut feelings. You must've withheld information from your superior officers for one reason or another at least once in your career. We all do it – including the chief of police. It doesn't make us bad cops, captain. It actually makes us real cops.' He studied her. 'What's your gut feeling telling you now?'

Captain Blake closed her eyes and let out a long sigh. 'Let me ask you something, detective. Do you think that reporter from the *LA Times*, Claire Anderson, knew where to find Mollie? Maybe knew you'd taken her to a hotel?'

Hunter tilted his head, reflecting. 'Possible. Reporters have their own sources, their own investigative team. Claire is certainly ambitious enough. Why?'

Barbara Blake faced Hunter. 'She was found murdered this afternoon.'

'What?' Hunter cocked his head forward as if he hadn't heard it correctly.

'Her throat was cut open.'

'No way?' Garcia murmured, his eyes wide.

'That's all the information I have at the moment. Detectives and forensics are still at the scene. But if our killer is really after Mollie, and Claire Anderson had any information that could've led him to her, the possibility he killed her for that information has suddenly become very real.'

Hundred and Twenty-One

The tension in the room was broken by a knock on the door. Captain Blake let Hopkins in.

'Did I come at a bad moment?' he asked, sensing the dark atmosphere.

'What have you got?' the captain commanded.

Hopkins nervously walked over to the picture board. 'Our only suspect is now James Reed.' He pointed to his photo.

'What?'

'Robert told me to keep digging at establishing the whereabouts of the other three in the suspects' list before he left,' Hopkins explained. 'Marcus Tregonni, Phillip Rosewood and Harry Lang—' he indicated the photos as he mentioned their names '—are now accounted for, and they all have alibis for at least one of the crime nights. They couldn't have done it. The only one left is James Reed.'

'He ticks all the right boxes,' Garcia said with a pinch of excitement. 'He's six-two, he's a loner, never married, lived with his mother until she died five months ago.' He faced Hunter. 'Which could easily have been the "last straw" you talked about. He's strong, highly intelligent, resourceful and very good at planning and calculating. When young, he was bullied and taunted by Strutter's gang in and out of school, and so was his mother. Can you imagine the sort of hate his household had towards Strutter and his gang? Certainly strong enough to have left very damaging psychological scars in his subconscious. He also blames them for his pet dog's death. The dog was called Numberz.'

'Hold on.' Captain Blake raised her hand. 'What's this about a dog called Numberz?'

Garcia ran through the story Kelly Sanchez had told them in her office earlier in the day. The captain immediately made the connection to the *numbered* victims and the decapitated pet dog.

'Makes you wonder, doesn't it?' Garcia concluded.

'There's an APB out on his car, right?' Captain Blake asked. 'Has it been spotted yet?'

'Not yet.' Hopkins shook his head.

'We've gotta find him,' she said, her voice filled with anticipation. 'OK, James Reed is now officially our main suspect in the Executioner Killer's case. Let's reissue the APB. If he's sighted, I want him stopped and arrested. We need him off the streets as quick as possible. Do we have a recent picture of him?'

'We can get one from Cal Poly's website,' Hunter confirmed.

She faced Hopkins. 'Do it. Let's get a copy of it to all bureaus.'

Furtively, Hopkins's eyes sought Hunter, who gave him an almost imperceptible nod as confirmation. 'I'm on it.' He dashed out of the room.

Captain Blake directed her stare at Hunter, her expression stern. 'I really hope my gut feeling is still as good as it used to be. Do what you have to do, Robert.' A short pause. 'Let's hope we can save Mollie and whoever it is this psycho is after.'

'Captain—' Hunter stopped her before she left '—if you get any more information on Claire Anderson's murder, please let me know.'

She nodded and calmly closed the door behind her.

Hunter returned to his desk and rubbed his face in frustration. He wanted to be out there, physically hunting the streets of LA for a suspect or searching for Mollie, but he knew that at the moment there was nothing else he could do but wait. And he hated waiting. It made him fidgety. He reached for the photograph pile Hopkins had left on his desk and purposelessly started flipping through them. His eyes weren't really looking and his mind wasn't really concentrating. He was just keeping his hands occupied while his brain worked overtime trying to piece the puzzle together. *Garcia's right.* James Reed did tick all the right boxes. His mother's death five months ago could've easily been the trigger that freed his bottled hatred. But why didn't Hunter get the feeling he always did when he knew they were chasing the right guy?

Hunter stopped flicking through the pile of photographs in his hands and held his breath. His stare locked at the top picture, studying the person's face, looking for something he knew he'd seen before. He almost choked when he finally saw it. 'Oh my God,' he murmured before springing to his feet and showing Garcia the photograph.

'Carlos, who's this?' he asked. 'Why wasn't this picture on the suspects board?' The urgency in his voice made Garcia tense.

'I don't know. I didn't set them up, but the names are on the back of the photos.'

Hunter checked. 'Michael Madden?'

Garcia consulted the list Hopkins had prepared. 'Here he is. The reason why he wasn't on the board is because he died a long time ago.'

Hunter refocused his attention on the picture. 'I don't think he did.' He showed Garcia the picture again. 'I think this guy's alive and well. And if I'm right, we both know where he is.'

Hundred and Twenty-Two

Garcia stared at the picture in Hunter's hands, confused. 'What are you talking about? Who's Michael Madden?'

'Look at the eyes, Carlos. You can change everything on a person's face but the eyes stay the same. They're like fingerprints.'

Garcia did as he was told, concentrating harder this time. 'Nope, I still have no idea who this guy is.'

Hunter looked at the photo one more time. Was his mind playing tricks on him? He would have only one shot at this. He needed to be one hundred percent certain. 'Let's go.' He rushed out of the office.

'Where are we going this time?' Garcia asked, following Hunter, who took the stairs going up in giant leaps.

'SID. I need to be sure. We need to talk to Patricia Phelps.'

Garcia frowned. 'The composite sketch artist?'

'That's her.' Hunter nodded.

The LAPD Scientific Investigation Division is responsible for the collection, comparison and interpretation of physical evidence found at crime scenes or collected from suspects and victims. It's located on the top floor of the RHD building. The LAPD composite artists are part of the SID team.

Patricia Phelps was the most senior and most experienced of the SID sketch artists. She was getting ready to go home after doing a couple of hours' overtime when Hunter and Garcia burst through her office door.

'Pat, we need your help,' Hunter puffed, half out of breath.

The short-haired brunette with a stop-traffic figure looked at Hunter through the top of her thin-rimmed designer glasses. 'Did you just run up six flights of stairs, Robert?' she asked in her husky voice that made most men melt. 'I guess if you ran all the way up here this can't wait until tomorrow, can it?'

Hunter took a deep breath but didn't reply.

'I thought not. What do you need?' She undid her coat.

Hunter handed Patricia the photograph. 'I need you to alter this picture.'

She studied it for a second before shrugging. 'OK. Let me scan it in.' She returned to her desk and a minute later the image appeared on one of her computer screens.

'How advanced is your software?' Hunter asked.

Patricia chuckled proudly. 'State of the art. As good as any animation studio in Hollywood. I can turn him into Brad Pitt if you like.'

Hunter smiled and motioned Garcia closer, who still looked puzzled. 'OK, guys, now here's the scenario. When you were young, everyone made fun of you, mainly because of the way you looked. It happened in school, on the streets . . . everywhere. Girls wouldn't give you the time of day and boys pushed you around, called you names and beat you up. It went on for so long and it got so bad that you ended up hating yourself and the way you looked. You wished you could be somebody else. Are you with me so far?'

Garcia and Patricia both nodded.

'What if you became rich early in your life? What if you had enough money to do anything you liked, including drastically changing the way you looked? You could finally become that someone else you always wanted to be? No more laughing or name-calling or being beat up. People you knew wouldn't even recognize you. Would you go through with it? Would you change your face?'

Hundred and Twenty-Three

Garcia thought about it for a moment, his eyes on the face on Patricia Phelps's screen. 'Probably.' He didn't sound very sure.

'Most definitely.' Patricia nodded enthusiastically. 'I've seen the kind of damage severe bullying can do to someone. The daughter of a friend of mine committed suicide a few years ago because of it.'

'I'm sorry,' Hunter said.

Patricia gave him a soft smile.

'Alright, so if you're this kid—' Hunter pointed to the computer monitor '—what would you have changed?'

Garcia crossed his arms and chewed on his bottom lip while studying the young student's face.

'Those umbrella ears would have to go,' Patricia said, leaning back on her chair. 'He probably got some real heat for them. They're quite – shall I say? – predominant?'

'Yeah, OK. I'll have to agree.' Garcia nodded.

'Can you change that?' Hunter asked, resting a hand on Patricia's left shoulder.

'Watch me work.' She entered a few algorithms into the software and used a device that looked like an electronic pen to draw on a flat board on her desk. Like a painter stroking a canvas, her movements were precise and graceful. Moments later the student's ears were completely different.

'Wow, that's cool,' Garcia said.

'Yeah, that looks much better.' Patricia smiled.

'OK, so what else would you change?' Hunter pushed.

'Probably that bump on his nose,' Garcia offered. 'It looks as if it's been broken.'

Patricia nodded and made the change.

'Good. Any other problems either of you would like to fix?' Hunter asked.

'His teeth.' Patricia this time.

'You can't see his teeth.' Garcia shook his head, frowning at her.

'That's true, but see the way he closes his mouth?' She used the electronic pen to indicate it on the screen. 'He's not doing it naturally. He's forcing his lips together in a pouting movement, which tells me his teeth were bigger than normal and pushed forward.'

Hunter and Garcia squinted at the picture.

'Trust me, guys. I work with this sort of stuff every day.'

'OK.' Hunter shrugged. 'But how can you change his teeth on the picture if you can't see them?'

'I can change the shape of his mouth, push his lips back a fraction and do away with his pouting. You'll see,' she said as her perfectly manicured fingers punched several keys on her keyboard. A few more strokes with the magic pen and the kid had a new mouth.

'Wow, he looks quite different from the original,' Garcia agreed.

Hunter shook his head, unsure. 'Something is not fitting.'

'His jaw,' Patricia noted. 'Because of the alterations I made to his lips and teeth, I'm certain a surgeon would suggest a small redesign of his jawline to fit his new smile. Maybe square it a little.'

'Can you do that?'

'As I said, with this pen I can do anything.' She smiled confidently and made the alterations. When she was done, they all took a step back from the monitor. The image they were staring at was that of a very different-looking boy from the one they'd started with.

'That's it,' Patricia said. 'I don't see anything else to add or subtract, do you?'

Both detectives shook their heads.

'We just turned a geek into a hunk.' Patricia laughed.

'That's perfect,' Hunter agreed.

Something had changed in Garcia's expression, but the recognition still wasn't there.

'Do me a favor now, Pat.' Hunter hunched his body over her desk. 'Darken his hair to a brownish color, add some gray over his temples and make it a shorter, combed-back style, will you?'

They waited while Patricia tweaked the picture once again.

'Can you hypothesize age?' Hunter asked.

'Of course.'

'Great. Let's age him about twenty-five years.'

The ageing process took a little longer. When it was finally done, Garcia's jaw dropped open.

'No fucking way.'

Hundred and Twenty-Four

Susan Zieliski read the letter for the tenth time, and again her emotions got the better of her. She couldn't believe it was really happening.

Susan hadn't had the easiest or luckiest of lives. She was born in Cripple Creek, Colorado, twenty-two years ago. Her parents were Polish–Jewish immigrants and very strict when it came to her upbringing. She did her best to respect their laws, but for a young girl growing up in today's America they were very restrictive, to say the least.

From a very early age Susan had two great ambitions in life. One – she wanted to be on stage and sing. Two – she didn't want to become like her mother, a very obedient, somewhat submissive wife who'd do anything her husband told her to without questioning.

At thirteen, Susan was already attractive. She'd inherited her mother's hair – so blond it was almost white – and her father's deep blue and captivating eyes. Plenty of boys had asked her out, but Susan wasn't allowed to date. Not until she was eighteen, and even then it had to be under her parents' supervision and the boy had to be Jewish.

Susan was no angel, though. Her first kiss came when she was fourteen. Bob Jordan took her behind the school gym during their lunch break and they made out like they were the only two people on earth. She allowed him to touch her breasts, and as he did she was overcome by a warm and exciting new sensation. But when he tried to slide his hand up her thigh and between her legs, she panicked and ran away. That panic didn't last long, and soon the touching became more intense, the breathing more emphatic and the excitement impossible to control. At fifteen Susan had her first full sexual experience. It'd been quick, painful and not very satisfying, but certainly promising.

Cripple Creek is a former gold-mining camp. A bedroom closet society with a population of fewer than two thousand people. That, together with her strict family rules, made it very hard for a girl like Susan to express herself. She wanted to see more, to explore more, and for the time being the answer came in the form of softball.

Susan didn't care much for sports, but when she found out her school's girls' softball team got to travel all over the state for the high school championships, she made sure she was a part of it.

Susan was sixteen when the team traveled to Colorado Springs to play a series of three games over a long weekend. On that Saturday night, the Bomber Gang, a young and upcoming LA rap group, was playing at the Underground. Susan, together with two other teammates, sneaked out of their dorm and made it to the show. It was Susan's first-ever live gig and it blew her mind. They got to meet the guys in the band and party with them. Susan spent the night with Kool Roxx, the band's lead rapper. He said all the right words and promised all the right things. They made love several times before she went back to the team's dorm.

When she missed her next period later that month, she didn't give it much thought, but soon the morning sickness, the fatigue and the tender breasts kicked in.

Susan's father, Jacek, was an old-fashioned man who believed in obedience, respect, honor and above all the purity of his bloodline. Susan knew that there was no way her father would understand. It didn't matter if she thought she was in love. To him she had disrespected and blemished his family's name in the worst way he saw possible. She decided not to wait for her father's reaction.

In Susan's childish, backyard-America naivety, she believed that Kool Roxx had told her the truth that night when he'd said he'd fallen for her. She believed he'd be happy to see her again and even thrilled to learn he would be a father. She had enough money saved up from her job at the local bookshop to get her to Los Angeles. She'd look up Kool Roxx and they could decide together their next move. But the address he'd given her didn't exist. The phone number he'd given her was of a Chinese restaurant. Four weeks later, alone in the public bathroom of a subway station in east LA, Susan self-aborted.

She stayed in Los Angeles. She was determined she could still make one of her dreams come true. She took a job at a diner in Lynwood and spent her afternoons auditioning for musicals. She had a great voice, very powerful and a little quirky, but her acting skills let her down. As soon as she was able to afford it, Susan started taking classes, and after five years it was all starting to pay off.

'*We are delighted to inform you that you have been chosen for the new cast of* In the Heights, *the Broadway musical.*'

Susan never got tired of reading that line. The letter had arrived this morning, and since then she'd been walking on clouds. Ironic that *In the Heights* was a show about chasing your dreams and finding your new home in a different place.

The knock on the door startled her. She wasn't expecting anyone, especially not at this hour. As Susan opened the door of her small apartment in Downey, her eyes widened in shock.

'Oh my God!'

Hundred and Twenty-Five

'Do you know this guy?' Patricia asked, hitting the PRINT button on her keyboard.

Hunter nodded and she watched as his eyes suddenly widened in realization. 'Damn, the book,' he said, bringing both hands to his forehead.

'What book?' she asked.

'The Compton High yearbook.'

'It's downstairs,' Garcia confirmed.

Hunter faced Patricia. 'Don't go anywhere. I'll be right back.'

Patricia glanced at her watch. 'You gonna owe me big time for this, Robert.' But he was already racing out of the door and down the steps.

He was back in forty-five seconds flat.

'Wow, that was fast,' Patricia said and frowned. 'How come you're not even out of breath?'

Hunter didn't reply. His attention was on the Compton High yearbook pages as he flipped through them, scrutinizing every photo.

'Who are you after now?' Garcia asked, taking a step closer and peeking at the book.

Hunter finally stopped turning the pages and rushed over to Patricia's desk. His face set in concentration. 'Can you scan this picture?' He pointed to a photo in the middle of the page. 'And do the same that we did to that one?' He nodded towards the printout on her desk.

'No problem.'

They watched as Patricia Phelps took her time airbrushing and retouching, once again transforming the student on the picture into a completely different one. As she completed the ageing process, Garcia felt his body shiver.

'You've gotta be shitting me.'

Hundred and Twenty-Six

Garcia made the trip from the SID to Holmby Hills in less than twenty minutes. They weren't sure what they were hoping to find, but they needed to talk to him again. Just like James Reed, he'd also lied about his previous knowledge of the victims.

They had no problem finding the house, a white-fronted, two-story, movie-star-style mansion in Beverly Glen Boulevard. The house was in total darkness, but the lights in the beautifully kept suspended front yard were on, and so were the Christmas decorations on the perfectly triangular evergreen trees that flanked the front door.

They took the long left-bending stone steps that led to the house two at a time. The doorbell wasn't working, and after a minute of constant knocking Hunter skipped over the small hedge to the left of the door and checked both large windows – they were locked and the closed curtains kept him from seeing inside.

'Let's give the garage a try,' Hunter said, running back down the steps to the two-car garage to the right of the house. Again, it was locked and so was the wooden side door to the right of the garage that no doubt led to the house's backyard. Its padlock looked flimsy, though.

'What're you doing?' Garcia asked, surprised, as Hunter

took a step back and shoved his right shoulder hard against the door.

'Having a better look,' he said matter-of-factly as he stepped through the door frame. 'You coming?'

'Are you nuts?' Garcia called as he doubled his step to catch up with Hunter.

The house's backyard was impressive. The centerpiece was a grand teardrop-shaped pool illuminated by underwater spotlights. To its left, a spacious beechwood, off-ground sun deck, and at the back of it a large barbecue area. All of it surrounded by high Raywood ash trees and sculptured hedges. The perfectly mown lawn sloped down several yards to a tennis court. No houselights were on. Hunter tried the glass sliding double doors that led into what looked to be a party room – locked. He cupped his hands over the glass and tried to see inside. It all looked lifeless. Taking off his jacket, Hunter rolled it around his right elbow

'Woah,' Garcia said, lifting his hands in a 'stop' gesture. 'What are we doing here, Robert?'

'I have to have a look inside.'

'Why? This may not be our guy. We have as much reason to doubt James Reed as we have to doubt him.'

'You saw the transformation on both pictures,' Hunter shot back calmly. 'That was no coincidence. This story goes way deeper. And I think it goes murder deep.'

'Fair enough, but breaking and entering isn't the solution.'

'We have a reason to knock on his door, Carlos.'

'This ain't knocking. This is kicking the damn door down, and it isn't legal.' He looked at Hunter as if he didn't recognize him. 'Even if he's our guy, any lawyer could get this case blown out of the water because we fucked up and didn't follow procedure, Robert. Is that what you want? We do this and we might be handing this guy a free out-of-jail card.'

Hunter glanced at his watch. 'I understand, Carlos. And usually I'd be the one giving that speech, but I'm running out of time here. Mollie's missing, the killer's after her and she believes he's gonna get to her tonight. That doesn't give me a lot of time.' He stared deep into his partner's eyes. 'I promised her nothing would happen to her. This is a good lead. I don't have time to go through the right channels and do background research. If I do, she dies. There's no way the DA's office will give us a warrant to even search his trash can.' He paused and breathed in deeply. 'Go back to Parker Center, Carlos. I'll deny you had any knowledge of my actions.'

'What?'

'You said so yourself: this could all be a mistake. I'm not gonna drag you into this. You've got a wife to think about, Carlos. You can't fuck up. I can.'

Hundred and Twenty-Seven

Garcia could barely believe what he was hearing. It was because of Hunter's stubborn attitude that he was alive today. If Hunter thought Garcia would simply turn and walk away, he had another think coming.

'Well, knowing that you can't properly fuck up if I'm not with you,' he joked, 'I'm coming with, *partner*.'

'Are you sure?'

'Who knows? Traffic duty might be a blast. Let's fucking do this.'

Hunter smiled and handed Garcia a pair of latex gloves before elbowing the door. There was a muffled crash and shards of broken glass hit the floor. They both looked around instinctively.

Hunter slipped his hand through the glass, unlocked the door and pulled his pen flashlight from his gun holster.

Garcia did the same and gingerly followed him inside.

The first room was a spacious rectangular structure with black marble floors, a few seats and a bar against the east wall. *Definitely a party room*, Hunter thought. Opposite the bar, a new set of double doors. These ones were hand carved in dark wood. Hunter carefully tried the handle – unlocked. They stepped through into a large and rich foyer decorated with antiques, fine porcelain, silver objects and a few paintings, no photographs. An imposing crystal chandelier hung above the split-level staircase that led up to the next floor.

'This place's too big. We'd better split up,' Hunter whispered, leaning towards Garcia. 'You stay down here, I'll check upstairs.'

Garcia nodded. As Hunter cautiously took the steps to the next level, he took the door directly in front of him.

The main sitting room was as ostentatious as the rich foyer he'd just come from, filled with expensive furniture, oil paintings and sculptures. Garcia crossed the room silently and made his way through the French doors at the far end of it. They led him into a sprawling den, warmed by a black marble fireplace on the east wall. The white carpet was lush and spotless. The north wall was framed entirely in full-length windows. On the opposite side of the room Garcia noticed a strange wooden door, not as high as a regular house door. Faint spots of light were coming from underneath it. Tentatively, he walked over, put his right ear against it and listened for a moment – some sort of distant hum. He looked back at the den's entrance as if debating whether he should go back and get Hunter. He decided to check it out by himself first.

As Garcia twisted the doorknob, he felt his blood warming and his pulse race. Every bone in his body was telling him something was wrong. He reached for his gun.

The door opened soundlessly, revealing a long and narrow flight of concrete stairs dimly lit by a single bulb that hung from a wire. At the bottom, another closed door. Garcia took the steps one at a time. The air was damp and heavy with a musty smell. His left foot caught the edge of a worn step and he slipped. His body was catapulted forward awkwardly, and he reached for the dirty walls, desperately trying to stop him from tumbling down. It worked, but he smashed his flashlight. His heart went into overdrive. Despite the cold, Garcia was sweating.

His eyes quickly moved from the door at the bottom to the one at the top several times, his finger tight at the trigger of his semiautomatic. He took a moment to calm his breathing and reassess the situation. He was sure that if the house wasn't deserted, his clumsiness had given away his position.

'Smooth, Carlos, very fucking smooth,' Garcia whispered between clenched teeth. He stood still for a while, listening for footsteps, waiting for somebody to come from one of the two directions – nothing. He wiped the sweat from his forehead with the back of his gun hand and descended the last few steps. At the bottom he pressed his right ear against the door once again. The humming sound was coming from inside.

Extra-cautiously, he tried the handle – unlocked. He pushed the door open just enough for him to be able to take a peek inside. It was a large basement room. Garcia observed from the door for a long moment but saw no movement. Satisfied, he took a deep breath, steadied his trigger finger and stepped inside. A series of brass lanterns mounted at uneven intervals on each of the two long side walls lit the room with a pale glow. He walked forward slowly, giving his eyes time to get accustomed to the poor light. Something caught his eye on the north side of the room and he stopped dead, his gaze fixed on the display in front of him. He knew exactly what it was.

'Oh God!' He shivered.

At the edge of his peripheral vision he saw a smudge of movement, too fast for him to be able to react. The first blow hit him perfectly across the face. He heard something crack and blood spurted from his nose. Out of balance, Garcia stumbled backwards, but not far enough. The second blow was delivered a split second later, hitting the tender spot on the back of his head with military precision. Garcia's world faded to darkness.

Hundred and Twenty-Eight

Hunter stopped suddenly, as if sensing something wasn't right. He'd been through three of the six upstairs rooms and so far he'd found nothing to substantiate his theory. He unholstered his H&K USP Tactical pistol and turned around, half expecting someone to walk in on him. He heard something, he was sure of it. Some sort of crash.

Carlos. He quickly and quietly moved back downstairs.

'Carlos?' he whispered at the bottom of the stairwell.

No answer.

He moved into the next room – a large sitting area. 'Carlos?'

Silence. The house was still. Stealthily, Hunter made his way through the French doors at the end of the room and entered the den.

'Carlos, goddamnit. I'm getting tired of saving your ass. Where the hell are you?' But if Garcia was in this room, he wasn't talking.

On the opposite wall he saw the dimly lit, small doorway that led to the stairs going down to the basement.

'I hate basements,' he murmured and moved down the steps as quietly as he could. Halfway down, Hunter saw broken pieces of thin glass on one of the steps. He also noticed scratch marks on the walls and a small dent, where Garcia's flashlight had hit it.

What the fuck happened here? His internal danger sensor started to scream at him.

The door at the bottom was ajar, and through the small gap Hunter could see that the room was large and in half darkness. He steadied his back against the wall and pushed the door open with his fingertips. From his outside position, he took in as much of the room as he could before checking his corners and finally stepping through the door. Crude brick walls surrounded the spacious area that was twice the size of the large party room upstairs. The air was saturated with a gagging, fusty smell. But there was something else in that basement room Hunter couldn't identify. Something that made his skin crawl. Something very evil.

At the far end he could see a long metal table that served as a counter for several instruments, but he couldn't make them out from where he was. There were seven life-sized dummies lined up against the wall. To their right there were drawings, sketches, timetables and plans. Hunter recognized what they were for before he saw the pictures. Large photographs of seven different people taken from all angles. The photos were divided into distinct groups clearly numbered one through seven. The first five had been marked with a large red cross over them. Hunter held his breath as he stared again at the photographs of the first five victims of the killer the press was calling the Executioner. The killer's research had been impeccable.

From behind the wide pillar that sat three-quarters of the way down the room, Hunter heard a mumbling sound. A split second later an office chair was wheeled from behind it. Hunter stood fast as he saw Garcia. He was unconscious and bleeding from the nose – it looked broken. His ankles had been tied to the base of the chair, his hands cuffed behind his back to the chair's backrest. Hunter lifted his gun in expectation. What else would come from behind the pillar?

He saw a black Sig P226 Elite pistol being pointed at his partner's head. Hunter recognized the weapon as Garcia's semi-automatic.

'Put your gun down, detective,' the man commanded from his hidden position. Only his arm was visible. In such dim light, Hunter didn't have a clear shot. 'Put your gun down nice and slowly or I'll scatter your partner's brain all over the floor.'

Hundred and Twenty-Nine

Hunter stood still, his aim as steady as it could be. He only needed one chance.

'You've seen what I've done,' the man continued. 'I'm sure you know I'm not bluffing.' His voice was as serene as it'd been the first time they'd met. 'I'll give you only a second.' He cocked the gun.

'OK,' Hunter called out before cautiously placing his pistol on the floor.

'Now kick it this way.'

Hunter did as he was told and his gun stopped just a foot away from the chair Garcia was on.

Finally, Dan Tyler, the owner of the house in Malibu and the person who tipped Hunter and Garcia about the photographs on the fireplace, stepped out from behind the pillar and picked Hunter's pistol up from the floor. 'Walk towards me, slowly. Any sudden movements, your partner dies first.'

Hunter took baby steps towards Tyler and, as he did, Tyler walked backwards, approaching the metal table. 'That's far enough,' he said as Hunter came side by side with Garcia. 'Get your handcuffs from your gun holster and throw me the keys. I don't have to tell you to do it very slowly, do I?'

Hunter followed the instructions.

'Now cuff your hands behind your back.'

A clicking sound echoed through the room.

'Turn around and show it to me.'

Hunter obeyed, snapping at them to show they were secure.

'Now kneel down next to your partner and sit on your heels.'

Hunter's determined eyes never left Tyler's face.

'It's over, Michael,' he said evenly. 'You know you won't be able to get away with this.'

Tyler looked undisturbed. 'No one has called me Michael in a very long time.' He chuckled. 'I don't want to get away with anything, detective. I don't have anything or anyone to get away to. After I'm done, I don't care what happens to me. My life ended a year ago.'

Hunter remembered the first time they talked. Tyler had told him that his wife had died twelve months ago.

'Killing these people won't bring Katherine back.'

'*Kate*,' Tyler shouted. 'Her *name* was Kate.'

'Killing these people won't bring Kate back.' Hunter tried again.

Tyler's eyes flashed fire. 'You have no idea what I'm doing or what this is all about.'

'We know more than you think.'

Tyler smiled defiantly. 'Is that so?' He placed both guns on the metal table and checked his watch. 'OK, I still have some time. Entertain me.'

Hundred and Thirty

Hunter saw this as an opportunity to buy time and maybe fill in some blanks.

'Alright.' He spoke slowly. 'You used to be Michael Madden. Your wife used to be Katherine Davis. You were both students at Compton High. Like several other students you were bullied, pushed around and made fun of, and that extended way beyond the school gates. Back then, there was a particular group of kids who took bullying to a whole different level. They humiliated both of you to such a degree you ended up hating the way you looked. You couldn't stand looking at yourselves in the mirror.' Hunter paused, searching his attacker's face. 'That group of kids was known as "Strutter's Gang".'

Tyler didn't look surprised. 'So you finally found out about them? I'm glad. I was worried no one would.'

'And that's why you directed us to the pictures on the fireplace. We missed them at first and you couldn't have that. You couldn't have those victims being attributed to someone else. You needed us to find out about the bullying.'

Tyler smiled.

Hunter kept his voice steady as he continued. 'Then you became rich. Very rich. You had money to do anything you wished, including starting a new life someplace else. Someplace no one knew who you were, far away from the bullying, but that wouldn't be enough. The damage had already been done. Every time you looked in the mirror, you still hated what you saw.'

'Money can buy anything, detective.'

'Including a new face,' Hunter admitted.

Tyler laughed. 'Please don't stop now,' he teased. 'My life story is just getting interesting.' He leaned against the wall. A relaxed gesture. Hunter carried on buying time.

'You created a new identity – Dan Tyler. From then on you had a good life. You'd even forgotten about Strutter and his gang for twenty-five years, hadn't you? But something brought them back.' Hunter paused, waiting for some sort of reaction from Tyler. He got none. 'Was it Kate's death? Is that why you decided to go after them and their fears? Because your worst fear had become a reality?'

Intrigue colored Tyler's face. 'My worst fear?'

Hunter needed to choose his words carefully. 'Losing the person you loved the most. Your wife. That was your worst fear, wasn't it?'

Tyler clapped his hands slowly while cocking both eyebrows and nodding. 'I'm impressed. You do know more than I thought you did.' He reached for something on the metal table and Hunter tensed. 'Did you figure that out by yourself or did she tell you?' Tyler lifted the copy of the *LA Times* with Mollie's picture.

For the first time Hunter's eyes left Tyler's face and quickly searched the room for a hiding place – nothing.

'Where is she? Where's Mollie?' he asked tentatively.

Tyler frowned. 'You think she's here? Why would I have her?'

'Because she was a threat to you and your plan. Because she knows who you are.'

Hundred and Thirty-One

Tyler threw his head back and laughed a strange, gurgling laugh. Hunter grimaced at the sound.

'No, she wasn't a threat, and, no, she doesn't know who I am.' His voice was confident. 'I got close to her, detective. We shook hands. She's quite a sweet thing.'

Hunter felt a knot start in his throat.

'Even after touching my hand, there was no recognition. She had no idea who I was. Whatever she was helping you with, whatever she sensed wasn't clear enough to make her a threat.' Tyler chuckled. 'If I wanted to kill her, she would be dead.'

Hunter held his stare with equal determination.

'You think you figured this out, detective? You have no idea what really happened or what Strutter's gang was capable of. You didn't dig deep enough.' Tyler's voice had deepened to a chilling tone. 'This didn't start in high school. It started on the streets when we were much younger. They used to push and push until we couldn't take anymore, and then they'd push some more.' He licked his cracked lips. 'Almost every day I saw Kate crying on her way back from school. They'd always come up with something to make her cry: name-calling, face spitting, physical abuse, sick humiliation . . . they didn't give a fuck. Do you have any idea what being laughed at and treated like a worthless piece of shit every goddamn day feels like? What kind of psychological damage that would do to a terribly shy girl like Kate? They were happy to scar her for life just for a laugh. One day they even covered her in human excrement, just for the hell of it.'

Hunter closed his eyes for a moment. Kate had been the same Katherine that James Reed had talked about that day in his house.

'And then there was Kate's father,' Tyler continued. 'That drunken and pathetic asshole. She'd come home from school with tears in her eyes and he'd scream at her and beat her up even more. Her mother was never around to care.' Tyler was grinding his teeth in anger. 'They shot her confidence to pieces. She was made fun of and called "ugly" for so long and so many times she truly believed she was. But Kate was the sweetest and the prettiest girl I'd ever seen and I'd do anything for her.' He paused to compose himself. 'I was intelligent, very intelligent. I figured out very early that I could make a lot of money without having to have a job. I could make money from my bedroom or from the street just by using a pay phone.'

Hunter remembered what Tyler did for a living. 'From the stock market.'

'That's right, detective,' Tyler agreed. 'I'm brilliant with numbers, better than anyone you've ever seen. And my brain understood the market. It was so simple I couldn't figure out why everyone else wasn't making money from it. Soon a few dollars turned into hundreds, hundreds turned into thousands, thousands into tens of thousands, and by the time I started my junior year I had almost a hundred thousand dollars in a bank account.'

Hunter read the satisfaction in Tyler's voice. 'You had already created a different identity even before leaving school.'

'You're quick, detective.' Tyler smiled. 'Just like Kate's father, mine was another drunken, good-for-nothing bastard. After my mother died when I was thirteen, the drinking and the beatings just got worse and worse. If he ever found out that I had money, or that I could make money, he'd no doubt stab me in the back so he could get his dirty hands on it. But he would never get anything from me.' He paused and wiped his mouth. He was over-salivating with anger. 'All you need to get a driver's license in this country is to pass the test and show a birth certificate, which can be easily forged or obtained from a dead child. With a driver's license and a false birth certificate you can apply for any other documents you'll ever need.' He gave Hunter a proud smile. 'In school I was still Michael Madden, but outside I had already become Dan Tyler.'

Hundred and Thirty-Two

Hunter needed to keep him talking. As long as Tyler was talking, no one was dying.

'But for Dan and Kate Tyler to exist, Michael Madden and Katherine Davis had to disappear,' Hunter offered calmly, careful not to sound challenging.

Tyler started pacing the room. 'And it took me a while to convince Kate we could do it. I told her we could go anywhere. I had more than enough money for us to start a new life, and I didn't need to be in LA to carry on making money. But her fear was stronger than her hope . . . until that day in English Lit class.'

'English Lit class?' Hunter pressed, gaining more time.

Tyler's gaze became distant as he remembered. 'As a teenager Kate developed a common hormonal imbalance – estrogen and progesterone. Do you know the consequences of such an imbalance, detective?'

Hunter shifted his weight from one heel to the other. 'It can cause excessive bleeding during the menstrual period,' he confirmed.

'That's right.' Tyler looked impressed. 'In Kate's case, the kind of bleeding that no pad could stop. And that day she was unprepared. It happened four days earlier than expected, inside our fourth-period class.'

Hunter could only imagine the embarrassment that would've caused Kate. He sensed the anguish in Tyler's voice.

'Blood was everywhere as if she'd been shot. And the word spread around like wildfire. Strutter and his gang had a new weapon to torment Kate with. And that's exactly what they did. They started a rumor that Kate was a little slut and that she'd miscarried in the classroom.' Tyler ran a hand through his hair and breathed in deeply. 'They started calling her "Baby Killer" and making jokes of how ugly the baby would be because she was the mother . . .' Tyler paused to let Hunter dwell on the gravity in his voice suggesting the subtext. 'After so many years of abuse she couldn't take anymore. She wanted to die. She thought about suicide. So I told her we could both die, at least to everyone we knew. Three weeks later we went camping and mountain climbing in Arizona and no one ever heard of Michael Madden or Katherine Davis since. Though they did find traces of an accident.' Tyler chuckled proudly. 'Did you know that when a body goes missing in the mountains, rescuers only hold a fifty percent hope of ever finding it?'

Hunter knew the statistic.

'We started a new life in Colorado. A few years later we flew to Rio for our operations. No one would ever again look at us and laugh at our ears or nose or anything. But there were complications during one of Kate's procedures.'

Hunter's eyes narrowed with interest.

'She almost died, and the fear I felt when I thought I'd lose her was something like I never felt before. It petrified me down to my core. She was everything to me.'

Hunter shifted his weight again. He was slowly seizing up: numb legs, sore spine, cramping muscles.

'Even though we had a brand-new life away from every-thing and everyone we hated,' Tyler continued, 'we never really managed to escape our past. We tried for years to start a family, but Kate just couldn't get pregnant. The doctors told us that there was nothing physically wrong with her. The problem was psychological.' Tyler rubbed his face with both hands in an agitated manner. 'She was scared that the baby would be born ugly, just like Strutter and his gang had said. She never forgot it. We had our appearances changed, but that didn't change our genes, which would've been passed down to the baby. She didn't want our baby to go through what we'd been through. Do you see, detective? We couldn't start a family because of the psychological damage Strutter's gang had caused.'

The light in one of the brass lanterns went off and the room got a fraction darker. Tyler moved to the front of the metal table, but that was still too far for Hunter to try anything.

'A psychologist suggested that we relocated back to LA. She said that we should face our fears, that avoiding them would only feed the uncertainty; it would only keep us from moving on. She said that being in Los Angeles could be the first step. It took years for Kate to agree to come back here. But the psychologist was right.' Tyler's lips spread into a half smile. 'Thirteen months ago Kate called me in the office. She was crying. She'd never been so happy in all her life. She said she'd bought a whole drugstore's shelf worth of pregnancy tests just to be sure. They all gave her the same result. We would finally be a family.'

The joy in Tyler's voice gave Hunter goose bumps.

'We celebrated every day. But I made the mistake of taking her out to a restaurant in Santa Monica Boulevard one night.' He paused and Hunter saw anger in his eyes. 'As we were having dinner, we heard a customer curse at a waiter who'd made a simple mistake. He made sure everyone in the restaurant heard him humiliating the poor kid. I saw Kate go rigid. She recognized his voice before I did.'

Hundred and Thirty-Three

'Strutter,' Hunter said, already knowing he was right.

'He never changed.' Tyler was fidgeting. 'After all that time he was still a fucking bully. He made a scene and the manager asked him to leave. Everyone was staring at him, but for some reason he noticed Kate. He walked over to our table and said, "*What the fuck are you looking at, you ugly pig?*"' Pain and anger erupted through Tyler's body and he shuddered. 'He made the same pig noises he used to taunt her with all those years ago, as if he'd recognized her.' He shook his head in disgust. 'Stupid me. I froze and didn't do anything. I just sat there and watched him walk away after humiliating my wife once again. Kate wouldn't stop crying after that and a week later she miscarried.'

Hunter shivered. *Here comes the 'last straw'*.

'She wanted that baby more than life itself. And to numb the pain, last New Year's Eve she swallowed a bottle of sleeping pills.' Tyler stood before the pictures on the wall, drooling with anger. 'The psychological damage they did to Kate when she was young had been such that even after all those years it took only his voice and a few seconds to rip her apart.' Tyler turned and faced Hunter. 'I thought I had nothing else to live for. My nightmare had finally become a reality. And then I saw an article in the paper with a picture of a smiling priest – Brett fucking Nichols.'

Hunter remembered he and Garcia had found that same article inside Father Fabian's room.

'I realized that while I suffered, while Kate took her own life because of what they did to us, Strutter and his gang were living normal lives. All of a sudden I had a reason to live again.'

'Revenge,' Hunter whispered.

'Yes.' Tyler smiled. 'The strongest reason of all. I swore I'd find them all and I'd make them pay. By the anniversary of Kate's death, they'd all be dead. I'd mark Strutter with the blood of the family he killed, my own blood, and number the rest of them with their friends'. I'd make them suffer in the most grotesque way I could. I had money, lots of it, and in my world money is power. I hired people to dig into their lives. To find out where they were and what scared them to death. Everyone is scared of something, detective. Not necessarily a phobia, but if you dig deep enough you'll find that everyone is scared of something. They had no right to destroy our lives.'

Tyler's voice started to quiver. He was losing control. Hunter shifted uncomfortably on his knees, tugging at his cuffed hands.

'Kate and mine were only two, but how many lives do you think they destroyed? Did they think they could do anything they wanted with no consequences? Well, they can't. I'm their fucking consequence,' he shouted while punching his chest with a closed fist. 'They created me. They created the anger and hate that run through my veins. Hatred gave me something to live for again. Seeing the fear in their eyes as they recognized Kate's picture, as they realized they were about to die their worst imaginable death, filled me with a mind-boggling pleasure. It changed me. And suddenly I wanted more than their lives and their fears. Torturing and killing them alone didn't satisfy me. I needed to taste their blood and savor their flesh. It made me feel . . . powerfully different. You should try it sometime, detective. It's a high like no other. Literally consuming your enemy – very addictive.' Spit flew from his mouth as Tyler lost control. He approached the table and grabbed Hunter's gun. 'And no one will stop me from finishing this. No one will stop me from having the rest of their blood. NO ONE.'

Time was up.

Tyler took a step forward, aimed the gun at Garcia's head and squeezed the trigger.

Hundred and Thirty-Four

Mollie Woods closed her eyes and allowed the strong jet of hot water to massage her stiff muscles. A thin gauze of steam had filled the tiny bathroom and was now creeping under its door and into the small hallway. It'd been a few hours since she had the vision, and still she couldn't stop shaking. She knew he was coming for her. She saw blood and panic and fear, and she had to run away.

She leaned against the white tiles and wondered if she'd done the right thing. She didn't know many people in LA. In fact, the only real friend she'd made since she arrived three years ago had been Susan Zieliski. Susan had told Mollie once, who she knew as Monica, that if she ever needed anything she could always count on her.

Mollie was shivering and crying when she knocked on Susan's door less than an hour ago. Her friend was instantly worried, and Mollie fed her a silly story about an argument and a breakup with her boyfriend.

'I didn't even know you had a boyfriend,' Susan said, giving Mollie a comforting hug. 'He didn't hit you, did he? Because if he did we should call the cops on the jerk.'

They talked for a while over a pot of freshly brewed coffee. Mollie had to snowball her story into a much bigger lie.

'You should stay here tonight, Monica,' Susan said.

'Actually, you can stay for as long as you like. I'd love the company.'

Mollie's smile said a silent 'thank you'.

'You look cold. Why don't you go and have a hot shower and I'll fix us something to eat. Then I can tell you about some great news I had today.'

Mollie turned off the water and slid open the cubicle door. Her clothes lay coiled on the floor where she had stepped out of them. Susan had supplied her with clean towels, so she wrapped one around her body and used the other as a turban around her wet hair. With her right hand she cleared a circular patch on the misty mirror and stared at her face.

She had decided that she'd call Hunter, at least to let him know she was OK. She'd been unfair with him when all he'd tried to do was help her. And in her fear of what might happen, she'd broken her promise to him and turned off her cell phone.

Suddenly, a disturbing sensation ran the length of Mollie's body. Frightened, she turned around and faced the bathroom door as if someone was there, staring at her. She was sure she'd heard something that sounded like a muffled scream. She stood perfectly still for a moment listening, but the only sound she could hear was the slow drip from the showerhead. With trembling hands, she reached for the handle and pulled the bathroom door open just enough for her to be able to peek outside. All the lights were off.

'Susan?' Mollie called in an uncertain voice.

Silence.

Cautiously, she stepped into the corridor and waited.

Nothing.

To the left the small living room and the kitchen, to the right the bedroom, but the apartment looked lifeless – it felt lifeless.

'Susan? Is everything OK?' Her voice had started quivering

with tears. With frail steps, Mollie went left, leaving delicate, wet footprints on the hardwood floor. She wasn't familiar with the apartment's layout, which was now illuminated only by the light that escaped from the bathroom. She used her hands to warily feel her way forward and stopped as she reached the living room. An uncontrollable rush of fear made her convulse and she tried in vain to fight the tears that blurred her vision.

'Susan, where are you?'

Mollie cleared her eyes and took one more step forward.

The bathroom light went off behind her.

Hundred and Thirty-Five

Hunter had run out of time.

With deadly determination, Tyler raised his weapon, aiming it at Garcia's head and pulled the trigger.

Click – nothing.

Tyler's face burned with rage and confusion as he tried one more time, but again the gun didn't fire.

In a flash, Hunter jumped to his feet, his hands magically freed from the handcuffs. Before Tyler could react, Hunter delivered a well-placed punch into his ribs, crushing the air out of his lungs. He tumbled to the floor but managed to swing his right leg around with tremendous force, hooking away Hunter's legs. Hunter hit the ground hard with the small of his back, the impact sending a sickening shudder through the rest of him. Awkwardly, he immediately rolled left, anticipating and escaping Tyler's follow-through head-crushing kick.

Tyler never let go of the gun. He finally realized what had happened. Before Hunter placed his weapon on the floor and kicked it over as he was ordered to do, he'd skillfully thumbed the safety into the lock position. *Clever*. It gave Hunter the precious seconds he needed to react. But Tyler wasn't about to make the same mistake twice. He unlocked the weapon, swung his arm around and fired.

Hunter rolled right this time, but not fast enough. As the

deafening gunshot noise echoed through the basement room, he felt a searing, nauseating pain envelop his left arm. He had to think quickly. He knew a second shot was coming fast. Before Tyler could aim the gun again, Hunter's instincts took over and he kicked out. His left boot found the same patch of ribs as his fist moments earlier.

Winded, momentarily powerless and propelled by Hunter's kick, Tyler's defensive reaction was to roll away towards the metal table and underneath it to the other side, creating a temporary barrier between him and Hunter.

They both got to their feet at the same time. Blood was dripping down Hunter's arm, but he knew he'd been lucky. He'd heard the bullet explode against the wall behind him, which meant that despite the excruciating pain the bullet had exited his arm cleanly. No bone or major arteries were hit. He saw the gun in Tyler's right hand rising towards him again. This time Hunter was certain luck wouldn't be so kind. In a desperate survival reaction, he jumped forward. His good arm stretched high above his head in a diving position. He knew he couldn't get to Tyler from where he was, but he could get to the metal table. And that's exactly what he did, pushing it and smashing its edge into Tyler's upper thighs. Unbalanced, Tyler stumbled back, crashing hard against the brick wall. But he still held onto the gun. His eyes burned with murderous hate as he lifted his head, searching for Hunter, his finger tense against the trigger once again.

Left – nothing.

Right – nothing.

Where the hell was he?

Hunter's sweeping floor kick came from under the table, taking Tyler's legs from beneath him. Tyler flew up in the air and hit the floor awkwardly with a cracking noise. Shoulder first followed by his head. The impact strong enough to fill his vision with splashing balls of light for a couple of seconds. As they faded, his eyes focused on the barrel of a gun.

'As I said before,' Hunter said, holding Garcia's gun that'd fallen to the floor when the metal table was pushed. 'It's over, Dan.'

Hundred and Thirty-Six

Hunter cuffed Tyler's hands behind his back using the same handcuffs he'd escaped from less than a minute ago.

'Carlos, wake up.' Hunter tapped his face.

A nervous twitch followed by incoherent mumble.

Another face tap. 'Carlos, are you OK?'

Garcia coughed, spitting out blood. He blinked several times as his eyes adjusted to the poor light.

'What the fuck happened?' he asked, looking at the mess in the room, a captured Dan Tyler and a bleeding Hunter.

'You don't really wanna know,' Hunter said, freeing Garcia from the chair.

'You need a hospital.'

'So do you.' Hunter chuckled. 'Your nose doesn't look too good.'

'It doesn't feel too good either. Actually, it hurts like fuck,' Garcia replied, touching it with the tips of his fingers and recoiling with pain.

'Let's call this in first.'

Before Hunter had a chance to dial, his cell phone rang. The display showed Mollie's number.

'Mollie? Where are you? Are you OK? Where did you go?'

'He . . . he's here.' Her voice was just a trembling whisper.

'What? What're you talking about, Mollie? I can barely hear you.'

'He's here.'

'Who is where? And why are you whispering?'

'Because he's here. He's in the apartment,' she said between terrified, shallow breaths. 'He's after me. The killer came after me.'

'Mollie, calm down.' Hunter tried to keep his voice steady and winced as a new surge of pain burned through his left arm. 'He isn't after you. We've got him. He's right here in front of me and he isn't going anywhere. You don't have to be scared anymore, Mollie.'

'No. You've got someone else.'

Her tears were making it harder for Hunter to understand her. 'What? What do you mean I've got someone else?'

'He . . . he's here in the apartment.'

Hunter's gaze met Tyler's. Only then he realized the challenging grin on the stockbroker's lips.

'You made a mistake, detective.' The grin widened into a cold smile. 'It wasn't me who she should've been afraid of.'

Garcia shuddered. 'What the fuck is he talking about?'

Hunter's mouth went dry. 'Mollie, talk to me. Are you still there?'

Mollie was so afraid she'd lost direction and wandered into the bedroom. The darkness was almost complete, except for the dusty sliver of colored light that crept in through the opening in the curtains. Confused and shaking, she turned around, not really knowing what she was looking for, and fear paralyzed her. From the corner of the room, hidden in the shadows, a pair of eyes blinked at her.

Hundred and Thirty-Seven

The tires of the Type R Honda Civic screeched loudly as Hunter took the turn and sped down South Beverly Glen Boulevard. He had no time to explain, taking Garcia's car and leaving him to call Captain Blake and run her through what had happened in Dan Tyler's house.

Trevor Tollino called Hunter as soon as he and Mollie had disconnected.

'Talk to me, Trevor,' Hunter shouted, hooking his phone to the car's speaker system. 'Where the fuck am I going?'

'She's in Downey, Robert, but I still don't have an exact location. Her phone only came back onto the grid a few minutes ago, but the good news is that it's still on. If it stays that way for another ten to fifteen minutes, with the phone's GPS I'll get you to within five feet of her.'

From San Diego Freeway Hunter took the exit onto I-105 East and joined Glenn M Anderson Freeway doing ninety miles an hour.

'Trevor, how're we doing? I'll be in Downey in a couple of minutes.'

'Almost there, almost there. Somewhere in Stewart and Gray Road. Do you need directions?'

'No, I know the road. What I need is an address.'

Hunter's left arm burned with a sickening pain. The bullet

had cut through his triceps, so any arm extending movement was pure agony. He'd driven most of the way using only his right arm.

'I got it, Robert,' Trevor's husky voice came through the speakers. '9160 Stewart and Gray Road. It's a complex comprised of seven buildings called Villa Downey Apartments. The signal is coming from the second building on the right as you drive into the parking lot from the main road. Second-floor apartment on the farmost end of the block.'

By the time Hunter turned into the road, rain was coming down in blinding sheets. 'I'm right on top of it. Get me some backup, Trevor.'

The improvised tourniquet Garcia had tied around his arm had loosened and Hunter was bleeding again. Pausing to use his teeth and right hand, he retightened the knot as best as he could. The piercing pain sucked the air out of his lungs and everything spun for an instant.

The second-floor corridor was long, narrow, eerily silent and in darkness. All the lights had been smashed. Hunter had no time to wait for the backup. Gun in hand, he moved down the corridor as cautiously and fast as he could. At the end of it, he tried the door Trevor had indicated – unlocked. He slowly pushed it open with the barrel of his weapon. From outside, he hooked his hand around the door frame, searching for the light switch. When he found it, he flicked it up and down a few times – still darkness.

Shit!

He had two options: put up with the pain of a torn triceps and use his pencil flashlight, or take his chances in a pitch-black apartment. Hunter gritted his teeth while inhaling a long, deep breath. Flashlight at the ready, he stepped inside.

The living room was small and sparsely furnished, but with

enough hidden corners to set alarm bells ringing. From the entrance, Hunter noticed an open-plan kitchen and a short corridor that led to a closed door. He needed to check those hidden corners before proceeding. Tightening his grip around his weapon, he moved forward watchfully. He'd taken only a couple of steps when something made him stop dead. He picked up a heavy metallic scent and his heart sank. He knew that odor extremely well.

Blood.

From the strength of the smell he knew there was a lot of it. He spun around slowly, the beam of his flashlight searching everywhere. He almost choked when he finally saw her.

'Oh God, no.'

She was naked and kneeling against the corner. Her breasts and abdomen covered in blood that'd cascaded from her slit throat.

Hundred and Thirty-Eight

Hunter ran towards the girl. Only when he got closer and kneeled down beside her he realized her hair was blond, so blond it was almost white. He aimed his flashlight at her face. Her deep-blue eyes were open. Frozen in eternal terror – a snapshot of her horrifying final moments. But it wasn't Mollie.

Clunk.

Hunter jumped to his feet. His senses on high alert. The noise had come from the small hallway next to the kitchen. Quickly and quietly he placed his back against the wall to the right of the corridor's entrance, took a deep breath and rotated his body into it. His gun searching for a target. All was still, but something had changed. The door at the end of the hall was open. Hunter was sure it was closed when he'd entered the apartment. Weak, flickering lights illuminated the bedroom. Candles, Hunter decided. A trap, he was certain of it, but he had no choice.

He heard a choked whimper, and a shock of hope shot up his spine. He knew it was Mollie, but he sensed a second presence. She wasn't alone.

As he took his first step into the hallway, Hunter's head whooshed. He had no idea of how much blood he'd lost so far, but he was fast becoming light-headed and weak. He took a moment to regain his balance. All of a sudden, Mollie was dragged into his field of vision by a tall and well-built figure. A gun pressed firmly against her head. She was naked, terrified and crying.

'Mollie,' Hunter murmured. And though his protective instincts told him to go to her, he held his position. His gun trained at the mysterious figure hiding behind her.

'Drop the gun, detective.'

Hunter hesitated.

The man pressed the barrel of his weapon hard against Mollie's temple. 'Drop the gun or she dies – right here, right now.'

'OK.' Hunter loosened his grip and his gun rotated around his trigger finger. 'I'm putting my gun down. Let's talk. No one has to die here.'

Mollie choked on her tears and her body jerked forward violently, but it was held by the man's strong hand.

'Put the gun on the floor and kick it this way with enough strength for it to reach me. If it doesn't, she dies and then you die.'

Déjà vu, Hunter thought and did as he was told.

As Hunter's weapon slid across the floor, the man stepped from behind Mollie and stopped the gun with his right foot. His eyes moved down for a fraction of a second, not long enough for Hunter to react.

'H&K USP Tactical?' The man sounded impressed. 'The favorite weapon of Navy Seals and special government operatives. Good choice. I can see you know your guns.'

'So do you.' Hunter shot back.

'That I do.' He smiled viciously.

Through the dim light, Hunter could finally make out the man's features. A face marked by a hard and unhappy life. Deep lines, rough skin, cold and sad eyes and an ugly scar that ran from the top right-hand corner of his left eye to the middle of his forehead. Hunter didn't need to search long to see the resemblance. There was something of him in Mollie. Maybe the mouth or the nose, but it was certainly there. He was her father.

Hundred and Thirty-Nine

John Woods kicked Hunter's gun to one side.

Hunter kept his hands away from his body, around head height with his palms facing forward. Showing he was no threat.

John's eyes settled on the bloody rag on Hunter's left arm. 'That looks painful and you look pale. I guess you lost a lot of blood, huh?'

Hunter didn't reply.

'Slowly, lift the edge of your trousers.'

'I don't have a backup weapon.'

'I'll check that for myself. Now lift them.'

Hunter did.

John grabbed Mollie by the hair and violently pushed her out of the way. She stumbled to the ground with a loud thump. 'Go back to the corner, kneel and pray,' he commanded. 'I ain't finished with you yet. Pray for your mother and for your sins, you little whore.'

Hunter could hear her desperate attempt to suppress her sobbing, as if the sound of her crying would enrage her father even more. John was too far away for Hunter to attempt any physical reaction at the moment. He had to think of something. While John's gaze was on Mollie, Hunter took a shallow step forward.

'You don't have to do this,' he said tentatively.

'YES I DO,' John shouted back. 'I failed my task the first time, but the Lord has given me a second chance. A chance for me to redeem myself. And this time I won't fall short.'

'You failed your task because you didn't understand it,' Hunter replied in a secure voice, being careful not to match John's aggressive tone, knowing it would only anger him further.

The doubt in John's eyes was brief, but enough to give Hunter a chance to carry on.

Another shallow step. 'You thought your task was to punish your daughter, to rid her of her affliction, or what you considered to be an affliction – the fact that she can sense other people's pain.'

'She's got the devil inside her, that's why she sees things – demoniac things.' John's aim never left Hunter.

'No, she doesn't. That's where you got it wrong.' Hunter knew John Woods was an extremely religious man. He had to play John's game if he was to stand a chance of saving Mollie. 'You misunderstood what God has asked of you. Your task wasn't to punish her. It was to help her.'

A moment of uncertainty.

'I understood God's words clearly. He talks to me,' John said confidently, stabbing his left index finger against his head. 'She was a test from the moment she was born.'

'Exactly,' Hunter confirmed. 'A test to see how you would cope with having such a special child. To see if you could understand.'

'THERE'S NOTHING TO UNDERSTAND,' John shouted back.

'Yes, there is. It's been part of our history since the beginning of time.'

A glimpse of curiosity washed over John's face.

'Think back to all the stories in the Bible. How many saints, how many people who only wished to do good were misunderstood, persecuted, even considered hell-sent and executed before they were finally seen for what they really were and given the credit they deserved? And that's simply because people didn't want to understand. Don't make that same mistake with Mollie.'

'There's nothing special about having the devil inside you.' John's speech was becoming faster, more excited. 'I was supposed to rid her of her curse, but I failed and I've lived in hell ever since. My task is now to see that she asks for forgiveness, and then send her to the only one who can forgive her.'

'Your task is to kill her?'

'Praise the Lord. The devil shall be no more.'

Hundred and Forty

The argument was slipping away from Hunter. If it did, he knew he and Mollie were as good as dead.

'Why would God give you such a vain task when he's omnipotent?' he asked steadily. 'Isn't God almighty? Doesn't God have the power to give and take life at the blink of an eye? If God wanted Mollie dead, why would he need you? A snap of his fingers and she'd be gone. And what would you have gained from that?' Hunter paused for a split second and saw doubt flourish in John Woods's eyes. He quickly pressed on. 'Nothing. No knowledge, no experience, no lesson learned. A futile task that would've taken God a nanosecond to complete. My understanding is that God doesn't hand out futile tasks.'

The concern in John's face grew.

'Your task was to understand your daughter. To help her control and comprehend the gift she'd been given. Who do you think gave her that gift in the first place, John? The devil doesn't have that power.'

Another head whoosh. Hunter could feel the blood running down his arm. He could hear it dripping onto the floor and he felt his legs starting to lose their strength. He knew he didn't have much time left.

'She cursed her mother,' John shot back with rage. 'She told her she would die.'

'No, she didn't. She tried to prevent it, and if you had listened to her your wife would be here now. Don't you see, John? Hidden in Mollie's gift is the ability to help people. She can help prevent some people from suffering, but she can't do it alone. She needs others to listen to her.'

'Like you did?'

'Yes, like I did. She was crying out for your help. And she still is. All she needed was your support, your understanding. Your task was to see beyond the masquerade. To overcome your own prejudice and find good in what you thought was evil.'

John shifted his weight from one leg to the other. He looked uncomfortable, doubtful of his actions. His grip on the gun slackened a fraction and Hunter ventured a new step forward, but John snapped back as if waking up from a dream.

'NO.' His shout was full of anger. 'I followed the task as it was given to me. She has to die. Like all the others had to die.'

Others? Hunter thought.

'They had to die so I could find the devil child.'

And suddenly it dawned on Hunter. The blond girl in the living room – on her knees – her throat slit open. Claire Anderson – her throat slit open. The girls in the paper. Hunter read it so quickly he'd forgotten about them. They were all brunettes. They were all around Mollie's age. And they all had been found naked, on their knees, hands tied in a prayer position with their throats cut open. John Woods had been in LA for days searching for Mollie. His frustration and anger exploding inside him as he failed to locate her. He projected his hatred onto girls that looked like her. He was killing Mollie over and over again. But more than that, John did believe his daughter was special, that she could sense other people's suffering. He knew she was a good person. He knew she would always try to help. He killed those girls not only because they looked like Mollie, but so Mollie would sense it. He was flushing her out. John Woods was the Slasher.

'And die she will,' John said, lifting his gun. 'And so will you.'

Hunter saw the determination in John's eyes as he tightened his finger around the trigger.

Game over.

Hundred and Forty-One

The thunderous gunshot was muffled by the torrential rain that drummed the windows. The wall behind him was splashed with blood, bits of flesh and skin. The air was instantly filled with the smell of cordite.

Hunter's body slumped forward, but in a last charge of strength he managed to hold onto the wall with his good arm. The combination of the loss of blood and the adrenalin of the moment gave him an incredible headrush and he lost his balance for an instant. As his eyes regained focus, he saw John Woods fall to his knees. Blood dripping from the gunshot wound in his right hand that'd obliterated three of his fingers. His mouth was half open, his eyes staring up in horror. Only then Hunter saw her. Mollie was holding Hunter's gun John had kicked to the side. He saw her cock the hammer, ready for a second shot.

'Mollie, don't,' Hunter called, dashing forward – both of his palms facing her in a wait gesture. 'Don't do it.'

She was shaking. Tears streaming down her face. 'He killed Su . . . Susan. He was going to kill you.'

'I understand, Mollie. But this time it's really over. Let me deal with this.'

From the floor, John Woods let out an animalistic grunt before vomiting explosively. The pain of lost fingers, broken bones, torn ligaments and the loss of blood proving too much for him.

'He raped me so many times.' There was no anger in her voice, only pain. Mollie's gaze flipped back to Hunter. 'I'm so scared.'

'I know, honey.' Hunter's voice was tender and concerned. 'But there's nothing for you to be scared of anymore. It's really over, I promise you. He won't ever hurt anyone else.'

There was a sudden rush of footsteps along the corridor.

'Drop the gun. Drop it now,' two LAPD officers shouted. Their aims fixed on Mollie.

'Hold on.' Hunter turned and faced them with his hands up in surrender, putting his body between their guns and Mollie. 'I'm Homicide Special Detective Robert Hunter.' He gestured towards the badge on his belt. 'This situation is under control. Lower your weapons.'

The officers exchanged anxious looks. 'It doesn't look under control to me, sir,' one of them replied.

'This is how I control my situations.'

Both policemen frowned.

'Keep *him* under watch.' Hunter nodded in John's direction. 'He's the Slasher killer you guys have been looking for.'

'What?'

'You'll probably find a knife on him with blood traces from all the Slasher's victims.' Hunter tilted his head sadly. 'Unfortunately, there's another victim in the living room.'

After a quick hesitation their guns moved their aim onto John Woods.

As Hunter spun around and faced Mollie again, he heard one of the officers radioing in the surprising news and requesting an ambulance.

'C'mon, Mollie,' Hunter whispered, stepping closer, grabbing a towel from the floor and offering it to her.

The tense moment between them seemed to last a lifetime.

She uncocked the gun and placed it in his hand. 'You're the only one who's ever believed me. You're the only one I trust.'

With tears in her eyes she hugged him.

Hundred and Forty-Two

Christmas Day

Garcia opened the door wearing the tackiest sweater Hunter had ever seen – a purple, red, pink and lime-green furry monstrosity that looked at least two sizes too big. His nose was bandaged as if he'd been through a nose job. Dark bruises under both of his eyes.

'Whoa.' Hunter jumped back pointing at Garcia's sweater. 'Does that thing bite?'

'I know, I know.' Garcia put on a face. 'My mother knitted it for me. She brought it over this morning. I have to wear it or else she'll be upset.'

'She's punishing you, that's what she's doing.'

'Yeah, probably. Come in,' Garcia said, showing him into the apartment. The Christmas tree in the far corner of the room was alive with flickering lights and decorations. Soft, old-fashioned seasonal music and a rainbow of mouth-watering smells warmed the room.

'How's the arm?' Garcia asked.

'Still hurts, but nothing I can't handle. I have to give the gym a miss for a few months, though.'

'And that's what worries you the most, isn't it?'

Hunter shrugged. 'How's the nose?'

'Broken. I'll have to give up head-butting for a few months,' he teased. 'I heard you got a call from the mayor, and it wasn't to talk about his wife.'

An indifferent shrug this time.

'You're flavor of the month, Robert. You're in everyone's good books, including Captain Blake and Chief Collins. Two serial killers in one night? That's gotta be a new record. Did you hear they finally found James Reed?'

Hunter nodded.

'We were right; he never left Los Angeles County. His lover lives in Ranchos Palos Verdes. We couldn't find the car because it was in her garage. How's Mollie?'

'She's OK, considering. She's been sedated for the past two days.'

'What's gonna happen to her?'

A subtle shake of the head. 'She will decide. She's eighteen today, legally an adult. But I've already talked to a very good friend of mine who happens to be one of the best psychiatrists in Los Angeles. She agreed to see Mollie free of charge for as long as it takes. Mollie's been through a hell of a lot and she'll need a lot of help. I'll do my best to be there for her.'

'I know you will.' Garcia smiled. 'She can also count on me.'

'I'm dropping by later this afternoon to wish her happy birthday and merry Christmas.'

'Great. We'll sort her out a huge plate with a bit of everything. Hospitals' Christmas meal must suck. Besides, when Anna and my mom get together in the kitchen, they cook enough food to feed a platoon.'

'I can see.' Hunter nodded towards the table overcrowded with colorful dishes.

'And there's still more to come.' Anna came out of the

kitchen wearing a blue and white apron with the words 'Kiss the chef' across the front of it.

'Don't mind if I do,' Hunter said with a smile and kissed her on both cheeks. He was introduced to Garcia's mother, Janet, a tall and authoritative woman with perfectly styled short blond hair, dazzling blue eyes and the sweetest, most calming voice Hunter had ever heard.

During lunch, Hunter was amused by Janet's stories of a young Garcia in Brazil.

'So you used to be good at soccer?' Hunter asked as he and Garcia did the dishes.

'I still am,' Garcia shot back proudly.

'I'll take your word for it.'

A few silent seconds went by.

'There's something I wanted to ask you, Robert.'

'Shoot.'

'I was handcuffed to the chair when I came to. It's logical to assume Tyler cuffed you as well.'

'He did.' Hunter nodded.

'How the hell did you get out of those handcuffs?'

Hunter smiled. 'A trick I learned a long time ago.'

'Care to share?'

'I always keep two sets of cuff keys with me.'

'Huh?'

'I keep a set where everyone expects to find one – together with my handcuffs on my holster. That's how I could throw Dan the keys when he asked for them. But here's my magic trick.' Hunter undid his belt.

'Hey, hey. If Anna or my mom walks into the kitchen right now, this ain't gonna look good.'

'Relax.' Hunter showed Garcia the secret pocket in the back of his belt. A set of handcuff keys safely tucked inside. 'It happened to me once before a long time ago. So I decided it'd never happen again. If you ever get caught off guard and you end up handcuffed, nine out of ten times your hands will be cuffed behind your back.'

'Clever sonofabitch.' Garcia chuckled. 'I'm definitely stealing that idea.'

Hundred and Forty-Three

Mollie was standing by the window, silently watching the drizzling rain, when Hunter poked his head through the door.

'May I come in?'

She turned around and forced a thin smile. 'What's the secret password?'

Hunter thought about it for a second. 'Now, let me see . . . It's either *happy birthday*—' his right hand appeared holding a birthday cake '—or *merry Christmas.*' He pushed the door open, revealing a nicely wrapped box under his injured left arm.

Her eyes widened. 'Oh my God. That's all for me?'

'Uh-huh.' Hunter stepped into the room and placed the cake on the small table by the bed. 'Here, merry Christmas and happy birthday.' He handed her the present. 'I hope you like it.'

Mollie sat on the bed and unwrapped it eagerly, her jaw dropping as she stared at the box.

'It's a laptop,' Hunter said.

'I can see that.' Tears flooded her eyes.

'A word processor and several other applications are already preinstalled. You said you wanted to be a writer. I hope this will help.'

'Oh my God. I can't believe you remembered.' The joy in her voice was contagious. She leaned forward and kissed Hunter's right cheek, and for a brief moment he looked embarrassed.

'I hope you're hungry,' he said with a wait gesture before stepping out of the room again. Two seconds later he reappeared holding two massive food dishes wrapped in cling film. 'Compliments of Carlos and his wife.'

Mollie did a double take. 'Wow, that's a lot of food.' She smiled. 'Maybe I can offer some of it to the other patients. There'll be a lot left over.'

'That would be very nice of you,' Hunter replied with a smile. 'Mollie, I wanted to ask you something,' he said in a more serious tone. 'The safety on my gun was on. I know it was on because I flicked it on.'

She nodded shyly. 'I know. I flicked it off.'

'How did you know?'

'Mr. Higgins.'

Hunter frowned.

'He and his wife own the diner I used to work at in Lynwood. They'd been robbed at gunpoint so many times they kept a pistol behind the counter and one in the kitchen. They made sure everyone who worked there knew how to use them just in case. I know how to reload, chamber and unchamber a round, cock the hammer and check the safety.'

Hunter chuckled. 'I'll be damned. Only in the United States of America you'd be able to get a job in a diner and be taught not only how to wait on tables but also how to use a firearm.'

A kind-looking nurse knocked gently at the door. 'I'm sorry, detective, but she needs to rest now.'

'It's OK.' Hunter grabbed his jacket. 'I'll check on you tomorrow, kiddo.'

'Robert,' Mollie called as Hunter reached the door. 'Thank you for everything. For the present, for remembering, for believing in me, for being there and for saving my life.'

Hunter faced her and smiled. 'Thank you for saving mine.'